P9-CAO-205

MORE...

St. Martin's Paperbacks Titles By

Lora Leigh

ELITE OPS SERIES

Black Jack

Heat Seeker

Maverick

Wild Card

SEALs TRILOGY

Killer Secrets

Hidden Agendas

Dangerous Games

RENEGADE

Lora Leigh

St. Martin's

This is a work of fiction. All of the characters, organizations, and events portrayed in this novel are either products of the author's imagination or are used fictitiously.

RENEGADE

Cover photograph of man © Shirley Green
Cover photograph of Berkeley Pier, dusk, with Golden Gate Bridge © David Sanger/Getty Images

For information address St. Martin's Press, 175 Fifth Avenue, New York, NY 10010.

ISBN: 978-1-61664-808-4

Printed in the United States of America

For a wonderful editor, Monique.

For all the help, the guidance, the advice, but even more your friendship.

And for two excellent lawyers who defy the stereotypes:
Eileen O' Brien
Douglas Ballantine
Thank you for all your advice and all your hard work.
The two of you together saved my life.

PROLOGUE

The dresses were gorgeous.

Mikayla Martin stood back from the finished products and rubbed at her lower back as she let a small, pleased smile curve her lips.

They were the dresses that romantic dreams were made of. Miles of frothy lace, satin, silk, and chiffon. Thousands of tiny seed pearls had been hand-sewn onto each one. Love had gone into the creation of each of the three wedding gowns, and the jade bridesmaid dress had been sewn with extra attention to detail. It was her favorite color, and one of her own designs.

Finally, after so many years of hard work and dreams, and the designs she so lovingly crafted, Mikayla's Creations was beginning to get a small measure of notice. Mikayla had no dreams of runway success. What she did have were dreams of a small, exclusive reputation that would keep her clothing shop open and thriving.

She breathed out a deep sigh and fought to let the dresses go. She wanted to pack them up and take them home with her. She didn't want to let a single one of them out of her sight.

"I know that look on your face, Mikayla." Her assistant, Deirdre Maple, pushed back her hair, propped her hands on her hips, and gave Mikayla a knowing smile.

With her kittenish expression and long red-gold hair, Deirdre was the advertising drive behind the shop. While Mikayla kept the customers happy, Deirdre brought them in by showcasing the wedding gowns and exclusive ball gowns Mikayla created. The bridesmaid gown she had been fondling was one of those. A one-of-a-kind that had been designed for one woman, one body.

There was a small section of the shop dedicated to less formal clothing. Exclusive designs of more casual attire and a small selection of unique, one-of-a-kind footwear and other accessories. But the majority of the shop was dedicated to the formal dresses and wedding gowns Mikayla so loved.

"Yeah, I know, I gotta let it go." Mikayla forced a grin as she stepped back and gave it one last regretful look. "Go ahead and call our future bride and our lucky bridesmaid and let them know their dresses are ready for pickup. They'd better hurry, though, because I just might steal them after all."

Deirdre gave a low, light laugh, her hazel green eyes twinkling with laughter as she shook her head. The girl wore a sleeveless silk emerald blouse, no collar, the tailoring sewn to match her slender figure. The taupe above-the-knee slim-line skirt and matching pumps drew attention to the blouse and to Deirdre's lush head full of red-gold curls as they cascaded nearly to her hips.

"You told me to remind you that you have to pick Scott up after work today." Deirdre glanced at the clock on the wall. "If you're going to get there on time, then you'd better rock and roll."

Mr. Unreliable. Of all her brothers, Scotty had to be the most irritating, if the most lovable one. The baby of the family, he was always happy, always laughing, and rarely took anything seriously. He was forever needing a ride, advice, or a loan. Their mother called him the "needy one". Mikayla just called him lazy—although she did it affectionately.

"You know you'll have to listen to him whine if you're late." Deirdre laughed. "Better hurry."

Mikayla grimaced before looking around the interior of her "baby." This store was her life.

"You could hire a cab to go after your brother," Deirdre told her. "That way you could stand here and admire your handiwork a while longer."

Mikayla laughed, though her gaze lingered a moment longer. She turned away and strode across the plush chocolate carpeting of the floor.

She moved around the display of dresses and gowns and toward the counter where she pulled out the invoices from the shelf below.

"Everything has been paid in full," she told Dierdre as a sense of accomplishment filled her. "Now, if we could just get a few more of these orders in, I could breathe a little easier."

"They'll come in," Deirdre assured her, and Mikayla couldn't help but believe it.

The shop was growing slowly, but it was growing. The sense of fulfillment she felt was overwhelming at times. Mikayla was doing something everyone had told her she didn't have a chance of succeeding at in the current economy.

"Do you think either of us will ever wear one of those wedding gowns?" Deirdre nodded toward them. "Hell, Mikayla, aren't you tired of waiting for Mr. Right yet? I think I am. Mr. Almost Perfect might do it for me."

Mikayla turned her face away, hoping to hide her own doubts. She sometimes feared that Mr. Right was a figment of her dreams. That the incredible sex, deep romance, and shared bonding she dreamed of was the stuff of fantasies and romance novels, not real life.

"Not for me." Mikayla shook her head at the very thought of settling for less, though. "Some things last forever, Deirdre, if you know how to work for your dreams."

That dream didn't *have* to be a marriage, children, a life spent sharing the day-to-day adventure of simply living together. But it was a dream Mikayla found hard to let go.

Deirdre's sigh was heavy. "You have to be the only pragmatic romantic I've ever heard of," she accused. "Come on, Mikayla; it never lasts forever. Why not take what we can get?"

"It" being marriage. Deirdre thought in terms of marriage. She wanted the dress, the wedding, the little gold band on her finger, the little white picket fence.

For Mikayla, marriage, like any commitment, took a lot of work, understanding, and patience. She'd seen that in her parents' marriage all her life. Her mother and father had set a perfect example of what real love and a real relationship was. That was what Mikayla wanted. Not just the wedding, the gold band, or even the white picket fence. It was that sense of belonging, that feeling of being a part of something that was larger than herself. Something that she could be a partner in.

She wasn't dependent. She didn't want to be taken care of, and she didn't want to take care of anyone. At least not in the sense of accepting responsibility for him. She wanted to take care of his heart with the promise of her own, and she wanted a partner willing to share each day with her and, perhaps, one day, to share children with her.

She wanted the whole dream, and she was willing to wait for it. She just hoped that while she was waiting there was someone out there actually making his way toward her. She wasn't getting any younger, her grandmother often reminded her. Just as her grandmother reminded Mikayla that twenty-six was too old to still be a virgin.

How Mikayla's grandmother knew Mikayla was still a virgin she hadn't yet figured out. Did she have a red V painted on her forehead that she couldn't see?

"I don't know, Mikayla." Her assistant leaned against the counter, her hair falling around her face as she grinned impishly. "I know what I'm missing by sleeping alone."

Mikayla laughed. "As if you sleep alone that often. You and Drake aren't exactly abstaining, last I heard."

Deirdre and Drake Marshal had been on-again, off-again since high school. They couldn't seem to make up their minds if they loved each other or hated each other. Just as Deirdre couldn't seem to decide if Drake was Mr. Right or just Mr. Available.

"Okay, I'm out of here then." Mikayla straightened the paid invoices again before gazing around the shop a last time.

Grabbing her keys, she turned and opened the old-fashioned glass front door and stepped out onto the sidewalk. Hagerstown was in its full flush of late-spring warmth. The trees were fully budded, many already showing their bright green foliage and swaying with the gentle wind that pushed through the historic town.

Mikayla loved it here. This was home. She had been born in Hagerstown, raised in it. She had gone to design school in New York, and the whole time she had been away all she'd wanted to do was come home.

It was sprawling, often loud, filled with tourists on the best of days, and pulsing with life. It wasn't as exhaustingly busy as New York or D.C., but Hagerstown still thrived with life and hummed with excitement.

At least, she felt the excitement.

Pulling her keys from the pocket of her light jacket, she hit the remote and unlocked the doors to the cherry red Jeep, she'd finally allowed herself to buy, before stepping onto the running board and lifting herself in.

Her skirt tightened above her knees before she swung her legs in and closed the door behind her. Starting the engine, she almost grinned at the feel of the motor throbbing through the vehicle.

Pulling into the stream of traffic, she eased through the busy streets, heading for I-70 and the job site her brother was working on several miles along the interstate.

The building site for the newly designed office space was a major deal for the company her brother worked for, as well as for her father. Her father had won the plumbing contract for the building, and a cousin had won the interior design contract for part of it.

Hagerstown was booming, and growing, though sometimes Mikayla feared it was growing too fast. Still, she loved watching its progress.

Flipping on the CD player, she slid one of her favorite CDs in. The soft-rock eighties tune filled the interior and soothed the weariness that was beginning to blur at the edges of her mind.

She had put four months of steady, hard work in to make the deadlines for the early-spring weddings of the brides whose dresses were waiting at the shop. Ordering, fitting, sewing, adjusting. From late winter through late fall the store, though not booming, was definitely busy. This year had been their best year yet.

She wanted to get home, relax in a bubble bath, and let that sense of satisfaction work through her before she started on reconciling accounts, bills, and orders.

It might be Friday night, but Mikayla still had work to do. Not that she had much else to do. The dating pool had been relatively dry lately, she had to admit.

Or maybe, as Deirdre accused her of doing, she had perhaps just set her sights too high.

That was always a possibility, she admitted to herself. She wanted something that might not even exist in the real world.

None of her friends had ever been swept mindlessly off their feet with a kiss. Sex hadn't made the earth move beneath them. They didn't love with a devotion that canceled out the thought of ever being with anyone but the one they loved. They were often unfaithful and saw the practice as a game of sorts. The thrill of the chase, of being chased, and being smart enough not to get caught.

They played with their own lives and with their children's lives, and it was something Mikayla wanted no part of.

She wanted the romance, the excitement, and she wanted honesty. She hated being lied to, and the thought of having the man she loved being unfaithful to her was enough to make her take a third and fourth look at any man offering to fill her life.

Was she as deranged as her friends often accused her of being? Were her standards simply set too high and dooming her to failure as well as to a life of loneliness?

Perhaps not deranged, but she was definitely beginning to worry that she was that hopeless romantic who was going to turn into an equally hopeless spinster.

What had her brother Scotty said? She was going to end up living alone in her perfect house, surrounded by her dresses, and still waiting for her perfect Prince Charming the day she died a perfectly lonely death.

And she was very afraid that was definitely the future she was looking forward to.

And in those moments she wondered if Deirdre wasn't right . . . if perhaps Mr. Almost was good enough. Except Mikayla hadn't even managed to find a Mr. Almost, either. If she ever laid eyes on him, then she might consider it. Just to say she had tried.

Shaking her head at the thought, Mikayla took the exit along a newly developed business site and drove along the rough, uneven road to the hulk of steel and metal rising from the dirt at the end of the dirt drive.

She pulled her Jeep alongside the six-story skeletal frame of the office building where her brother Scotty had all but ordered her to meet him.

Why her youngest brother couldn't manage to keep his own ride running she hadn't figured out yet. He was always tinkering with this, tinkering with that, and it never failed that he called her when he managed to tinker it into complete auto failure.

One of these days she was going to do as she threatened and get the family together for a mechanical intervention where her brother was concerned. He was going to have to learn to keep his hands off his vehicle's guts. If something wasn't truly broken, then there was no need to fix it, right?

Pulling into the muddy mess at the front of the unfinished building, Mikayla blew out a hard breath.

Mr. Unreliable had struck again. As usual, he wasn't where he was supposed to be or doing what he was supposed to be doing.

In this case, waiting for her to pick him up.

So where was he? Where was anyone? The place was utterly deserted.

Turning down the lush, wild strains of Barry White on the CD player, Mikayla tapped her fingers on the steering wheel. Pursing her lips, she stared around the muddy mess of the job site, eyes narrowed against the dim light as she searched for her brother.

Her lips thinned as she mentally counted to ten.

She wouldn't get upset, she told herself. Her day had been too good to let this ruin it. She'd just finished two of the most gorgeous wedding gowns she had ever created and the last bridesmaid's dress. Rows upon rows of seed pearls, yards of satin, silk, and lace, and miles of tucks to go along with the hefty payment she had received.

Two months of sewing delicate rows of tiny pearls and witnessing the tearful smiles of two brides who would treasure those dresses for the rest of their lives.

She sent up a little prayer that those dresses would be treasured through a lifetime of wedded bliss.

Now, where was her brother?

She wanted to get home, pour a glass of wine, and relax in her new hot tub just long enough to ease the tension that still hadn't worked its way out of her body. She had meetings tomorrow with several brides, a groom, and four society princesses looking for the perfect dress to wear to the perfect party.

She grinned at the thought. The women scheduled to go through the dozens of books filled with ball gowns, slinky satiny gowns, and silky clouds of perfect creations tailored to bring a gasp to the most jaded lips would bring a much-needed boon to the shop.

The financial crisis hitting the world at the moment

hadn't seemed to affect the sale of dresses, gowns, and various accessories that were "must-haves" for the well-put-together society princess.

Mikayla checked her watch, tapped her fingers on the steering wheel again, and blew out an irritated breath.

Scotty better hope he didn't need her to ever pick him up again. This was it. She had been sitting here for ten minutes already. Where was he?

Turning the CD off, she opened the door to the Jeep and stepped out of the vehicle.

Her nose wrinkled at the smell of oil, mud, and what she swore was sweaty men. What was it about construction sites? Every time she had been forced to come out after her brother she swore the place smelled like guy BO.

This was the last time she would allow herself to be guilted into this. Scotty was going to have to get himself a girlfriend or something. Someone willing to make this drive and go searching for him, again, because he needed a ride.

The last time he had needed a ride Mikayla had ended up waiting an hour for him to finish what he swore was an important project before he left. She'd learned later he'd been playing poker in one of the toolsheds.

The rat.

Gritting her teeth, she pulled her cell phone from the holder at her hip and hit his number.

It rang.

"This is Scotty; leave a message." Voice mail. She hated it. She hung up without leaving a message. She would end up saying something she was certain she would regret.

Dammit, the least he could do was answer his phone.

"Listen, I told you I was taking care of it."

The sound of an angry voice above had Mikayla stepping back to stare up at the building, searching for the source of it. Perhaps Scotty was up there.

She was going to kill him.

A quiet murmur of another voice had her straining to hear what was said.

"Look, you owe me already. It's time to fucking pay up, you ignorant bastard. I told you, I need the fuckin' money. I did my part; now you do yours."

Mikayla's nose wrinkled as she searched for bodies to go with the vulgar words.

There was a low, quiet murmur in response.

"Look, I've had about enough of this. Pay the fuck up before I let him know exactly what's going on here."

The voice belonged to Scotty's boss. Eddie was his name. The foreman, Eddie Foreman. All three of her brothers snickered over the name.

Her lips parted to speak, to let the foreman know she was there and, she hoped, to find out where her brother was.

"What the hell are you doing? Put that gun the hell away. Have you fucking lost your mind?"

Mikayla stared up in horror as the pair came into view.

"You're costing me too much, Eddie." The voice was low, a harsh, angry growl that sent a shard of fear racing up Mikayla's spine, but what met her eyes had terror streaking through her. The gun in his hand, even from five stories up, drew her gaze, the dull black reflecting the last rays of the sun with a wicked, vicious light.

She jerked her gaze from the gun to the man holding it, her mouth going dry at the shadowed face she recognized despite the steadily dimming sunlight. It was Maddix Nelson, the owner of the construction company her brother worked for, and Maddix was holding a gun on his foreman.

She could see Eddie Foreman's face clearly. His heavy features were twisted into lines of disbelief and fear. Maddix Nelson's face, on the other hand, was cold. Colder than Mikayla could ever remember seeing it. And she had seen him many times over the past several years. All three of her brothers worked for him. The oldest brother, only two years younger than Mikayla, had worked for Nelson Building and Construction for over four years now.

Her father worked with Maddix through the plumbing business he owned.

She could feel her hands shaking, her stomach clenching in horror, as she watched Maddix lift the gun until it was pointed directly at Eddie Foreman's chest.

"You're crazy!" Eddie wheezed. "Put that fucker down, man. All I want is my friggin' money. You owe it to me."

"You owed me results, Eddie," Maddix snarled, his lips pulling back from Eddie's lips in anger.

Mikayla watched in suspended disbelief as Eddie stepped back, though there was no way to escape. A thick steel beam met his back. There was only one way to go, and Maddix Nelson had that way blocked.

She had to do something. What could she do?

Mikayla could feel her chest tightening in fear, in total and complete disbelief, as Maddix took a step closer.

Mikayla backed to the Jeep, gripped the door, and scrambled inside. She had to give Eddie a chance. There was no one else around.

She had to do something.

"Don't do this, man!" Eddie cried out.

Mikayla laid on the horn, praying. . . .

She screamed at the sharp retort of gunfire. Throwing the Jeep into gear, she screamed again, hysteria threatening to overtake her as Eddie fell five stories to the rough ground below, obviously dead.

He fell faceup, his eyes wide, staring blankly as Mikayla hit the gas. She heard the bullets hit the driver's side door. One tore through, cracking the hard plastic of the gearbox, sending shards of sharp plastic flying.

Ducking over the steering wheel, she raced from the job site. Mikayla's hands shook as she tore at the cell phone at her side. Pulling it free, she hurriedly hit the programmed speed dial as sobs tore from her chest.

"Hey, Miki, Scotty called—" Her father's voice came over the line.

"Oh, my God! Oh, my God! Daddy, he killed him! He killed him! I saw it. I saw it all!"

Heavy sobs shook her body as she raced off the rough dirt road onto the interstate and raced for home, for her parents.

"Miki, settle down." Her father's voice tightened, firmed, and became commanding. "Are you driving, Miki?"

"Oh, God, Dad, he shot at me," she cried out as she checked the rearview mirror, her body shuddering so hard she was surprised she could keep the Jeep on the road. "It was Maddix Nelson, Dad. I saw him."

"Miki, where are you?"

"I was supposed to pick up Scotty." Then a horrible thought pierced her mind. "Where's Scotty, Dad? Where is he?"

"Miki, settle down," he snapped then.

The sound of his voice, commanding, reminding her of her childhood years, when she knew when her father was at his most serious. He was at his most serious now.

"Now, listen to me. I'm getting in the truck, honey. Me and Mom are coming. Tell me where you are right now. We'll meet you."

She hurriedly gave him her location.

"Keep heading toward us, honey," he ordered. "Keep talking to me. We're on our way."

"Where's Scotty?" she sobbed. "Was he there?"

Oh, God, her brother couldn't be dead. She couldn't bear the thought of it.

"Scott called me earlier, Miki," her father promised her. "He got a ride. His phone died while he was talking to me and he couldn't reach you. Scotty's fine. Now concentrate on driving. I'm almost there. When you see me, just pull over."

She could hear her mother in the background, her tone calm but the concern in it heavy.

She was safe. She would be safe. Her father wouldn't let anyone hurt her.

She was amazed that she wasn't pulled over. They would surely think she was intoxicated if they had. Panic was pulling at the edges of her mind, and Mikayla never panicked. She had been raised with three younger brothers. Three younger brothers would make a girl crazy if they had half a chance. Mikayla had never given her brothers a chance.

But her chest was so tight she could barely breathe. Tears filled her eyes and blurred her vision. She felt as though she were in a nightmare she couldn't wake up from.

"He killed him," she whispered again.

"Keep it in your mind, Mikayla Ann. Remember it until we get to you and get you to the police." Her father's voice firmed again, the use of her first and middle names snapping her out of the hysteria threatening to overtake her again. "Where are you, honey?"

She quickly gave him her location once again.

"Pull over at the gas station just ahead of you," he told her. "We're coming up on it now."

"I see it. I see it." She was crying harder.

She couldn't believe it. Eddie Foreman's face kept flashing before her eyes, his eyes unseeing, the blood soaking his chest, his body bent and broken.

"Mikayla, pull over!" her father snapped.

Mikayla shook her head, blinked, and with a hard twist of the steering wheel whipped into the gas station. The Jeep tilted at the hard turn, rocked, then righted itself before she pushed it into park and threw the door open.

She fell out of the Jeep as her father and two of her brothers raced from the two pickups they had arrived in. Behind them were two state police officers she hadn't expected—officers her father or brothers had obviously called. Mikayla ran to her father's arms, desperate; she felt his arms close around her.

She was safe, she told herself. Her father and the police would take care of everything.

Maddix Nelson wouldn't kill anyone else.

CHAPTER 1

Four weeks later

Nikolai Steele pulled the wicked black Harley into a vacant parking spot on Washington Street, let the engine throb for several seconds, then turned the bike off slowly, ignoring the curious looks of several women walking past him on the sidewalk as he stared across the street at the office front of Nelson Building and Construction.

Sometimes, past favors sucked. This was one of them. He owed Nelson for some rather important information the man had provided several months prior. Nik almost shook his head. That IOU was now about to become a pain in the ass.

"I'm here." He spoke quietly into the comm link built into his helmet.

"Carry the helmet in with you, Renegade. Leave the comm on so I can pick up the conversation and see what he wants." Tehya Talamosi, the red-haired sprite working communications, spoke quietly into the link.

He nearly rolled his eyes at the new code name. Unlike the others, his code name had changed several times over the years to reflect the differing areas of the missions assigned. For this more personal job

"Renegade" reflected the fact that this time, he was working alone.

His initial meeting with Nelson would be overseen by his commander, Jordan Malone, until it was ascertained whether or not this was indeed a personal contact or if it was something more. Something that could possibly risk the Elite Ops unit or Nik's cover.

Pulling the key from the ignition, Nik swung from the bike and slowly pulled the helmet from his head, careful to leave the sensitive electronics inside active.

He had no idea what Nelson wanted; all he knew was that he had contacted Nik in a manner in which he shouldn't have been able to contact him. It's what had put Jordan on alert, and it left a hell of a lot of questions for the man to answer.

Holding on to the helmet, Nik waited for a break in traffic before strolling across the street. At six and a half feet it was impossible not to draw attention to himself. Add that to his well-conditioned body, long white blond hair, and what he knew were his unusually strong Nordic features and Nik was impossible to hide in plain sight.

This was why he preferred the shadows. Nik had the ability to blend into those shadows, to watch, to wait, and to garner the least amount of attention possible.

The shadows were safer. There he wasn't forced to interact with others. He didn't have to risk friendships, loyalties, or possibly the drive to fill the unnamed hunger that plagued his soul.

Stepping onto the sidewalk, he was aware of the pedestrians who cleared a path around him. They watched him with wary curiosity, sensing instinctively that this was a dangerous man.

Nik stepped inside the offices of Nelson Building and Construction and walked up to the receptionist's desk.

"Maddix Nelson." Nik's voice, normally dark and

rough, sounded more dangerous as he stood over the petite young receptionist.

She swallowed tightly as her brown eyes widened, youth still fresh enough that she felt no fascination for the monster staring down at her. She felt only that inherent fear, that need to run.

"M-m-may I ask—"

"Steele." He gave only his last name. The name and identity he had been given eight years before.

She jerked the phone from its cradle, punched in a number with a jerky movement, and stuttered his name into the phone.

"Mr. Steele, Mr. Nelson's assistant will be right here." She laid the phone on the cradle as she glanced desperately at the small seating area off to the right. "It will be just a moment."

Nik had mercy on her. He stepped back from the receptionist's station, but he didn't sit. He moved to the edge of the lobby, placed his back against the wall, and waited.

He didn't have to wait long.

Maddix Nelson's assistant, Alison Chenkins, moved down the staircase that led to the upper floors rather than using the elevator. Dressed in slim black slacks and a white tailored blouse, with low heels, she gave the impression, a correct one, of quiet efficiency and confidence.

"Mr. Steele." She moved right to him, a slender hand reaching out in greeting. "Thank you for coming so promptly."

Nik's brow arched sarcastically as he accepted the handshake, careful not to pinch her hand in his much larger one.

"We can use the elevator or the stairs," she offered. "Mr. Nelson is in his office."

"Stairs are fine with me."

"Excellent." A friendly smile tugged at her lips as she turned and moved for the staircase. "If you'll follow me."

He followed, keeping a careful distance between himself and the assistant, his gaze constantly searching his surroundings.

Nik hadn't expected Nelson's favor to be called so quickly. Nor had Nik expected the message to come through a contact whom only a few people were aware of.

"I always take the stairs whenever possible." Alison Chenkins grinned back at Nik as they moved past the second floor. "The elevator is quicker, but the stairs are better for my hips."

"And give Maddix Nelson time to prepare himself," Nik stated quietly.

She almost paused on the steps before her smile turned cooler and the chatter stopped. She turned, and her pace quickened until they were pushing through the fourth-floor door and moving into the plush assistant's office outside Maddix Nelson's office.

Maddix didn't make Nik wait. He was standing in the door to his office, his dark hair brushed back, but not as neatly as Nik remembered it being before. There were added lines on Maddix's face, his brow creased with worry. Six weeks had wrought an almost devastating change to the man's face.

"Nik, thank you for coming." Maddix invited Nik into his office with a wave of his hand.

Nik glanced into the office, then to Maddix in a signal that the other man was to go first.

The other man gave a mirthless smile before stepping into the office.

Nik stepped inside as he tucked the motorcycle helmet under his arm to provide Tehya with clearer audio and visual coverage of the room.

"You contacted me through an unusual source, Mr. Nelson," Nik stated as he moved to the side of the room, putting the wall at his back. "Care to tell me why?"

Maddix ran his fingers through his hair, and it was obviously not the first time.

"I tried to reach you through Lilly Harrington and her fiancé, Travis Caine, but they were out of the country and unavailable," Maddix stated quietly. "That only left the few contacts that I could find of Caine's to get a message to you."

Nik arched his brow again, remained silent, and waited. Maddix ran his hands over his face before sitting in the large chair behind his desk. His suit jacket lay over the back of the chair, and his shirtsleeves were rolled up haphazardly. The shirt was wrinkled, as were the slacks he wore. He looked like a man under pressure.

"It took a while," Maddix finally sighed. "I finally learned Caine was in Aspen last year and possibly knew Bailey Serborne Vincent. I contacted her husband, John Vincent, and looked into the possibility that he could help me contact you."

Nik leaned back in his chair then and watched Maddix silently for long moments. So that was how Maddix had known to contact John Vincent, code-named Heat Seeker, an undercover agent with the agency Nik worked in as well.

Maddix's knowledge of John had caused an edge of concern when Maddix had contacted Nik.

"How did you learn Travis was in Aspen?" Nik asked.

"Raymond Greer," Maddix answered. "I knew his

wife, Mary, when we were younger. They were in D.C. several weeks ago, when Mary mentioned Bailey's marriage to John Vincent and John's friend Travis Caine standing as best man in the wedding."

How small the world was becoming, Nik thought.

"So, who do you need to rid yourself of?" Nik asked.

Nik's reputation had been created long before he had taken the identity. Nik Steele had been an assassin and thief, willing to take almost any job.

Maddix's expression reflected disbelief for several seconds. "No, you misunderstand, Nik. I don't want to get rid of someone. I want to find out why someone wants to get rid of me. Have you heard about the murder that took place at my building site outside of town?"

Nik narrowed his eyes. "A bit."

Tehya's information on it was as thorough and in depth as only Tehya could make it. He knew about every piece of evidence collected, the entire depth of the investigation, and the fact that Maddix was seen committing the murder at the time that he had an airtight alibi.

Maddix gave a mocking laugh, a bitter, angry sound.

"I can't understand it. I know that girl. I know her family. Her father worked for me, her cousins. Her brothers." He shook his head wearily. "She seemed like such a good girl, Steele. Mikayla Martin has never seemed like a psycho before, so what the hell happened?"

"I take it you're saying you didn't kill your foreman?" Nik asked as though he really didn't care.

"No, I didn't kill my damned foreman." Maddix shot Nik a disgusted look. "As I'm certain you already know, I was in an impromptu business meeting with the mayor, the chief of police, and several of our city leaders. But that damned girl refuses to believe it."

Maddix was out of his chair and pacing to the wide, historically old windows of his office and stared down at the traffic bustling below before turning back to Nik.

"I need your help," Maddix said, his wide, tanned face creasing in tiredness. "When you needed information, I provided it for you. When you needed the blueprints on the estate the Harringtons were using, I provided it, quietly. I was there when you needed me; now I need you. You said you owed me. Now I'm calling in the debt."

Nik pursed his lips and stared back at the other man thoughtfully. Yeah, Nik owed him the favor; there was no denying that. And Maddix wasn't scrimping when it came to hiring the best. Nik was the best. He took care of things, all kinds of things. If a man wanted the best personal security, he called Nik. If he wanted the best assassin, he called Nik.

"You want the girl killed then?" Nik pressed.

"Fuck no!" Maddix looked like he was going to have a seizure. Shock and disbelief transformed his face as his brown eyes widened once again until they looked as though they would bulge from his face. "I don't want her hurt. I want to know what the hell is going on with her. Why did she target me?"

Nik sat back as he stared at the other man in confusion.

"If you had me investigated, Maddix, then you know what I'm known for. What makes you think I can help if you don't want this girl to simply disappear? You're hiring a sledgehammer here when you need a flyswatter."

Maddix shook his head as he stared back at Nik as though horrified.

Maddix swallowed tightly, his Adam's apple bobbing

in tight reflex. "I don't know who else to turn to that could actually do the job. Look, Nik, I've helped you in the past, and I don't want that girl hurt. I simply want to know what the hell is going on. Mikayla has never been caught in a lie. Someone is trying to destroy me. Mikayla or someone else, I don't know. I want to know who and I want to know why."

Fuck, Nik didn't need this.

As Maddix said, he'd provided invaluable information weeks before, during an operation that had threatened one of their own. An operation that had been of vital importance to the security of several nations. Nik did owe Maddix, but as Nik stated, Maddix was hiring a sledgehammer to swat at a fly.

Nik propped his ankle on his knee, set the helmet on his leg, and angled the face shield in Maddix's direction.

"Did you kill the foreman, Mr. Nelson?" Nik asked coldly, holding his hand up to forestall the words on the other man's lips. "Let's not protest yet, because I warn you, you lie to me and I find out, and I'll kill you as well as those lying for you. Tell me the truth and tell me what you really want before we go any further."

Maddix shook his head, frustration lining his face as he moved back to his desk and took his seat. A position of control, Nik thought. This was where Maddix Nelson felt the most in control.

"I didn't kill my foreman." Maddix wiped his hands over his face again before leaning back in his chair and laying his arms on the sides. "I swear to you, I wasn't there. And I don't want the girl hurt. Not so much as a bruise or a moment's fear. But I do want to know what the hell is going on. I've lost three damned good builders, one of the best contract plumbers in the business, and an interior designer I was salivating to get for that office project. All because of Mikayla Martin. They've pulled from the project because of their belief in her. And I swear to God, I don't even blame them. If I were someone else, I'd believe her, too. That's how honest she has always been. How good her reputation is." Confusion filled his face now. "If you asked me if I knew a good woman, then Mikayla would be the first that came to my mind."

Maddix shook his head as he sighed heavily, his lips tightening for long moments.

Damn if Maddix didn't act as though he was telling the truth. Nik watched curiously as Maddix lowered his head and stared at the desk for long moments.

As he lifted his gaze back to Nik, Maddix finally sighed, confusion evident in his dark brown eyes. "You know, I helped that girl get a loan for that dress shop of hers. My wife and I sent all our friends there for dresses, tuxes, suits, whatever we could do to help her. My wife, Glenda, and Mikayla were fast becoming friends before this happened. I just can't understand why she'd lie like this."

"And this is what you want me to look into?" Nik asked incredulously. "Do you know how much I charge, Maddix? I don't come cheap, even for a fucking favor. This is like putting a junkyard dog in a cage."

Maddix's eyes narrowed. "You owe me, Steele; you made that statement yourself. That you owed me one. I'm calling in your marker."

"That marker gets you a discount," he grunted. "And a slim one at that. This isn't a cut-and-dried job. You're talking about indefinite work here."

Maddix leaned forward. "Nik, I put myself in a spot when I helped you before. I risked my business, my family, when I went against Lilly Harrington. If she had learned what I was doing, she could have convinced friends to pull out of some very important D.C. contracts I have. I went out on a limb for what you were doing. Remember that while you're setting your price."

Nik rose to his feet. "I'll take eighty percent of my normal fee for the job in cash."

For a moment, grief flashed in Maddix's eyes. "I don't have enough in personal cash at the moment, and too many eyes are watching the business funds since this murder," he finally said, his voice low. "Give me fifty, Steele. Come on; I know a lot of people. I'll owe *you.*"

"I don't want your favors, Maddix." Nik stood to his feet as he stared back at the other man coldly. "I'll be at the Suites until morning if you change your mind."

"Steele." Maddix rose as well, his movements jerky. "Look, I don't have a good feeling about this. I've built my business using my gut, and my gut is twisted into so many knots it's painful. Whatever the hell is going on isn't going to threaten just me; it's going to threaten her." He reached to the desk and tossed a picture across it with an angry jerk of his hand.

Nik shouldn't have looked. He knew he shouldn't look, but he wanted to make certain the helmet was angled correctly for Tehya to get an image of the picture. However, his eyes went straight to the photo as well, narrowed, and something inside him became intrigued.

Thick, long dark blond hair fell straight as a ribbon, thick and healthy, over her shoulder and across her breasts like a soft, warm, living curtain. She had a wide, clear forehead, a pouty lower lip that drew the male animal inside him. Brows a shade darker than her hair arched over eyes that seemed to suck him in. Amethyst eyes. Eyes that glowed even in that damned photo. They were surrounded by thick, naturally long lashes. Her face was makeup free, innocent, honest. Pure.

Purity, he knew in many cases, was only skin-deep,

but somehow, even that cynical part of his soul wanted to believe the purity he saw in her went clear to the bone.

"She has three younger brothers and her parents are damned good people," Maddix snapped. "That girl." His finger stabbed at the picture. "She's decent, Nik. I've known her all her life and she's known me just as long. She's investigating me, for God's sake. Talking to people. Refusing to relent on her belief that I was the shooter she saw." His hands were shaking in anger, and perhaps in a little fear. "She's costing me contracts, clients, and more damned sleep than I can afford at my age."

"Eighty percent of my fee," Nik repeated, fighting back the gut-clenching need to go lower. "I'll be at the Suites."

Nik forced himself to turn around and walk out of the office, leaving an astounded Maddix Nelson behind him.

Striding from the building and across the street, Nik straddled the motorcycle and pulled the helmet on.

"Give me," he told Tehya as he buckled the strap beneath his chin and started the Harley.

"I'll have what I can get by the time you get to your room," Tehya promised. "I'll drop it off myself."

Nik pulled into traffic, his jaw set in lines of tension as he headed for the hotel.

"What do you have already, Tehya?" he questioned her firmly. "I know you're not empty-handed."

A chuckle came through the link. "Renegade, trust me, this time, I'm well and truly empty-handed at this point, but I'm still looking. Fix me a cup of coffee and we'll discuss it when I get there."

Mikayla stood outside the home of the deceased foreman, Edmond "Eddie" Foreman. Her lips didn't curve into a smile at the thought of his name now. She felt that familiar sinking of her stomach, that flash of fear at the memory of his face as he hit the ground. His eyes had been wide in surprise, blank in death. Blood had continued to saturate his shirt; one leg was twisted at an odd angle.

The fall had broken his back, his hip, and his leg. What had killed him, though, had been that bullet in his heart. The bullet that Maddix Nelson had put there.

Breathing in deeply, Mikayla pushed her hair back, straightened her shoulders, and strode up the cracked walkway to the two-story duplex Eddie had owned with his wife, Gina.

Mikayla had only met Gina once, at a company picnic Maddix Nelson had thrown for his employees and contractors and their families. She was a quiet woman, Mikayla remembered. Gina hadn't smiled a lot and had spoken even less. Eddie had insisted on being the attention getter of the family. He was loud and brash, but he hadn't deserved to die as he had.

Mikayla was hoping Gina would be willing to discuss her husband's death with her. So far, most people were highly uncooperative when it came to answering her questions about Eddie Foreman or Maddix Nelson. They watched her suspiciously or in some cases with outright dislike.

Strangely, Maddix himself was staying particularly low-key about the entire event. He had somehow managed to convince several city officials to give him an alibi, as well as the chief of police.

Maddix wasn't vociferously protesting his innocence. He was being rather smart, she concluded, by keeping quiet and allowing his friends to cover his murdering butt.

Moving to the front door, Mikayla knocked firmly at the rough wood door, noticing the peeling paint, the crack in the door frame, and the state of disrepair that the wood porch was in.

Eddie Foreman hadn't done much for the upkeep of his own home.

The door opened slowly.

"Miss Martin." There was a hint of a sigh in Gina Foreman's voice. "I had a feeling I would be seeing you soon."

Dressed in jeans and a T-shirt, the police dispatcher looked harried and tired. No doubt she was staying awake at night, perhaps worried that she was in danger herself. Mikayla knew she would have been.

Dark blond and brown hair framed Gina's pretty features and fell to just below her neck in a layered straight cut. Her chocolate brown eyes were somber, the shadows beneath them attesting to her lack of sleep.

"Mrs. Foreman, I'd like to talk to you for a moment." Mikayla stared back at Gina earnestly. "I just have a few questions."

Gina Foreman closed her eyes briefly. She was dressed for work. The black T-shirt she wore carried the insignia of a dispatcher, and Mikayla only hoped the woman cared more about her husband's death than she did about her job. Mikayla wasn't holding her breath, though.

She was doomed to disappointment, though. It was a good thing she hadn't held her breath.

"You know I can't talk to you," Gina finally stated regretfully as she laid her arm against the door frame and rubbed her forehead against it.

"I understand no one wants you to talk to me," Mikayla agreed painfully. "But he was your husband and he was killed in cold blood." Mikayla wanted to scream. Anger was like a parasite inside her, spreading, eating away at her control.

"Miss Martin, let it go," Gina advised her softly as she straightened. "The police are investigating his death, and I have every confidence that Chief Riley will find his killer."

Mikayla couldn't let it go. She couldn't get that image of Eddie Foreman's sightless gaze staring up at her out of her mind. It haunted her.

"Are you sure?" Mikayla asked, doubt heavy in her voice. "Or will he simply continue to cover for your husband's murderer?"

Gina Foreman's face tightened as grief flashed in her dark eyes once again.

There was no doubt she was mourning her husband, even though from what Mikayla understood, Eddie Foreman hadn't exactly been a loving, faithful husband.

"I can't talk to you," the other woman repeated. "Don't do this to me. Don't make me doubt people I trust. . . ."

"Do you think I didn't trust Maddix Nelson as well?" Mikayla argued softly, desperate to convince the woman to talk to her. "Mrs. Foreman, I watched your husband die in front of my eyes. I saw the man who shot him. Perhaps you can ignore that, but I can't. I see it every night in my nightmares. I can't escape it."

She couldn't forget it. She had tried. She had fought sleeping just to escape the dreams. She couldn't get the image of Eddie Foreman's dead body out of her mind. She couldn't forget that evening, the sounds, the smells, the horror of it. The feel of complete terror enveloping her as Maddix Nelson had shot at her next was still an ever-present reminder that nothing was certain. Especially tomorrow.

Gina lifted her hand to her trembling lips as tears gathered in her eyes. Eyes that were shadowed and dark with weariness and grief. Mikayla hated seeing that pain; she hated adding to it.

"God, don't do this to me." Gina shook her head, her dark blond hair swaying just below her neck as she shook her head.

She was a pretty woman, Mikayla thought. She'd often thought Gina Foreman was too pretty for her portly, overbearing husband.

"Mrs. Foreman, I need answers," Mikayla whispered, her fingers curling into a fist as she pressed them against her stomach. "I have to know why so many people would lie for Maddix Nelson."

"And I can't let myself believe you," Gina said, refusing the request, though her voice was thick with tears now. "I can't let myself believe that what you say is true, Miss Martin. Because if it is, then it means not just Maddix Nelson, a man I've trusted for years, is a murderer, but it means my boss and other people I respect are lying for him. And that I just can't believe. I know them. I don't know you. Good-bye."

The door closed in her face.

Mikayla raked her fingers through her hair as she turned and stepped from the porch, her teeth gritting at another dead end.

She'd put off coming to talk to Eddie Foreman's wife for three weeks after the funeral, hoping that in that time Gina Foreman would begin questioning the excuses Maddix Nelson and his friends had given her.

The lies, Mikayla amended. There could be no excuse for murder, or for covering it up.

Moving back to her Jeep, she wanted to stomp her feet, scream. Even her family argued with her over the questions she asked, the people she had tried to talk to in the past weeks.

Her parents were beside themselves with worry, and she couldn't blame them. It seemed as though the entire city council was covering for Maddix Nelson rather than trying to bring him to justice.

The police force patronized her if she even tried to question them. They followed her at times, watched her, though as of yet no one had threatened her. She had a feeling it was a good thing she strictly obeyed traffic laws or she would be paying a hell of a lot of fines.

She was expecting trouble soon, though. She was surprised it hadn't happened yet. The police were actually all very polite, cool, and apparently quite dismissive, but she could see the promise in their eyes. Mikayla knew she would never be able to depend on them if she needed protection.

As she moved around the front of the Jeep, her head lifted at the sound of a motor throbbing up the street. The wicked black Harley was cruising down the street, pulling attention to the extra tall, broad form of the man riding it.

His entire face was shielded by a black helmet, but nothing could hide the incredible body covered from shoulders to feet in matching black leather.

It was almost enough to steal her breath. It wasn't every day a woman saw the perfect male form, but if this wasn't the perfect male form, then it didn't exist.

Long muscular legs, broad shoulders, powerful arms, and, if she wasn't very much mistaken, a corded, muscular flat stomach beneath the snug black jacket he was wearing.

Wow.

She had only seen men like him in magazines.

If only she had seen him before her life had gone to hell four weeks ago. Before she had seen a man murdered and realized that her word meant nothing in the town she had been raised in, the town she loved.

There were days that she wondered if her life would ever be the same again. Nothing seemed to matter anymore but justice. And as her friend Deirdre told her daily, she was searching for justice for someone she didn't even know.

Or was she?

There were days she wondered if she wasn't searching for justice for herself as well.

No one believed her. No one believed she had seen Maddix Nelson shoot and kill his foreman that evening. Oh, they were nice enough about it. Most people were quite good at patronizing her.

Perhaps it was someone who resembled him, they said.

Had Mikayla been drinking? Doing drugs? Those questions had been asked often.

Her lips tightened as she jerked her attention from the fine specimen on the motorcycle and pulled herself into her Jeep.

She didn't have time for a man. She didn't have time to fantasize or to long for one right now. A man couldn't help her. Until Mikayla found out why everyone was lying to her, no one could help her.

Because nothing else mattered.

She wasn't a liar and she wasn't deranged, and it seemed as though it was up to her alone to prove it.

CHAPTER 2

Nik tossed the black helmet to the bed before striding to the refrigerator just inside the door of his hotel room. The small suite wasn't luxurious but clean and comfortable.

"What have you found?" He turned to Tehya as she watched him from the sofa across the room.

"Pretty much nothing." She shrugged her slender shoulders as she brushed back her long fiery red hair and watched him with brilliant emerald green eyes. "She's honest, pays her bills on time, never bounces a check, and until four weeks ago devoted herself to the clothing store she owns in town. She's the oldest of four children; her father is considered dependable and honest, as is her entire fucking family. Two of her brothers have had speeding tickets, nothing more. They're your average American family, Nik." Tehya shook her head and stared back at him as though confused. "I don't think I've ever investigated anyone without a shady past, secrets, or a blemished reputation. I could be going into shock."

He grunted at that as he pulled a beer from the fridge and closed the door with a snap.

"Bullshit," he growled. "There has to be more."

She stared back at him with offended mockery. "I know how to do my job, Renegade, and I'm damned good at it. If there was something to find on her, I would have found it. The extremely interesting part here is that there's simply nothing to find."

Twisting the cap from the bottle, he moved into the small area and sat down in the chair across from her.

"Maybe she was sleeping with Maddix Nelson? Scorned love perhaps?"

A strange smile quirked Tehya's lips as she shook her head. "I accessed her gynecological records. Your mark is a virgin, my friend. Lily-white and pure."

Shock widened his eyes. "There are virgins left in the world?"

Tehya's brows lifted, her own gaze reflecting her surprise. "Well, there are few over the age of sixteen," she agreed with a laugh. "But she's one of them."

"Damn." He reached back, released the leather thong holding his hair at his nape, and shook his head in bemusement. "She's not a hag. Does she have a disease of some sort?"

"No diseases." Tehya shook her head. "She's just your typical nice girl next door. It seems they're not extinct after all."

Nik couldn't fathom it. He wondered if he had ever known one of those nice, innocent girls and decided he hadn't. He sure as hell hadn't ever known a virgin.

"Why would your typical all-American girl next door want to destroy the reputation of the man who provides jobs to practically her entire family?" Nik asked Tehya as he rubbed at his jaw thoughtfully. "From what Maddix said this afternoon, her brothers, her father, even her damned cousins are working for his company."

"They *were* working for it," Tehya amended as she crossed her blue jean–clad legs and leaned back in the corner of the couch. "Her father broke his contract with the company the week after Mikayla's accusations against Nelson. The next day her brothers quit, and two days later her cousin pulled out of negotiations on the design contract Maddix was ready to sign. Two other cousins, heavy-equipment operators, quit the next week."

Nik rubbed at his upper lip with a forefinger as he considered that information.

"She was at Eddie Foreman's home this afternoon after I left Maddix's office," he told Tehya. "I drove past the house and saw her leaving."

Tehya nodded as she adjusted the shoulder of her loose white shirt. "She's been questioning a lot of people. Most of them seem to simply tolerate her and her questions. They're torn between believing her and believing Maddix. It doesn't help her cause that Maddix as well as his alibis seem genuinely confused by her accusations. Of course, those involved in a conspiracy always look better when dealing with such things in a gentle manner."

Nik arched his brow at her statement. "I don't think I'd be nearly so patient."

"Of course you would." She grinned. "You'd pull the trigger real slow and easy."

He grunted in amusement before tipping the beer to his lips and considering the information they didn't seem to have.

"What about Maddix Nelson?" he asked.

"According to him, the chief of police, and two council members, they were in an impromptu business meeting at the time of the shooting. Neighbors swear they saw each individual enter Maddix's home and saw him open the door for them. It appears he has nosy neighbors."

"Most neighbors are nosy," Nik mused.

Tehya inclined her head in agreement as Nik tapped a finger against the arm of the chair.

"Interesting," he finally stated. "Your sweet girl next door accusing an upstanding business figure of murder and he has the perfect alibi that places him in his home in a meeting. Does it seem a little pat?"

"A little." Teyha shrugged. "I'll be honest, Nik, I pulled every contact the Ops has in the area and a few we don't. I've covered this from back to front since you received the call from Maddix Nelson through Jordan's personal line. I can't find anything on him, or on the girl. If you accept his request, then you have your work cut out for you. And Jordan sent a warning. You're in this one on your own. The team's being pulled to Dallas on another op and we won't be free to help you."

Hell, he didn't want a damned thing to do with this. He wanted to pack up and fly back to Texas rather than deal with the woman he had seen leaving Gina Foreman's home that day.

He unwillingly remembered that long, thick dark blond hair. Almost because her eyes had caught his attention and immediately held it. Those amethyst eyes that were prettier in person. And evidently the innocence he had glimpsed in that photo went further than skin-deep.

"Jordan needs you to take care of this quickly." Tehya rose to her feet as she stared back at him. "We miss you when you're not with us, Nik."

His lips twisted at the message before he finished his beer and leaned forward to place it on the wood tray that sat on the large padded stool between the couch and chair.

Of course they needed him, Nik thought. Jordan's team was small and specialized; having even one member out during a mission could make it more difficult.

"I'll do my best," Nik promised, though he had a feeling this little favor was going to cost him much more time than he had.

"Look, Nik, maybe you should just walk away from this one," Tehya suggested as she walked to the side of his chair and laid her small hand on his shoulder. "Most of us owe a lot of people a lot of favors that we can never truly repay. This might be one of those cases."

But something inside him clenched at the thought of leaving. Mikayla Martin's image flashed before him, determination notching her small chin.

He stared at the wall across the room rather than the woman who often saw too much. "We'll see."

"Sure you will." She patted his shoulder before moving to the door. "Give me a call if you need anything. And remember, the ladies from Elite Two are leaving town day after tomorrow. If you need their help, they're available until then."

The three women who had once been a part of the European Operation, Elite Ops Two, had been assigned permanently to Jordan when their former commanders had been assigned to another unit. They were now 100 percent American on paper and awaiting their next assignment.

If Nelson came up with the money, Nik mused, then he was stuck here. Nikolai Steele did not work for free, but he owed Maddix, and Nik believed in paying his debts.

Stripping, he stepped into the shower, adjusted the water, and began washing away the grime that hours on the Harley had managed to accumulate on his body.

After leaving Maddix's office, Nik had ridden around, checking out locations and residences of the players involved. That's how he had run into Mikayla Martin as she left Gina Forman's house. As the water beat over his body, Nik opened his eyes to stare down at the heavy erection that hadn't abated since he had gotten his first true glimpse of Mikayla.

He'd never gotten so hard so fast in his life. Especially for a woman he knew he couldn't have.

But then, no one had ever dismissed him as Miss Martin had done. Her expression had at first been interested, admiring, and though Nik wasn't the least bit conceited, he had been irritated when she had turned from him, her expression twisting into a grimace.

It had only made him harder.

She was too tiny. Hell, she couldn't weigh a hundred pounds soaking wet if her life depended on it. But still, she was curvy. Nicely rounded breasts had pressed against the tailored white blouse she wore, while a flirty spring green skirt had flounced just below her thighs. Matching strappy sandals had complemented her legs, short though they were.

If she was five four it would shock the hell out of him. That long mass of straight, thick dark blond hair was the kind men dreamed of. Hair that would wrap around a man, hold him to her, bind him.

Nik grimaced, his fingers going to his dick as warm water sluiced down his body.

As tiny as she was, he could think of nothing but seeing her above him, lowering herself on the heavy shaft of his cock, her cries of pleasure echoing around him. Her pussy would be snug. His fingers tightened on his cock at the thought. She'd be hot and slick. He'd make sure she was wet enough to take him, but she would still feel the bite of erotic pleasure-pain.

Her face would flush. Would those amethyst eyes darken? Hell yeah, they would.

He stroked his fingers over the heavy shaft as he imagined her taking him, easing her hot little pussy down the thick stalk of his dick as her heavenly lashed eyelashes fluttered in pleasure.

He'd watch her. His fingers tightened further. He'd have to watch her take his cock. Watch plump, flushed folds of flesh part for the wide crest as she worked herself down it. Her heavy juices would coat his shaft, ease along it to the tight sack of his balls.

His jaw tightened at the thought as heated water ran over the taut sack.

God, he could get into fucking her.

Once he was lodged inside her to the hilt he'd watch her face as she rode him. Watch all that long hair as it flowed around her. Maybe it would cover her breasts, her tight nipples peeking through the strands.

And he could brush her hair back so his fingers could touch her tender nipples. Nipples that would be reddened, swollen from his earlier suckling of them. He would have caressed them, tasted them with his tongue as his hands stroked her body. Every inch of it. No part of her sweet flesh would go untouched by him. His hands, his lips, his tongue, would know every sweet inch of her flesh.

His hand moved faster, the thought of the pleasure that could be had building in his balls until they were tight, tortured with the need to come.

He would grip her shapely hips in his large hands. He bet he could span her waist with his fingers. He'd hold her, keeping her from moving too fast, from finishing it too soon. He'd press her tightly onto him as she filled herself with his erection, ensure that her delicate little clit rubbed against him. She would cry out then. Her soft pussy would ripple around the hard flesh, suck at it as she fought for release, as the tight portal grew hotter, slicker.

He pumped his hand down his dick as he imagined it. Imagined her crying out his name, her hands pressing into his stomach for leverage, her head tossing, reddened lips parting as she fought to breathe.

He would give her what she needed then.

Hell yes. He'd hold her hips tight and buck beneath her, driving deeper and harder inside the heated depths of her sweet cunt as he felt her unravel around him. Her pussy would clench and flex. It would spasm with convulsing, heavy strokes along his dick as she arched back.

And he would fuck her harder. He would thrust his cock inside her as hard and deep as possible as he felt her release, felt her juices spilling along his shaft before he came with her.

"Fuck, yes," he groaned, eyes closed, his balls tightening, surges of sensation racing up his spine as his cock jerked in his grip and his seed began to spurt.

He'd drive in hard. A groan tore from him. He'd lodge inside her to the hilt. His come spurted again as his hand tightened, moved faster. And he'd fuck her as he came. He'd pump into her with all the ferocious hunger and building need he'd denied himself for so long. A heavy snarl of hunger echoed around him as his abdomen clenched and the last harsh convulsions of release shot from his dick.

Ah, God. He'd give it all to her.

He leaned against the shower wall and fought to catch his breath.

As tiny as she was, as tender as she would be, he'd not be able to hold back.

You're a monster. My God, Nikolai. Do you care

nothing for me? Do you not care that you hurt me every time you touch me? Is it not enough that I suffer in your arms?

Nik flinched at the memory, the harsh words tearing through his head as sanity returned.

Would Mikayla see him as a monster as well? A man whose needs would only hurt her?

Of course she would. Disgust tore through him. He wouldn't be able to help but hurt her. She was too small, and he was much too large.

And there was no future for it.

He was a dead man. Dead men didn't hunger. Dead men didn't need.

He stared down at his dick in surprise. Dead men might not do any of those things, but that wasn't a dead man's cock he held in his hand. It forcibly reminded him that his hand was ineffective in stilling a hunger he shouldn't have.

"Fuck." He muttered the word with an edge of disgust before jerking a cloth from the rack inside the shower and soaping it quickly.

He didn't have time for this.

There was always a chance that Maddix would come up with the two hundred and eighty thousand dollars that his fee worked out to—with the discount. He should have ignored the call, he thought as he began to wash himself roughly. He should have forgotten that he still possessed some measure of honor. He should have denied the debt and moved on to the next mission.

There were so many things he should have done and hadn't. His biggest mistake had been staring into amethyst eyes and forgetting that he was a dead man.

Shaking his head, Nik finished his shower, dried off

roughly, then dressed in jeans and T-shirt before moving to the bedroom and lacing hiking boots on his feet.

On the off chance Maddix managed to come up with the fee, Nik needed to be prepared. He needed more information on the players involved in this little game. There had to be more than Tehya had managed to come up with.

Someone was lying, Maddix Nelson or Mikayla Martin, and Nik needed to at least have a place to start. Maddix had been too damned sincere perhaps, though it wasn't easy for most people to lie to Nik. He'd seen and heard every lie and knew the expressions and contradictory reactions that went with them.

Mikayla Martin had accused Maddix of murdering one of his employees, and rather than being enraged, Maddix had been confused. He hadn't struck out at the girl; neither had the chief of police. Maddix was playing a damned good game, Nik had to admit.

But then, so was Mikayla.

Moving to the small kitchenette, he was in the process of moving his backpack when a firm knock sounded at the door.

Nik turned and stared at the dark green panel in disgust. It seemed as though Maddix Nelson may have come up with the funds after all.

Nik moved to the green steel door and checked the peephole. Sure enough, the other man stood there, his expression stoic as he stared at the closed door.

Gripping the knob, Nik opened the door slowly and moved back to allow the other man to enter.

Maddix entered, his shoulders straight and tense as he reached back with one hand to rub at the tense muscles in tight circles. In the other hand, he carried a briefcase.

Nik stared at that briefcase, knowing what it contained.

Hell.

"Two hundred eighty thousand dollars." Maddix set the briefcase on the small table just inside the door as Nik moved to the other side.

Maddix stared at the case, sighed heavily, then looked back to Nik. "There it is," he said. "It's yours."

Nik stepped to the table, laid the briefcase flat, then flipped open the locks.

He flipped through the stacks of bills. Yep, that looked like two hundred and eighty thousand dollars to him. A fee for a favor owed.

Fuck.

There were days he wished he hadn't been raised to understand what honor meant. To understand what a favor owed truly was. Because standing there now, Nik could feel his gut clenching at the knowledge that he was stepping over a line.

He clicked the locks back into place and pushed the briefcase toward Maddix with a disgruntled glance toward the other man.

"It's all there." Maddix stared back at Nik in confusion.

"So hold on to it," Nik growled.

Maddix stared back at Nik silently, confusion darkening his eyes. "But you demanded the fee up front," he reminded Nik.

That line was staring him in the face, tempting him to cross it, to be the bastard the past was turning him into. To cross it now meant crossing it forever. There would be no turning back.

There would be no sunlit wheat-colored hair spread across his chest. No amethyst eyes staring back at him with true trust. Trust that wouldn't be later marred by the money that now sat between him and a job he knew better than to take.

"Take your money and get the hell out of here." Nik injected enough ice in his voice to ensure there was no chance of detecting the conflicting emotions raging inside him or the choices he didn't want to make at the moment.

"What . . ." Panic reflected in Maddix's face.

"I owe you the fucking favor," Nik stated coldly. "No fee required. Keep your money, Maddix. Maybe you can try to pay me off if I find out you're lying to me." He made certain his smile was colder than his eyes. "But I doubt it would work."

He'd hoped Maddix couldn't access the funds. Nik knew, despite Maddix's alibis, that there were indeed federal eyes watching for large withdrawals of personal funds that would hint at a hired killing.

He'd stared into eyes that hinted at dreams, at innocence. If he found out the innocence was true, then heaven help anyone daring to harm her.

Where the fuck had that come from?

"She gets to you, doesn't she?" Maddix shook his head. "I knew that picture would do it. It's the eyes."

Nik stared back at him, realizing now, as he had instinctively suspected earlier that day, that he was being played.

"I'll call you if I need to talk to you," Nik informed Maddix. "Until then, get the hell out of my face and pretend you don't know me. Or I'll walk away, Maddix. Right after I help her string your ass up."

And he could do it. He would do it. It wouldn't matter how many alibis Maddix had; Nik could destroy every damned one.

"I don't have to worry about that, Nik." Maddix picked up the briefcase and moved for the door. "And I can honestly say I have no damned idea who you are."

Nik stood back and watched as Maddix moved past him to the door. Maddix left the room, pausing only long enough to throw Nik one last confused glance before leaving.

Nik kicked the door closed, a curse escaping his lips as he raised his hands and linked them behind his neck before pacing into the bedroom.

The wildness burning inside him was only growing as the years passed. He managed to hold it back most days by throwing himself into a mission, by becoming the cold, unemotional robot he'd turned himself into ten years before when Jordan had offered him the chance of a lifetime.

A chance to walk away. To fight without rules. To make a difference.

Had he made a difference?

Not enough of one.

He still couldn't sleep at night. He still awoke to the sounds of gunfire, of his daughter's screams before he could reach the car she had died in.

If he had made enough of a difference, wouldn't those nightmares have left him by now? Wouldn't he be able to sleep in peace?

He stared at the bed, perfectly made, large, comfortable. The Suites had near-perfect beds. And he knew from experience he would find no sleep in them.

He left the helmet lying on the couch as he grabbed the keys to the Harley and left the room. Closing the door tight behind him, Nik made his way from the hotel to the shadowed back lot where he'd parked, and quickly checked the bike over before straddling it and giving the key a quick twist.

If he couldn't sleep, that left work. And he had plenty of work to do here. If he was going to figure out if Maddix was lying, then the place to start was with the girl.

All good girls had their secret little vices. There was no such thing as innocence or purity. Mikayla Martin might have a lot of good in her, but Nik was betting she was hiding a lot of bad as well. The key to getting past the good girl's defenses was to find her vices.

She might not party, but she did like to dance. She didn't have a steady boyfriend, but she was prone to date quite often. She was definitely a mystery.

Pulling from the parking lot, Nik hit the brightly lit streets of Wesel Boulevard while heading for the Cancun Cantina just minutes away.

Tehya's initial investigation into Mikayla showed a girl who loved her job, her family, her friends, and having fun in general. She was serious when she had to be, but she enjoyed her social life.

She was a different kind of woman, he thought. He wasn't certain if he knew how to deal with a woman who enjoyed her social life just as well as she enjoyed her job.

He was used to women who were somber, cynical, bitter, and/or psychotic. Women who had lived on the dark side too long, for whatever reason. Even those who worked with the team had their mental scars, their dark sides. They'd seen too much, knew too much about the evil that existed within the shadows.

She didn't look like a woman who knew anything about evil. She would be the type of woman that would provide a man the calm within the storm. Or would she remind him of everything he had never known or had and the innocence would be something to resent?

As Nik pulled into the Cantina lot he couldn't imagine that. He couldn't imagine resenting the peace that could be found in her arms.

He shook his head. His father had once told him that peace came from within a man. It was a peace Nik had yet to find within himself.

Securing the Harley, he strode into the Cantina, the loud music, weekend gaiety, and dim lighting similar to nearly every other club he'd been in during his time with the Elite Ops.

The dance floor was packed, bodies gyrating to the music pounding out from the surprisingly good country western group performing.

He scanned the room, searching for hair the color of wheat. Mikayla was a creature of habit, so he should find her here tonight.

She worked diligently at her shop five days a week and most nights. On Sunday she had lunch and dinner with her parents and she was available for her brothers and friends whenever they needed her.

She had a full social life and a broad base of friends. She truly was your everyday girl next door, from all accounts.

It was now Nik's job to delve beneath those accounts and find the truth. All he had to do was protect his soul in the process.

CHAPTER 3

Mikayla tapped her fingers against the table as her date, Thad Dawson, stood beside the table talking to friends. He worked in a law firm all week and then socialized on the weekends with the same people he worked with which made little sense to her.

At thirty, Thad was charming, appeared sincere, and seemed to have all the qualities of a Mr. Right. Not that she was looking for Mr. Right. She truly wasn't. But as her father often reminded her, she wasn't getting any younger.

She was his baby girl, and he just wanted to see her settled.

Mikayla just wanted to bring a killer to justice so she could get back to her life. She had dresses she wanted to make, unfinished designs waiting for completion. She had a life to get back to.

She should be doing something besides sitting here on a date with a man more concerned with the cases he'd been working on through the week than he was with hitting the dance floor, where she could at least expend some of the nervous energy still raging inside her.

At least she was still dating, she thought mockingly.

It seemed people were divided where she and Maddix Nelson were concerned. Those who believed her, or simply considered her amusing, were inclined to allow her within their circle of friends. The other side simply gave her a wide berth.

Thad, she suspected, only still asked her out because the owner of the law firm he worked for was still close friends with her father and hadn't, so far, seemed to take a side.

Things had definitely changed between her and Thad, though. The last few weeks, the budding relationship had become strained, and after tonight she doubted seriously she would see him again.

She might as well have not been here for all the attention he was showing her.

"The bastard was so guilty, Emily." Thad chuckled, breaking into Mikayla's thoughts, and rather than angry, or with a sense of offended justice, Thad sounded merely amused and almost in awe.

The bastard in question had murdered his wife.

"Hey, baby, the prosecutor knew he didn't have enough evidence. I simply pointed it out. That's why we're paid the big bucks. To make certain our clients have every advantage." Thad's friend and co-worker Emily Shaltz was filled with smug satisfaction.

As the daughter of one of the partners of the law firm, she was arrogant and self-important. Something Mikayla had always been able to overlook in Emily. Her parents were friends of the family, and Mikayla had always tried to overlook some of Emily's more grating qualities. Until the past weeks.

Mikayla's lips tightened at the obvious, in her eyes, miscarriage of justice. No wonder so many people hated lawyers. All that mattered to them was winning. Well, to some of them. There were a few, she had to admit, who were the good guys. They just weren't a part of this circle.

"And that's why Emily is moving quickly into a partner's position." Thad was clearly impressed.

"I'm not the only one." Emily turned to Thad, her gaze raking over him with obvious interest. "Thad is heading there quickly himself. He clearly has what it takes to make the partners notice him."

Mikayla sat back and watched the display. Tall, svelte, and slender, Emily Shaltz, with her clear dark blue eyes, curvy, tall body, and so obvious superiority, had no doubt of her charisma and sexual charm. The fact that Thad was obviously falling quickly beneath the promise in that cool gaze was really no surprise.

She could slip away and no one would notice her, Mikayla thought with a slight edge of amusement. She could go home, do a little work, and actually go to bed at a decent hour and she doubted Thad would even know she was gone.

"Ma'am." The waitress at Mikayla's side drew her attention but received no more than a passing glance from those standing at the other side of the table.

Mikayla glanced up. "Yes?"

"The gentleman at the bar has offered to buy you a drink." The waitress pointed toward the extremely tall, had-to-be Nordic, blond man sitting casually at the bar. Even from across the room he presented an imposing figure.

Mikayla glanced back at Thad, gave a little smile, and shook her head. "Nothing for me, thank you." She rose to her feet. "I believe I'm heading home for the night."

Light blue eyes, rakishly long white blond hair, and a body guaranteed to stop women in their tracks at thirty paces. There wasn't an ounce of give in those broad shoulders, nor in the hard, savage lines of his arrogant face.

A dark overnight growth of beard and mustache shadowed his lower face. He looked entirely too confident of his own sexuality, and dangerous.

Danger exuded from his pores. It surrounded him. It was so much a part of him that Mikayla felt her heart racing at the impact of it.

She had seen similar men. Not as hard, not as dangerous. Men who had been in war for too long, who had returned home unable to fit back into the steady, peaceful routine they had known before they left. But they were a pale imitation of this man. This man was the essence, the very definition, of danger.

The dark rider she had seen on the motorcycle earlier had had a body to die for. This man had the body, but those hardened features, the cool ice blue eyes, and the expression of hardened purpose held the warning that he was more than just a hard, gorgeous body. This man was a weapon.

It was definitely time she headed home. If she had drawn the attention of this man somehow, then she could be in more trouble than she already thought she had gotten herself into.

Thad didn't even notice when she left the table. Damn if that wasn't enough to prick a girl's ego. He'd harassed her for weeks for a date before she'd given in. Thad was a good friend, she'd known him most of her life. He was a nice guy, but too intent on impressing the boss's daughter to pay much attention to his date. She understood. She wasn't tall and curvy and a part of the social sphere Thad wanted to enter. She was short, perhaps too curvy. Her long hair wasn't blond; it wasn't brown. It was what her mother called dirty blond.

It was straight; it wasn't silky. Her breasts weren't large, and she wasn't available for a quick one-night stand.

That pretty much canceled her out for most men.

Slipping through the throng of dangers, she headed for the exit.

The Cantina sat below the major convention center and hotel in the county. It was connected to it and provided a major source of entertainment for the guests there.

It was often a major source of entertainment for Mikayla. In the past weeks, she hadn't quite been in the mood for entertainment, though.

Pulling the keys to her Jeep from her jeans pocket, Mikayla was suddenly thankful that Thad had been running late today. It meant she'd had a reason to drive her own vehicle to the club rather than riding with him.

It gave her a ride home.

Moving through the shadowed parking lot, she pressed a key between two fingers defensively, prepared, just in case. She'd learned the hard way that nothing was really safe. That at any second something could happen. Something one didn't bring on oneself.

Watching the shadows warily, her gaze canvassing each area that could hide a threat, she moved as quickly as possible to her Jeep.

It had been impossible to park close to the entrance of the Cantina. She'd been forced to park in a lot across the street. The only place available at the time was far, toward the other end.

She should have gone home when she realized she couldn't park close enough to the bar to be safe. But Thad had been so insistent.

This would teach her.

Quickening her step, she waited until she was close

enough to the vehicle before hitting the automatic door locks. She heard the click as she rounded the car. Her hand was reaching out for the door latch when she'd realized how serious her error had been.

Hard hands grabbed her from behind.

"Fucking troublemaking cunt!" A harsh growl sounded behind her.

Mikayla didn't have three younger brothers for nothing, and she sure as hell wasn't going to be a victim who didn't fight back.

Fear roiled through her. Terror became a creature, snarling, fighting, as adrenaline surged through her bloodstream and nothing but the instinct for survival ruled.

She swung her fist with the key tight between two fingers.

A male grunt sounded in the darkness as she felt herself being thrown, flipped around as she slammed into the back of the Jeep.

Her face raked against the side of the canvas top as her breast was driven against the spare tire. A cry of pain tore from her lips, and with the next breath she was screaming, kicking, scratching, the key gripped between her fingers as she lashed out. In the dark, she couldn't see much: a shadowed face. Her attacker wasn't much taller than she, but he was strong.

His fingers wrapped around her throat, clenched. Mikayla drove the keys into a soft midsection. A hard grunt, the fingers loosened, but a second later it felt as though a sledgehammer had driven into the side of her face.

A fist. Distantly, she realized it was a fist. Every muscle in her body went lax for precious seconds as shock and pain traveled through her body. The keys fell from her fingers, her only weapon of defense gone as she felt those fingers, too strong, wrap around her throat once again.

She was going to die.

Mikayla could feel that knowledge rattling inside her brain. She couldn't fight against strength. She was too weak now. Her senses felt scattered, her breath so short.

She was definitely going to die.

Nik walked out of the Cantina, his gaze searching the brightly lit front entrance of the club as he looked for Mikayla. Cars whizzed by, their headlights flickering through the shadows as he narrowed his eyes in his search for her.

Mikayla had managed to get out of the bar before he realized she had left. She had disappeared into the throng and he'd lost sight of her. By the time Nik realized she was leaving he was too far behind to catch up with her.

She must have been parked close, he thought. The only way she could have gotten away from him so quickly was if she was parked directly in front of the Cantina.

His jaw tightened.

He was turning to stalk to the far end of the lot to his Harley when he heard it: a muted cry.

He stopped, pausing, his gaze searching the parking area across the street.

Where had it come from?

There. Again.

Moving, Nik raced across the street, seeing two shadows struggling at the far end of the parking lot. He was pounding across the blacktop when he heard a strangled cry of feminine rage.

The taller shadow fell back briefly. But only briefly.

Nik wasn't close enough.

"Mikayla!" He called out her name as he raced between the cars.

The shadow paused, twisted, and in less than a second sprinted off.

Nik watched in horror as hair the color of the softest wheat shone for the briefest second in the flashes of the car lights on the other side of the parking area.

Almost in slow motion she crumpled to the ground just before he could reach her.

Fuck. Fuck.

He was too late.

Horror raced through his system as he hurriedly crouched beside her, his hands running over her quickly as he searched for the telltale dampness of blood, the sign of broken bones. The hilt of a knife.

"No." Weak, panting, she pushed at his hands as they moved over her breasts. "What are you doing?"

She sounded muffled, strangled. His eyes had adjusted to the darkness. He could see her face now, no blood. One hand pushed at his as the other rose to rub at her neck.

"Miss Martin?" He brushed her hair back from her face as he helped her sit up. "Are you okay?"

If he were a lesser man, a normal man, he would have been shaking.

His hands framed her face as she stared up at him, her head wobbling as he felt her shuddering.

"Mikayla?" He tried to smooth out the ruined sound of his voice, compliments of a fire that had burned too bright, too hot, too long ago.

"I'm fine." Her voice was low, weak. "Who are you?"

"Nik. Nik Steele."

Fuck, he knew her name, but she hadn't met him. She was going to be suspicious as hell.

"The waitress was nice enough to tell me your

name," he told Mikayla as he watched her fighting to catch her breath, her hand still massaging her neck. "Are you okay?"

She nodded jerkily, the movement halting as she grimaced in pain.

"He tried to strangle me," she rasped, fear quaking in her voice. "You scared him off."

He hadn't scared the fucker off fast enough. She could have been killed. It took only a second to use a knife, but whoever had attacked her hadn't wanted to kill her the quick, easy way.

Thank God.

"Help me up." She pressed her hands to the ground to push herself up.

"Here." Nik gripped her beneath her arms and lifted her carefully to her feet, holding her as he watched her find her balance. "You should go to the hospital."

Her head lifted slowly.

"Oh, my God, no!" The ragged sound of her voice had rage striking through his chest. The sound of irritated vocal cords. The struggle to breathe as she was being strangled had done minute damage as well.

"You should be checked out."

"My entire family would show up like avenging angels." Her hand lifted shakily to her brow.

"It would be better to make certain you're not hurt."

"I'm fine." She took a deep breath. "I'm just shaky."

"Too shaky to drive—"

"I have to find my keys." She shook her head slowly. "Help me find my keys."

Her keys were at her feet.

Bending, Nik picked them up, holding them away from her as she reached out for them.

"Hospital, or I can drive you home. Take your pick."

Mikayla stared up at the stranger. There was a sense

of familiarity in the way he acted toward her. It didn't make sense. She didn't know him. She knew she had never met him before. She would have remembered if she had.

"Who are you again?"

"Nik Steele," he answered, his voice, despite its roughness, incredibly gentle.

"That doesn't tell me who you are." She stared at the keys in his hand. "Could I please have my keys?"

He shook his head slowly. White blond hair dusted against his shoulders as his dark clothing blended in with the night.

"I told you, I can drive you home or to the hospital. There's always the option of calling an ambulance or the police."

"No." Her response was quick.

The last thing she needed was the police. She doubted very seriously they'd help her anyway. They would probably give her assailant a medal.

"No police." She just wanted to go home.

"Come on." His hand gripped her arm, not roughly but in a grip of steel as he steered her to the passenger seat of the Jeep. "Get in. I'll take you home."

He helped her into the passenger seat, hiding a smile as she watched him warily, suspiciously.

There were options. She could feel her cell phone in the back pocket of her jeans. She could call one of her brothers.

No. No way. Any of the three would freak out, call her parents, and she would end up in the hospital whether she wanted to be there or not. And her father would definitely call the police. He'd curse and yell at them when they showed their lack of concern. Her mother would be shocked. She knew most of the police officers in town by first name. There was no sense in allowing more of them to disappoint Mikayla's gentle mother.

Jorrey Martin had cried last week when Mikayla had called to report a break-in attempt at the shop. No one had showed up. Her father had been forced to call and threaten them with a report to the state police.

Not that that would help.

The driver's side door opened and the huge form of the strange man was forced to release the catch on her seat, shoving it back the full length before he could fold his frame into the seat.

"Address?" He turned to her as he pushed the key into the ignition and turned it on.

Mikayla gave him her address quickly, then watched as he put the Jeep into gear and backed out of the parking space.

"Know where that's at, do you?" she asked.

She didn't live in Hagerstown. She'd bought her first house in the small town of nearby Williamsport.

"Actually, I do. I just rented the house next to you this afternoon. I was waiting until tomorrow to move in." His teeth flashed in the dim glow of the dash lights as he glanced over at her. "Hell of a coincidence, huh?"

She so did not believe in coincidence. The house beside hers was definitely for rent. The single-story brick and stucco, like her own, was set behind a screen of evergreen and decorative privacy pine.

"And how do you intend to get back to your car?"

"My Harley," he told her. "Call a cab and have it waiting on me when I get there. I'll see you safely inside your home; then I'll leave. I'm not moving into the house until tomorrow."

"And you care why?"

That didn't make sense. At the moment, Washington

County and the surrounding area was rather divided over whether to kill her or to laugh at her.

She had witnessed a murder and seen the murderer, and no one wanted to believe her because the murdered hadn't been well liked and the murderer was a powerful member of the community with an unbreakable alibi. And it seemed someone definitely wanted to shut her up.

"Why wouldn't I care?" Nik asked as he pulled to a stop at the intersection. "Not all men are assholes, pretty girl."

Her brows lifted. Pretty girl?

Mikayla watched the traffic, her hands clenched desperately in her lap as she fought to hold on to her control. Fear was a wild creature inside her, barely contained. This was a stranger. He wasn't the man who had attacked her. If he had been, she would have been simply dead. His hands were huge, a fitting match to the extra tall, corded length of his body and his rough-hewn face.

"I didn't say you or anyone else was an asshole." She touched the bruise she could already feel forming on her face. "Except the person who decided to use me for a punching bag tonight."

"You went out without a purse or anything to steal; it's hard to believe it was a mugger," Nik commented. "Why do you think you were attacked?"

Mikayla glanced at his profile before sighing tiredly. "You're not from around here, are you?"

He chuckled at that. "Nope. Texas."

"Figures." For some reason, it was hard to see him as a Texan, though. "Been here long?"

"Long enough to rent a house." He grinned as he slid a look her way before returning to the traffic. "And you haven't answered my question."

She bit her lip in indecision. "I might have made some people angry." She shrugged, feeling defensive. Angry.

The store was thriving more from curiosity than from her designs. She no longer trusted friends to hold her secrets, because too many had repeated things she had confided to them. She had tried to play the game as Maddix Nelson was, keeping her reserve in public and trying to find the truth by talking to those she knew were connected to the foreman. But no one would talk to her. And Maddix had the perfect alibi. An evening business meeting with the chief of police and two of the members of the city council. It was an alibi she would have believed herself if she hadn't known better.

"Might have?" Nik shot her another glance as he turned onto the interstate and headed for the exit to nearby Williamsport. "How did you 'might have' pissed someone off?"

"Something I'd rather not talk about." Mikayla gave a quick shake of her head. "I'd rather know why you're here from Texas."

"A job." In profile, the hard, sharp planes of his face held a wicked, sexy edge.

The sight, the image of him, had a strange effect on her. Her stomach tightened in response; she could feel her heart racing. It was pounding against her chest, making her breathing short, as she became aware of a peculiar sensitivity within her body.

"What kind of job? What do you do?" She sounded a little breathless, but she could excuse it. She had just been attacked. She'd been struck. God, her father had never even spanked her. That was the first time she had ever been struck in her life.

"I'm in private security," Nik answered, his voice

rasping along her senses, almost broken. It was one of the most arousing sounds she had ever heard.

"What kind of private security? Like a bodyguard? A security guard?" She brushed back her hair as the aches of the strikes against her flesh began to actually hurt.

At least nothing had been broken.

"Installation of customized security systems in this case," he told her. "I'm good with electronics."

"You said 'in this case'?" She lifted her hand slowly to the ache in her ribs. "Do you sometimes do other things?"

"Bodyguard, deliveries. I'm pretty well rounded." He made the turn onto the exit, then headed through the small town Mikayla called home.

"So you're here to install personal security systems. Who are you working for?" She needed a distraction until she could get rid of him.

"Privileged information," he drawled as he glanced back at her. "Sorry."

"Not a problem." She shook her head as they drew closer to the house. A part of her regretted that the ride was almost over.

She felt safe here with him, despite the fact that she didn't know anything about him.

"You're hurting," he stated, his voice hardening as he pulled the Jeep slowly into her driveway and slid it into park before turning to look at her.

She almost jerked her hand back from her ribs.

"Some guy just knocked me around for the hell of it," she pointed out with an edge of bitterness. "Yeah, I'll have a few bruises."

"I think you should go to the hospital," Nik suggested, his gaze intent as he stared back at her. "You could be seriously hurt and not know it."

She shook her head. "It's bruises."

"You don't know that, Mikayla," he chided her, his voice lowering. "It could be something far serious and you wouldn't know."

"He slammed me against the Jeep and hit me in the face," she said, rejecting the idea. "There are no internal injuries or broken bones. I'm just going to be sore."

"You're just going to have a bruise across the whole side of your face." He reached out then, his fingertips almost brushing against the ache in her cheek. "He should be killed for that alone."

Mikayla's lips parted before she could control it, her heart speeding up, racing until she swore she could feel it in her throat.

It wasn't racing in fear. It was racing in excitement at the thought of Nik's fingers touching her flesh.

"Let's not talk about killing." She almost gave a hard, bitter laugh. The last thing she wanted to even think about was killing. "I forgot to call your cab. You're going to have to wait awhile for it to arrive."

His lips quirked in amusement. "Not a problem." He pulled his own cell phone from the holster at his side before hitting a number.

"Pickup," he notified the other end before giving the address. "Yeah. Good thing I caught you. I'll be waiting outside."

He flipped the phone closed.

"A friend?" she asked.

"A co-worker. She owes me a favor." He pushed the phone back into the holster before turning back to Mikayla. "I'd ask for coffee, but I can almost feel the word 'no' on your lips."

She had to grin at that. No matter how much she wanted to spend more time with this intriguing man, she wasn't as brave as she wished she were.

"Sorry," she sighed, hearing the heavy regret in the sound. "My dad is already going to go ballistic because I didn't call him first thing. If he finds out I let a stranger into my house, he'll begin to question how well he raised me."

"A woman who listens to her father. A strange concept." Nik grinned, causing her stomach to turn flips at the quirk of his hard, bitable lips. Damn, she would love to taste those lips.

"There are a few of us left," she promised him, letting a small laugh pass her lips despite the ache in her ribs.

"Yes, so it seems." He tilted his head in agreement. "Ah, well, my ride will be here in two more minutes. I have to say, I was glad to meet you, Miss Martin."

"And I have to say, thank you for saving me." She grinned back as she held her hand out. "Can I have my keys now?"

Pulling the keys from the ignition, he placed them slowly in her palm, his fingers touching her flesh as she felt a subtle, low rush of energy as it passed over her skin.

Her fingers curled over the keys, brushing his as his hand lifted.

"Thank you again," she said, her voice more breathless than before.

"I'll see you soon," he promised. "Remember, I live just next door. Come on now; let me see you inside so I can be sure you're going to be okay. Like your father, I'll worry."

"You have children?" Was he married? Oh, Lord, was she lusting after a married man who was going to move in next door with a wife and children?

His expression stilled, though. Something hard and brutal flashed in those icy blue eyes.

"I did once," he finally said before giving his head a hard shake and pulling the latch to the door and stepping out quickly.

He didn't want to talk about it; that was obvious.

He was a father once, he said. His child was dead or somehow lost to him then?

She held her questions, her curiosities. Some subjects were too sensitive, especially between two people who didn't know each other.

Her door opened; then he reached inside and gently helped her from the Jeep.

"Nik, I'm sorry." She laid her hand on his arm.

"For what?" His eyes narrowed in the dim light.

"For whatever hurts you," she said softly before stepping aside and moving gingerly along the sidewalk, aware of him behind her.

Her door was still locked. Inserting the key, she unlocked it, stepped inside, and pushed in the code for the alarm system. Everything was still secure. Her lamps were still on; her cat, Biskus, meowed from the arched doorway into the kitchen just as he did every time she returned.

"Everything's fine." She turned back to Nik, aware of him staring down at her, tall and broad. Protective. "Thank you again."

"Thank you." He reached out, touched her unbruised cheek, then turned and left.

A car pulled up at the curb and as Mikayla watched the door open she saw the redhead inside. Tall, of course, and pretty.

And then they were gone.

Closing the door behind her, Mikayla reset the locks and the security system before staring down at the rather large black and white long-haired cat that had adopted her.

"Well, it's just you and me again, Biskus."

He meowed again, then turned and loped back to the kitchen.

A clear indication he felt he deserved a treat for being left at home alone.

She felt perhaps she deserved a treat herself. For the bruise on her face, the one she felt forming on her ribs, the fear she had experienced that night, and the man she had been forced to walk away from.

Her father would have been horrified.

She could hear him raging even as a smile tipped her lips.

Her brothers would go crazy.

And that still wasn't enough to dim her interest.

Or her arousal.

CHAPTER 4

"Oh, my God!" Deirdre's voice was horrified, her expression slackening into lines of complete disbelief as Mikayla walked into the shop early the next morning.

She had timed her arrival to coincide with Deirdre's and to ensure she could take care of customers while Mikayla hid for the day.

"It's not as bad as it looks," Mikayla assured her assistant.

Mikayla knew her face looked damned bad. The bruise spread across her cheek to her jaw and then to the side of her lip. Her lower lip was split and, though not grotesquely swollen, incredibly uncomfortable.

"It's not as bad as it looks?" Deirdre's eyes were wide, her hands moving from her silk-clad hips as she rushed across the plush carpet to Mikayla.

"Mikayla, what in the world happened to you?" Her friend's green eyes, the color of a summer leaf, filled with threatening tears as her hands lifted to Mikayla's shoulders and turned her more fully to the light. "My God. Who hit you? Do I need to start collecting bail for your brothers?"

"They don't know, and you're not going to tell

them." Mikayla suppressed a shiver; she was doing everything she could to keep her family from finding out.

"You think you can keep this from them?" Deirdre propped her hands on her hips again, the cream silk of her skirt stretching over her hips as her shoulders straightened beneath the light blue sleeveless blouse she wore.

"I'd better keep it from them," Mikayla muttered. "They'll make my life hell otherwise."

"So what happened?" Deirdre demanded again, following Mikayla as she gave a brief shake of her head and moved to her office at the back of the shop.

"I was attacked in the parking lot of the club," she told the other woman as they entered her office. "Maybe it was a mugger."

"And maybe it was a Nelson fanatic," Deirdre snapped, anger filling her tone now. "That's who it was, wasn't it?"

"I really don't know, Deirdre." Mikayla plopped her purse on the less-than-tidy desk and sat down gingerly in the softly padded chair behind it.

"What else is wrong?" Deirdre would have to notice the careful way Mikayla took her seat.

It never failed. Her family and friends were like overprotective bears at times.

"Look, I was just knocked around a little bit," Mikayla assured Deirdre. "A white knight showed up, rescued me, and delivered me home safe and sound."

And that was enough to distract Deirdre.

"White knight?" Deirdre plopped her rear on the corner of Mikayla's desk, the open door giving her clear sight of the front door, and gave Mikayla a demanding look. "Give deets, girlfriend."

Mikayla laughed. "Deets, huh? What makes you think there are any details?"

Details such as height, hair, eyes, pure male sex appeal. Oh, Mikayla had deets.

"Well, duh." Deirdre laughed. " 'White knight' is the key word here. Tell me all about him."

Mikayla's lips parted as the light tinkle of the bell at the door sounded. She started to laugh at the pout that formed on Deirdre's lips, until she saw a look of complete awe fill her face.

Mikayla leaned forward tentatively and restrained a sigh at the sight of the man walking across the carpet. In black leather pants, biker boots, and a T-shirt that stretched across his hard, broad chest, Nik Steele walked into the dress shop.

"The white knight," she murmured in amusement as Deirdre seemed locked in amazement.

"Mikayla?" He stepped into the office, looking between her and Deirdre.

Ice blue eyes. Mikayla wondered if there was actually any emotion behind that gaze. The night before, she hadn't seen the ice there, the hard, almost cynical light; instead, she had felt something, sensed it, in the way he acted, the tone of his voice.

But she remembered what he had said. He'd once been a father. Losing a child would destroy the soul, she thought. But would it leave anything for anyone else?

"Can I help you, Mr. Steele?" Leaning back, she let her gaze rove over that gorgeous hard body just one more time.

His lips quirked as though he was well aware of his effect on her and Deirdre as well. It would be hard to miss it; Deirdre was staring at him as though he were a sweet and she was dying for a sugar rush.

"Yes, ma'am, you can." A flicker of warmth glimmered in his icy eyes. "I was wondering if you'd like to join me for steaks tonight? I thought I'd throw a few on the grill. Break out a couple of bottles of beer."

"If she's not interested, then I am." Deirdre suddenly found her voice. "She's not real smart sometimes, ya know." There was a wealth of amusement in Deirdre's expression as Mikayla frowned at her.

"She appears extremely intelligent to me," he drawled, that sexy grin still tugging at his lips as he crossed his arms over his chest and leaned against the door frame.

The flesh between her thighs heated, grew damp. That rat-a-tat-tat of her heart made her breathless. He had an effect on her that no other man ever had.

"Yes, she's extremely intelligent," Mikayla informed him as though participating in the conversation.

"I don't know." Deirdre leaned her hand against the desk and glanced back at Mikayla. "Look at her face. See, she knows better than to be in dark places by herself. I bet that was where you found her, huh?"

"It was indeed." Nik's gaze sliced back to her. "Parked in the darkest area as she played punching bag for some asshole. She hasn't told me why yet."

Deirdre's gaze swung back to Mikayla in amazement. "He doesn't know?" She switched back to Nik. "You don't know?"

"I didn't say I haven't been checking into it."

He knew.

Mikayla swallowed tightly before drawing in a deep breath. At least, as deep as sore ribs allowed.

"Figure anything out yet?" she asked.

"A few things," he answered. "Enough to know why you were attacked last night."

"You work fast." A sense of disappointment filled her. She couldn't tell if he believed her or not.

"So who do you believe?" Deirdre voiced the question Mikayla was only thinking.

Nik stared back at Deirdre as though in surprise. "I tend to believe the punching bag. They rarely get used without reason."

Mikayla's heart melted. It was totally illogical, but he wasn't laughing at her, and he wasn't questioning her honesty.

"There you are, a smart man." Deirdre waved her hand toward Nik as she stared back at Mikayla, satisfaction filling her gaze. "Now, if you don't show up for that steak, then I'm gonna."

Deirdre bounced from the desk at the sound of the bell tinkling once again. Nik straightened and stepped into the office. Deirdre got as far as the doorway and froze and Mikayla could have sworn she whimpered.

Mikayla knew who it was. Deirdre turned to Mikayla, her expression filled with pity. "Can I have the day off?" she asked as Mikayla's father and brothers stepped into the store.

Dread filled Mikayla. "Can I?"

Nik was standing on the back deck of the rented house, the grill heating, steaks lying on the small grill ledge, as he heard the gate between the two properties squeak as it opened.

He restrained a grin.

He'd left that shop that morning just after giving her father the details of the night before. First, Nik had been required to show ID and subject himself to an in-depth interrogation on why he was there and how long he was staying and even provide references. They were references Nik had no doubt Mr. Martin would call.

The man was extremely protective of his only daughter, and the three young men with him had been almost as intense. There was no doubt Mikayla was well cherished by her family.

She had humored them, though there had been desperation in her gaze as she looked at Nik. A plea to rescue her as her family descended upon her.

He'd been amused, he had to admit. A part of that amusement had been overshadowed by grief, though. He would have been just as protective of his own daughter. Seeing Ramsey Martin's fear and love for his child had sent a shaft of guilt tearing through Nik.

What would he do had he ever learned a man was intending to use his child as Nik was intending to use Ramsey Martin's child?

He'd kill him.

That was an easy question to ask.

But Mikayla wasn't a child any longer. She was a grown woman, one with an innocent appeal that drove him insane.

He couldn't equate Mikayla with a child, his or any others. He was man enough to see the woman in her, and to be aroused by her.

"I was wondering how long it would take you to break free." He didn't turn as he sensed her moving toward the deck.

"I completely blame you for the entire debacle that my day has been." The accusation in her voice had a grin tugging at his lips. There was no true heat, more exasperation and irritation than anything.

"That's why I have your beer extra cold." He turned to her, and he swore his cock surged harder, faster, than it had the night before.

Son of a bitch. Look at her. That fall of soft wheat blond hair over one side of her face as those amethyst eyes watched him with narrowed intent.

That look sliced right through him. Like fire snaking through his body. He felt sweat begin to dot his shoulders, felt his balls tighten painfully.

Hell, he wanted to taste her so damned bad he could barely stand it. The need for it was a hunger raging through him with a force that almost left him shaking.

He'd never wanted anything like he wanted this woman right now.

"How do you like your steak?" He had to turn from her. If he didn't turn away from her, then he was going to lift her up on the long wooden table, stroke that flimsy dress up her thighs, and peel it from her plump breasts.

"Medium whatever," she answered as she stepped up to the deck. "I hope you have salad and a potato to go with that. You owe me after the hell I went through today. Do you know they made me go to the hospital? Do you know what hospitals are like? I hate those damned places."

He turned back, just for a second, he told himself. He was just going to look at her for another second.

She stood at the top of the steps, her hip cocked, one hand resting against it as her hair fell around her shoulders like a sunlit cape.

She was so damned short. And so fucking petite he was almost scared to touch her. Hell, she'd be the death of him. He was going to expire from sexual hunger before the night was over.

"Salad and potato are waiting inside," he promised her.

He'd done his homework. He knew how she liked her steak before he'd even asked her. He knew she preferred Caesar salad and baked potatoes. She liked ranch dressing on her salad, butter and ranch on her potato. She preferred rolls with honey and liked lemon with her sweet tea.

She wore dresses, rarely wore jeans, and she liked silk and French lace beneath her clothing.

He was dying to get under her dress.

"Where's that beer?" The irritation in her voice only made him harder. Made him feel challenged.

"Here you go, pretty girl." Pulling open the door to the minirefrigerator beneath the grill, he opened the beer, then turned and handed it to her.

Her fingers glanced his as she took it and he swore his body tightened further. His cock was going to explode at this rate.

Nik swore he could smell the sweet, soft aroma of arousal reaching out to him, or perhaps it was just the innocent curiosity in her gaze and his own imagination.

"God, they made me crazy." She plopped down on the seat at the picnic table, crossed one slender leg over her knee. Her strappy soft blue sandals were an attractive contrast to the white and pale yellow sundress that barely met her knees.

The fluttery dress was pretty as hell, feminine and soft, tempting. It made a man want to slide it right off her body.

"They love you." Nik tossed the steaks on the grill, hoping to distract himself before he ended up trying to seduce her right there on the back deck.

"To death." She gave a charming little puff of air behind him. "Mom showed up just after you left. She cried when I didn't want to go to the hospital. Then she cried some more when she got a good look at my face. Do you have any idea how hard it was to escape them? Do you know Dad is threatening to move my brothers in with me? Can you imagine how irritating my brothers are?"

"They seemed concerned." He could see her killing them in three days flat. The three of them had postured, growled, and frowned at him the entire time he had been at the shop.

"They seemed mentally retarded." That little puff of air again.

He chuckled at the accusation.

"I swear I think Dad must have dropped them on their heads when they were babies. Those three have the combined IQ of a brick."

Mixed with the irritation was affection. She loved her brothers, but Nik could understand why they made her crazy. Once upon a time, he had had a sister himself. One he had hovered over and protected.

"You managed to hold them off, though?" Damn, he hoped she had, because he had every intention of seducing the hell out of her. That would be rather hard to do if she had three brothers living with her.

"I threatened to cook for them." He caught her shrug from the corner of his eye.

"You can't cook?"

"Not as far as they know." She tipped the beer to her lips, took a long, refreshing drink, and he almost came in his jeans. He could only imagine how sexy those pretty lips would look on his body. On his cock.

That told him a lot, though. She protected herself against the overprotection of her family. She had deliberately allowed her brothers, men who enjoyed their food, to think she couldn't cook.

He tested the steaks, judged their doneness, then pulled them from the grill and placed them on the china. Moving to the table, he set the steaks in front of her, moved back into the house, and gathered the rest of the meal.

The first beer eased her irritation. The second was enjoyed with the steak as early evening began to dim. Nik lit the citronella candles he had waiting on the far edge of the table, pulled two more beers from the mini-fridge, and cleared the dishes.

"You should be punished." A little pout crossed her lips as he returned to his seat. Even the bruise marring her face did nothing to detract from the seductive image.

"Why is that?" He chuckled as he leaned closer. "I didn't tell your father anything."

"No, you told the owner of the bar as he was leaving this morning, who then called my father in like five seconds flat. You have to be careful around here, Mr. Steele. There are no secrets."

"I'll remember that." He watched her carefully. "The owner of that bar had some very interesting information, though."

He watched her eyes. In less than a second the guileless amusement turned to wary suspicion.

"I bet he did." She tensed, her eyes filling with disappointment.

"You've had a lot of problems like this, haven't you, Mikayla?" Nik asked gently.

Her lips twisted mirthlessly and for a second he saw a flash of grief.

"Yeah, I have." She shrugged, causing the filmy strap of her dress to slip partially over her silken shoulder. "Maddix has the perfect alibi." Her head lifted, her eyes meeting Nik's head-on then. "Are you sure you're on the punching bag's side here?"

There was a wealth of cynicism in that look, and hurt. She believed in what she had seen. She truly believed Maddix Nelson had committed that murder.

"Let's say I'm in the 'I wasn't there' camp," Nik finally answered her, wondering at that prick of guilt he suddenly felt. "And I tend to lean to the side of the underdog. I have to say you're definitely the underdog here, sweetheart."

"Underdog" was an understatement.

Mikayla stared back at Nik Steele, wondering at the shadow that briefly darkened the light blue of his eyes, that made them appear not so cold or lacking in emotion.

What did he hide behind those eyes?

"Yes, I'm the underdog," she agreed, shrugging before reaching to her shoulder to readjust the strap of her dress.

He watched her. Those eyes focused on her movement, lightning swift, and with another flash of that brief, dark emotion. And hunger. Mikayla glimpsed the hunger in his gaze. That flash set a charge within her own nerve endings. It was like flash fire. It tore across her flesh, tightened her nipples, and for a second literally stole her breath.

"I should go." But instead of jumping to her feet as she knew she should, she sat there instead, allowing his gaze to hold her trapped.

"Why?" Eatable lips. The man had completely eatable lips. Just a little bit full, just a little bit sexy, hinting at restraint, and a tempting hunger to lose control.

She could feel it, that knowledge, sense it with the raging feminine need coursing through her body.

"Because you're dangerous," she whispered, feeling her fingers shake as she lifted them from the table. "And I think I've had enough danger in my life lately."

She had to force herself to begin standing.

"Are you sure you want to leave now, Mikayla?"

He stood, leaned closer, and for that moment she was lost.

She was lost in his eyes. Icy, icy blue eyes that at first were as frozen as the Arctic. Until he came closer. Until she glimpsed for a second that flame of blue in their depths.

Until his lips touched hers.

That kiss.

She had read about *that kiss*. She had seen movies that revolved around *that kiss*. But she had never known it herself before this. This was the first time.

As his lips brushed against hers heat seared her senses and some unknown narcotic began to infuse her blood. Wild, impossible pleasure began to pound through her body, focusing between her thighs, swelling in her clit, dampening her sex. Sensual, sensuous, the heavy lassitude washed through her, allowing her lips to part, to accept that first brush of his tongue.

She had kissed before. She'd had lots of kisses. She was a virgin; that didn't mean she had never been kissed. It didn't mean she had never been touched or tempted.

But never had she been tempted like this. Parting her lips further, she allowed her senses, her curiosity, to take control. A kiss like this was once in a lifetime. It was a kiss that personified danger, broken hearts, and star-crossed hungers.

She trembled as he moved around the table, never breaking contact, the kiss growing only deeper as he took deep, drugging sips of her lips. He rubbed his lips against hers, licked at her tongue with his. Then his lips slanted over hers and he took them as a man intent on seduction.

Mikayla wasn't going to fight it. This was more man than she had ever had so close. More man than she had ever dared to approach, ever wanted to approach. Mikayla had always wanted nothing more than to live a safe, steady, sane life.

Life hadn't been any of that lately; why not grab some of the pleasure to be had from it?

She gasped as she felt herself being lifted. The smooth planks of the picnic table were under her thighs as Nik's hand cupped her neck, holding her in place as his kiss deepened.

Summer heat whipped not just around her but also through her. The feel of his strength, the touch of his lips, were heady. She wanted more.

Mikayla couldn't resist reaching up to his hair, her fingers tugging at the leather strap holding it back. The coarse, cool strands flowed around her fingers, down the sides of his face. The sensual feel added to the pleasure beginning to build in her body.

"Such a brave little beauty," he murmured, his head lifting as her eyes opened.

What had ever made her imagine his eyes were cold? Icy? That wasn't ice. It was a steel blue flame blistering in its heat.

"Brave? Stupid maybe?" She was breathless, but it was the feel of his hands on her thighs, pushing the hem of her dress higher, that had her losing her breath.

The heated rasp of calloused flesh sent fingers of blistering pleasure racing through her nerve endings. Her gaze jerked down. She had to watch. Eyes wide, her lips parting, she watched as his large, broad hands slid her dress slowly up her thighs until his thumbs met at the damp center of her silken panties.

He stood between her spread knees, his legs shifting to part her thighs as his thumbs moved subtly against the center of her panties.

"Nik . . ." She tried to breath. She had to convince herself this was a bad thing. She had remained a virgin all these years, waiting until it was right.

Was this right? Or was it just a man who knew exactly how to play the human body?

"Shh. I just want a taste, pretty baby," he crooned. "I've never tasted innocence before."

Her gaze flashed back to his. That pale blue flame licked over her senses as his head lowered.

His lips stroked along her jawline to her neck. Flash points of pleasure seemed to tear across her nerve endings, streaking to alternate points of her body as she began to ache with sensual heat.

His thumb pressed against her clit as it throbbed for attention. The firm, knowing touch sent spirals of sensation tracking lower, invading the depths of her sex and clenching through her body with near-violent desire.

She had never wanted like she wanted this touch. The heated warmth of his fingertips against her inner thighs, his thumb pressing against her clit as his kiss sank inside her.

It was incredible.

He was the ultimate bad boy bringing the ultimate pleasure, and Mikayla, like any good virgin, was much too susceptible to it.

The exquisite sensation raced through her body like a narcotic she couldn't resist. It weakened any thought to protest, any need to deny. It sensitized her flesh, heated it, and had her lying back for him as he came over her, his knee pressing against the table, replacing his thumbs as one hand gripped her hip and dragged her closer to the firm pressure of that diabolical knee.

For twenty-six years she had remained a virgin and she was ready to throw it all away right now, right here.

Her head tipped back as his lips moved from hers, to her jaw, to her neck. The heated rasp of his unshaven jaw brushed against her neck as his lips waged a path of sensual destruction along the tender flesh of her neck.

It was incredible. It so surpassed pleasure, came so close to orgasmic bliss, she could barely breathe for it. She couldn't think. She couldn't do anything but *feel*.

Oh, God, it felt so good.

His fingers played at the edges of her breasts as his lips moved lower, brushed against the rounded tops, licked over them. His tongue painted a trail of fire that sent a quicksilver rush of sensation tearing through her womb.

"You have to be the sweetest thing I've tasted in my life," he growled as he pushed the strap of her dress over her shoulder, revealing more of her breast, daring to nudge her dress lower until the tender bud of her nipple was revealed.

She was doing this on his deck? Letting him touch her like this, taste her like this, on his picnic table? And she was loving it.

The side of his finger rasped against her nipple as she arched closer, feeling his tongue lick between the valley of her breasts. She wanted his tongue on her nipple. She wanted to feel it enclosed in the heated cavern of his mouth. She wanted it like she had never wanted another touch.

Was it the danger she had faced? The knowledge that tomorrow had almost not arrived for her? Was it the danger? Was it simply the man?

The man was incredible.

A low, muted groan, or a growl, vibrated against her breasts as his lips smoothed over her nipple. Racing pleasure raked over the tender tip, sent an incredible mix of sensations flowing through her.

Her head tipped back, her back arching as she bit her lips to hold back a cry. Her nipple lodged between his lips as his tongue stroked over it. Stroked, like a wet, heated flame.

She was on the verge of begging for more. Begging was clearly becoming an option when she suddenly stiffened at a sound she couldn't believe she was hearing.

"Mikayla, are you out here?"

Her brother? Scotty?

Her eyes flew open, watching as Nik's head lifted just enough to allow his eyes to glance through the veil of his lashes toward the gate that separated their yards.

"Mikayla, your car's out front. Where are you?"

Her lips parted in shock. "He called the police the last time I tried to ignore him."

Nik's expression tightened with predatory intent, a glint of danger flickering in his gaze.

What was she allowing herself to get into here? Where had her common sense gone?

"She's not here, Neil," Scotty called out. "Get Beau; we'll call the sheriff. He might actually help us this time."

Her eyes widened. All her brothers were there?

Oh, Lord.

"Let me go." She wiggled beneath Nik, still feeling too fragile, too feminine, against him. "They really will call the sheriff."

They didn't care how they embarrassed her, but she was lucky. They cared. For all their overprotectiveness, for all their irritating ways, her brothers loved her.

Nik's gaze slid slowly back to her. She imagined she saw a war waging in his gaze, whether to release her or to hold her, to ignore her brothers or to tempt her further.

Finally, between one breath and the next he eased up, straightened, then lifted her from the table.

His hand slid the strap of her dress up as the other adjusted the neckline, hiding the rounded flesh of her breast as he stepped back.

"A lucky save," he told her, his lips quirking. "Go do what you have to do, pretty girl. We'll talk later."

Talk? She could just imagine where that conversation would lead.

"I think the best thing I could do is stay away from you," she said softly. "I don't need a broken heart, Nik."

"Do any of us?" He glanced behind her. "There are your brothers."

"Mikayla." Suspicion laced Beau's voice as he opened the gate. "What are you doing here?"

Nik stepped back. "Good night, pretty girl."

He turned and stepped into the house, the doors sliding closed behind him.

Mikayla turned, faced her brothers, and breathed out wearily.

A lucky save? Or simply a reprieve?

CHAPTER 5

Maddix Nelson's home was in the most exclusive part of Hagerstown. The rising mansions and gated estates were lavishly rich and heavily secured.

The Nelson home was on the lower end of lavish, situated in a gated community, surrounded by other similar homes, just as expensive, just as secured.

As Nik pulled the Hummer into the Nelson driveway behind several other vehicles, he was clearly able to see why his neighbors had been so certain Maddix had been home the evening Eddie Foreman had died. They were intensely curious. Even now Nik counted no fewer than half a dozen watching as he stepped from the vehicle and made his way along the precisely placed sidewalk that led to the front door.

The door opened as he stepped onto the ornately decorated front porch.

"Nik." Maddix opened the door and stepped inside. "They're all here." "They" being the two city council members, chief of police, and mayor, as well as Maddix's son, Luke.

Nik followed Maddix through the quiet, understated

luxury of the house to the back of the house where the office was located.

Nik stepped into the room, paying particular attention to the heavy, closed drapes, the dark wood walls.

"Nik, Councilman John Cooker, Mayor Dempsey, Chief Daniel Riley, Councilwoman Caroline Faulkner, my wife, Glenda, and my son, Lucas. We were all here the night Eddie was killed."

"This is ridiculous, Maddix." Glenda Nelson, Maddix's younger second wife, was clearly his trophy bride. At thirty-three the former model with her dark chocolate skin and rounded dark eyes was an exotic beauty who was clearly put out at being asked to attend this meeting.

His son, Lucas, sat slumped in a chair in the corner, his brown eyes narrowed with spoiled defensiveness. His expression bespoke a man who considered himself far beyond being required to attend to anyone else's schedule.

The councilman and -woman watched in interest from their places on a love seat. There was a heavy sense of familiarity between the two that bespoke of lovers, despite the fact that they were married, to other partners.

The chief of police sat in a chair next to a cold fireplace, his lips set in a thin line, his hazel eyes watching Nik suspiciously as Mayor Dempsey nodded his head in greeting.

The gang was all here.

"Thank you for meeting me," Nik said, making an attempt at a polite greeting.

"It wasn't as though some of us had a choice," Maddix's son sneered.

"No, it wasn't," Nik agreed. "But I'm certain we all appreciate your cooperation."

Cooperation his ass. Nik had warned Maddix he would drag the son there by his hair if he wasn't in attendance. It was a threat Maddix had evidently relayed.

"Why must Luke and I be here, Mr. Steele?" Glenda crossed her arms over the soft pale cream blouse she wore with stylish white shorts. "I'm certain we weren't needed."

"You were all here the night Eddie Foreman died," Nik said. "I have some questions I wanted to ask."

"Yes, we were all here, which means Maddix obviously killed no one," Glenda continued to protest. "That makes this an exercise in futility if you ask me."

So much for cooperation.

"Did I ask you?" Nik queried with cool softness.

"Enough, Glenda," Maddix growled. "Let Nik do his job. If he asked you to be here, then it's for a reason."

"We should have invited Mikayla." Luke's lips tightened into a smile of clear male appreciation. "Then perhaps I wouldn't be so bored."

Nik turned his head and stared at the other man. "And why do you say that, Mr. Nelson?" he asked.

The smile shifted to one of anticipation. "Once this is over, it would be nice to take what's owed me. The little bitch was teasing the hell out of me before she dropped me cold after she accused my father of murder."

"Shut your damned mouth, Luke," Maddix ordered his son furiously before Nik would make a move to shut his mouth permanently. "I told you to stay away from that girl before any of this happened. She's too good for your spoiled, whorish ways."

There was an edge of contempt in Maddix's tone that surprised Nik. Luke was Maddix's only child, a son at that, and obviously spoiled past redemption. The fact that Maddix was taking a stand when it was obviously too late made no sense to Nik.

"His mother raised him," Maddix explained with a glare toward his son. "Until she couldn't do a damned thing with him, either."

"He's twenty-seven years old. Throw his ass out and let him figure it out on his own," Nik stated coldly. "For now, he can sit tight and keep his mouth shut or he'll deal with me."

He slid Luke a cold, hard look as the other man opened his mouth to speak again. Just as quickly, Luke settled back and merely glared mutinously back at them.

"Why are we here, Mr. Steele?" the councilwoman asked then, clearly as bored with events as Nik was becoming.

Nik turned his gaze to her, revealing nothing. "To satisfy my curiosity, perhaps," he stated.

The real reason was to gauge the honesty of Maddix's alibi. Guilt was never as cleverly hidden as others believed it was. Bringing them all into the same place as they had claimed they had been the first time gave Nik a chance to decide if they were lying or if that meeting had truly taken place.

"I wasn't even in this damned room," Luke muttered. "I was upstairs. If I remember correctly, Dad was rather insistent that I not stay."

Maddix's lips tightened as his expression turned reproving. "He was drunk."

"I was." Luke smiled sardonically.

"I was by the pool." Glenda waved a graceful hand toward the pool outside the office. "I don't involve myself in Maddix's business affairs."

No doubt. Not for the first time Nik was amazed at familial interactions. They were nothing like his family, back in Russia, before he'd lost all he held dear. His may not have been willing to stand up to their government to help Nik, but they all knew better than to disrespect their parents. He and his brothers and sisters had worked from an early age and learned to take care of themselves. Nik had never been able to make sense of men and women like Luke Nelson and Maddix's trophy wife.

"Was there anything in particular that you needed to know, Mr. Steele?" The chief of police watched him with barely disguised animosity. "Or are you just checking us out?"

Nik allowed his lips to quirk mockingly. No doubt the police chief had investigated *him*. Nik could see it in Riley's eyes, in the hunger to make an arrest that could possibly be the turning point of his career. Possibly. If he could actually come up with any proof to back the rumors that circulated in certain circles where Nik Steele was concerned. Thankfully, they were rumors. Even the U.S. government, armed forces, and law enforcement agencies often depended on the information he provided and even, at times, his services.

"Just checking you out," Nik agreed as he crossed his arms over his chest and turned his gaze back to the son. "You know Ms. Martin then?"

"I spent the better part of three months wining and dining her," he grunted. "She was ready to put out when she decided to try to ruin Father for whatever reason." He glared back at Maddix. "Not that I could blame her much."

Nik watched Maddix roll his eyes. "He begged that poor girl for a date for two years. She finally gave in to him just to shut him up."

Luke snickered at the comment, his gaze filled with sarcasm as he stared back at Nik. "She's a frigid thing, I have to say, but I could have melted her."

Frigid? Mikayla?

There was no doubt in Nik's mind that Luke Nelson hadn't had a chance at Mikayla. She had been anything but frigid the week before on Nik's back deck.

"Did any of you know Eddie Foreman?" Nik asked as he turned to the others in the room.

"I rather doubt it," the councilwoman informed him as she smoothed back a strand of her carefully colored blond hair. "Our meeting that night concerned city business interests that Maddix is a part of, not his construction business."

That was pretty much what Nik expected. His reasons for being here had very little to do with the questions or any information that could be gained on the foreman.

Nik was learning quite a bit, though, more than he had expected. There was a lot to be learned from simply watching.

"What do you have so far, Nik?" Maddix rubbed at his forehead at he cast the others a disgruntled look.

"Nothing yet." Nik cast Luke Maddix another look, one he was certain was filled with confidence. "I've moved in next door to her, though. She's a nice girl."

"I told you she was." Maddix shook his head. "I thought she was too good for this."

Luke was glaring back at him now.

"How long before she learns why you're here, do you think?" Luke grunted with bitter amusement. "It's not as though you're hiding it. Do you think she's going to thank you for lying to her?"

Nik arched his brow. "In this situation, lying isn't an option." He shrugged. "She'll learn soon enough and I won't deny it. I've told her no different."

He would give Luke Nelson no ammunition against him, or Mikayla. It wouldn't matter whether others knew why he was there or not. Maddix had called Nik to find out why Mikayla was lying. The problem was, he couldn't tell which one of them was lying, her or Maddix. It was a disturbing realization.

"Do you think we haven't checked you out, Steele?" Animosity thickened Luke Nelson's voice.

"Enough, Luke," Maddix growled.

"Tell him, Riley." Luke's sneer in the chief of police's direction was snide and filled with derision. "You can't arrest the bastard, though, can you? Can't or won't. Maybe you're just too damned scared?"

Chief Riley's wide, square face tightened in anger as Nik merely shook his head. "He can't arrest me." Nik stared back at the chief. "I have yet to break a law."

Which wasn't entirely true.

"That we can prove," the chief muttered. "You know, Steele, I'm only here because Maddix is a friend and I want this cleared up just as much as he does. Otherwise, I'd be trying to find a way to fry your ass, no matter the fact that certain government agencies find you useful."

"That you can prove. And fortunately for me, I have many friends," Nik agreed as he inclined his head mockingly. "And on that note, before I murder this little bastard of Maddix's, I'm leaving."

Fury stiffened Luke's expression as he jumped to his feet and turned to his father.

"I feel sorry for you, Maddix," Nik stated, pitying the man. "Try suspending his allowance for a while. Maybe he'll act like a decent human being rather than the disgrace he's turning out to be."

Nik walked out of the room as Maddix lowered his head and pinched the bridge of his nose. Almost simultaneously Glenda and Luke began raging. It didn't surprise Nik that Glenda was joining in on Luke's side;

like the two council members, Glenda and Luke Nelson were making a little happy time between the sheets.

Nik wondered if Maddix was aware of it.

On second thought, Maddix wasn't a stupid man; he probably was.

Leaving the house, Nik walked back to his Harley, swung on, and twisted the key. The engine flared to life with a heavy, deep roar.

Maneuvering out of the wide driveway, he headed for the security gates and what he considered freedom beyond. Hell, he'd prefer to pledge the rest of his life to the Elite Ops than to live like this. Accepting deceit and selfish bickering such as what he'd glimpsed in Maddix Nelson's life.

The man hadn't raised his son with the same values he lived by; that was for damned sure.

But Mikayla had those values.

Where the hell had that thought come from?

Nik felt his enter body tense, tightening involuntarily at the thought of the too-small, too-fragile woman he had held in his arms the past week.

He hadn't been able to get her out of his mind, nor had he been able to keep from watching her. He was spending more time tracking her than he was tracking a killer. And that wasn't even Nik's job. His job was to figure out why she was lying about a man who hadn't, or at least who swore he hadn't, committed murder.

This was turning into a hell of a job, and one that was clearly going to take more time than Nik had anticipated. His commander, Jordan, was already questioning how much longer it could possibly take. The team had already been sent out to the next mission without Nik. That was something that hadn't happened in all the years they had fought together.

It was something that shouldn't be happening now. Except Nik couldn't seem to pull himself away.

The bruises on Mikayla's face were only now beginning to fade a bit. He knew that because he spied on her. As disgusting as it seemed to him, he couldn't help but watch out for her, to check up on her.

Someone much larger, much stronger, had dared to attack her in the darkness. Because of what she had seen or because of what she thought she saw?

Nik knew the surrounding area was divided on the subject of Maddix Nelson committing murder. Many thought he was capable of it. Some thought he was capable, but that in the case of Eddie Foreman he hadn't actually acted. Others thought the idea absurd but were amused by the battle being waged over it.

And at least one night, someone had decided to put a stop to the small woman who had instigated that battle.

A cold, hard knot of rage formed in Nik's stomach at the thought of the harm that could come to her. Something dark and protective welled inside him despite his battle against it.

Hell, he'd lost enough in his life. Did he really need to allow himself to become attached to a woman he knew he could never allow himself to have fully?

He could fuck her. He could take that shining innocence she had saved for so long and mar it with the darkness that lived within his soul, but he couldn't keep her. For a brief moment in time he could let the warmth and light that flowed through him when he touched her fill his soul, but he would have to walk away soon.

His life wasn't his own for two more long years, and even then he couldn't call it his own. There was no chance that once that time was past he could ever live a life even resembling happy.

He'd made enemies. He'd walked a line that no man could walk and expect to find peace later.

He was known in many dark corners of the world as a killer, a purveyor of war and destruction. And he wanted to bring that into the life of a woman who seemed to vibrate with warmth?

And yet how could he walk away?

His jaw ached at the force of his teeth grinding together. His hands flexed deliberately around the handgrips of the motorcycle handlebars as he turned toward town and the shop he knew Mikayla would still be working in.

Creating dreams. That was what she did there.

She created dreams in the form of dresses for both the innocent as well as the jaded. In each stitch of each design that she created herself, she lived her own dreams.

Dreams of romance and adventure, dreams of candlelit nights and passion.

And he knew, in a back room of her own home, she was creating her own dream. The first fragile form of a white gown that she would one day wear as she walked down the aisle herself.

He'd seen it when he had slipped into her home. His fingers had touched the fragile lace of the underskirt she had begun as his eyes had memorized the sketch on the table.

Mikayla was making her wedding gown. A creation of satin and lace, of beads and ivory. A gown she would wear for the man who would claim her heart forever.

Nik couldn't allow himself to be that man.

There was a part of himself that clenched in fury at the thought of any other man claiming that place in her life, though Nik knew it was a place he could never claim himself.

Damned if he did, damned if he didn't.

His job here was to find out why Mikayla Martin was lying about what she had seen.

His opinion was, if she was lying, then she was the best damned liar he had ever laid his eyes on. Or simply a woman he wanted more than he had ever wanted any other woman.

The potential for destruction was only growing.

Mikayla stared at the plate-glass window of her shop, feeling the tears that threatened to flood her eyes.

"LIAR." The word was brilliant crimson. The defacer wouldn't be caught. Mikayla had been through this too many times now to even bother calling her lawyer to once again demand the security tapes from the bank across the street. They always showed the same thing. Whoever used the paint wore a now-familiar black face covering. They had run across the street, painted, and run back while Deirdre and Mikayla were closer to the back of the store.

"LIAR." The letters were like a brand on her soul as the door opened and Deirdre stepped out with a bucket of hot sudsy water, a scraper, and sponges.

"I'm sorry, Mikayla," Deirdre said softly as pedestrians walked by slowly, whispering.

Everyone whispered.

"It's not your fault, Deirdre." It was her own fault, she thought. She must not have been careful enough when she stopped by the new foreman's house, a friend of her father's, and tried to discuss Eddie Foreman with him.

That or he had called Maddix Nelson after she had left.

"Luke Nelson told some of the guys at the bar that his father had hired a private investigator," Deirdre said as Mikayla dampened the window, then went to work with the scraper. "Have you seen anyone?"

She shook her head. No one had talked to her. A part of her wished they had, then that evening wouldn't seem more like a too-vivid nightmare than reality.

There were days she had wondered if it had even happened. If it hadn't been for the fact that Eddie Foreman was indeed dead, then she would almost be convinced she had imagined the entire thing.

"What about Nik Steele?" her friend asked. "Have you seen him again?"

"Coming and going." She scraped at the stubborn paint as Deirdre began working on the other side. "I haven't spoken to him again."

"Not since your brothers cock-blocked you." Deirdre snickered.

Mikayla knew what her friend was trying to do. Deirdre was trying to ease the hurt. This had happened so often now that there were times Mikayla wondered if it even hurt any longer.

"I don't want to talk about that, Deirdre." Perhaps she had made a mistake in telling her best friend about the deck fiasco with Nik Steele.

"Of course you don't." Deirdre grinned. "Then you might have to admit you miss him."

Of course she missed him. There was no doubt about that. But the sane part of her brain realized that the absence was for the best.

"Doesn't matter." She finally shrugged, keeping her eyes firmly on the job at hand. "Some things are better off unknown."

Nik Steele was better off being one of those unknowns. Like aliens, the mysteries of the universe.

As she watched the water smear across the red, mixing with the color, looking like blood running in rivulets to the sidewalk, the image of Eddie Foreman flashed in her mind.

She swallowed tightly, her heart thudding sluggishly at the remembered fear.

"Mikayla, you don't mean that," Deirdre said softly.

"I mean it," she whispered as she fought to shake off the nightmarish image of Eddie Foreman's dead body. "He's a bad boy, Deirdre. I'm the good girl. Doesn't that suck? Sounds like a recipe for trouble if you ask me."

"Sounds like a recipe for some incredible sex to me, but I'm prejudiced toward the idea."

The dark rasp of his voice sent a rush of sensation up Mikayla's spine. She swung around, her gaze hitting directly in the center of his chest before lifting, slowly, to those incredible light blue eyes.

What had ever made her believe his gaze was icy? It was hot. Filled with hunger, with sex, with trouble.

Deirdre was so dead. That wench had totally betrayed her.

Blood rushed to her face, heated her body. That was all well and good, but the flush afflicting the flesh between her thighs was terribly uncomfortable. It was lush, damp, so heated. The need for touch began to rock her system, to travel across her nerve endings and throb in areas of her body that she was certain shouldn't be throbbing.

"You weren't supposed to hear that," she muttered irately, turning back to the window, scrubbing at the paint, promising to make sure Deirdre paid for this one. Somewhere, sometime.

"We need to talk, Mikayla," Nik stated as he moved closer, the heat of his body surrounding her. "Could you leave the cleanup to your assistant?"

"No, actually, I can't." She was too close to proving just how thin that layer of her good-girl persona was. It was barely skin-deep, and the flames burning beneath it were melting it away as quickly as a fire softened butter.

He had an effect on her she knew no man should have on a woman. He made her weak. He made her need things she knew she shouldn't need.

She had plans. Her plans did not include having her heart broken, her future forever marred, by the man she couldn't have.

"We could always discuss this on the sidewalk." He turned, leaning his back against an unpainted section of the window, crossing his arms over his chest. "I could tell you in detail exactly what I had planned last week when your brothers decided to become inquisitive and protective. For instance, I didn't have time that night to tell you how soft your pretty thighs are."

Mikayla froze. For one horrible second she could only imagine who was standing behind them. Her breath stopped. Her eyes widened; then she sneaked a peek around them, nearly giving a hard breath of relief when she saw no one.

Her gaze jerked back to him.

"Come inside and talk to me, or we'll talk out here."

"You don't want to talk," she hissed.

"Talking is the last thing on my mind," he assured her, his fingers curling around her wrist, his eyes locking onto hers. "Isn't this where the bad boy kisses the good girl in public and begins sullying her pristine reputation?"

There was a twinkle of amusement in his gaze, but it was hesitant, as though in teasing her he was enjoying something he hadn't expected to enjoy.

"Sorry, someone else already took care of sullying

that pristine reputation. At least, the honesty part of it." She sighed as she attempted to pull her wrist from his grip. "Let me go, Nik. I don't have time for this. I have a window to clean."

"And I have a discussion I want to have with you. Come along, sweetheart." He pulled her into the shop as she stared at his back in amazement.

The black T-shirt he wore stretched across the hard, well-defined muscles, catching her gaze. Otherwise, she assured herself, she would have never followed him, at least not without the fight she should have given him, into her office.

As the door closed behind them and he began to turn, her lips parted to inform him of her opinion, in blistering detail, of his high-handed tactics.

He was quicker than she. Between one breath and the next he was lifting her to him, his lips catching hers, his tongue slipping between her lips with rapacious demand, with hungry sexuality.

And she wasn't fighting him. She didn't have the strength to fight him. Instead, her fingers gripped his shoulders, her lips parted further, and her tongue stroked against his, tasted him, drew him into her like the sweetest nectar.

It was exquisite. The taste and the feel of him.

It was like drowning in dark heat and forbidden hunger, and for precious seconds Mikayla allowed herself the sheer luxury of having exactly what she wanted, exactly how she wanted it.

She wasn't going to fall in love with him, she promised herself. This was not going to mess up her plans for her future, because she simply wouldn't allow it to.

It was just a moment out of time, she promised herself.

She could have this moment.

She could have his lips on hers, his arms wrapped around her, holding her against the rock-solid heat of his chest, feeling his heart beat against her breasts, the hard outline of his erection beneath his jeans, pressing into her lower stomach.

God, she wanted him.

Straining closer, she fought for a deeper kiss, more touch. She wanted to feel him against every inch of her body. She needed him at this moment like she needed the very air to breathe.

Just for a moment.

"Such a good girl," he murmured as his lips sipped from hers, his hands shaping, then cupping the rounded curves of her rear as he lifted her, pressed her against the wall, and let her feel him.

"Aren't you supposed to be fighting, Mikayla?"

The hard wedge of his cock pressed firmly between her thighs, hot, thick, a solid weight of arousal behind the leather pants he wore.

The thin silk of her stylish short skirt rode up her thighs, leaving only a narrow band of silk between the leather and her dampening flesh.

Her panties were no barrier. She felt too much; the sensations traveled too deep.

"I am fighting." She bit at his lips for not kissing her, for daring to pull away from her.

At the nip, he seemed to freeze, then a harsh growl of hunger tore from his lips and he was kissing her as though the sheer act of thrusting his tongue inside her mouth, stroking against hers, mimicking the act their bodies were suddenly desperate for, would somehow assuage a hunger Mikayla knew she was never going to be free of.

His hand slid beneath the skirt, calloused fingertips touching bare flesh only a breath from the elastic band of her panties.

She wanted his fingers there. She wanted them sliding beneath the material. She wanted him touching her.

Rocking against the press of his erection, she allowed her fingers to bite into his shoulders as his lips slanted over hers, the hunger deepening, the need tearing through her.

She couldn't have him.

She couldn't have this.

She wanted it.

She wanted it with a force threatening to drive her insane as she suddenly found herself free of him, standing against the wall, staring back at him in shock.

His hair was loose and flowing along his shoulders. Had she done that? Slipped the leather strap free of his hair?

She must have. It was tangled in her fingers, the warm leather gripped in her hand as she stared back at him, drawing in deep, ragged breaths.

He was no less affected. His eyes blazed with need.

No man had ever burned for her like this. Mikayla had never inspired great passion until now.

And God help her, if she didn't have more of it, then she just might do something she rarely did.

She was going to cry.

"How much do you want, good girl?" His fingers slipped just beneath the edge of her panties, feathering over the swollen, curl-laden flesh that dampened further at the feel of his touch.

"How much?" How much did she want? She wanted everything. All of it. She wanted to forget why she was supposed to protest, and take everything she could get.

"A little?" He breathed a kiss over her lips as his

finger feathered against the curls with the lightest ca-ress. "Or a lot?" His finger slipped past the curls of her swollen sex and slid gently between them.

Her lips parted on a gasp of shock, of exquisite pleasure.

"So which do you want, good girl?"

CHAPTER 6

Nik wanted it all.

Staring into Mikayla's exceptional violet gaze, he watched the slumberous sensuality take over as his finger rubbed against the snug entrance of her slick, heated pussy.

He wanted nothing more than to slip his finger inside her, to feel the tight grip of intimate flesh, the ripple of pleasure as it raced through the velvety flesh.

Instead, he only caressed the clenched entrance. He only touched her gently, easily.

"You should wax here," he suggested, watching her eyes flare again, watching the mingled shock and hunger as it raced through her. "You would feel the lightest breath of a touch then. Your sweet, sensitive flesh would be bare for me, Mikayla. No matter the touch of my fingers, my lips, my cock. You'd feel it as though each nerve ending were naked to my touch."

The sweet, heated flow of her juices trickled against his fingertips, slickening them further as a little gasp of breath parted her lips.

"Please." The little plea was a rasp of sound from her throat.

"Please what, sweet baby?" He brushed his lips against hers.

"Please, don't do this to me."

He stared down at her, seeing the confusion, the pleasure, in her gaze, and he knew in that heartbeat that it had taken everything inside her to make that plea.

He heard the words, just as he felt the response in her slender, fragile body. She was arching to him, reaching for him, her body shuddering as it fought for orgasm, even as she whispered the plea that he let her go.

He could give it to her. Just a little. With nothing more than his fingers he could bring her to climax, showing her what she was attempting to deny.

That would be cheating, he thought. He wanted her begging for what he could give her, tortured with the need to know what waited on the other side.

Not knowing, imagining, wondering what she had pulled away from could in ways be more powerful than knowing.

His finger slid from the clenched opening, slipped upward, circled her straining clit, then pulled away.

He wasn't finished with her, not by a long shot. As she stared up at him, that beautiful gaze sinking into his soul, he brought his fingers to his lips and let himself taste her.

The taste of her exploded against his tongue like liquid sunshine. Fresh, vibrant, a hint of sweetness and spice that he knew he could so easily become addicted to.

Her eyes widened as she watched, her lips parting. Swollen cherry red lips. He could easily imagine them parted, those eyes staring up at him as he let himself fuck the sweet recess of her mouth.

His balls tightened at the thought. She was so innocent, she would be hesitant. He would be her first taste of true passion, and he'd ensure she knew every ounce of pleasure possible.

"A little then?" He kept his voice quiet, the rasp of his nearly broken voice more of a growl.

Her lips trembled. It was sexy, and vulnerable. That vulnerability touched him in a place he hadn't known existed. In the heart he had sworn he didn't have.

"Why are you doing this?" She tugged at her skirt, straightening it, her hands trembling as she stared up at him in confusion.

That look did something to him. Something he couldn't explain. It pierced a part of his soul that had remained frozen hard, solid, for so many years.

"Why am I doing what?" Brushing her hair back from her face, he had to admit Mikayla Martin could make even a dead man dream.

"Why are you messing up my life, Nik Steele? I was fine before you arrived."

"You were bored," he assured her, his fingers brushing along her jawline. "I saw you at the bar, baby. I watched. If your eyes had become any more glazed you would have been comatose. Tell me, have you even heard from the bastard since that night? The one you were there with?"

She hadn't. Nik saw it in the nervous way her tongue peeked out to touch her upper lip.

"I heard he was dating the daughter of one of the firm's partners after that night." Her shoulders lifted in a tight shrug. "No big deal."

Her date hadn't even called to see if she had arrived safely, Nik knew. Actually, the man had spent the night in the other woman's bed. And every night thereafter. He'd preferred the barracuda to the gentle woman he'd been with.

The good girl. The virgin.

God help him, Nik wanted to be the man to share that first climax with her. The one who watched her eyes widen, watched her body shudder, and heard her cries as she came around him.

"This isn't over," he told her as she shifted away from him, his gaze locked on her. "You want to think it is, Mikayla, but you know as well as I do that it's not."

"Why?" Pushing her hair back, she watched him in dismay. "You can have any woman you want, Nik. Why me?"

"Why me?" he asked instead. "Why are you opening a door I didn't know existed inside me? Why, Mikayla, are you making a dead man dream?"

He froze. He hadn't said that. *Fuck.*

He jerked the door open without another word and stalked through the shop and out the door.

This was finished. It was simply over.

And he knew better.

It wasn't over. It couldn't be over until he had the scent of her out of his head, the taste of her from his tongue. And he knew he couldn't stay away from her long enough for that to happen anytime soon.

Striding to the parking lot at the side of the shop, Nik swung onto the Harley and within seconds roared down the street. He wore the helmet, though he wished the wind were in his hair, the scent of a coming rainstorm filling his senses. But rather than wiping the smell and the taste of Mikayla from his mind, it would only remind him of her. She was as wild and as free as the storm, beneath that good-girl exterior.

In her eyes he saw more than the dressmaker, more than the virgin. He saw the woman fighting to hold on to safety when safety was the last thing she truly wanted.

He should leave her alone, but he knew he wouldn't. He knew he couldn't. The part of him that had been dead was slowly coming to life for her. Staying away wasn't an option.

Reaching up to the side of the helmet, he activated the link to the base and the woman manning communications.

"Jordan is getting nervous, big boy," Tehya informed Nik as she answered the link. "He needs you back here."

"Not yet," he answered, his voice hardening at the thought. "I need you to get some intel for me."

"Jordan finds out that I'm fucking around working on your 'favor' then he's likely to punish me," she drawled.

Nik waited.

"Okay, maybe he'll actually get around to that spanking he keeps threatening me with." She laughed lightly. "What do you need?"

"Luke Nelson, Maddix Nelson's son," Nik answered her. "You didn't tell me he had dated Mikayla."

"Baby, your little Miss Martin dates a lot," Tehya informed him with a thread of amusement. "In the past year she's gone out with eight different men. Even the little controversy between her and Nelson hasn't slowed down her social life. Rarely the same one for more than a few dates, though. She's very popular. She attends many of the parties that her dresses are worn to. Before Eddie Foreman was killed she was a very popular guest in many homes. That's actually risen since she accused Maddix Nelson of murder. This war between them keeps everyone highly entertained, it seems. If you want to know more about the families you should ask Eleanor Longstrom."

Eleanor Longstrom owned the antique store down from Mikayla's shop. An ex-CIA agent and contact for the unit, she could dig up information others only dreamed of acquiring.

"Check him out. While you're at it, see if you can

dig up anything on Maddix that I don't already have. Something's wrong here, Tehya. Both of them can't be telling the truth."

Tehya was silent for long moments. "She's a pretty girl," she finally said softly. "Are you falling, Ice Man?"

It was a nickname Tehya used with fondness, as she did now. But it reminded him how dangerous Mikayla was to his self-control.

"That has nothing to do with the truth," he told Tehya. "They're both sticking to their story and I need to get to the bottom of it. See what you can find out for me."

"Will do," she promised. "It's going to take a few days, though. The team is on mission and I'm providing backup intel."

"Understood." The mission came first. "Work on it when you can."

The link disconnected as Nik turned the bike to the interstate, taking the exit to the house he had rented. He was going to have to finish this, quickly. Otherwise, the little fairy stealing his self-control was going to end up stealing his heart as well.

Mikayla pulled the Jeep into her driveway, glanced at the house next door, and saw the lights that blazed inside as well as the glow of the back porch lights.

It was well after dark. She had deliberately stayed at the shop as long as possible, trying to restore the defenses she had never had to worry about falling at a man's touch.

But no man had ever affected her as Nik Steele did.

Shaking her head at the thought, she lifted her keys from her purse, pulled the strap over her shoulder, then stepped from the Jeep.

As she closed the door and hit the automatic door

locks, Nik's front door opened. Leaning against the door frame, his arms crossed over his chest, he watched her.

He looked tall, forbidden, shadowed.

Turning from him, she hurried up the sidewalk to the house, her gaze moving carefully along the yard, the porch, watching for anything out of the ordinary.

She wasn't as wary as she normally was. She wasn't as frightened. Nik was watching her. He was there, and for some reason that gave her a sense of security that she hadn't even felt when her three bruiser brothers had escorted her into the house, checked it out, and made certain all her doors and windows were locked.

Nik was dangerous. He was more dangerous, she felt, than anyone who could possibly be waiting in the shadows.

Unlocking her front door, Mikayla stepped inside, closed the door, punched in her security code, then locked the door behind her. The house was too silent.

She felt completely alone and too restless.

The urge to step back outside and walk to the one next door was overwhelming. It was an urge she forced herself to ignore.

She'd waited until late to come home for a reason, hoping she would be tired enough to just go to sleep.

It looked as though that wasn't happening anytime soon, though.

Moving to the small office area between the living room and kitchen, she dropped her purse to the small end table by the door and moved to her computer.

Powering it up, she moved to the kitchen, poured herself a glass of sweet tea, and walked back to the office.

By the time she took her chair, the computer was loaded and ready to go.

The file marked: "NELSON" glared at her from the desktop.

How could she further her research into Maddix Nelson? She'd pulled everything she could find on him as well on Eddie Foreman, and still there was nothing she could use.

The best she had been able to find had been a few articles mentioning production and material problems with a few jobs. Nothing that wasn't found with countless other construction companies as well.

Propping her elbows on the desk, she covered her face with her hands and wondered where she should go from here. There was nothing to tie Maddix Nelson to Eddie Foreman's murder other than the fact that Mikayla had witnessed it.

And no one believed her.

She was at a dead end.

Maddix Nelson was going to get away with murder.

A heavy sigh slipped past her lips as she stared at the still-unopened file. She was concentrating so hard on it that when the firm knock came at her door she nearly jumped out of her skin.

She stood up, her eyes going to the clock on the computer before swinging to the door.

She knew who it was. She could feel him with every fiber of her being.

"Mikayla." The rasp of his voice, like sandpaper over velvet, stroked up her spine with sensual destruction.

That didn't keep her from moving across the room, her fingers punching in the code to the alarm before she unlocked the door and pulled it open.

He wasn't wearing riding leathers anymore. He wore snug jeans and a white shirt tucked into the low-riding waistband. Long sleeves were rolled to the elbows and a hint of light-colored chest hair peeked from the buttoned edges of the material at his chest.

His long white blond hair was loose, falling around his hard-boned face with delicious rakish appeal.

"It's almost eleven, Nik. What do you want?" she asked wearily, tiring of the battle inside her to resist his magnetic appeal.

"We need to talk." He stepped into the house without an invitation.

"We can't talk tomorrow?" Sometime when her willpower was stronger perhaps? That would definitely be a better time to talk as far as she was concerned.

"No. We need to talk tonight."

Mikayla closed and locked the door before turning to face him.

"Do you want a drink?" she asked.

Every nerve ending in her body was standing to attention now. The sheer act of walking, of feeling the silk of her skirt against her thighs, was becoming sexual.

Geez, how had she managed to live this long without knowing the effect a man could have on her?

"I'm tired," she stated, though she didn't feel in the least tired at the moment. Excited. Filled with anticipation. But tired was running in last place.

His gaze raked over her. She could feel the hunger in that look, a dark need that at once terrified her and made her breathless in anticipation.

It was all Nik could do to keep his hands off her. His palms itched with the need to stroke her silken flesh, to lay her beneath him, to fuck her until they were both sated, exhausted from satiation.

His cock throbbed with the need. Every nerve ending in his body throbbed for it. Standing before him, her amethyst eyes curious, hot, she made him burn inside for her.

He wasn't here to fuck her, though. He was here to finish this. He'd already called Maddix. There was nothing to be found, no reason for her accusations other than the fact that she believed she had seen Maddix Nelson kill his foreman.

The attack on her the night she and Nik met had been in response to her allegations against Nelson, the attacker striking in anger. Nothing else made sense. The graffiti on her shop window, all of it. She needed to step back, she had to let this go, and Nik had to leave.

Nik believed Maddix hadn't been there. His alibi was too solid. But Mikayla's belief in what she had seen went too deep.

There was nothing to tie either of them to anything suspicious, which meant the killer was still on the loose. He had nothing to fear, though, because the only person who saw him thought she had seen someone else.

She was no threat, and there was no reason for the killer to harm her.

It was time for Nik to go.

"Why are you here this late, Nik?" She moved farther into the living room, her expression still and calm despite the arousal blazing in her eyes.

Her long dark blond hair flowed down her back like a heavy cape. The image of a fairy came to mind once more. A fragile, innocent little fairy too good for the world she suddenly found herself within.

"I'm leaving." Hooking his thumbs in his belt, he fought the need to touch her.

Surprise filled her eyes then. "Your job is over already? It was hardly worth renting a house for, was it?"

Confusion filled her voice, as well as disappointment.

"I managed to wrap things up faster than I expected,"

he told her, wondering at the tightening in his chest as she continued to watch him with such somber intensity.

"I see." She nodded slowly. "When are you leaving?"

"Tomorrow evening."

She asked, still watching. "So why are you here tonight?"

He almost grinned. She was smart as hell. She knew something wasn't quite right about the job he had claimed to have versus the fact that he was leaving so soon.

"I'm here because of what you saw, Mikayla." He tried to say the words gently, to lower his voice enough that she knew he wasn't there to hurt her.

She flinched. Hell, so much for trying. "You're here because of Maddix?"

Nik clenched his teeth for long seconds as he watched the feelings of betrayal fill her beautiful eyes.

"I've known Maddix for a while," Nik told her. "I'm confident enough in the man I know to believe he's innocent. I was here to check you out, to figure out why you would want to destroy Maddix by accusing him of murder."

Nik wasn't going to sugarcoat it. There was no gentle way to tell her. No easy way to break this to her or to keep her from hating him after he was gone.

As she took a step back, almost in defense, her arms wrapped over her breasts, her face paling, causing her eyes to appear larger, darker than before. Pain swept across her features as moisture glistened in her eyes, proof that he was piercing at the heart of a woman who had been hurt too much in the past weeks.

"I see," she whispered, obviously fighting against the hurt and anger he could see building in her eyes.

"The night at the club. The guy that attacked me. Did you know him, too?"

Nik's brows jerked down in a frown as he felt the ice he had built around him before coming here beginning to crack.

"You think I'd have someone attack you, Mikayla?"

Her lips tightened in a mocking grin. "Sorry, how silly of me. You like doing your own dirty work, don't you? Do you get more satisfaction that way?"

He couldn't blame her for her anger. He'd expected much worse than this. But he had to admit this silent pain tore at him more deeply than screaming accusations could have.

He could have walked away from the screaming. Walking away from this quiet pain was harder.

"I'd kill any man who tried to harm you," he told her. "I'd never hurt you, Mikayla, not intentionally."

"What more does a liar deserve?" Her fingers clenched on her arms as she held on to herself. "Isn't that how you see it? I dared to lie about your precious Maddix. What more do I deserve?"

He shook his head, hating this. He hated this worse than he had ever hated anything in this life. Seeing the pain on her face tightened every muscle in his body and tore at his determination not to touch her.

"I don't believe you're a liar, Mikayla," he sighed. "Any more than I believe Maddix is a killer. What I do believe is that you think you saw Maddix. It was evening. Shadows stretch over the building site at that time of day. That can give anyone, anything, a far different look."

A tear slipped free.

God, he hated that single tear, the proof that she was fighting so hard to hold back the pain he was inflicting.

"Of course, that's all it was." She nodded in agreement. A mocking, ironic agreement. One filled with betrayal. "You figured it out, Nik. Thanks so much for fixing this little problem for me." Her breathing hitched, breaking a heart he didn't know he had. "Now you can get out of my house and go back to where you came from."

Any other woman he knew, or had ever known, would have been cursing a blue streak at this point. Screaming. Throwing things. He could have escaped and thanked his lucky stars she hadn't actually managed to hit him in the head with anything.

But not Mikayla. Her shoulders straightened, her chin lifted defiantly, and she fought her tears and her anger with everything inside her.

And it was killing her.

Mikayla stared back at Nik, feeling as though she were going to be sick. Her chest felt tight, her heart straining at the agony resonating through her.

Had anything ever hurt this bad?

No, it hadn't. It hadn't even hurt this bad when her uncle had asked her the same question.

It didn't matter that it was a logical question to ask.

"Strange." Her voice sounded strangled. "You never asked me about what happened that night. You never even asked me about the possibility that I could have mistaken someone else for Maddix, did you, Nik?"

If he had asked, she could have told him why she was so certain. She could have told him how the sunlight pierced past the shadows, blazed across Maddix's distinctive face for those few, unforgettable moments.

But Nik hadn't asked her.

"There was no reason to ask, Mikayla," he stated; his expression seemed to be filled with pity. "I talked to Maddix, his family, his alibis, and his neighbors. He was at home, exactly as he said he was."

Mikayla nodded again. Whatever it took to get him out of her house, out of her life. She just wanted to hide and lick the wounds she could feel tearing through her heart.

She had known Nik Steele was a very bad idea. She should have followed her instincts. This would teach her to do exactly that.

She couldn't believe her heart had led her astray this way. That she had been poised so close to falling for a man who had been essentially lying to her all along.

At least he'd had the decency not to actually seduce her, she told herself. That final humiliation hadn't been delivered.

"Mikayla, you're going to have to accept that Maddix didn't kill Eddie Foreman," Nik told her, his voice harsh. The longer he stood there, the more forbidding his expression became.

"Hey, I'm agreeing with you." She was fighting her tears second by second. God help her, if she didn't get him out of her house then she was going to break down and humiliate herself by losing control of her tears. "You can leave now, Nik. You've explained everything. Why, Maddix should have called you earlier to fix this little problem of his."

She hated Nik. She wanted to hate him. She wanted to hate everything about him rather than to hurt this way. To feel those sharp talons of agony raking across her soul at the subtle lies he had practiced.

His jaw flexed, the muscles working furiously as he obviously held back whatever he wanted to say instead.

"Why don't you just leave?" she suggested as she walked to the door and jerked it open. "Go, Nik. Pack.

Go back where you came from. I didn't need you before you arrived here and I don't need you now."

She didn't need anyone else to remind her that Maddix Nelson had gotten away with murder. It was shoved in her face daily. It was spray painted on her shop window; it was left in messages on her answering machine at home every night.

The injustice of it boiled inside her like acid. Eddie Foreman might not have been a nice man, but he hadn't deserved to die like that. And she wasn't strong enough to bring his killer to justice.

The knowledge that there was nothing she could do about it ate at her mind like acid.

Nik stared at the door, then back to Mikayla.

He wanted to do as she ordered. God knew it was the wisest course of action. He should walk right out that door and be finished with this. It was obvious it was over.

Instead, the need to touch her was rising within him by the second. It would be his last chance to touch her, to taste her. The last chance to experience that incredible pleasure, that almost peace he found in her touch.

He moved for the door as though to follow the order. His gaze remained locked on hers, every cell of his body honed in on the warmth of her.

As he stopped in front of her, his hand gripped the edge of the door, pulled it from her grip, and closed it gently while she watched in shock.

"What now?" she whispered, the anger breaking through for a moment. "Do you still want an answer to that question you asked earlier? A little or a lot?" Her lips tightened, that spark of pain darkening her eyes further. "Guess what, Nik? How about none? Nothing. There's nothing more that I want from you. No, just leave, so I can forget you ever existed."

"Why do you think I'm leaving?" His voice was a harsh growl that surprised both of them.

In that tone, he heard what he watched her sense. A hunger such as he had never known in his life. A need that burned in his gut, in his balls, that tightened and engorged his dick to painful hardness.

The need to fuck her was ripping him apart. The need to possess her, to do the impossible, to protect her, tore through him with a power so strong that for a second it tore past the control he had promised himself he would hold on to.

Before he could stop himself, he pulled her to him. Before she could protest, he lifted her against him, covered her lips with his, and gave into a need so fierce, so overriding, that it was more animalistic than logical.

And Mikayla couldn't resist.

As his lips slanted over hers, she couldn't hold back the need to part her own, to taste him, to feel him, just one more time.

This one last time.

The hold she'd exerted on her tears slipped and the moisture fell from her eyes. The pain brewing inside her found release as the hunger she couldn't control tore past the barriers she had fought to place between her and this man she couldn't hold herself back from.

Pleasure raced across her nerve endings, raked through her system. Velvet-lined talons locked into her womb, sending sensation clenching into her sex, swelling her clit tighter and leaving her helpless in his embrace.

He was the bad boy. The heartbreaker. She had sensed it all along, known she couldn't give in to that temptation, no matter how she wanted to. Ached to.

Her lips parted further, her tongue licking against

his as a moan broke free and her hands gripped his shoulders desperately.

He tasted wild and dangerous. His kiss was dark and earthy, filled with dominance and lush ecstasy.

Arching to him, she could only moan as she felt his fingers jerking the hem of her blouse from her skirt. His big hand stroked beneath it, curving around her hips, lifting her against him as his other hand curved around the rounded flesh of her breast.

His thumb stroked her nipple as his fingers delved beneath the edge of her bra and lifted her flesh free. He was moving as he stroked her past reason. Moving her. Before she could process the information, process where she was, she found herself stretched out on the rich material of the microfiber upholstery of the couch, Nik moving over her.

Her blouse was unbuttoned, spread apart. The front clasp of her bra was loosened and his lips were traveling over one breast, licking, kissing, as she stared down at him in shock. She watched in bemusement as his lips parted, covered the tight, hard peak of her breast, and sucked it into the blistering heat of his mouth.

His tongue stroked against the tight bundle of nerve endings, sending fingers of electric pleasure to clench between her thighs as she felt her juices flowing from her inner sex. Her vagina clenched, burned, felt empty as Nik's hard thigh pressed against the sensitive mound firmly.

She was drowning in sensation. The pleasure swamped her, stilled any protests she could have even thought to have, and wiped away betrayal, hurt, anger, filling her instead with heat and hunger.

She found herself rocking against his thigh as her hands clenched in his hair to hold him to her breast. Her thighs tightened on him, stroking her clit against the denim of his jeans and the silk of her panties as ecstasy threatened to drive her wild.

She couldn't bear it. The need was ripping through her, rising, pulling her down into an abyss of pure sensation too intense to deny.

She wanted more. She wanted all of it. The hard wedge of his erection free, hot and hard, pressing into her, taking her. She wanted to feel the pleasure/pain of that first possession, wanted to feel the agony of that first orgasm.

"Oh, God. Nik, please . . ." She twisted against him as his lips moved to the valley between her breasts, his tongue licking, as his hand flattened on her stomach, his fingers stroking against her flesh.

"Mikayla." The growl of his voice weakened her further, pulled her deeper into the vortex of pleasure.

Her hands pulled at his shirt, the need to touch his flesh a hunger unlike any other she had ever experienced.

"Sweet baby," he groaned, his thigh easing back, his fingers sliding to her thigh. "Fuck, Mikayla, I need you."

The admission struck her womb like a sucker punch, causing it to clench, to flex with wild hunger.

She felt dizzy, desperate. Nothing mattered but his touch. The lies were forgotten, the betrayal pushed to the back of her mind.

"Mikayla, baby." His fingers stroked over the wet center of her body. "I would have loved to have time to convince you to wax this pretty flesh. To let me lick you, taste your sweet pussy."

She cried out. The pleasure that rushed through her was almost more than she could bear.

"Would you like that, sweetheart?" His lips moved down her body, licking to her belly button, stroking around it as his fingers pressed over her clit. "Do you want my mouth on you? Sucking your sweet clit, licking it? I'd fuck you with my tongue, baby. Drive it so deep inside your sweet pussy."

Her hips bucked against his hand as she fought to breathe, the images racing through her mind, stoking the hunger.

High enough that she was ready to beg. That she was ready to surrender herself, to surrender her heart to a man who had deceived her. Who had lied by omission.

She felt the tears that fell from her eyes now. Pain rose inside her, matching the hunger. He was going to break her heart. He would take everything.

"Mikayla." Tortured, broken, his voice drew her gaze back to him as he stared up at her.

His fingers lifted to stroke away the tears.

"I can't tell you no," she suddenly sobbed. "I can't. I need you, Nik, so much." Her breathing hitched, emotion tearing through her. "What do I do when I have to remember you lied to me? When you have to go? What do I do then?"

CHAPTER 7

Mikayla went to work the next day and hid in her office. She hadn't slept; she couldn't concentrate. She didn't cry, but God, she wanted to. She wanted to break down and scream and rage and curse Nik for ripping her heart from her chest.

By lunch, Deirdre had obviously had enough. When she walked into the office and closed the door behind her, Mikayla looked up from the accounting she wasn't even trying to focus on.

"I closed the shop for lunch," her friend informed her. "It's time we talk."

Mikayla shook her head. She'd told Deirdre that morning what had happened. Mikayla may have omitted details, but Deirdre knew enough to understand just how close Mikayla had come to giving herself to Nik.

A man she hadn't even known. One she still knew so very little about. A man who had deceived her.

"He's leaving this evening?" Deirdre asked when Mikayla said nothing.

"That's what he said." She leaned back in her chair and rubbed her hands over her face, knowing she looked like hell.

What the hell was wrong with her anyway? She couldn't be in love with him, but she was close to feeling something. . . . All she knew was that it was a good thing he was leaving; otherwise, she would end up begging him to take her.

"You're going to tell him good-bye," Deirdre stated, her voice fierce.

Mikayla sat forward slowly. "Have you lost your mind?"

Deirdre had to be crazy. The man's touch was like a drug. She couldn't resist. And her best friend thought she was going to tempt that danger further?

"If you don't, you'll always be watching for him, Mikayla," Deirdre stated firmly. "If you don't say good-bye, if you don't watch him leave, then you'll never let go of him, not really. He'll always be the one that got away. You don't want that. I watched my mother go through this with Dad. She wouldn't watch him leave and she never stopped watching for him to return."

Mikayla shook her head. "I'm not married to him," she retorted defiantly. "I'm not even in love with him."

"Doesn't matter." Deirdre propped her hands on her hips and glared back at Mikayla. "Listen, I know what I'm talking about here. Go home, shower, put on some makeup, and dress pretty. And tell that son of a bitch good-bye with a smile, even if it's killing you. I promise you, you'll sleep better for it tonight."

Would she? Or would it only hurt more?

Mikayla blew out a hard breath as she crossed her arms on top of the desk and laid her head heavily on them.

"I don't want to say good-bye," she muttered, her tone mutinous. "I might cry again."

How humiliating. She hadn't had the strength to simply tell him no; she had cried instead. Because she knew he was going to leave. She knew he had lied to her, that he didn't love her, that he was going to walk away from her whether she allowed him to become her lover or not.

And honestly, it was better that way. She had known from the beginning that he was a heartbreaker. All bad boys were. They broke hearts from the cradle, and if they ever gave their own then it was rare.

She had known that the moment she laid on eyes on him riding down Gina Foreman's street. The ultimate bad boy. Dangerous, hard-core, sexual, almost illegal.

"Come on, Mikayla, you don't want to fixate on him after he's gone, and you don't want to regret him." Deirdre sighed. "Go home, get ready, and when he leaves smile and tell him good-bye. Do this for yourself, or you'll always regret it."

Sitting up, she stared back at Deirdre, knowing how her father's desertion of her and her mother had affected her. She and Mikayla had been friends forever. They shared a passion for clothes and a passion for business. They had their separate dreams and their separate lives, and they were each other's support network.

And Deirdre was probably right. She and her on-again, off-again boyfriend, Drake, had had more than a tumultuous relationship. Drake had broken Deirdre's heart more times than Mikayla could count. If anyone knew how bad it hurt to be unable to walk away, then it was Deirdre.

"Think about it," she urged her friend. "Don't let him hurt you more than he already has, sweetie."

With that, Deirdre opened the door and returned to the front of the shop. Likely to her lunch as well.

Mikayla just wished she had an appetite. Her stomach protested at the very idea of food at this point. She didn't want to tell Nik good-bye. She didn't want him to leave. She wanted to return to the evening past, before she had ever known why he was there and what he was doing.

To the time when, in the back of her mind, she had wondered if she was enough to tame a bad boy.

The thought caused her to pause. God, she had known better than that; she had to have known better. She had never allowed herself to be interested in the bad boys, the charmers, the heartbreakers. She had focused on the nice, steady guys instead. Only to learn that many of them weren't so steady after all.

She was twenty-six and still living that child's dream of giving her virginity, that gift that she could give only once, to the man she would share the rest of her life with.

Unrealistic. No one could accuse Mikayla Martin of being a hard-nosed realist, could they?

Shaking her head, she rose to her feet as she heard the low, melodic sound of the bell over the door tinkling delicately. Deirdre had reopened the shop rather than waiting for the lunch hour to end.

It didn't matter. Mikayla was going home. She was going to take her best friend's advice and hope she knew what she was talking about.

After Mikayla gathered her papers together and refiled them, she turned to grab her purse and leave. The office door opened, and she stepped back in surprise as Deirdre followed the familiar male into the office.

"Talk about freakin' childish," Deirdre sneered at Luke Nelson as he glared back at her. "He just comes right in like he owns the damned place."

"If it hadn't been for my family she wouldn't have this shop," Luke retorted petulantly. She hadn't seen this side of him until she had made the mistake of actually going out with him a few times.

Luke was selfish, self-involved, and, as far as he was concerned, all-important.

Mikayla had never considered Luke quite so important, and had managed to garner his undying scorn in turn.

"What do you want, Luke?" Mikayla propped a hand on her hip and stared back at him in irritation. "I have things to do today and I don't have time to deal with you."

"Things like Nikolai Steele?" Luke snapped. "God, I thought you had more sense than to fool with such a lowlife."

Behind Luke, Deirdre's expression slackened in outrage as Mikayla stared at him in shock.

"She went out with you," Deirdre shot back at him. "Nik Steele can't be anything but a step up."

Luke glared at her again as she rolled her eyes and leaned against the door frame, obviously refusing to leave.

"Luke, what I do or who I see is none of your business," Mikayla informed him.

"Are you aware the bastard is no more than a criminal?" Luke told her, his gaze raking over her insultingly. "I thought better of you and your Miss Goody Two-shoes act."

Her Miss Goody Two-shoes act?

"It's not an act," Deirdre muttered defiantly behind Luke's back as she crossed her arms over her breasts and glared at him.

"Give me a break." Mikayla rolled her eyes at both of them. "What the hell do you want, Luke? I don't have time to deal with you."

"She said 'hell.'" Deirdre's eyes widened as she and Luke both stared at Mikayla as though she had committed a crime.

She always said "hell." Just never aloud. Her brothers had the corner on vulgar language. Mikayla had claimed the corner on not using it. That didn't mean she didn't think it.

"Luke, what's your problem?" She shook her head, uncertain how to handle either of them now.

"Your friend Nik Steele is my problem." Luke glared at Deirdre over his shoulder as though daring her to speak. "Are you aware the bastard was hired by my father to prove you a liar? That he's here to make a fool of you, Mikayla?"

Mikayla arched her brow. "I'm more than aware of that, Luke."

Her admission took the wind out of his sails for a moment. He stared at her, his eyes wide with surprise.

She had managed to throw him off. He hadn't expected her to know Nik's true reason for being here. He'd thought he'd found a way to hurt her. She had always known Luke was mean-spirited, but she hadn't expected him to be so blatant about it.

"You're no better than the rest of us," he sneered. "He's nothing but a terrorist wannabe and you're rolling around in the bed with him, aren't you? So much for all your high ideals."

She stared back at Luke archly. "Why? Because I refused to roll around in the bed with you? Sorry, Luke, maybe I was looking for a man rather than a spoiled little boy. Now get out of my shop before I call Nik and have you thrown out."

It was the best threat she could come up with, as well as the most insulting. Or at least, it was as mean as she was willing to get at this point. Luke had problems with his opinion, as well as others', of his manhood. There was no sense in damaging it worse by throwing him out herself. Besides, she rather liked the pristine look of the pale green summer dress and matching high heels she wore.

His expression twisted. Something dark and uncertain flashed in his eyes.

"He's trouble," Luke snarled back at her.

"But it's my trouble, not yours."

"Damn you!" Emotion almost shadowed his eyes. "Damn you, Mikayla."

Turning, he stalked from the shop, the door slamming closed behind him.

"He's a little boy in a body to die for," Deirdre said regretfully. "God was playing a hell of a joke on us when he made that man."

"He made the body, not the man." Mikayla shrugged, though she, too, felt an edge of regret and concern. "Luke let himself become what he is."

Deirdre stared at Mikayla doubtfully. "With Maddix and Annette Nelson for parents, what choice did he have?"

Annette anyway. But Mikayla kept the observation silent. Maddix Nelson had tried to raise his son with a few values. Mikayla knew that for a fact. For too many years the Nelsons and the Martins had been friends.

When Annette and Maddix had split up, Annette had gotten custody of Luke, who had been very young at the time, and proceded to raise him the exact opposite way Maddix would have wanted him raised.

Annette was a bitch; everyone had known it. She had been tolerated because so many had liked and benefited from Maddix. His son . . . had not been tolerated nearly as well.

"I'm heading home." Mikayla sighed in resignation as she stared back at her still-silent friend. "I'm taking your advice."

"It's about time," Deirdre informed Mikayla. "Give

him hell, sweetheart. He might walk away, but I promise, he'll never forget you."

Just as she wouldn't forget him. She had a very bad
feeling he was going to become the one who got away
no matter what she did. Her reaction to him went too
deep; her need for him was too strong.

She could have done without whatever quirk of fate
had set Nik in her path. She could have happily lived
her life not knowing such pleasure existed.

No, she amended. She couldn't have. She wouldn't
have wanted to miss this, wouldn't have wanted to exist in a state of ignorance. She knew now why no relationship she'd had so far had worked. Because that
kind of incredible pleasure had been missing.

And now it was walking right out of her life before
she'd ever known what it was supposed to be.

Nik watched from behind the sheer curtains of the window looking out to the front of the house as Mikayla's
Jeep pulled into the drive next door.

She was dressed as pristinely as ever, he noticed as
she walked to her front door. That beautiful long wheat
gold hair was done expertly in a French braid that fell
down her back, only her bangs left uncontained. The
soft summer sleeveless blouse she wore in a soft cream
complemented the mint green above-the-knees skirt
and cream-colored heels she wore. Her purse was the
same mint green as her skirt.

Damn woman was always color coordinated and perfectly put together. She gave the impression that there
wasn't a damned thing in hell that could ruffle her perfectly layered feathers.

Until he got her aroused.

She burned in a man's arms then.

Or rather, she burned in his arms.

"Nelson's son came to her shop before she left," Eleanor Longstrom, the owner of the antique store across the street from Mikayla's, stated behind him.

Eleanor had no idea who or what Nik was a part of, despite her former classified position with the CIA before her retirement ten years ago.

All Eleanor knew was that she had been "asked" to cooperate with Travis Caine and Nik Steele when they had been in town several weeks before. Nik had pulled her in for intel this time as well, knowing one set of eyes wouldn't be nearly enough.

It was the reason she had arrived this evening, to deliver information, unaware that he was leaving and that, as far as he was concerned, this job was completed.

"Do you know why he was there?" Nik asked as he glanced over his shoulder at the spritely grandmotherly woman who watched him with a knowing smile.

"He was rather angry, I heard," she stated. "I stepped in and spoke to Deirdre when Mikayla left. Luke was very insulting. He seemed to believe Mikayla was lowering herself to sleep with you."

Why did he want to know this? And why was he listening?

Nik grunted at the thought. "She just arrived home," he mused. "Where did she go after she left the shop?"

"She stopped by her father's office for a while," Eleanor reported. "Her mother was there. Mikayla and her parents are very close. Any man Mikayla falls in love with, or begins seeing seriously, will have to become close with her family."

Another reason to leave, Nik thought. He wasn't a family man—at least he wasn't anymore. He was a loner now. Mikayla didn't need a man who had sworn to never put down roots again.

"This isn't my business," he told Eleanor. "I'm leaving."

"And that's a shame." Eleanor sighed. "She needs you right now. If for no other reason than to figure out what is going on."

"She's in a hell of a mess," Nik stated as he stepped back from the window. "No one believes Maddix killed his foreman. Hell, even I don't believe it was Maddix she saw. But I don't believe she was lying. There are no leads, no suspects. It's a dead end."

"Mikayla's not a liar." Eleanor shrugged her graceful shoulders as she watched Nik with thoughtful blue eyes. "I used to babysit her father, and I've known Mikayla all her life. She's not as wild as her brothers and they're all basically honest, but Mikayla holds herself to a higher standard. She always has. She's a good girl, Nik, and she's in trouble."

"Is that a warning, Mrs. Longstrom?" He arched his brow at the disapproving look on her face.

Her lips tightened.

"On second thought, I think it's a good thing for Mikayla that you're leaving," Eleanor said somberly. "She doesn't deserve a broken heart along with the rest of the trouble she's had to deal with."

No, she didn't. And Nik didn't need to add to the regrets in his life, either.

"Do you have any further information?" Nik asked, making certain his tone indicated that their meeting was over.

"There's nothing more to report, Nik." She shook her head, the short cut of her gray hair brushing against the nape of her neck. "But as I told you when you arrived, Maddix was definitely in that meeting when Eddie Foreman was killed. It was an impromptu meeting that arose when the council members learned property they had been trying to buy for a city project was coming up for sale. It was actually arranged within hours of the actual meeting. Maddix has several neighbors who witnessed their arrival as well as the fact that Maddix answered the door himself when each arrived."

There had to be something he was missing, Nik thought. He'd investigated this as far as he could go. His job was to find out why Mikayla would lie about what she had seen. He couldn't give an answer, because she was certain she had seen Maddix.

It was unfortunate that Nik hadn't been able to resolve the problem and whoever had killed Eddie Foreman had gotten away with it.

"I'm leaving now," Eleanor announced. "If you need anything else, then you only have to let me know. It's unfortunate you can't stick around and figure out who murdered Eddie. He wasn't always a nice person, but he didn't deserve to be murdered."

"I have other things to do," Nik told her.

Eleanor nodded as she headed for the back door. "That's a good thing for Mikayla's heart, a bad thing for the situation itself. I have a feeling, though, if you don't leave you'll only end up hurting her."

Or himself.

Nik watched as Eleanor left the house before he turned back to the window to stare into the soft light of early evening.

He was packed and ready to roll out, though he hadn't figured out why he hadn't left yet.

There was a part of him that loathed walking out the door, nothing in hand but the leather bag he had arrived with. There was something he was leaving behind, but he was damned if he could figure out what the hell it was.

Shaking his head at the thought, Nik went through the house, secured it, then picked up the leather bag that held several changes of clothing as well as the weapons he had brought with him.

He had to force himself out the front door. Hell, walking away had always been easy, especially since his "death." He hadn't known it possible to possess a hunger for a woman the way he did for one tender, sweet little virgin at the moment.

He stepped outside, pausing on the porch to stare into the slowly dimming light of a summer evening. Rain was coming. He could feel it in the air, almost taste it against his tongue.

The scent of it reminded him of Mikayla.

He shook his head, trying to shake the regret growing inside him away as he strode to the driveway and the motorcycle parked there.

"Nik."

She stepped from behind the Jeep and moved to the strip of grass dividing the driveways, moving to stand beneath the heavy oak tree growing there.

Fairy princess. That was what she was. He couldn't get the idea out of his head. So damned petite and innocent, still believing, somehow, in the good of the world. He could have told her, would have told her, there was so very little good left.

"You should have stayed in the house, Mikayla." He secured the leather bag in the metal saddlebag on the side of the cycle.

"I shouldn't say good-bye?" There was the faintest edge of hurt in her voice now; it matched the hurt he had glimpsed in her amethyst eyes, in her pale face.

" 'Good-bye' is for friends," he pointed out to her as he straightened and stared back at her. "Are we friends, Mikayla?"

It was a challenge and he knew it. She was still angry. That spark of ire still lingered in her gaze, in the tightly controlled curve of her lips.

"Why are you here?" As he moved around the back of the cycle, he knew lingering here was a mistake.

He should leave now, before he was drawn in any further. Before he completely fucked the fragile peace he'd found after all these years.

"I say good-bye." Her fingers were laced together in front of her, her shoulders straight. The heels she wore barely got her to the middle of his chest. He wanted to protect her, he realized. He wanted to wrap her up, protect her from the world, and keep all that innocence and fire for himself alone.

He should be locked up for even desiring such a thing, because he knew how fragile that illusion could be.

"I told you, you say good-bye to a friend," he growled.

"Or someone you wished could have been a friend," she mused softly before pulling at her lower lip with her teeth and nibbling at it nervously for a second. "I won't forget you, Nik."

His stomach clenched; his cock, hard since the moment he laid eyes on her, tried to thicken further. Hell, he'd never been so hard in his life.

"You should." Anger was slipping through the tight leash he fought to keep on it. "You should forget me the moment I ride out of here, Mikayla. Or do you like it when men lie to you? When they hurt you?"

She flinched, her lips thinning. "Maybe that's why I'm saying good-bye, Nik," she suggested then. "Maybe I'm scared if I just watch you ride away, then I really won't be able to forget you."

That made more sense, but it wasn't going to work. He could tell her himself that there were points in a person's life that couldn't be forgotten. For them, what they hadn't had would always haunt them. It couldn't be helped.

Nik shook his head. "What the fuck do you want from me, Mikayla?" He sighed. "I told you the truth. You should have your brothers standing here rather than standing here yourself."

"And what would they do?" she asked bitterly. "If they tried to fight you, you'd decimate them. If they got lucky and hurt you, I'd never forget it. It's a no-win situation, isn't it, Nik?"

For a second, tears glittered in her eyes before she blinked them back. She turned her gaze from him for a second, then returned it with renewed strength.

She had to be one of the strongest women he had ever laid eyes on. Damn her. She made him remember the dreams he was ordered to throw away so long ago. That dream of finding peace amid war, safety in a world where safety was a liability rather than an ethereal dream.

"It's a no-win situation," he finally agreed. "What you do with it is what makes the difference, baby. When I'm gone, just forget. Otherwise, you'll only hurt yourself."

He knew inside he had begun the painful process though, watching the hurt that was building in her eyes. A hurt he wanted nothing more than to heal before he did exactly as she had told him to do. He was riding out of town, moving right out of her life. Unlike her, he wouldn't have his anger to hold onto. She'd done nothing to deserve his anger, therefore there was no shield between his hunger and her memory.

Her tongue slid over her lips again, tempting him to taste, to lose himself to the hunger rather than running away from it.

"Deirdre was wrong," she finally whispered as he forced himself to keep a distance between them.

"About what?" Fists clenched at his sides, his entire body so tight he wondered why he hadn't cracked.

"Saying good-bye won't help me forget. A woman doesn't forget her first hunger. Ever."

He moved to her. Just in time.

As he reached her there was a flash of light high to his side, a distinctive splintering of light where there should have been none as the fading sun struck against glass. The splintering of the tree bark as Nik jerked Mikayla to him and threw them both to the ground as the sharp retort of a sniper's rifle cracked through the air.

"Move!" Nik didn't give Mikayla a chance to move on her own despite the order.

Hooking his arm around her waist, he jerked her from the ground as the next bullet struck the ground at the exact spot her head had been and he pulled her around the tree, in front of the Jeep, then raced for the house.

Another round hit the cement of the sidewalk just ahead of him as he threw them both into the house, adrenaline and sudden racing terror streaking through him as Mikayla collapsed against the wall, a streak of red against her face, on her pretty, creamy blouse.

"Mikayla." Her name was a harsh, broken sound as he jerked the edges of her blouse apart, searching for a wound. There was none there. Nothing. Just blood.

Blood on her face, her head.

"Ah, God. Mikayla. Mikayla." She was staring up at him in horror, her eyes wide, shocked, the black nearly filling the amethyst color as her hand lifted to her head, the golden color stained.

His hands were shaking. Sweet Lord. Ah, God. She had to be okay.

"Wood." Her voice was strangled. "I think it hit me."

She touched her head again, her fingertips coming back marred red as she stared at them. They began shaking like a leaf at an oncoming storm. She lifted her gaze to him once more.

"Please," she whispered. "Please don't let them kill me, Nik. Please."

A tear fell. A single drop of fear and pain that slid slowly down her too-white face to mix with the smear of blood on her cheek.

Fear raked across his soul. Only once in his life had he ever known anything approaching the sheer agony, the horror, that filled him now.

He had no weapon but the small snub-nosed pistol secured just inside the top of his boot. It was no match for a sniper. And there was blood on his woman.

His woman.

He wasn't going anywhere. Not until he found who Mikayla saw that day, and who suddenly wanted her dead.

CHAPTER 8

Nik escaped just after midnight, Mikayla's father's vow that he wasn't leaving his daughter alone giving Nik the chance he needed to make a little visit.

Only one person had reason to want to silence Mikayla, and that was Maddix himself. He knew Nik was leaving the job unfinished. Just as he knew that Mikayla wouldn't stop trying to prove he had killed Eddie Foreman.

If it wasn't Maddix, then someone close to him. Someone who feared she would prove Maddix guilty. Or was it someone trying to make it appear as though Maddix had grown tired of her accusations?

The possibilities were becoming endless, and it was time to begin eliminating them.

Fury was cold and silent inside Nik. A murderous rage that he had only felt once in his life, burning in his soul. God help the shooter when Nik got his hands on him, and he would find him. And he'd kill him. Slowly.

The sight of Mikayla's blood would live in Nik's nightmares.

The police had been very little help, and that had only served to piss him off further. She had on more than one occasion called the chief of police a liar when he'd given Maddix an alibi. That had placed her in a very tenuous position now that she needed help from that same police force.

After Nik slipped into Maddix's gated community, it didn't take long to slide into his backyard and make his way to the glass patio doors that led to Maddix's study.

The chief of police's car was sitting at the front of the house, which meant Maddix had been warned about the shooting, as Nik had known he would be.

Hagerstown was a fairly large city, but some things just got around fast.

"Goddamn, Daniel! What the hell are your men trying to prove?" Maddix's voice rose in fury. "Son of a fucking bitch, get them under control!"

Maddix's tone suggested panic. His eyes were filled with confused astonishment, his expression furious.

"Dammit, Maddix, don't tell me how to do my fucking job," the chief growled back at him. "And what the hell do you expect from my men? How many times has that little bitch called me a liar? She insults the whole police force when she does that."

"I don't care if she personally insults every son-of-a-bitching man on the force, their ancestors, descendants, and future in-laws," Maddix yelled back, his hands flattening on the sleek cherrywood of the desk he stood behind. "Do something!"

Nik slipped to the entrance into the empty living room, his lips thinning at the piss-poor security of Maddix's home even as he took advantage of it.

Slipping through the darkness, he made his way to the heavy wood door that barred the study. Thankfully, it wasn't locked. Not that it would have posed much of a problem.

"Look, Maddix, she's bringing this trouble down on herself."

"Fuck you, Daniel!" Maddix sounded as though he were ready to have a stroke. "Find the bastard. Now."

Nik stepped into the room. "And when you find him, I want him."

Nik was armed. The Glock he carried easily in his hand wasn't missed as the chief of police turned to Nik in shock and Maddix sat down heavily in his chair.

"Thank God," Maddix muttered, shaking his hand as he pushed his fingers through his hair, not for the first time. "Is she okay?"

Nik closed the door, locking it carefully behind him as he faced the two men.

"Your chief didn't tell you?" The icy fury threatened to escape.

Maddix lifted his gaze to Daniel questioningly.

"It was minor," the chief snapped. "A scratch, nothing more."

"Sweet Lord," Maddix whispered. Leaning forward, he braced his arms on his desk and stared back at Nik. "She's going to be okay?"

"I told you it was a damned scratch, Maddix," Daniel snarled, his large, wide-boned face flushing in anger. "Do you think I'd lie to you?"

"What I think is that you'd encourage your men to take less care with Mikayla Martin than any other citizen in this town," Nik answered for Maddix. "Your detective was less than thorough and your crime scene unit negligent. Trust me when I say I'll make certain you pay for it."

"God, Daniel," Maddix muttered again. "You can't handle this in such a manner. You have to take care of her."

"I can't control this, Maddix," the chief argued.

"Hell, she's pissed off the entire force. You can't handle it, either."

"*I'll* handle it," Nik assured them.

It was already being handled. The phone calls Nik had made on the way over had ensured that the situation would receive its own special investigation.

"Why the hell are you here anyway?" Chief Riley snapped, his lips thin, his hazel eyes sparking in outrage. "I don't need you or anyone else telling me about my men or how they should do their jobs."

"I disagree." Nik shrugged. "And you can leave. It's not you I need to talk to."

"Like hell."

"Go, Daniel. You're about as much help as your men were tonight," Maddix growled.

Daniel threw Maddix and Nik both a furious glower before stalking to the door. It took the chief a moment to unlock it before he slammed it heavily behind him.

Nik holstered the Glock as he turned, relocked the door, then faced Maddix once again.

"Someone almost killed her tonight, Maddix," Nik said, his voice low, murderous intent clear in his tone. "I don't like how this game is going."

"And you think I do?" Maddix nearly came out of his chair in outrage. "God, Nik, if she dies, the whole world is going to believe I'm behind it. Do you think I'd be that fucking insane?"

Nik moved to the leather chair facing the desk and sat down slowly, propping his ankle on the opposite knee as he stared back at the other man for long moments.

"I think desperate men employ desperate measures," Nik finally answered. "Fortunately, I also don't think you're desperate yet. Which leaves it up to me to figure out who is. Who is so determined to take you down?"

Maddix leaned back in his chair, an air of exhaustion surrounding him.

"Hell, just every competitor I have. I've managed to snag some prime contracts in the past years. It's caused several other companies to feel the pinch. But nothing could be pinching them this bad. I know the owners of those companies, Nik—"

"We'll get to that," Nik broke in. "My job now is to protect Mikayla. That means finding out who murdered Eddie Foreman. I find that person, then I find the man who nearly put a bullet in her head. And when I do find him, you won't have to worry about him causing any further problems."

Maddix swallowed tightly.

"Now, we're going to go under the assumption for the moment that you didn't kill Eddie and that Mikayla isn't lying. She believes she saw you. That leads to the question, who looks like you?"

Maddix shook his head fiercely. "Not even my son resembles me. I take after my mother's side of the family, and she's an only child. There aren't even any cousins on that side."

"Illegitimate cousins or brothers?" Nik asked.

"Hell no. As much money as I make, I'd know if there were any. They crawl out like cockroaches when you have money."

Nik stared back at Maddix thoughtfully. It had been worth asking. He'd had to rule it out before he could begin his own investigation.

"I'll need any information you have on Eddie as well as the investigation your police department has put into this case, no later than tomorrow afternoon."

"I can do better than that." Maddix reached to a drawer at the side of his desk. "I have the file. Daniel has kept it updated as well. I've gone over every inch of it, though I can't find anything that points to anyone in particular, Nik. There are no suspects. No one saw anything except Mikayla, and I swear to God, she didn't see me there."

He pulled the file free. It was easily three inches thick. At least the police department had been doing something.

Nik took the file, glancing at it for just a second before tucking it under his arm and staring back at Maddix emotionlessly.

"Keep Luke away from her," Nik finally ordered the older man icily. "If he comes around her again, Maddix, he's going to get hurt."

Maddix sighed heavily. "He liked her an awful lot, Nik. Despite appearances, this hit Luke hard."

"I think he's a spoiled little bastard and the only thing that hit him hard was the fact that he couldn't fuck her. Keep him the hell away from her, or I'll fuck him up. Are we understood?"

Maddix swallowed tightly. "I'll make certain he stays away from her."

Giving a quick nod, Nik turned and left the room, disappearing into the shadows of the house and exiting out the way he had come.

He had his work cut out for him.

There were no easy answers here, and no suspects. All he had was a woman he knew was innocent, a friend he suspected was innocent, and a game with no rules.

Fortunately, those games were the only games Nik played well.

"Mikayla?" Deirdre's voice outside Mikayla's door held a hint of warning.

Mikayla lifted her attention from the dress form and the ball gown hanging on it.

"Yes, Deirdre?"

The door opened as Deirdre peeked in apologeti-
cally. "Um, there's someone here demanding to talk
to you."

"Who?" There was an edge of irritation in her voice
and she couldn't help it. She so didn't want to have to
deal with Luke again.

"Me."

Nope, not Luke, but perhaps just as bad.

Glenda Nelson stepped into the room. Maddix's trophy wife. She was easily twenty years younger than he,
model gorgeous with her dark cocoa skin and shoulder-
length raven black hair. Deep, dark brown eyes stared
back at Mikayla with a hint of anxiety rather than the
animosity she would have expected.

Glenda was just as arrogant as always, though. Pushing past Deirdre, she entered the room, looking around
the large sewing area curiously before turning back to
Mikayla with a haughty air.

"We need to talk," Glenda stated.

"I have this, Deirdre," Mikayla assured her. "Go on
back to the shop."

Mikayla waited until the door closed before turning back to the other woman. "What can I do for you,
Glenda?" she asked wearily. "If you're here to throw
your own little fit like Luke did, then I don't want to
hear it."

Glenda shook her head with a grimace as her chocolate brown eyes seemed to darken further. "I heard
about the shooting last night. I was worried, and concerned."

"Afraid I'd accuse Maddix of that, too?" Mikayla
gave a little mocking snort.

"Not hardly," Glenda assured Mikayla with a
slight shake of her head. "I'm as certain of Maddix's

innocence as I am of my own. As I said, I was concerned, as is Maddix. I wanted to see for myself that you were unharmed."

Glenda had almost been a friend, one Mikayla felt she would have cherished. Now, only suspicion and regret lay between them.

"Perfectly unharmed." Mikayla held her arms out from her body as she fought back the anger that continued to brew inside her.

How many women had come through that shop today out of simple curiosity? They hadn't even bought anything, which would have been the courteous thing to do, after nosing into her business. They stared, whispered, and pretended to browse. A few even attempted to question her, but they all left empty-handed. Mikayla had escaped to the sewing room simply to get away from it all. After more than a month of the whispers, suspicions, and questions, she was ready to run home and hide for a while.

Who could have believed that trying to be honest, trying to find justice, could result in this?

"I can understand why you're angry," Glenda said softly. "If you truly believe you saw what you think you saw, then this would be hard."

"Go away, Glenda." Mikayla had had enough. Either she was a liar or her eyesight was lousy. No one seemed willing to believe that she could have possibly seen Maddix Nelson commit murder.

"Fine, but before I leave, I want to look at the dress design we were working on before this bullshit started." Glenda placed one graceful hand on a slender hip as her expression became as superior and arrogant as always.

Mikayla's brows arched. "The dress design?" It was one of her best. It was still lying on her desk, a dress she couldn't possibly begin without a buyer, a dress designed for one person specifically. The person standing in front of Mikayla.

"Why?" she asked suspiciously.

Glenda wasn't one of the easiest people to understand. There had been a time when Mikayla had almost called Glenda a friend. But that had been before the former model married Maddix Nelson and moved up in the social sphere.

"Because it's my dress," she stated as though the reason were a foregone conclusion. "And I want it. The annual Autumn Ball happens in less than three months. That doesn't give us much time."

"You told me to shove this dress in places I don't want to mention," Mikayla reminded Glenda, her eyes narrowing in anger. "What makes you think I'm willing to do it now?"

Glenda's arms crossed over her breasts as she stared back at Mikayla with cool disdain. "That dress was designed for me, Mikayla. My body." One graceful hand slid down her side with the ultimate love for her own body. Mikayla almost rolled her eyes.

She needed the money, there was no doubt. Unfortunately, Mikayla truly did like Glenda. The woman, despite that air of superiority, had a kind heart and a wry sense of humor. Before she married Maddix, that was.

"I want my dress." Glenda's eyes narrowed in determination. When she got that look, it was rarely a good thing. "For the Autumn Ball." A pout formed on her lips. "Come on, Kayla; be nice to me. I'm trying here."

"Why are you trying?" Confusion washed over Mikayla. "Why do you even care?"

"The hell if I know. You accuse my husband of a heinous act, stick to your story, and nearly get killed for it. I figure, you're not lying, right? Someone's playing you, my friend. And if that's the case, I can still have my dress and remain loyal to my husband. I'll raise your asking cost by a thousand, and that's it. Final deal. Now do I get my damned dress or what?"

"Don't call me Kayla," Mikayla snapped back at her.

"Agree to my dress or the whole town will be calling you Kayla before the week is out. I'll make certain of it."

As a threat, it was a damned good one. Mikayla despised that nickname. It was the one her brothers had always used when they were playing tricks on her as a child.

Mikayla sighed wearily before glancing at the desk where she knew the design lay. It would be a major coup for the shop. That dress was a masterpiece, and there was no doubt Glenda would make certain everyone knew she had an exclusive no-one-else-could-ever-wear dress.

It was business. Business was business, Mikayla's father had once told her.

But then, her father had pulled out of Maddix Nelson's contract as well when he learned how easily the other man was getting away with murder.

And Mikayla needed the money desperately, as well as Glenda's support of the store. Mikayla was surviving, but the past month had been slow. Too damned slow.

"I can't." And she regretted it like hell. That dress was one of the most beautiful designs she had ever come up with. "I'm sorry, Glenda, but I can't."

"But you will." Glenda's brown eyes narrowed on her. "Look, until this is cleared up neither Maddix nor I want to see you suffer, Mikayla. Or this shop. I'm trying here; help me out. . . ." Glenda seemed to get to the very heart of the problem. "We were friends once. And your father is established, Mikayla. He has plenty of work to replace a few lost contracts. Do you?"

No, she didn't.

"This is just a dress," Glenda said softly. "For a friend. You gave your word before this happened. Your father hadn't even signed a contract on the new projects. Let's face reality here. It's not the same situation."

Mikayla's lips thinned as she stared back at the other woman. "I don't understand why you're doing this." She shook her head. "What are you gaining from it, Glenda?"

"Peace of mind, dammit," Glenda snapped back. "Now, I'll expect a call from you or Deirdre to let me know when fittings begin. Don't forget the date, Mikayla. And I'm not taking 'no' for an answer."

She breezed out of the room and seconds later the bell over the front door tinkled merrily to announce her departure. The scent of her perfume still filled the sewing room when Deirdre came to stand in the doorway.

"What was that?" she asked.

Mikayla explained briefly, trying to make sense of what was going on even as she debated whether or not to actually do the job.

"We need the money," Deirdre said softly. "Rent's coming up. A down payment on that dress would more than pay for it."

That was more than the truth.

"I have to think about it." Mikayla shrugged, her gaze going back to the desk where the design lay. "Give me a few days, Deirdre."

"A few days." Deirdre breathed heavily. "Maybe in a few days we can actually take a paycheck while we're thinking about this. What do you think about that?" She turned and strode back into the shop, just as the bell tinkled again

Mikayla snagged the edge of the door and carefully closed it. She wanted to slam it.

God, she hated this. She felt torn, worn, and completely unsettled. If it wasn't enough that her life had gone completely to hell, now Glenda was trying to push her deeper into the pit.

And she still had to go home and face Nik, since he'd decided he could protect her more easily while staying at her house.

She groaned at the thought. Home. Alone. With Nik. He had moved in, with her family's complete approval, it seemed. Not that her father was comfortable with it. But Nik he was still there. He was making her brain mush, and that made it even harder to deal with Glenda. Because coming up with a reason not to make that gorgeous dress was becoming impossible. Coming up with a reason not to touch Nik was even harder.

She was a virgin. She was saving herself for marriage.

Bullshit.

She'd never met a man who made her heart pound, made sweat pop out on her flesh, and her heart race with such pleasure and excitement that she feared it would pound straight out of her chest.

Pushing her fingers through her hair, Mikayla turned and paced to the back of the room. As she stood amid bolts of material, the scent of the luxurious fabrics filling her senses, suddenly it wasn't enough.

The shop was her dream. It was her career and her livelihood. But it wasn't her lover. It wasn't the excitement that filled her at the thought that when she left the shop there was more waiting for her at home.

And that was where she was getting ready to get into trouble.

She would finish the dress. She would take Glenda's extra thousand on top of the fee she had already quoted and would make damned certain the dress was worth every penny of it.

Mikayla's Creations would make a name for itself. She would have this at least when Nik was gone. She was under no delusions that this had turned into some kind of forever scenario.

A growl tore from her throat.

She was insane.

She wasn't doing this to herself.

She wasn't going to . . .

Was she?

She stared around the room and shook her head again.

She couldn't think about this now. She couldn't think about Nik like this, not right now.

She had a dress to start, a life to live, and once she got home she had a killer to catch.

Nik was living in her house, he had promised to find out what was going on, and that meant he would prove Maddix Nelson had killed Eddie Foreman. And she was going to help.

CHAPTER 9

Nik arrived at the shop at precisely eight o'clock, when Deirdre and Mikayla had finished cleaning the shop and adding up the accounts for the day. They were putting the finishing touches on a new window display when the Harley throbbed to a stop at the curb and the vision of "rough and ready" swung from the seat to rise to his full glorious height.

He pulled the wicked black helmet from his head and gave his head a hard shake, allowing the long strands of pure white thick, luscious hair to fall just below his shoulder blades carelessly.

"My God, do you think men get as hard when they see a woman do that as I just got wet?" Deirdre breathed out in awe at the sight.

Shooting her a disgruntled look, Mikayla forced herself to finish tucking the back of the summer dress over the mannequin and pinning it into place before the bell over the door announced that Nik had entered the shop.

"Are you ready?" His voice was a hard, deep rumble that had Mikayla's stomach flexing in a surge of pleasure.

Deirdre turned, caught Mikayla's eye, and lifted her brows as she mouthed, *Oh yeah.*

Mikayla didn't even bother to shake her head at her friend. "We're ready," she assured him as she strode to the counter and picked up her purse, watching as Deirdre followed.

Within minutes Mikayla was in the Jeep and headed home, all too aware of the Harley following close behind her.

As she pulled into the driveway she inhaled deeply, collected her purse and the large leather briefcase she used to carry her sketchbooks and supplies.

"I'll go in first," Nik told her as they moved toward the door. "Stay behind me. Once we enter the house, remain in the foyer while I check everything out. I'll come back to the living room and get you if everything is clear. If I call back to you that it's not clear, then I want you to run hell-for-leather and call Jordan Malone. I programmed his number into your cell phone before we left the shop."

When exactly had he managed to do that?

The thought of anything happening to him or any threat directed at him because of her suddenly had her heart racing in dread. What would she do if by chance he were hurt? If somehow whoever had shot at her the day before managed to harm Nik instead?

"And stop worrying," he ordered. That fierce, rasping statement couldn't be described as anything other than an order as he glanced over his shoulder and gave her a hard look before stepping onto the porch.

"Yeah, I'll get right on that," she muttered as he held his hand out for the keys.

"And don't bother arguing with me, either," he warned her as she handed them over. "I know what I'm doing, Mikayla."

She had only a glimpse of the lethal black handgun that he pulled from behind his back after he unlocked the door.

She did as he'd ordered, though. She stepped into the foyer, closed and locked the door behind her before resetting the alarm and waiting as he began going through the house.

Lights came on in each room. Living room, kitchen, and dining room. The half bath, the hall. She heard him going into each bedroom; then she heard the thud of his steps as he came up the basement stairs. Minutes later he was walking back into the living room, the gun no longer in sight.

"I hate this," she said as she tossed her purse and case on the nearby table and stalked to the kitchen. "It's ridiculous."

"The price you pay for being honest." His shoulders lifted in a shrug as he followed her. "You should have known there would be backlash when you reported what you saw, Mikayla."

Those pale, pale blue eyes watched her intently as she moved for the refrigerator and pulled an oven dish from inside. Sliding it into the oven, she set the heat and the time before shrugging her jacket off and glaring back at him.

She didn't bother answering.

"I need a shower. Dinner will be ready in an hour."

She escaped as quickly as possible. He was getting ready to ask questions, she thought; she could see the intent in his eyes. Questions she didn't want to answer again. She had no desire to see the suspicion in his eyes as he asked her if she was certain she had seen what she knew she had seen. What she thought she had seen.

Stepping beneath the water, Mikayla frowned at the

thought. She was certain she had seen Maddix Nelson, wasn't she?

She closed her eyes as water washed over her face, and let the image of that day flash through her mind once again.

She was staring up, the dying rays of the sun striking the upper floors of the skeletal building. And Maddix stood there, staring down at her as Eddie Foreman fell to the ground, his chest soaked with blood.

Maddix. His features were distinctive. The personable lines of his face, the way he brushed his hair back, the strong line of his jaw, his lips held in a rigid line of fury as he saw her.

Like a photo, but blurry after time, she admitted.

Shaking her head, she hurried through her evening routine. When she finished, her long hair was halfway dry and falling down her back rather than in the braid she normally kept it in. Light cotton sweats and an overlarge T-shirt completed her evening attire.

Normally, this was relaxing time. Tonight, she had a feeling relaxation was going to be the least of what she had to look forward to.

Moving from her bedroom, she was met with the sight of Nik leaving the guest room. He'd showered as well. Damp hair was pulled back to his nape, exposing the strong, harsh features of his face, the pale icy blue of his eyes.

"Dinner should be ready."

She rarely went out of her way for dinner. She normally ate late, so she kept it simple, a nice casserole. Tonight chicken dumpling casserole was on the menu. She'd prepared extra and bought a loaf of freshly baked bread to go with it.

She knew how much a man could eat. Her brothers had been proving it since they'd hit puberty.

Dinner was quiet. Thankfully. She needed time to unwind. The events of the past two days were beginning to eat at her. The harder she tried to forget that someone had actually tried to kill her, the sharper the memory became.

"What did you find out today?" she finally asked as she cleaned up the table and placed the few dishes in the sink for washing later.

"Not a lot," he answered.

Leaning back in his chair, the beer he'd opened held loosely between two fingers, he stared at her with a thoughtful frown. "I went through the file Maddix gave me last night, checked it against the information a source of mine had. The police have no suspects, as we already knew. Tomorrow, I'll head to the construction site, see what I can find out there."

"You'll find nothing there," she informed him. "The building is more than halfway completed now. The area where Eddie was killed is completely filled in, and the workers refuse to talk to anyone about it. Maddix has covered his tracks well."

She peeked over his shoulder as she started the dishwasher.

"Or someone else has." He sighed as he leaned forward and stared back at her intently. "Let's go under the assumption here that you're both telling the truth. That means, there's another player involved."

She shook her head. "How does that make sense? Only Maddix would have a reason to kill me. If someone else killed Eddie, then it wouldn't make sense for him to want to hurt me because I believe I saw Maddix?"

"That's one of the questions that now have to be answered," he told her.

"I wish I'd never seen it." Turning back to the dishes,

she fought back her anger and her tears. "It's been nothing but trouble for me as well as my family, Nik. No one believes me, and Maddix plays the game perfectly. He's getting away with murder and no one even cares."

Even Nik believed him. Mikayla could tell he did.

The tension in her shoulders was so clear that Nik swore he could feel it in the air.

Hell, he had no idea what the fuck to do here.

"Let's sleep on it, see what we can come up with."

"I know Maddix and Eddie argued hard for weeks before Eddie was killed." She swung back to Nik, her gaze fierce. "Loud enough that they were heard outside the office that sits on the construction site. Then again days later at the cantina. Maddix was angry at him over something. Has your buddy told you what they were fighting over?"

"Maddix hasn't mentioned it. And why are *you* just now mentioning it?"

"Because you're just now showing any interest in doing anything about it." She turned back to him, those incredible amethyst eyes damp and filled with pain. "No one wants to listen, Nik. That's what I keep trying to tell you. And no one wants to know the truth. The only reason I know about this is because my brother Scotty just happened to have been on the job site as well as at the cantina. He witnessed it."

Nik made a mental note to talk to her brother after he found out what he could at the job site.

For now, he had a hellaciously long night to look forward to, because God only knew it was going to be impossible to sleep. She was a single door away from him. The scent of her filled the entire house. The thought of her, sleeping alone in that big bed she had, spread out, tempting, and warm, was enough to drive him insane.

Fuck.

He drank the last of his beer, his gaze on her back as she finished the dishes and set them in the drainer.

The clothes she wore practically hung on her, but they did nothing to make him forget the sweet perfection of her body beneath them.

"You should let me go to the construction site with you." Turning, she wiped her hands on a small towel as she stared back at him challengingly.

"And you should hop up on this table and let me have you for dessert," he suggested as he allowed a hint of the hunger he felt to fill his voice.

Her face flushed. The prettiest shade of pink suffused her cheeks. Would the rest of her body flush so charmingly?

"I don't think so." Her voice was breathy, and he liked that. He knew she was at least thinking about it. That was a good thing. "And that has nothing to do with me going to the construction site with you."

"That's about as likely to happen as you letting me go down on you." He shrugged, watching her expression closely. "As a matter of fact, me going down on you is probably more likely."

His entire body tightened as he watched her catch her breath, watched her nipples tighten beneath her T-shirt. Hard, pretty little points that he knew were achingly sensitive. He wanted his mouth on them again. He wanted to lick them until they were cherry red and each breath caused a cry to part her pretty pink lips.

"I doubt it." She tried to sound firm, determined, but a virgin was no match for the sensualist Nik knew he was. He wanted her until nothing else seemed to matter. Wanted to taste her with a desperation that clawed at his balls.

"Don't make it a dare, Mikayla." He rose from his

seat before turning and tossing the beer bottle in the trash. "I might not walk away from that so easily. You want, just as bad as I do."

He left the room rather than standing there and watching that need fill her. Damn, it was all he could do to make himself walk away.

Mikayla had dreams. Whatever those dreams were, they didn't involve losing her innocence in his bed. At least not yet.

He was going to have her before this job was over; he could feel it. He knew it. Just as he could feel the knowledge that taking her could destroy both of them.

He didn't need this, he reminded himself, not for the first time. He didn't want to break Mikayla Martin's heart. He didn't want to steal the gift she was obviously saving for her husband. But the hunger was coming close to overriding his convictions. And that wasn't a good thing.

The next morning Mikayla stepped from the bedroom, in some kind of sinfully designed-to-stop-the-male-heart summer dress.

It was a soft lavender, sleeveless with a heart-shaped front that cupped her breasts and snugged up to them before flaring over her hips and ending just above her knees in a slim-line skirt that had his hands itching to draw it up her legs.

Three-inch cream-colored heels covered her tiny feet and still left her incredibly short. Her hair was braided again, the French braid pulling the strands back from her face and revealing the pretty, soft lines of her face.

Minimal makeup complemented her skin, but the hint of gloss on her lips made him hungry to lick it from the lush curves.

"Breakfast is do-it-yourself," she told him as she passed by him, her attention on the contents of the little cream-colored purse she carried. "Deirdre usually picks something up on her way in, so I don't cook in the morning."

Hell, he'd kept his distance last night; this morning was another thing. Those little buttons between her breasts tempted his fingers; the hint of sweet flesh between her breasts peeked out at him, and tempted his tongue.

He was about to have his breakfast right now. At least, a little taste of it.

Snagging her around the waist, he pulled her to him.

Before she could protest, he lifted her to the center island, pressed in between those pretty legs, and held her still for a kiss that fried every synapse in his brain.

All he knew, all he felt, all he tasted, once his lips touched her was Mikayla, heat, and sex. His cock, already hard, painfully so, seemed to thicken further. His balls drew tight and his body became one hard ache where she was concerned.

A moan of surrender was the answer to his kiss. Her arms wrapped around his neck, her breasts pressed into his chest, and Nik was lost in her.

God, she tasted of pure heat. A man could become lost in her forever if he allowed it.

One hand cupped the back of her head to hold her in place while the fingers of the other moved to those buttons. They were meant to intrigue, designed to tease.

He had them loosened in about three seconds flat, and when he figured out she wasn't wearing a bra his breath stopped in his chest.

His hands filled with the lush mounds. He couldn't help it. Slanting his lips across hers, he shaped the firm, heated flesh, his thumb raking over tight nipples as she flinched beneath the caress.

He felt like a schoolboy. Hell, like a teenager, copping a feel for the first time. His hands were almost shaking as she arched against him and shuddered in pleasure.

Pulling back from her, Nik stared down to where the swollen, feminine curves filled his hands. His thumb moved slowly, firmly, over a nipple, and he watched as a hard breath pushed her breasts tighter in his grip.

"Like ripe little berries," he whispered, his gaze lifting to stare into her mesmerized eyes.

Pleasure was swamping her. Nik knew the look, knew the flush of arousal out of control, the swollen lips parted to breathe easier. But there was more. Her eyes darkened to near purple, a wild glitter of hunger flickering in them as her little pink tongue moistened her lips.

"What are you saving yourself for, Mikayla?" he asked her.

He needed to know. He had to know those dreams before he committed the ultimate sin of destroying them.

A sharp little inhalation.

"Nik . . ."

"Tell me, baby," he growled. "Tell me what you've saved yourself for."

She destroyed him when she answered. "You. I think I've waited forever for you, Nik."

One of these days, he'd learn not to push his luck, not to tempt fate, and to never question a woman, Nik thought as he pulled the Harley into a parking slot in front of the business and sales offices of Martin's Plumbing and Water Works.

The store was on the outskirts of town, housed in a rough-hewn building reminiscent of days gone by. The appearance was deliberate, though, rather than a result of the building being run-down.

Before moving on in the investigation, Nik had a few questions for Scotty Martin. The three Martin sons were now working for their father's business. Before they had joined their father they had each worked in other construction areas. Their father had insisted they get the experience.

Scott was working the main store with his parents this week, Nik had learned. He had a few questions for the youngest son of the Martin clan. Namely, why the hell he had left his sister to hang out to dry after he'd found a ride that day.

Striding into the store, Nik found the younger man immediately. Scott stared back at Nik with the same suspicious look the rest of the family had given him several nights before when he had assured them he would be looking after Mikayla's safety.

None of them trusted him, and that was fine. But other than the father, Nik had not noticed anyone protesting too vociferously.

"Steele." Scott's eyes narrowed on Nik as Ramsey moved from the office in the back.

Nik nodded to the father before turning back to the son. "Could we talk for a minute?"

Scott shifted nervously. He was man enough to know exactly why Nik wanted to talk to him.

"I'll be back in a sec, Dad," Scott told his father before glancing at the parking lot.

"This can be taken care of in the office," Ramsey informed them both, obviously as sharp as any father. "Where I can watch you two."

Nik almost let his lips quirk into a smile. Instead, he

strode to the office, expecting the other two to follow and not really giving a damn if they did so agreeably.

"Mikayla doing okay?" Scott cleared his throat nervously as he and his father stepped into the office and the door closed behind them.

"She's doing fine," Nik assured Scott. "But all you had to do was call her to find that out, wouldn't you think?"

Scott cleared his throat again before glancing at Ramsey as he moved behind the desk and sat down.

"Scott's paying for his negligence that day," Ramsey stated firmly. "I trust you're not here to go over this, Mr. Steele."

Nik arched a brow and looked at Scott mockingly. The knowledge that Nik was deliberately courting Scott's father's protectiveness wasn't lost on the boy. He squirmed, ducking his head in shame before lifting his gaze to Nik's once more.

"I have some questions," Nik told them both as he took a seat in one of the leather chairs facing the desk. "First and foremost, who knew Mikayla was picking Scott up that day?" He deliberately posed his question to the father rather than the son.

"Scott?" Ramsey asked, frowning as he glanced back at Scott.

"He can ask me," Scott growled. "Why is he asking you?"

Ramsey continued to frown.

"When dealing with a child you go to the parent," Nik stated softly. "If you're a man, then we can dispense with a third party."

Ramsey glared back at Nik. "I think we're both aware Scott is no match for you, Mr. Steele."

"And I think we both know that the thought of Mikayla's ire is a far better deterrent in smacking that kid upside the head for his negligence than your anger or anything you could do, Mr. Martin," Nik said. "I have some questions, nothing more. But if you feel you must protect him, then neither of you should object when I deal with the matter as one adult to the other, and exclude him as much as possible."

It was a tactic Nik's father had used on him, his brothers, his cousins, on more than one occasion.

"I can handle this," Scott protested, his shoulders squaring as he tried to tell himself as well as his father that he was a man.

Ramsey gave Nik another hard, warning look before standing slowly to his feet, nodding sharply, then leaving the room.

Nik remained in his seat, staring back at the young man with knowing mockery. Scott knew he'd just come face-to-face with judgment if he was lucky. A hell of a lot of hurt if he wasn't.

Nik got straight to the point.

"Why didn't you call your sister and let her know you had a ride rather than leaving her to arrive at a deserted construction site where anything could have happened to her?"

This had nothing to do with the investigation and everything to do with the primitive protectiveness rising up inside Nik for her.

"I forgot." Scott crossed his arms over his chest before tucking his hands beneath his armpits defensively, his shoulders hunching as though he carried the weight of that decision and it didn't sit well. "I was on the phone with Dad when she called. My phone was dying. I asked Dad to call her back. By then, she was already there and it was too late."

The boy shook his head before swallowing tightly,

his gray eyes darkening with remembered fear. "I almost got her killed."

"Let it happen again, and it won't matter where I am, or what I'm doing. I'll come for you, Scott. You got that? I'll kill you."

The boy paled. "Yeah, you and the rest of the family."

"Your family will leave you breathing. I won't," Nik told him before gesturing to the chair next to the desk. "Tell me what you know about Eddie Foreman."

Scott blinked but did as he was ordered. He sat down slowly, the awareness that he had gained no more than a reprieve from Nik evident in his gaze.

"He was an asshole," Scott breathed out heavily. "Always cutting corners, always trying to make deals and earn an easy buck."

"Mikayla said you witnessed an argument between him and Maddix Nelson?" Nik reminded Scott.

Scott nodded. "I don't know exactly what it was over. I only caught bits and pieces. Maddix was accusing him of something from what I heard. I heard Eddie yelling from the construction office that he didn't do it, and that Maddix was crazy. I heard Maddix yell back that he'd pay for it, if he did."

"And you told the police this?" Nik pressed.

"Hell yes, I did." Scott frowned, anger darkening his gaze. "Bastards just blew me off. Said it didn't matter because Maddix didn't do it. My sister doesn't lie—"

Nik held his hand up, recognizing that Scott was in danger of losing his temper. He needed Scott calm. This information wasn't in the police report. There were too many holes, too much information missing.

"Anyone else?" Nik asked. "Who could have wanted Eddie dead beside Maddix?"

Scott shook his head. "Hell if I know. Probably everyone. Like I said, he was an asshole. . . ."

"What about that evening?" Nik asked. "Who else knew Mikayla was picking you up?"

Scott snorted at that. "Everyone. The guys like Mikayla, but she was late that day. I caught a ride, thinking maybe she had forgotten about me while she was sewing. She does that sometimes. Me and the boys I left with were the last ones out. Even Eddie had left before us. I have no idea why he came back to the job site."

To meet with someone, evidently.

"What about Maddix?" Nik asked. "Did he come out to the site often?"

"Always after everyone else left," Scott replied. "And yes, I tried to tell the police that, and they still wouldn't listen."

But Nik had something to start with now. Unfortunately, that something was against Maddix himself.

Nik didn't trust anyone unconditionally, especially a man he owed a favor to. The suspicion had been cast, and now Nik had to figure out where it went.

"Scott, what about the chief of police and the council people he was meeting with that night? What do you know about them?"

"I know they're all in bed together." Scott leaned forward, his expression mutinous. "One way or another, through either business or sex, they're all up each other's asses and they have a damned good reason to lie for Maddix Nelson. He's one of them; Mikayla's not. That's why she's being treated like shit and that's why the police won't believe her."

If Maddix Nelson was lying to him, Nik would make damned certain he made good on that threat. There was a steel-hard core of determination riding inside Nik, one he didn't bother to fight. Strike against

Mikayla and Nik would be the one to strike back. He'd always warned Maddix what would happen; Nik would leave it up to the other man to heed the warning or not.

Calling Nik had been a bad mistake if Maddix was involved in any way in the murder of Eddie Foreman or the attempted shooting of Mikayla. Of course, from a certain standpoint, it could have been considered a wise move. Hire someone to come in to prove Maddix was innocent with the excuse that he simply wanted to know why he was being targeted? That was damned good.

If Maddix and his alibis were lying, then Nik would make certain they all paid.

When he rode out of town he would make sure there were no threats left against Mikayla.

When he rode out of town.

That thought left a sour taste in his mouth, and a regret inside him he had been certain he wouldn't let himself feel.

He couldn't let himself feel. Because there wasn't a chance in hell he could stay.

CHAPTER 10

Mikayla walked into the house early that evening. Standing aside, she waited as Nik went through the house and then returned to the living room. One more evening that she had returned to find her home unviolated.

Lucky her. If only she could claim the same for her shop. There were more of Maddix Nelson's friends and their friends tripping in and out than there were of her own.

Financially, it was good, but her nerves were shot.

"I have to go out for a while," Nik told her as he came back to the living room, his jaw flexing as though he were clenching his teeth.

"Fine. I'll leave your dinner in the oven." She shrugged as though it didn't matter.

She wasn't going to let it matter. After the completely humiliating episode that afternoon, the less time she had to spend with him the better.

"I'll be sure to remember that." There was a dark, hungry sound in his voice, a rasp that sent a shiver racing up Mikayla's spine as he neared her.

She breathed in deeply, drawing in the dark male

scent of him. A hint of winter in the summer. A hint of heat on a cold winter's night.

"Mikayla." He paused before her; the way he towered over her should have made her feel something other than intensely feminine, protected.

"I thought you had to leave?" She stared up at him, the three-inch heels she wore doing very little to add enough to her height to make her feel a bit more on common ground with him.

She was cursed with her short stature, she determined. And before a man like Nik, so tall and broad, his towering over her and making her feel feminine and protected could be hazardous to the heart.

"You're a dangerous woman." His voice lowered, the ice in his eyes seeming to unthaw for just a second.

"And what makes you think I'm such a dangerous woman?" she asked, her voice stronger than she knew she actually was.

"Because you make me forget some hellacious lessons," he stated as his hand lifted, his thumb brushing against her lips gently.

They trembled at his touch. She couldn't help it. The need for his touch had been rising since he had walked away from her that morning.

Who was she kidding? The need for his touch was about to drive her positively insane. She had never ached like this. To the point that her entire body was sensitized, hyper, on fire. She was burning alive.

"I thought you were leaving," she repeated, the little squeak in her voice as her lips brushed against his thumb.

Oh man, she needed desperately to tighten her thighs, to put just a little pressure on her clit to ease that tingling little burn going on down there.

The way he was looking at her was driving her crazy.

As though he could see straight to that hungry, sexual part of her. The part that had wicked, nasty fantasies about him.

"We'll talk later." That sounded like a threat. A sensual, hungry threat that had her sex clenching involuntarily as she forced herself to slide out of the way, to allow him to open the door and leave.

As the door closed behind him Mikayla could have sworn that some of the life in the room went with him.

That was exactly what she didn't need, she told herself as she forced herself to the bedroom. The life couldn't leave the room when he left; otherwise, how much worse would it be when he left her life, not just the room?

Guard against a broken heart, girl, she told herself as she stepped into the shower.

The shower might not have been the best idea, though, as the water sluiced over her naked flesh, heated and warm, caressing, her hands rubbing from her shoulders down, over her breasts, her waist.

The rasp of the washcloth over her flesh reminded her of Nik. The calloused heat of his hands coursing over her body, touching her, feeling her.

Eyes closed, inhibitions lost, a muted moan left her lips, shocking her with the hunger rife in the sound.

She had never wanted as she wanted at this moment. A man's touch, his kiss.

No, not just a man's, Nik's. Nik's touch. Nik's kiss. His hands smoothing over her stomach, hips, to her thighs and beyond.

Dropping the cloth, she let her fingers touch, so desperate, so on fire, now that nothing but flesh on flesh could come close to giving her what she needed.

Her head tipped back against the shower wall, the feel of her hair caressing the tops of the rounded globes of her rear another caress. Another reminder of a touch she wanted, a touch she had no hope of attaining if she didn't have Nik.

Brushing her fingers over the swollen curves of her sex, Mikayla drew in a hard, broken breath at the whispered caress against her clit.

Sensation shot through her, clenching her stomach and tightening her thighs as her fingers parted the slick, dew-rich curves of her pussy and delved inside.

It was good, damned good, but not as good as Nik.

A needy moan fell from her lips again as she dragged her free hand to her breasts, her fingers brushing against first one nipple, then the next. She let her nails rake against them as she fought to find the feel of Nik's calloused, roughened fingertips against them.

Almost. She almost had the sensation. The pleasure.

Water pounded around her, hot and wet as her fingers slid through the slick layer of juices that eased from her vagina. She wanted, ached, to be touched there. To be taken. It was a hunger unlike anything she could have imagined.

"Mikayla!"

Her eyes flew open in shock to meet the searing blue flames in Nik's gaze.

One hand still cupped her sex, the other her breast, her fingers on her nipples as her brain tried to comprehend the sudden change.

To assimilate the fact that Nik was stripping. His T-shirt tossed aside in the space of a breath, his jeans loosened with one hand, unzipped, his cock springing free as he pushed them over his hips, his gaze refusing to release hers, his expression filled with hunger, with something more than pure lust.

"I . . ." She tried to talk, to explain, as his hand gripped hers and drew it from between her thighs.

Heat flushed her face. She had been standing there, still touching herself, as he undressed. How mortifying. And yet how sexy.

The water shut off. She blinked back at him as he drew her from the shower.

Mesmerized. That was what she was. She was mesmerized. She knew damned well what was getting ready to happen and she was suspended between disbelief and helpless anticipation.

When his lips met hers, adrenaline jacked through her veins, pouring into her senses as she felt his hands stroking over her.

No, those weren't his hands. Well, they were, but he held a towel between his flesh and hers.

Drying her.

A moan tore between their lips as she cried out at the friction against her sensitive flesh. She felt weak, uncertain. The rasp of the towel over her skin was almost too much; sudden, sharp spears of pleasure tore through her.

Her gasps of surprised pleasure were silenced by his lips on hers, but the jerking of her body, the hard inhalation, wasn't lost on him. It seemed to make him harder, hotter. His lips slanted over hers, his tongue pressing against her and stroking in rapid-fire motions that stoked her own need higher.

Mikayla stopped trying to make sense of it. The hard naked press of his cock against her stomach was like a brand. His hands were wide, strong, holding her to him as he lifted her, turned, carried her to the bedroom.

Mikayla was shaking. She could feel the tremors racing through her body as his lips continued to ransack hers.

"You'll be the death of me." He pulled back from the kiss as he laid her on the bed, staring down at her, the broad, bronzed width of his shoulders shad-owing her.

She had to touch them.

Her nails raked over the tough flesh, felt the flesh of muscle beneath.

"How?" She forced the word past her lips, question-ing his statement rather than begging for him as she wanted to.

Watching his hand move, his long fingers cup her breast, Mikayla lost the ability to reason anything then.

"This . . ." The answer was lost on her. "This sweet, sexy little body. That innocence in your eyes. I don't know if my conscience can survive you, Mikayla."

"Then make it worth it," she whispered, fighting the whimper in her voice. "For both of us."

She had to touch him as she spoke. She had never imagined pleasure like this, never imagined such need to touch a man. Her hand slid down his chest, his hard abs, to the thick stalk of flesh rising from between his thighs.

She couldn't encircle it with her fingers. It was heavy, strong, and hot, throbbing beneath her fingers with life and pleasure.

Mikayla's neck arched as his lips came to hers again, his kiss hungrier, hotter, than ever before.

It was going to happen, she thought. Her ideal of romance had been shot to hell. The white dress she had planned was dust in the wind.

Would antique white work? she wondered, because she wasn't about to deny herself this.

She wanted to touch him. All of him. All over.

His hair-roughened thigh stroked against her softer one as she ran her foot up his lower leg, feeling the strength, heat, and soft male hair against her foot. She hadn't known her feet could be so sensitive.

But she had known her neck was sensitive. Still, when his lips brushed down it, moved from her lips, she couldn't halt the cry that escaped her lips.

She wanted to rub her entire body against him.

His shoulder tasted of a hint of salt, a lot of hard, vibrant male, and of life. The taste of his flesh was almost an aphrodisiac, drawing her further into the sensual vortex wrapping around her.

"You don't know what you're asking for," he groaned as his lips brushed along her skin, moving unerringly to the swollen curves of her breasts.

She didn't know what she was asking for?

"Everything you have to give me," she demanded, her head grinding against the pillow as his hands cupped her breasts, lifting them as his mouth descended on one hard, violently sensitive nipple.

"Look at me, Mikayla." His tone was darker, rougher.

Forcing her eyes open, Mikayla stared into the pale blue flames of hunger in his gaze.

"You don't want everything," he whispered, his cheek brushing against her nipple.

"Everything." No matter how dark, no matter how lusty. She wanted all of him.

His eyes narrowed on her, his tongue licked out, stroking over her nipple a second before his lips covered it, drawing it into the liquid fire of his mouth.

Mikayla arched, her arms wrapping around his neck to hold him to her as she felt one hand move from her breast to her thigh. She tried to pay attention; she really did. She needed to have an idea of what to do to him when she got the chance. What would make him crazy. Deirdre said it could be done that way. That men would sometimes touch how and where they liked being touched.

If that was true, then she was doomed to failure.

What was he doing with his mouth on her nipple? The way he suckled it, the way his teeth and tongue rasped over it, was making her insane. The deep drawing strokes were sending sharp bolts of sensation tearing into her belly, her clit.

She was helpless beneath him. Mikayla hadn't imagined pleasure could be so sharp, so deep. As his lips moved from nipple to nipple, caressing and tormenting each in turn, she found herself growing desperate for more. More touch. More pleasure.

Her fingers dug into his hair, holding on to the strands as his hips rolled between her thighs, the hard wedge of his cock pressing into her lower stomach.

The pleasure was extreme. It rolled through her in waves of sensation too strong, too shocking, to assimilate as his lips moved from her breasts, lower, down her stomach, then to her thighs.

"You think you can handle it, little innocent?" he growled as his lips brushed over her thighs.

"Anything you want to dish out." Lightning was going to strike her dead for that lie, because just the feel of the ends of his hair brushing along her thighs was throwing her senses into chaos.

That amused quirk of his lips was almost worth the lie, though. It was so sexy, wicked, dominant.

And just that quick sensation speared along her clit, jerking her body to high alert and drawing her knees up along his hips.

"Good?" he asked.

Good? His fingers were milking her clit. Gently she gave him that. But the effect was catastrophic. She would have retaliated if she had enough of her brain left to figure out how to retaliate.

Instead, her fingers tightened in his hair as her hips arched, driving her clit closer to his lips instead.

His lips stroked along either side of it, brushing her thighs, sparking flames along each nerve ending he encountered.

"That's not fair," she moaned.

"Fair would have us on opposite sides of the earth, sugar," he crooned as his tongue swiped against her flesh. "Do you want me to play fair?"

"No." Her head shook quickly. If he left her now, she might have to actually turn into the bitch her brothers swore she was becoming.

"Then what should I do?"

"Taste me."

Mikayla froze. Nik even froze, as though the very idea that she had said such a thing stopped the world on its axis somehow.

Shy virgin Mikayla? Talking dirty?

She knew how to do it, she thought mutinously.

"Taste you?" he whispered a second before he placed a gentle kiss directly over her clit. "Mikayla, playtime is almost over. Are you very certain this is what you want?"

"I told you, do your worst." She was insane and she knew it.

She wanted the memories, though. Every one of them. When he was gone, she wanted to know she had for the first time been who she wanted to be. That she was herself. That for once she threw caution to the wind and lived for the moment and grabbed the chance she had at true sensual pleasure.

Do his worst? Nik had varied and wicked scenarios he'd replayed in his imagination more than once where Mikayla was concerned.

Having her beneath him, naked, wild, was but part of it. He'd never imagined she was so courageous, so daring, as to challenge him to do his worst.

Because his worst could be bad. Sexual, dominant, and hungry, he was a man who knew the depths of his own hungers, just as he knew that holding back with this woman would be next to impossible.

She had dared him. Under normal conditions that wouldn't be enough, but with Mikayla it was the switch that unlocked the sexual beast prowling beneath.

Staring up at her, he gave her one last level look from beneath his lashes, gauged her true courage, then parted the swollen folds of her pussy and laid his lips to the sweet pink sensitive flesh of her clit.

Her hips arched, strong and fast. Holding her thighs firmly, Nik held her in place as he placed kiss after delicate kiss against the throbbing nubbin.

Her hips jerked in his hold, strangled cries falling from her lips as he used his tongue with each kiss, flicked at the delicate knot of nerves, and began priming her body.

She was a virgin, not an idiot, Mikayla assured herself desperately as she felt her senses burning beneath the destructive kisses Nik placed on her swollen clit. She may not have physical experience, but she read. She listened. She watched television and she had her own fantasies. And she sensed what she liked. Which was pretty much anything with Nik.

Lifting her hips closer to him, she let herself revel in the pleasure racing through her, even as she fought to keep herself from becoming catatonic within it.

She wanted this. Every touch he would give her. But she wanted more as well. She wanted to touch as well as be touched. She wanted to drive him just as crazy for her as she was for him.

Broad shoulders were wedged between her thighs, holding her open to him as his lashes lifted, his gaze meeting hers as he licked around her clit. Stroked it, lashed at it in a caress so wickedly hot there should have been flames flickering over her flesh.

Watching, barely able to process anything but the pleasure, Mikayla arched closer, needing more.

And Nik was more than willing to give her more. As her juices eased from her vagina, his lips and tongue licked lower, drawing closer to the center of the vicious ache whipping through her body.

His fingers parted the folds of flesh as a moan tore from her lips once again. And he licked. Long, slow licks, his tongue flickering over the entrance, dipping inside, a harsh groan tearing from his throat as she arched closer.

God, she needed closer.

"Nik!" His name tore from her lips as his tongue thrust inside her, penetrating with a heat that tore the last shred of restraint from her mind.

Her thighs fell open further, knees lifting as her fingers buried in his hair to hold him closer to her. The feel of his tongue inside her, stroking flesh that had never been touched, exciting nerve endings just newly awakened.

She twisted against him, loving each caress, relishing it as her fingers bunched in his hair to hold him to her. Each lash and impalement of his tongue drove her closer to the edge, stoked the fires inside her higher, and built the need for more higher with every stroke.

She was going to come. She knew she was riding the edge, knew that once she slipped over it then there wouldn't be a chance that this would be a shared adventure. It would become her adventure alone.

She wanted to touch him as well. Wanted to watch her hands stroke over his chest, feel the strength of his cock beneath her hand, her lips.

"Nik, please," she moaned as shudders of near ecstasy began to wrack her body. "Please, Nik."

"Please what, baby?" His head turned, his lips stroking against her inner thigh once again.

"Let me touch you. Please, Nik, before I come, I need to touch you."

He couldn't bear it.

Nik stared up at her, seeing his demise in dazed amethyst eyes and flushed feminine features. He didn't dare allow her to touch him yet. Not yet.

As he held her gaze his fingers stroked into the tender slit of her pussy, parting the folds, following the shallow valley to the wet entrance of her sex.

Slick and heated, the little opening clenched at the touch of his finger, flexing against his caress. Her eyes dazed further. Hunger surged through him as her hips arched again, need tightening her body, then surprise as his fingers dipped lower, the tip of one stroking against the tight entrance of her rear.

She was close to orgasm. Close enough that he was confident he could restrain her need to touch as well.

Tucking the tip of his finger against the little rosette, he turned his attention back to the sweet, lush flesh of her pussy. The taste of her was incredible. Drawing him, intoxicating him as her knees lifted, one delicate foot rising to his hip as she opened herself further to him, testing every ounce of self-control that he had ever possessed.

He was losing himself to her; he could feel it. His cock throbbed with vicious need as his balls drew tight, the scent, the feel, of her making him insane for her.

Gripping her hip with one hand, he held her to him as his tongue flicked over her clit before drawing it into his mouth. He sucked at it gently, licking it with firm strokes as the tip of his finger eased inside the tender entrance lower.

She was trembling in his grip, her thighs tightening as muted cries fell from her lips. The flesh gripping the tip of his finger flexed and milked at the tip, tempting him to penetrate her further.

Sensual hunger was rising inside her. As her pussy became wetter, her anus eased, making his impalement of her easier, drawing him deeper as he pushed her closer.

Pleasure was a demon burning beneath Mikayla's flesh, drawing her tighter, deeper, as she felt the impalement at her rear, Nik's lips and tongue at her clit. She was drowning in sensation. Raking talons of pleasure were racing across her flesh, surging through her bloodstream until they exploded through every cell of her body.

His name tore from her lips. Her hips arched, a strangled scream escaping as electric surges of intense, overwhelming ecstasy raced through every nerve ending and threw her into a vortex of complete rapture.

It seemed never ending. A chaotic clash of sensations and pleasure that left her shaking, trembling in an aftermath she had no idea how to handle.

And it wasn't enough.

She needed more.

Before he could grip her hips and hold her in place once again, before he could retain control and come over her to throw her senses off balance, Mikayla moved.

Nik straightened between her thighs, giving her the perfect opportunity to sit up quickly, her hands flattening against his hard abs, her gaze drawn to the thick erection rising hard and powerful from between his thighs.

"Mikayla." His voice was strangled as she leaned forward, her lips pressing against the hard, muscular flesh of his lower stomach. "This isn't a good idea, my love."

She didn't answer him. She didn't have the ability to answer him. As she opened her eyes, her head turned, the fingers of one hand attempting to curve around the heavy flesh.

She was hungry for him. She needed to feel him, to taste him. As his fingers threaded through her hair, she feared in an attempt to pull her away from him, she lifted and pressed her lips to the heavily veined shaft.

Nik stilled. His fingers bunched in Mikayla's hair, his gaze locked on her as he felt the satin heat of her lips against the tortured length of his cock.

Sweet mercy, she was destroying him and didn't even know it. Even her touch was innocent, tentative, yet so damned sensual and hungry it was all he could do to not pull her head back and push the head of his cock into the sweet heated draw of her mouth.

He needed to hold her still, to keep her from taking him with such intimacy. Possessing her, stealing the veil of her innocence, was one thing. Actually stealing the core of her innocence was another thing. Entertaining fantasies of unleashing the wild, wanton side of Mikayla Martin might get him through the night, but doing it was a risk to his soul and he knew it.

Still, he felt helpless to do anything but watch as her tongue licked the engorged, darkened crest of his dick before swiping over it in a long, slow lick that sent a sizzle of pure lust electrifying his balls.

Staring down at her, he watched as her eyes fluttered closed and her lush, pert lips slowly covered the throbbing head of his cock.

He wasn't going to be able to pull her away. He

couldn't pull her away. It was too damned good. Her mouth was liquid heat, her lips like hot silk, the draw of her mouth like pure ecstasy.

Son of a bitch. He was supposed to walk away from this? What had ever made him believe such a thing was possible?

The nails of one delicate hand raked down his abs as she held the hard shaft with the fingers of the other. Her lips and snug mouth drew on the engorged crest, her hot little tongue flickering over it as every muscle in his body tightened with the riptide of sensation washing through them.

The tentative, innocent movements were more destructive than any touch he had ever known in his life. He'd been with women whose experience more than matched his own, but even then he hadn't been as affected as he was now.

Now, he was drowning in the fucking pleasure. It was tearing through his system with wildfire destructiveness and tearing at his determination to hold back, to ease the damage that could be done to her heart when this was over.

There was no holding back with his dick in her mouth, though, or the innocent movements that sucked him to the back of her throat, the murmur of a little moan vibrating against the tip before she pulled back and then took him all over again.

Before Nik could rein the hunger overtaking him, his fingers tightened in her hair and he was fucking her mouth with tight, controlled movements. Movements that taught her what she didn't instinctively know.

As he watched her lips move on him, watched the hunger that filled her face as her lips enclosed him, Nik could feel the control he fought so hard to hold on to slipping out of his grip.

Electric fingers of sensation were racing from his balls up his spine and back again. Hunger was a ravenous need tearing at his mind now, demanding more than her lips, her slender fingers trying to enclose him. That hunger demanded that veil of innocence, as well as that core.

Buried beneath that hunger was a flame he fought to deny. A surge of possessiveness, of tenderness. A knowledge that in his life he had never felt anything like he was feeling now.

"Enough." His voice was harsh as he pulled back, forcing his cock from the heat of her mouth as he pushed her to her back and moved between her thighs, his knees pressing her legs farther apart.

As she lay spread out before him like a luscious offering to the hunger raging through him, Nik couldn't help but take a moment to appreciate the unique beauty of her.

Her slumberous amethyst gaze gleamed with violet fire. The long strands of her wheat gold hair spread out around her as her swollen lips parted to breathe in roughly.

Firm ruby-tipped breasts rose and fell heavily, the pale globes tempting his lips, even as the curl-shrouded, dew-glistening mound of her pussy drew his gaze and the throbbing length of his dick.

"Are you sure?" It was the most insane question he could have asked. If she changed her mind now, then he was going to explode in agony rather than pleasure.

She reached down, her slender fingers gripping his cock as her hips lifted.

Searing feminine heat brushed against the head of his cock, causing him to grimace in erotic agony. The need to thrust inside her was making him crazy.

"Do you think I'm sure?" Her voice was breathy,

breathless, as his hips shifted, his cock parting the swollen folds of her pussy to press against the tight, clenching entrance to her body.

He prayed for patience. His hands tightened on her thighs as he shifted closer, watching as his cock began to press inside her.

Heat surrounded the engorged crest, streaked up the shaft, and tore through his entire system.

Some instinct inside him was screaming, *Mine.* It broke past the shields he had kept around his soul for so many years and speared straight to the center of his spirit.

His. She belonged to him.

Mikayla stared up at Nik, feeling the slow, steady stretching at the entrance of her pussy. Pleasure/pain began to wash through her as he forged inside, his cock taking her, possessing her in ways she hadn't expected.

She struggled to keep her eyes opened as she watched the folds of her sex part, watched the slick, juice-laden folds part and hug his flesh as he entered her.

"Nik." Her hands gripped his wrists as he held her thighs, his hips pressing steadily forward. "Nik, I . . ." She licked her lips. She didn't know what to say, what to do.

Pleasure was tearing through her; a tight, pinching burn was mixing with the violent eroticism and stoking the arousal inside her higher. Heat washed over her, burning beneath her flesh as a painful pleasure began to deepen.

"Hold on, baby." Nik's voice was deep, dark, stroking over her senses and pushing her higher. "Hold on to me, Mikayla."

Her hands tightened on his wrists as she thought she knew what was coming. Deirdre and other friends had assured her there would be pain. The larger the man, the greater the pain, she had been assured.

Nik pushed inside her, his cock pressing against the thin shield of her virginity. His thumb moved to her clit, pressing against it, rotating and sending her senses screaming in sudden, vibrant sensation.

The orgasm that washed over her shocked her. It threw her into a pleasure so extreme she lost her breath, her voice, and any pain she would have felt as Nik surged inside her, breaking through the virgin shield she had saved for him.

A part of her acknowledged that. She hadn't known him, hadn't known who he was or when he would come into her life, but this was what she had saved herself for.

Wild, exquisite sensation crashed over her, arching her hips and burying his cock deeper, harder insider her as his hips thrust against her once again.

Pain was submerged in brutal pleasure. It was disguised in agonizing ecstasy as one orgasm surged through her even as she began to build toward another.

The feel of his cock stretching her, thrusting hard and deep inside her, had her entire body arching toward him as he came over her. His hard body surrounded her, his arms gathering her close as his lips covered hers.

A brutal male groan joined the tortured moan of pleasure that tore from her throat as his tongue thrust hungrily into her mouth.

His chest hairs rasped against her nipples; the stubble on his face rasped against her; his thighs caressed hers; his cock speared inside her. Hard. Deep. Triggering a climax that tore her from the very foundations of her soul and sent her flying into pure ecstasy.

Nik stiffened in her arms, his erection burying deep when she felt him tense, felt his cock pulse and throb inside her.

It was a rush of adrenaline and rapture. A high that Mikayla could have never imagined. One her friends had never warned her of. It was like flying into the sun and piercing paradise as Nik groaned her name, whispered something foreign, and collapsed against her.

It was like finally belonging.

CHAPTER 11

She was sleeping.

Nik stared down at Mikayla's relaxed face as he moved back to the bed, a warm, damp cloth in hand.

Cleaning her gently, he couldn't help but marvel at the softness of her skin once more. Unblemished, lightly tanned, her muscles toned with a feminine softness he could barely resist.

He'd nearly forgotten to wear a condom.

As he moved back to the bathroom, that thought tortured him. Not since he was a teenager had he forgotten to wear a condom. Not since the conception of the daughter he had lost. But he'd nearly forgotten with Mikayla.

Disposing of the damp cloth, he turned and braced his hands on the decidedly feminine sink and stared into the mirror above it.

What he saw there bothered him in some elemental way. The lack of emotion that had been in his eyes, hell, in his soul, for the past years was now replaced with too much emotion.

The pale blue orbs looked tortured. As tortured as he felt. He could feel the nightmares of the past moving in on him now, brewing from behind that closed door that had his nightmare emotions locked behind it.

That door was no longer locked. Mikayla had opened it, and now he had no idea what the hell he was supposed to do with the emotions welling inside him. What the hell was he supposed to do with Mikayla?

Stepping back into the room, he had every intention of walking out of it and back to the cold, lonely bed in the guest room. *Why compound the mistake?* he thought. Sleeping with her would only make it harder to leave later.

Amethyst eyes were opened now, watching silently as he stared back at her, as though she knew what he was about to do.

He had just taken her innocence, taken a gift that she could only give once. One she had saved all these years only to bestow it on a lost cause.

She would remember this night forever; he didn't want it to end with her regrets.

Like a man walking to a death chamber, he moved back to the bed and the woman. Slid into it and gathered her against his chest as he wondered if sleep would ever hold anything but regrets after this.

"You have no responsibility to me, Nik," she whispered in the darkness as he flipped the small bedside lamp off.

God, was she so wrong.

"I didn't say I did." He kept his voice low, fought to keep his emotions in check as he buried his fingers in long strands of hair that flowed out from her head.

He felt her lips against his chest as her fingers played softly against the light mat of hair on his chest.

"Tell me something about you," she whispered.

Nik stared up at the darkened ceiling and realized

how little she truly did know about him. How little he allowed anyone to know about him.

"I was married once." He grimaced, wondering where the hell that admission had come from.

Rather than jumping in and questioning, Mikayla remained silent.

"I had a daughter. Her name was Nicolette." He hadn't told anyone about his child. He never talked about her. Sometimes, he felt as though Nicolette had been nothing but a dream.

"That's a very pretty name," Mikayla breathed softly against his chest.

Nik could feel the pain inside, just as sharp, as bright, as ever, but this time it seemed tempered by time, or by Mikayla.

"What happened to her?" she asked softly after several minutes had passed, an edge of sadness in her voice that warned him that she knew his baby was already gone.

"How do you know anything happened to her?"

Mikayla lifted her head from his chest until she could gaze down at him, the dim light from the moon spearing through the windows, giving her just enough perhaps to see by.

"If nothing had happened, then she would still be with you," Mikayla said softly. "You wouldn't be dodging bullets for a woman you barely know if you had a child depending on you to come home."

God, how right she was.

"I was in the army." He cleared his throat, remembering too clearly the decisions he had made because of his daughter. "I transferred out of the unit I was in for a desk job when my wife became pregnant. Nicolette was five when her mother decided marriage didn't suit her. She was having an affair while I was working long hours to try to provide as much as I could for her and Nicolette. It wasn't enough.

"I was at work when she left. The man she had been sleeping with had been mixed up in some bad business. Some of his enemies thought he was in the car with her and Nicolette. They intercepted it. Nicolette was shot."

Her body was torn apart by the power and speed of the bullets that had ripped into her tiny body.

Nik could still see it. The blood, the horror. The knowledge that he hadn't protected his child.

"It was my fault," he finally whispered, accepting that guilt now as he had never before. Accepting it because he realized the care it took to hold a woman's heart.

He hadn't taken that care. He had nourished his job, nourished his position, and given his free time to his child, while his wife had been left on the outside looking in.

"How is it your fault?" Mikayla asked.

Nik stared back at her. "Because I wasn't the husband I should have been, Mikayla. I wasn't the man I should have been."

"Nik, I'm so sorry," she whispered, and he swore he saw the glimmer of a tear that eased down her cheek. "But it wasn't your fault. Your wife made that decision, not you."

Someone other than he shed a tear for the child who had never had a chance to live. The delicate little girl who wanted to be a ballerina. The laughing mischief maker who waited each evening for her "poppa" to come home.

"It was a long time ago." He had to blink back the moisture in his own eyes.

Mikayla shook her head. "It happened yesterday. That's how clear it is in your heart, Nik. You loved your daughter."

He nodded slowly and said, "Yes."

It happened almost nightly in his dreams, almost daily in his memories. And the ache never completely went away, though over the years it had softened.

"Lay down." He pressed Mikayla back to his shoulder. "Nicolette would have loved you. You look like one of those damned fairies she was forever reading about."

And Mikayla did. In that moment Nik realized how much she did resemble one of the little sprites in those long-ago books Nicolette used to make him read to her.

"A fairy, huh?" He felt Mikayla grin against his chest.

"A very beautiful, very wild fairy." He almost smiled himself. "Flitting around and finding trouble every chance she has. You need a full-time keeper."

"Are you applying for the job?" The laughter in her voice, the gentle teasing, was almost more than he could bear.

"Too many jobs already." He had to close his eyes against the refusal he forced past his lips. "Let me get you out of this one first, baby. Maybe you'll learn how to stay out of trouble after that."

"You can hope." Her voice had sobered, the realization that he wouldn't, couldn't, stay a silent reminder that nothing lasted forever.

"I can hope." He kissed the top of her head gently before tucking her closer to his body.

He could hope for many things, though he had stopped doing so long ago. If one didn't hope, then disappointment didn't visit. Hoping meant you had something to live for, and living for something or someone else was asking for pain.

He'd make certain she was safe; then he would make certain someone watched over her. Someone other than him.

The next day Mikayla assured herself she had gone into this with her eyes opened. She wasn't in love, she promised herself. When Nik left, and she knew he would leave, then she would be able to go on without nursing a broken heart.

It didn't help to know she was lying. As autocratic as he could be, as dominant as he was, she was still falling in love, and that knowledge had the power to terrify her.

He was so much more than most men she knew. Hell, more than any man she had ever known. In the dark the night before, she had learned something about him that she hadn't expected. Something that might explain that dark, tortured air she glimpsed around him.

He'd lost so much. A whole life in some ways. A wife and a child. He'd obviously left the army after their deaths and now worked privately. But he was still alone. And a niggling little warning at the back of Mikayla's mind whispered that he seemed to like being alone really well.

When he drove off after following her to the shop, Mikayla stared at his back with a frown for long seconds. He'd drawn away that morning. He'd already showered and had coffee when she got up, his gaze as frosty as ever as she fixed her own.

Perhaps frostier, she told herself as she stepped into the shop and greeted Deirdre before heading to her office.

There were phone calls to make. Nik was searching for Eddie's killer, but that didn't mean she couldn't help him in other ways.

She hated being on the sidelines where her own

protection was concerned. Mikayla didn't hide from the realities of life. This was her life, and she was the one who had now become a killer's target.

But why?

It took a while, but she finally managed to reach a friend of Eddie Foreman's who had been elusive for so many weeks.

"Look, Mikayla." Robert Cronin sighed after realizing who she was trying to get hold of him. "Let the police investigate this one."

"Robert, they're not investigating anyone," she informed him wearily.

She had known Robert for years. Before his divorce, his wife had often come to her for dress alterations. As Robert was another construction foreman, though now no longer with Maddix Nelson, there was information as well as gossip that he had to be privy to.

"Why did you leave Maddix Nelson's company?" she asked. "Just give me information, Robert. Help me."

"Son of a bitch, you're gonna end up dead," he said and she could almost imagine the grimace on his craggy face. "Maddix Nelson ain't no killer. If his granddaddy was alive, then I'd say be looking at him. That man was a pure black-hearted son of Satan if you ask me."

She didn't want a dissection of the family tree. Just information, she thought in frustration.

"Maybe Maddix is just better at hiding it," she suggested.

Robert was quiet, though the distant sound of machinery in the background could be heard.

"There's some talk," he finally said. "Maddix has been seen in places that he shouldn't be seen, maybe talkin' to people he shouldn't be talking to. The illegal sort. Eddie was at a party a few months ago; he used to get pretty drunk, ya know?" Robert cleared his throat.

"Anyway, he said he had something on Maddix. Didn't say what, but said it would bring him down."

Mikayla bit at her lip. "Do you have any idea what it was?"

"He didn't say, Mikayla," Robert growled. "Whatever it was, though, Eddie was sure he could hurt Maddix with it. If Eddie told anyone what it was, then it would have been Steve Gainard. He's the only one Eddie would confide in, if he was going to confide in anyone."

And Steve had been out of town for months. Mikayla had left several messages with his service as well as on his cell phone.

"I can't believe Maddix did this." Robert sighed again. "But I can't believe you lied about it, either. That puts a lot of us between a rock and a hard place, Mikayla. Like I said, his granddaddy was a real bastard. I wouldn't have put anything past him before his death. That old bastard went so far as to threaten to disinherit Maddix's father if he dared decide to have another child. He didn't want Maddix's daddy, Lowell, to have a large family. Felt it would take away from the company they were building."

"But as you said, he's dead," Mikayla pointed out. "And it wasn't Maddix's grandfather I saw, Robert. It was Maddix."

"Yeah, I hear ya." Confusion filled his voice then. "I wish I had answers for ya, girl. I don't like nobody takin' potshots at ya. Drop this, before you get killed."

She couldn't drop it. The injustice of it, as well as the knowledge that dropping it would only convince everyone she was lying. She couldn't do that. She wasn't a liar. She knew what she had seen.

"Thank you for your time, Robert." She ended the

call with a sense of falling further into the rabbit hole her life had become.

"Anytime, Mikayla," Robert promised her. "Tell your daddy I said hi. I'll be prayin' for ya."

She ended the call and stared at the phone for long moments before calling Nik.

She gave him the information quickly and didn't have to wait long for his reaction.

"You were to stay out of this," he growled, anger surging in his voice.

"Look, I'm texting you Robert's cell-phone number. He's willing to talk to you as well."

"I told you to stay out of it," he snapped again.

"And I told you, this is my life," she retorted. "You don't know the people to talk to, Nik; I do. I may not be able to get all the answers, but this is something we didn't have before."

"Text me the damned number," he snarled. "Then get off that fucking phone and keep your ass out of trouble until I get back. Do you understand me?"

She almost grinned.

He sounded protective rather than angry.

"I'll do my best," she told him, knowing he knew better. She knew better. If she could manage to think of another direction to go in this, then she would make the call or the visit or send the e-mail. As she told him, this was her life, and she wasn't giving up.

Texting the number after hanging up, she stared at the phone, rubbed her brow, then made a quick note of the information Robert had given her before adding it to the file she was keeping.

Disregarding Nik's orders, she made a few other calls, but the information Robert had given her couldn't be confirmed by the few sources she had to talk to whom she could rely on. That left her with yet more dangling threads to this.

Threads she would have to pick at later, she thought as she hung up the phone an hour later.

The rest of the day was spent like most others. Mikayla worked on the dresses in the back, kept several fitting appointments, and even managed to sell two more of her own designs before closing time came.

As she and Deirdre were standing at the register counter waiting for Nik, an explosion shattered the quiet of the store.

Glass rained into the shop as the mannequins standing in front of the window toppled over, knocking a rack of dresses to the floor and leaving Mikayla to stare at it all in shock as the sound of tires squealing seemed to echo around her.

Deirdre was screaming something. Cursing was more like it, as Mikayla stared in shock at the destruction.

"That was a fucking gunshot!" Deirdre screamed at her. "My God, Mikayla!"

"Call the police, Deirdre." Mikayla felt almost numb inside.

She couldn't have avoided the shot if it had been for her. She would have been dead. But it wasn't her they were after this time. It was her store. Her livelihood. Her security.

Someone was trying to frighten her, trying to force her into backing off.

She pulled her cell phone from her purse and pulled up the address book and Nik's number.

"Mikayla? I'm on my way to pick you up," he answered immediately.

"I might be a while leaving," she told him. "Someone just shot into the shop and destroyed the front window. I have to call Dad to get this boarded up for the night. I can catch a ride—"

"I'm on my way." The line disconnected.

As Deirdre stood over the rack of dresses that had fallen, Mikayla watched as she pushed in her father's number and called him. Just as with Nik, she had no more than gotten the explanation out than he had hung up with a terse, "We're on our way." Which of course meant the whole family was arriving.

At least the window would be boarded up quickly, she thought wearily.

She hadn't moved from the counter. She had no intention of moving.

"Go home, Deirdre." Mikayla stared at her friend as she looked at the pile of clothing helplessly once more.

Deirdre's head snapped up, her expression disbelieving as she turned back to Mikayla. "Do what?" she asked incredulously.

"Go home. Dad and Nik will be here soon. Don't bother coming back in for a while."

It wasn't a brick thrown at the window. This wasn't spray paint on the glass. That had been a bullet, and Deirdre could very well have been in the way of it.

"Like hell," Deirdre snapped as she stalked back to the counter. "I'm not going anywhere. I'll be damned if some jackass is going to run me off."

"You'd rather one of them kill you?" she asked her friend point-blank. "That was a bullet."

"No fucking shit," Deirdre yelled back at her, her hands going to her hips. "And I saw the car they were in and got part of the plate number. Fuck 'em." Rage was glittering in her green eyes. "I'm not going anywhere."

The end of her sentence was punctuated by the hard, furious throb of the Harley as it jumped the sidewalk and came to a hard stop.

Mikayla watched as Nik jumped from his seat and through the opening where the window had been and strode quickly to her.

He'd done that so smoothly, she thought inanely. Stepped up on the seat, those long legs stepping onto the window frame, and in the shop he came. As though he owned the place.

"Are you okay?" His hands gripped her shoulders, his eyes, no longer frozen but burning with rage, going over her quickly. "Dammit, Mikayla. I told you to let me take care of this."

Mikayla felt herself shaking then. She was gripping his forearms as though they were a lifeline.

"That makes twice since Eddie's murder," she whispered shakily as she stared up at him. "What do they say about the third time?" *A charm?*

"It's okay, baby." He pulled her against him, his hand at the back of her head, pressing her to his chest as he sheltered her with his harder, stronger body. "God, baby, you have to stop pushing buttons here. Let me handle this."

It hit her fully then. If he hadn't been supporting her she may well have fallen to the floor in hysterics. Someone had shot at her again. What if that bullet actually hit her the next time?

Nik could feel the rage tearing through him as he looked past Mikayla to the other girl.

Deirdre Maple was watching him closely, her green eyes curious, knowing. And suspicious. She didn't trust Nik at all, and that was probably a good thing. It was a quality Mikayla should have developed before she let him into her bed.

Not that he had any intention of betraying her, but she was so fucking trusting.

"The car was a late-model Civic," Deirdre stated as

Mikayla continued to hold on to him. "Maryland plates." She quickly rattled off the first three numbers. "It was a grayish or silver color, hard to tell in the low light." She nodded to the busy street. "They shot up a side road and disappeared rather than continuing on Washington Street."

"I didn't see anything but the glass exploding into the shop." Mikayla pulled.

"I was watching the street." Deirdre shrugged. "Since the last time someone tried to gun you down, I've been trying to watch things better. I saw the guy stick his arm out the window toward our window, but I didn't see the gun and I didn't see his face."

In the low light, it would have been easy at that angle to miss the gun, Nik thought as he turned and stared out the door.

"This is crazy," Mikayla whispered as she moved back only as far as Nik allowed her to go. "Why try to kill me now? I've been questioning people for weeks."

"Because you're getting too close," he snarled. "For God's sake, you have to stop this!"

It was a warning to him as well, Nik knew. A warning to back off, just as that first shooting had been a warning to Mikayla. To back off the investigation.

"And here's our friendly neighborhood Detective Dumbass," Deirdre's tone was nearly a sneer as several police cars pulled up as well as an unmarked car.

Detective Robert Denover stepped from the unmarked vehicle, his bald head shining dully in the overhead lights as he propped his hands on his hips and stared at the front of the shop with a frown.

Deirdre moved back to Mikayla's side as Nik slowly stepped away from her to meet the detective as he entered the shop.

"Ms. Martin." He nodded back to Mikayla before

his gaze swung to Nik, his gray eyes narrowing in suspicion. "Mr. Steele. I'm surprised to see you here."

Mikayla's gaze flickered between Nik and the detective. "You know Detective Denover?" she asked him faintly.

"We've met." Nik nodded shortly. "He's investigating the Foreman murder as well."

Mikayla knew that, and she wasn't pleased with the efforts she knew he had put in on that investigation. He had been almost insulting the night she had reported the murder once she had told him who she saw.

Denover gazed around the shop, shaking his head before turning back to the officers behind him. "Find the bullet," he ordered them with a hint of frustration. "Get the statements. I'll go over your reports when I get back to the office in the morning."

He turned to leave.

"You'll take care of this yourself." Nik wasn't about to let him leave without properly investigating the matter. He'd just about had enough of this bastard's attitude. "You'll do it, or I'll make certain your chief hears about your neglect."

The detective's lips curled mockingly. "He won't be surprised."

"But he may well be surprised when federal agents descend on his office with an investigation into how he's running it," Nik offered with mocking pleasantry. "I can arrange that, Denover. And I will arrange it."

He had every intention of arranging it anyway once this was finished. Mikayla wasn't being protected and Foreman's death wasn't being investigated as it should be. The fact that Maddix was good friends with both the mayor as well as the police chief and doing business with the city had given him a cachet he shouldn't have possessed.

Denover's lips tightened as he threw Mikayla an irritated look. Shaking his head, he proceeded to at least oversee the search for the bullet and the statements Mikayla and Deirdre gave.

As they finished, Mikayla's father's pickup pulled in outside and the entire family spilled from the crew cab of the vehicle. Three brothers, a furious father, and a concerned mother.

For a moment, déjà vu whipped through Nik. His parents had arrived at his home in a similar manner, his brothers and sisters close behind, the night his wife and daughter had died. They had gathered around him; they had sworn to support him. Until he'd gone against several politicians in his determination to find the men responsible for his wife's and daughter's murders. It was then that his family had turned their backs on him.

Mikayla's family hadn't turned their backs on her when they saw how difficult the fight was, though. They were there. Her brothers lifted sheets of plywood from the back of the truck while her parents rushed inside.

"Nik." Ramsey Martin nodded in his direction as his wife, Jorrey, rushed to Mikayla's side. "I want to take her home."

It was a similar conversation that had been conducted the last time someone had shot at Mikayla.

"She's not a child." Nik shook his head. "Whatever Mikayla decides, I'll help her. But it's her decision."

"And I'm not moving back in with my parents." Mikayla pulled back from her mother's embrace with a frown. "I told all of you that."

Ramsey dug the fingers of one hand into the back of his neck in frustration, worry and love apparent on his face, in his dark gray eyes.

"Mikayla, someone is trying to kill you," her mother argued.

"If someone was trying to kill me then I'd be dead," Mikayla pointed out, and Nik couldn't help but agree with her. "Someone is trying to scare me, and though they're doing a damned good job of it, I'm not running away and hiding."

Mikayla said "Damned." Nik stared at her in surprise, as it seemed her parents did as well. Mikayla just simply never cursed.

"They're going to get serious," Ramsey protested. "I don't want to have to bury my own daughter, Mikayla. I'd appreciate it if you'd hang around long enough to make certain your brothers pay for my funeral."

Mikayla's lips twitched as she glanced at Nik. "He swears my brothers will sell his business and live high on the money for the few days it will last."

"Few hours," Ramsey snorted as he turned and looked at the three young men working quickly to close the front opening where the window had been. "And that's beside the point. The point is, this isn't going to work. I don't like knowing some bastard is shooting at my daughter."

"Hiding won't change anything," Mikayla argued, though Nik could see it was hard for her to argue with her father. "It just puts you in danger as well."

"I'll take steps to make certain this doesn't happen again, Mr. Martin," Nik spoke up, and nearly snapped his own teeth no sooner than the words came out. What the hell was wrong with him? The best thing he could do was turn her over to her parents, finish this investigation, then ride off into the fucking sunset. He hoped without breaking Mikayla Martin's heart.

But he couldn't do it.

"She's been shot at twice since you came to town," her father stated, his look accusing. "She wasn't having problems then."

"Dad, please." Mikayla stepped in front of her father, as though she thought she could protect one of them. As though there were a reason to feel one of them needed protecting. "I'll be fine."

Her father stared down at her, much as Nik realized he was staring down at her. Patiently.

Then her father reached out, gripped her beneath the arms, and set her gently out of the way. Like a child.

If Nik hadn't been watching her face he wouldn't have seen the pain that flickered over it at her father's casual disregard of her position.

It was enough to make Nik want to lift her and put her right back. He didn't doubt her father's love for her, but Nik did doubt her father's ability to understand the woman she was, rather than the child he wanted her to be.

"Ramsey." Her mother moved to her side. "You can't force her to come home."

Ramsey frowned back at his wife, before turning the look on his daughter.

Mikayla shook her head, that look of wounded pride glittering in her amethyst eyes.

"I'm not a bone to fight over," she said, the hurt thick and heavy in her voice. "I'm going to *my* house. Thank you, Dad, for bringing the boys to fix the window. And thank you for being here for me. But you can't help me this time. And I won't hide under your bed like I did as a child when the kids at school picked on me. I have my own bed now."

She turned and walked regally, as regal as a fairy could be as her wings drooped from a father's lack of respect. Ramsey Martin loved his daughter, but to Ramsey she was still a little girl. And his little girl was in danger and refusing to listen to his advice.

Nik turned to her father slowly. He was staring at

Mikayla as though she had just robbed him of his heart.

"You're going to get her killed," Ramsey accused Nik, his voice low, vibrating with fear and anger.

Nik shook his head. "I'm the only one who can save her, Mr. Martin. You can't help her; your sons can't help her. I can."

Ramsey rubbed at his neck once again, a grimace tightening his face. "I can't help but think you're the reason this is happening to her." He looked to the closed office door. "But she's not going to let me take care of her, is she?"

"She doesn't want to be taken care of," Jorrey Ramsey stated, though her gaze stayed on Nik. "She wants to be a part of her life. Not a spectator."

And what the hell that meant Nik could only guess.

Shaking his head, he turned back to the investigator as he moved from the back of the room.

"We found the bullet," Denover informed him. "Ballistics will take over from here. But I wouldn't expect anything more than we got on that last one."

"Which was?" Nik stared back at him coldly. There still wasn't a report on the last shooting.

Denover smiled mockingly. "Nothing." Nodding, he moved for the door, the officers standing behind him following closely.

Which essentially meant anything concerning Mikayla Martin was not high priority.

That would change the minute Nik had a chance to make a phone call. If Jordan wanted him back anytime soon, then his commander could see about getting this case moved a little higher on the list of priorities where the police department was concerned.

"That is what is wrong with the world today," Ramsey Martin growled as the investigator and his officers left the shop. "A complete lack of respect. I knew that little bastard's father. He'd be rolling in his grave to see his son acting that way where the law is concerned."

It didn't surprise Nik in the least. It only went to reaffirm his belief that the world, politics, and the police had much in common, no matter the nation one was in.

"Mr. Ramsey, take your family home." Nik turned back to Mikayla's father. "I'll take Ms. Maple and Mikayla home. And I'll get to the bottom of this. One way or the other."

One thing was for damned sure. If he managed to get his hands on the person shooting at Mikayla, then he was going to kill him. There wasn't a force on this earth that would be able to keep Nik from tearing the bastard's head off.

Nik had no doubt there wasn't a special place in hell reserved for men who dared to threaten to harm pretty little fairies. On the off chance that there wasn't, Nik would make certain the shooter suffered before he died.

"Think she'll say good-bye to me?" Ramsey wondered aloud as he glanced at the office door once more.

"I'd say she'd be more hurt if you didn't go to her," Nik responded as he moved away to test the plywood barrier the brothers had put up.

He left the Martins alone now as they moved for Mikayla's office. Perhaps, if the father tried, he could erase the hurt he had put there earlier.

"You know, you're going to break her heart," Deirdre said as she moved behind Nik.

Nik turned and faced the redhead, seeing the concern in her eyes for her friend.

Deirdre Maple and Mikayla Martin had been friends

since childhood. The report he'd put together on Mikayla showed an endearing friendship between the two. Deirdre was the sister Mikayla's parents hadn't been able to give their daughter. And at the moment Deirdre was playing the big sister, just as she always had.

And Nik didn't have an answer or an assurance for her.

She shook her head at his lack of response. "I know that look. She won't be the only one left with scars, will she, Mr. Steele?"

"No," he finally answered her softly. "She won't be alone, Miss Maple."

He moved away from her and left the shop to check the work the boys had done. As he moved out, they went in, eyeing him suspiciously as they did so.

They were men; they knew he wouldn't be questioned where their sister was concerned, just as they knew that he was an entity to be wary of.

He'd never harm Mikayla, but if her brothers got in the way of his protecting her, then God help them.

God help another living soul that dared to hurt her again.

He was sick and damn tired of people picking on his fairy.

CHAPTER 12

People saw her as a pushover, and Mikayla knew it.

As she stepped from the shower that night, dried, and dressed in a long cotton nightgown and robe, she admitted she might well be too damned nice.

Even Nik treated her with kid gloves. There was a difference between needing to be protected from a killer and needing to be protected from life.

She had no desire to be protected from life. She wanted to live life, experience it. She wanted to laugh and she wanted to love, and if that meant getting her heart broken, then she wanted that, too.

She'd had plans, she admitted. Plans to be a virgin on her wedding night, plans to wear her white dress, but those plans had changed. She had a very bad feeling there was every chance Nik wouldn't be sticking around for a white wedding.

Not because he was a heartbreaker. Not because he had any desire to hurt her, any desire to spoil the plans she had made. Because the darkness inside him might not allow him to love with the same need, the same intensity, as Mikayla could allow herself to love with.

Moving through the house, she was aware of Nik in

the living room sitting on the edge of the couch as he cleaned his gun at the coffee table.

He had done that the night before when they left the bed for a snack. While Mikayla made sandwiches, he had cleaned his gun. He took exceptional care of his weapon.

"I ordered pizza," he called out as she moved for the fridge. "It arrived a few minutes ago."

She had to admit, she hadn't been looking forward to cooking at midnight.

"It's a good thing I'm not on a diet," she muttered as she poured herself a glass of sweet tea and moved into the living room.

Sure enough, a pizza box sat on the end table next to the recliner, along with several paper plates.

Mikayla made short work of a slice, sipped at her tea, and watched Nik finish cleaning the gun.

He'd showered as well.

His hair was nearly dry, fanning around his face as he bent his head to his task and carefully put the weapon back together.

"What are you doing tomorrow?" she asked as he laid the weapon aside.

"I'm heading to the job site to talk to the new fore-man and a few of Eddie Foreman's friends. There has to be a reason someone wanted him dead; I just have to figure out what that reason is."

"What have you learned so far?" She knew what he had learned, the same thing she had. Not a damned thing.

"Just a few rumors." He sat back on the couch and stared at her thoughtfully. "Foreman wasn't well liked by a lot of people. I called your friend. He gave me the same information he gave you, but I haven't been able to verify it, or find Steve Gainard."

"Steve's out of town," Mikayla stated before breathing in deeply. "For a man so unliked, no one wants to discuss Eddie."

"We'll see." Nik shrugged. "I have a few more leads to follow."

"I'm going with you." She straightened her shoulders and stared back at him in determination. "Deirdre has dared me to come back to the store until this is taken care of."

"No. You're not." Steel encased his voice as he watched her with warning, icy eyes. "You're in enough danger, Mikayla; I won't allow you to compound it. Your brothers will be at the store with you tomorrow, and you'll do as you've been doing; you'll work in the back room. I'll pick you up myself once I get another vehicle tomorrow and begin taking you to work and back myself."

"No, you will not." She surged to her feet. "I won't like that, Nik."

"Then you'll die," he growled as he came to his feet as well. "And that's not an acceptable trade as far as I'm concerned. You'll only endanger yourself further by going with me."

"It's my business and my life." Her arms went across her chest as she lifted her chin.

She was going to help him; it was that simple.

"No."

She wasn't going to do anything of the sort, and it was that simple. The very thought of Mikayla putting herself that much closer to danger was enough to send terror racing through him. It simply wasn't going to happen. Even if he had to tie her to her office chair and release her himself at the end of the day, it wasn't going to happen.

Damn, she was stubborn, though. He could see that

militant little light in her amethyst eyes, the determined angle of her chin, the pure fire in her eyes.

His cock, already rock hard and engorged, seemed
to thicken that much more and ached with a hunger he
wondered if he would ever sate.

He had tried to tell himself throughout the day that
he had a job to do here and that job did not include rolling around the bed every chance he got with Mikayla.

His imagination proceeded to place her on the kitchen
counter, the couch, the coffee table, wherever he could
get to her, if the bed was such a problem.

"You can't just tell me no," she stated, incredulity
coloring her voice. "This is my life, Nik, and it's my
problem. I was the one shot at three times already and
I'm the one who will die if this isn't fixed."

"I won't let you die." The ice in his eyes was replaced
by fire just that fast. Before the words left his lips he had
crossed the distance between them, his hands gripping
her arms as he glared down at her. "That's why you will
not be going, Mikayla."

"I won't accept—"

Before she could finish the sentence her mind was
being blown by a kiss that stole her breath and her
senses.

This kiss was unlike any he had given her yet. It
was a full-blown sex act, a hungry devouring of her
lips and tongue by his own as he pulled her closer
against his body and intoxicated her on the white-hot
heat of his kiss.

There were no allowances for innocence with this
kiss. There were no excuses made for the hunger that
began to sizzle and burn between them.

There was definitely no permission asked as he un-
tied the belt to her robe and pushed it from her shoul-

ders and lifted her in his arms, turned, and sat down in the large chair.

Mikayla would have been shocked if she had been given the chance. Nik pulled her over him until she was straddling his lap, the sensitive mound of her sex pressing against the hard wedge of his cock as it strained beneath the cotton sweatpants he wore.

This was pure, unadulterated lust with a little old-fashioned dominance thrown in on the side. Well, maybe more than a little. This was complete dominance.

Her ass cheeks flexed in his palms as he cupped them, pulling her closer, grinding her against the throbbing flesh pressing between her thighs and sending her clit into a complete overload of sensations. The little bud swelled instantly, coming to full blazing, aching life and demanding satisfaction.

Beneath her hands his bare chest rose and fell swiftly as his lips slanted across hers, his tongue stroking against hers as Mikayla threaded her fingers through his hair and held on for the ride.

One of these days, she thought, she'd have the experience, the knowledge, to destroy his senses just as effectively. Until then, she would greedily take every kiss, every caress, and learn from it, even as she reveled in it.

And reveling in it she was.

Her thighs tightened on his at the feel of his calloused palms pushing beneath the hem of the gown and pulling it upward, sliding it from her body until her arms lifted and he tossed it away as though it didn't matter.

He didn't pause in his attack against her senses. Not Nik. He was a man who knew exactly what he wanted and how to attain it. And he was definitely attaining it now.

His lips drew back from hers as his hands moved to her shoulders, bracing her as his lips moved down her back, heading swiftly to her breasts.

Tremors shook her body as pleasure began to suffuse it. Like a flame beneath her skin, consuming her entire body, shards of sensation began to sizzle and electrify. The velvety feel of his lips moving over the curve of one breast had her shaking. Fingers of electric impulse were shooting straight to her womb, clenching it in need and dragging a cry from her throat as his tongue stroked over one nipple enticingly.

"I could devour you." His voice was a growl of pure hunger. "I swear to God, every time I touch you it's like being burned by pleasure."

She was going to melt like butter all over him. The sound of his voice, the stroke of his lips and tongue over her nipple, and the eroticism of his words combined to have her juices flowing and dampening the silk of her panties. Her vagina clenched in hungry need and she swore her nipples tightened further.

"Then devour me," she whispered, the ache in her voice unmistakable as she watched him.

His lips were poised over her nipple, his hard bronzed face dark with lust, with need.

If only it were simple lust and nothing more, she thought. But she saw more, and ached to understand what the emotion in his eyes meant.

His lips quirked before he bestowed a suckling kiss on the sensitive tip of her breast, causing her to catch her breath in excitement.

"You like the pleasure, don't you, baby?" His cheek rasped against the curve of her breast as his lips lifted from her nipple. "Sweet little innocent."

The stroke of his hands down her spine to the upper curve of her buttocks had her inhaling in anticipation.

Of course, Nik didn't miss the reaction, she thought in dazed excitement. His fingers began to play there, drawing circles, the blunt tips of his nails raking against her skin as she shuddered in reaction.

"I'm going to take you right here," he promised her then. "I'm going to drive my cock up that sweet pussy, Mikayla, while my fingers play in other ways." One finger traced the narrow cleft of her rear to her thighs.

Mikayla cried out in sensory overload as he chose that moment to cover her nipple with his lips. His teeth rasped it gently; his tongue stoked and laved. He sucked the tender bud into his mouth, drawing on it with heated destruction as Mikayla lost even the ability to process thought.

She felt her panties tear. He didn't bother taking them from her, he just ripped them from her body, and she swore she almost came from the excitement of the act.

Mikayla couldn't retain even a semblance of control where her responses to him were concerned. Each touch had adrenaline racing through her bloodstream, spurring the need for more, making each touch a bounty of pleasure.

Her hands stroked along his shoulders as he sucked at first one nipple, then the other, drawing it into his mouth, laving it with his tongue, setting fire to her womb with each draw of his mouth.

Anticipation began to thunder in her head as she felt his fingers move between her thighs. She thought he would release the heated length of his erection, thought he would take her then, ease the burning pain for his possession.

Instead, his fingers cupped between her thighs as his head pulled back, his lips releasing her nipple as he stared down at her.

His fingers stroked inside the slick, soaked folds of her flesh. They glided through the moisture, eased back, flicked over the hungry opening, then stroked against her clit with near-devastating results.

"How sweet and hot," he crooned. "You make a man want to burn inside you, Mikayla."

Burn, burn, she chanted silently as her hips moved as though on their own, pressing against his fingers and demanding more.

"Is this what you want, baby?" One finger pressed high and hard inside her, filling her with a sudden fiery ecstasy that had her back arching, his name falling from her lips.

Oh, God, that was what she needed.

The rasp of his finger against tender, sensitive nerve endings was nearly more than she could bear. It felt as though electricity were surging inside her, searing her.

"Ahh, you do want that," his voice rasped, approval and hunger thickening the tone. "Do you want more, Mikayla?"

He gave her more. A second finger joined the first, pressed inside her, stretching her, burning her with the sensations as she gasped, her hips grinding down on the penetration.

It was exquisite. The feel of his fingers moving inside her, stroking her, parting the tight muscles, and finding hidden little nerve endings that had known no touch but his.

His thumb stroked around her clit, the roughened pad an intense friction that kept her hovering on the edge of release. Surging white-hot fingers of sensation were attacking her nerve endings, sizzling through her clit, her vagina, screaming in silent demand at the feel of his fingers stretching her apart.

She tightened on the invasion inside her, perspiration dampening her flesh as the heat surging through her body began to consume her.

She couldn't hold back her response; she didn't want to hold it back. She wanted to lose herself in him, in the pleasure.

Forcing her lashes open, she stared back at him, her body jerking at each surge of pleasure that rocked through her. Each thrust of his fingers inside her body.

"What you do to me," she whispered breathlessly. "I love it, Nik. I love what you do to me."

His expression tightened, his fingers reaching higher inside her, where he paused, stroked, and forced a cry from her lips at the incredible sensations that raked through her womb.

"There, pretty girl," he groaned, the hand that gripped the side of her rear moving until his fingers slid into the narrow crease. "There you go; just let it feel good."

All kinds of good.

Mikayla shuddered as the hand at her rear changed course, moved, and seconds later she felt the hard, naked length of his cock pressing against her thigh.

"Come here, sweetheart." His fingers slid free.

One hand gripped her thigh, the other the hard length of his erection as he tucked it against the entrance of her body.

"Ride me, Mikayla. Take me, baby, however you need me."

However she needed him. She needed all of him, wild and uncontrolled. Breaking that control wouldn't be easy, though. It wouldn't happen tonight. Tonight, though, she would know the pleasure.

All the pleasure. Controlling it, taking it, relishing it.

Lowering herself, Mikayla felt her lashes flutter uncontrollably at that first fiery, stretching entrance.

The feel of the engorged crest pushing inside the tender flesh burning as it parted sensitive tissue and caressed once-hidden nerve endings with exquisite force.

She moved on him slowly, taking him by increments as she watched his face. The way his eyes narrowed, the flush that bracketed his cheekbones, the harsh, tight lines his expression morphed into.

Savage hunger glittered in his eyes and tightened his face just as it began to roil through Mikayla's system.

She was wanton. She was hungry for him. Rocking against him, pressing down, lifting, slow and easy she took every hard, heavily veined inch of his cock inside and shuddered with the pleasure racing through her.

She had never known anything like this. Like controlling the strength and the power of the man beneath her, taking him, moving against him for her own pleasure, and watching the pleasure as it filled his face as well.

It made her want more. It made her want to see if his face could tighten further, if pleasure could brighten his eyes further.

Holding on to his shoulders, she breathed in roughly and fought to keep hold of just enough of her senses to watch him, to memorize his expressions, his response. The way the muscles of his shoulders tightened and bunched, the way sweat beaded on his forehead and ran in a small rivulet down the side of his face.

His finger slid to the rounded flesh of her rear, tightened, and parted them before sliding inward, meeting in the shallow cleft that parted the sensitive globes.

Her eyes closed. Color ricocheted behind her eyelids as she felt his fingers rasp against the delicate opening he found there before his fingers dipped to the point where their bodies were locked together.

She wanted to move, needed to move, but as his fingers caressed the edges of her stretched opening she could only feel and let the pleasure wash over her as he drew the heavy, slick moisture back.

As his fingers moved back once more, she lifted, her inner muscles tightening convulsively on his cock as the friction heated her further.

Sliding down once again, she felt his finger rub against her rear entrance, felt it tuck gently against her, using the downward pressure of her body to penetrate just enough to warn her of his intentions.

Her eyes flared open as she froze. The feel of his finger poised just inside the forbidden entrance had her breath catching as his narrowed pale blue gaze met hers.

"Do I stop?" he asked, his voice low, rasping deeper than normal as he pulled back and exited, only to draw more of the moisture that eased from her vagina back to the sensitive area.

She lifted again.

His finger tucked back into place.

Did she dare? Could she dare?

Closing her eyes, biting her lip, Mikayla slowly lowered herself once again.

The look on her face nearly had him losing his hold on the release that threatened to erupt from his balls.

Nik gritted his teeth as he fought that ache, felt her pussy rippling around him in nearing orgasm as it burned through the thin protection of the condom he had managed to roll over his dick before she began taking him.

Innocence marked her expression, filled her eyes. Despite the eroticism of the act, that innocence was still there. Despite the fact that she was slowly, hesitantly, taking his finger up her ass, his dick up her near-virgin pussy, she still looked like a virgin. Like a wanton, innocent fairy perched on his lap, driving him insane with pleasure.

It was all he could do to hold on. All he could do to hold back his release as he felt those tighter inner muscles gripping his finger as she began to move on him.

It was an agony of pleasure. Sharp shards of sensation raced up and down his spine, coalesced in his balls, and combined to drive him closer to release, to another nail in his fucking coffin.

Damn her, she was stealing every shield he had placed around his soul and he couldn't figure out how she was doing it. He couldn't stop her from doing it, and he couldn't leave her to keep it from it happening.

As he gripped her hip with his free hand, his head rested along the back of the chair. She was moving faster now, stronger. Her body undulated against him, rising and falling, her back arched, her face radiant, as though she loved the feel of his body. Needed it. Craved it as much as he craved hers.

God, he needed more of her.

He wanted to spend every second just like this. With her taking her pleasure of him. Riding him like she couldn't help it. Like the perfect vision of sensual enjoyment. Her face flushing, her amethyst eyes darkening, her breasts swollen, nipples so hard they were like berries.

"There you go, baby," he groaned. "Fuck me, Mikayla. There you go, hard and fast, darlin'. Fuck me. . . ."

It was tearing through him. He could feel the hard

pulses of electric sensation tearing up his spine, sizzling in his balls. His cock tightened, pulsed.

Gripping her hip tighter, he moved harder beneath her, faster. Surging inside the tight grips that clenched around his dick as well as his finger, milking them, destroying him with her response to him.

She was close. He could feel her rising, see it in her face.

Her hands gripped his shoulders as strangled little cries fell from her lips. Tight, hard nipples brushed his chest, burned into his chest.

"Oh, God. Nik." Tightening further, she began to shudder.

"Give it to me, Mikayla," he groaned as he fucked inside her harder, his hips surging beneath hers, driving his cock into the hot, almost-too-snug grip of her pussy. "Give it to me, baby. Come for me, Mikayla."

As though she needed nothing more, she exploded. He felt her climax, felt it tugging at his cock, his finger. Her juices flowed along his shaft to his balls as she tightened, arched, and cried his name as though only he could hold her to the earth now.

Wrapping his arms around her, he pulled her to his chest, held her close, and powered inside her. Once. Twice. The explosion shattered through him as Mikayla jerked and shuddered in his arms, lost in her own pleasure as he found his alongside her.

Holding back was becoming harder each time. Holding his heart and his soul behind the ragged edges of what shields remained was becoming next to impossible.

Cradling her in his arms, still buried inside her, Nik realized in that moment that he could never have enough of her. That losing her, walking away from her, would destroy what he had retained of his humanity in the past ten years. He would be nothing more than a shell of a man.

Just as he realized he would have no other choice. When this was finished, when she was safe, he would have no choice but to leave. In doing so, he would leave the last threads of his soul with her.

Rising from the chair, he held her close to his heart and moved to her bedroom, the big bed he had shared with her the night before, and the warmth he'd found in it.

Laying her down, he couldn't help but grin at the drowsy kiss she laid on his lips before he straightened and moved to the bathroom.

Minutes later, he returned with a warm, damp cloth and towel. He cleaned her thighs and the delicate folds of her silken pussy before drying her gently.

"Why do you do that?" She stared back at him, her lashes heavy as he straightened.

"Because I can." As he moved back to the bathroom he wasn't about to tell her the truth. That nothing mattered but taking care of her, but showing her what she deserved, what she should have if she takes another man to her bed once he was gone.

Of course she would, he told himself. She was a beautiful, vibrant woman. A passionate woman. She couldn't live her life alone.

But the thought of another man sharing her bed had rage eating at his insides like battery acid. No other man could need her as he needed her. No other could touch her with the same hunger, with the same driving desperation that he knew he touched her with.

No other man would see the delicate fairy beneath the strong, determined young woman she was.

And no other man could possibly love her as much as he did. As much as he always would.

Inside, he froze. A part of his soul burned like a white-hot flame as the knowledge of that emotion slammed into his mind. Into his heart.

God help him.

He loved her.

CHAPTER 13

Nik's reason for being in Hagerstown and on the Nelson job site where Eddie Foreman had died wasn't a secret. When he arrived at the job site the next afternoon and began questioning the employees after stopping to talk to Robert Cronin, Nik also learned that mixed feelings existed among the men there, as well as the normal suspicion he had faced since beginning the job of finding a killer rather than a liar.

Thankfully, Mikayla's brothers seemed to have gone a long way in loosening lips. As each man was pulled into the office trailer for Nik to talk to, he learned that the Martin brothers had already informed those they considered friends that Nik was more concerned with finding the killer and protecting Mikayla than he was with protecting anyone's reputation.

There were still those who weren't convinced, but at least they were talking to him.

"Mikayla always was a go-getter, even in school," one of the employees told him as he sat across from the small desk Nik was using to question the man.

"Yet you refused to discuss Eddie Foreman with her

when she tried to talk to you," Nik stated as he leaned back in his chair and watched the younger man.

David Melbourne was Mikayla's age. He'd graduated in the same high school class with her and known her most of her life. He was a friend of the Martin brothers and also known to have socialized with Eddie Foreman.

"Well, I didn't talk to her because her brothers didn't think she should be investigating things and I agreed with them." David shrugged with a grimace. "Hell, someone had already shot at her when he killed Eddie. I didn't want her hurt, and she was just poking her nose into trouble."

"So you'd rather Eddie's murderer went free?" Nik asked.

"That beats having Mikayla get hurt," David agreed with a definitive nod. "Besides, Eddie was an asshole. Someone was bound to kill him eventually. Mikayla's nice, though, ya know? She didn't need more grief. And now, someone's tried to shoot her three times. She should drop it already."

"You heard someone shot into the store last night?" Nik asked.

David nodded his shaggy head. "That's one of the reasons I'm willing talk to you now. Cops didn't want to hear what I had to say when Eddie was killed, but I figure you're going to hear it from someone else anyway."

"Such as?" Nik leaned forward, watching the other man carefully as suspicion reared its ugly head. Nik had rarely found anyone willing to talk just for the hell of it.

"Look, Eddie wasn't a great guy," David informed him. "He had a lot of enemies. He liked to make examples of people. Coupla weeks before he was killed he fired this one guy, Jarvis Dalton. I been thinking about that. Jarvis resembles Maddix a little bit. He's some kind of distant cousin to him. Anyway, Jarvis was here the day Eddie was killed, yellin' at him. Told Eddie if he didn't give him his job back, then he was going to pay for it. Maybe Jarvis made Eddie pay for it."

"There's a rumor that Maddix has been seen meeting a bookie in D.C. and possibly one here in Hagerstown. What do you know about that?" Nik asked, wondering if David could confirm the information Cronin had given him.

David shook his head. "I don't know anything about that one. But I don't mess with bookies, so what do I know?"

Nik wasn't certain how accurate the information either David or Robert offered could be. They weren't in the reports Nik had received from Maddix or the reports the investigating officer had made. But as the day progressed, it wasn't the first time Nik heard David's version, or the first time he couldn't confirm Cronin's.

Just as it wasn't the first time that Nik had heard the reason none of the men had told Mikayla was because of her brothers' fears that she was going to get herself hurt.

They'd protected her, and Nik knew the hell she would rain down on them if she ever found out about it.

When the new crew foreman made his way into the trailer, Nik was beginning to get sick of hearing of how helpless Mikayla was. "Helpless" wasn't a word he would use. "Vulnerable" definitely, but besides the point. The information he'd learned could have been useful if he'd had it when he first arrived, whether it came from Mikayla or Maddix.

"Mr. Wallace." Nik nodded as the middle-aged foreman took a seat in front of the desk.

"Let's get this over with so I can go back to work," Jack Wallace breathed out heavily. "I can't imagine why Maddix gave you permission to disrupt the job site like this."

"Perhaps to catch a killer? Or do you think Maddix did the killing?" Nik asked.

Wallace snorted at the idea. "I don't doubt Maddix would kill, but Eddie Foreman just wasn't worth the price of the bullet used on him. Maddix has better business sense."

"Can you tell me what you know about Eddie's meetings the day he died?"

As the assistant foreman, Jack Wallace should have been aware of any meetings Eddie had had.

"None that day." Wallace shook his head. "Eddie liked to have his meetings at a bar or track, if he could. He didn't like taking meetings here because someone was always overhearing things and that just pissed him off."

Which meant he was probably hiding something, Nik thought.

"What about Maddix Nelson? Did he come to the job site often?"

Jack Wallace shrugged. "Few times a week maybe. He'd talk to Eddie for a bit, check things out, then head back to town or wherever."

"What about Eddie then?" Nik asked. "What type of foreman was he?"

"He was a fucking bastard." Wallace grimaced. "Son of a bitch liked to talk down to the men and play himself up as someone he wasn't."

Sounded like a hell of a guy, Nik thought mockingly.

"He wasn't well liked then?"

Wallace nodded. "Not at all. Hell, even I didn't like him, and I can get along with everyone."

Nik rather doubted that.

"He argued with a former employee the day he died?" Nik probed. "What do you know about that?"

"Jarvis Dalton." The other man nodded. "Eddie had fired him a few weeks before. Accused him of stealing. Jarvis was pretty pissed off over it. He wanted his job back, but Eddie wasn't giving in. He was fed up with Jarvis for whatever reason."

"But you don't know that reason?" Nik pressed.

Wallace frowned. "Let's say, I'm not sure. I suspect Jarvis was stealing, but Eddie never said either way and he got pissed when I asked, so I just let it go."

"What about the day Eddie died? Were very many of the workers aware she was picking her brother up?"

Wallace snorted. "Probably everyone. Scotty had her pick him up pretty often, and the guys liked to watch her blush when they hooted and hollered at her. She's a pretty girl, and the boys here like a pretty girl."

Nik just bet they did. He clenched his teeth to hold back an anger and possessiveness he shouldn't be feeling. Mikayla was his for the moment, he reminded himself. He couldn't let himself hold any tighter to her than he already was, not if he wanted to retain his sanity when it was time to leave.

"Did Maddix meet Eddie often at the track or bars that you're aware of?" Nik asked.

Jack Wallace frowned. "Maddix Nelson doesn't gamble that I'm aware of. I've heard him say his business is enough of a gamble, he doesn't need to compound his losses."

"Thank you, Mr. Wallace." Nik rose from his chair and gathered his notes together. "And thank your men for talking to me."

"Well, the faster you get this taken care of the faster

I get some peace on the job," Wallace growled. "This situation has been a guaranteed spark to every damned argument that flares up on the job. Too many men here are prone to believe Maddix did it, while others are certain he didn't. Knowing one way or the other would be nice."

"And what do you think?" Nik asked curiously. "Do you think he did it?"

Wallace paused. "I think he's more than capable of doing it, like I said, let's put it that way," he finally answered. "Maddix has a temper, and if Eddie did something to threaten him or this job, then yeah." He nodded. "Maddix would be capable of it. But Maddix could have gotten rid of him by firing him, and Maddix normally takes the smartest route, no matter what he's doing."

Interesting. Nik hadn't expected the current foreman to make that admission.

"Thank you again, Mr. Wallace." Nik nodded as he headed to the door. "I'll return your office to you now."

He left the office trailer, slid his sunglasses on his face, and stared around up at the nearly completed building where Eddie Foreman had died.

Nik's investigation so far hadn't gotten much more information than he had gotten today. He'd spent the past week in the bars and cafés asking questions, sometimes simply listening to the local gossip. And there was plenty to be had.

Maddix Nelson and Mikayla Martin were subjects that were heavily debated. Both were well known. Mikayla was well liked; Maddix was an employer and well liked with the same intensity that he was well hated.

And murder was always fodder for gossip.

So far, Robert Cronin was the only one associating

Maddix with gambling tracks and underground casinos in Baltimore and D.C. No one else had heard of Maddix gambling.

Pulling the keys to the new GMC Sierra he had picked up that morning, Nik hit the unlock and auto start, waited, then moved to the vehicle.

He'd already lost everything that meant anything to him once. Losing it again wasn't high on his list of priorities. He hadn't stopped living by the sword. He doubted he would ever stop living by it. God knew what would happen to him, though, if anything ever happened to Mikayla.

Pulling the cell phone from the leather holster at his side, he pressed the speed dial and waited.

"Malone," Jordan answered on the first ring.

"I'm going to be awhile," Nik informed the other man. "I may need help as well."

Jordan was silent for long moments. "What's going on?"

Nik quickly outlined the situation without informing his commander that he was now sleeping with the woman he was here to investigate. More to the point, he was more concerned with protecting the woman than he was with protecting the man who had hired him.

Jordan was no man's fool, though. He'd been bitching for weeks over the fact that his agents couldn't keep their dicks in their pants or their hearts in their chests until they completed their commitments to the Elite Ops.

He was raging over the fact that Travis Caine, the most recent agent to succumb to Cupid, had hooked up with a high-profile lover.

Lady Victoria Lillian Harrington had once been an agent, until an attempted assassination had wiped her memory and allowed her to return to her previous life.

Not that the return hadn't benefited the Ops. It had. Her return had been a mission in and of itself. But that didn't mean Jordan had to like the fact that Travis had now placed someone above Elite Ops. Just as three other agents before him had done.

Jordan's branch of the Elite Ops, in Jordan's opinion, was weakened by the fact that his men had acquired the greatest weakness of all. Love.

"How close are you to figuring this out, Nik?" Jordan asked.

"Hell if I know," Nik breathed out roughly. "She's been shot at three times, but the more I've thought about it today, the more I can't help but think each time was a deliberate miss. Both times they had clear shots. They were close, but missed. I can't leave until I figure out who killed that damned foreman and created this mess. If I find him, then I find the person shooting at Mikayla."

"Your job was to figure out if Miss Martin was lying and if so, who she was covering for," Jordan reminded him. "You've completed the job you were hired to do. Now you can turn the information over to the local authorities and leave."

It was a subtle warning to drop the mission and return to base.

That wasn't happening.

"Jordan, I'm not leaving until she's safe."

Silence stretched between them for long moments.

"Fuck. I thought for sure you'd at least hold out until your commitment with the Ops came to an end," Jordan growled. "This isn't going to be easy to explain to Elite Command."

"What's there to explain?" Nik asked coldly. "I'm finishing a mission to repay a debt, nothing more."

"Then why do you need help, Nik?" Jordan asked. "If all you're doing is repaying a debt?"

"Explain it to Elite Command however you have to," Nik stated. "I need at least one agent."

"Everyone is out now," Jordan snapped. "The present mission has been hell where information is concerned. I might be able to pull one of the girls from the other unit, though. I think Raisa is returning from England tonight or tomorrow. I can send her out if she returns."

"She'll work."

The agents in Elite Two had been reassigned to Jordan's command for the few years they still had on their commitments. They were information gatherers, behind the scenes, support only. They were damned good, though. Nik would let Raisa cover his back anytime.

"Kira Richards and Bailey Vincent are in D.C.," Jordan mused then. "They're on a fact-finding mission. They headed out night before last. I'll see if I can contact them."

"That could work." Nik nodded. "I'll keep you updated on what I'm finding here, but it's a hell of a situation. I don't think Mikayla's lying, Jordan. That leaves Maddix holding a smoking gun and a dream alibi to say he didn't do it."

But there was nothing left but to suspect Maddix. His alibis were friends and business associates. If killing Eddie had benefited them as well, then they were all in on it.

"Nelson has some pull in D.C.," Jordan reminded him. "One of Elite Command's members knows him personally. That information won't sit well."

"I don't care if it doesn't sit well." Nik turned onto the interstate, his eyes narrowing in anger as he glared at the road.

"Your judgment is compromised," Jordan pointed out. "You're sleeping with her, aren't you, Nik?"

Nik's lips thinned. He wasn't answering that question. It was none of Jordan's business as far as he was concerned.

"My judgment hasn't been compromised," Nik snarled. "Maddix Nelson isn't above murder."

"And no woman is above lying," Jordan pointed out coldly. "Either way, figure out what the hell is going on. I'll see who I can get out there, but remember, Nik, they'll be sending in their own report. Make damned sure your judgment is solid. We can't risk anything less here."

His judgment was fine, it was his heart in question, Nik admitted silently.

"Let me know if anyone is headed out," Nik stated rather than debating the former. "I'll report back when I know something."

"Yeah, well, make it soon," Jordan ordered.

The line disconnected.

Nik breathed out wearily as he glanced at the keypad of the phone and hit the number to Mikayla's shop.

When he disconnected, he was almost snarling in fury.

Mikayla wasn't there, Deirdre had informed him. She had left less than an hour after he had, and Deirdre suspected Mikayla was once again investigating Eddie Foreman's murder.

How the hell was he going to keep her safe at this rate? She was risking her life as cavalierly as he did, and that wasn't acceptable.

He keyed her cell-phone number in quickly.

"Where the hell are you?" he questioned the minute she answered the phone.

She paused before saying, "Did I ask where you were?"

Her tone was candy sweet, immediately putting his

survival instincts on high alert. Male survival, that instinct that warned him he was pissing his woman off and she had the power to make him pay for it.

"Mikayla, we both know what I'm doing," he stated carefully. "I can't do that if you're not safe."

"I'm perfectly safe," she assured him. "I'm working."

"You're not *at* work," he ground out.

"I didn't say I was *at* work; I said I'm working," she pointed out, her tone still deliberately sweet.

"On what?" His jaw was clenched so tight his teeth ached. "Tell me where you are and I'll follow you back to the shop."

"I'm not ready to go back to the shop," she informed him with patient emphasis. "I have things to do, Nik. Things I've allowed you to delay for me. You want to work alone, that's fine. I can do the same."

Patience. He forced himself to patience. Growling at her wasn't going to do a damned bit of good and he knew it. Sensed it with an intimate knowledge that only a lover would have.

"You're endangering your life, Mikayla," he finally said calmly. "Is that what you really want to do? Do you really want to give the bastard shooting at you a clear shot? An opportunity to kill you the next time."

"I guess that's your choice, Nik," she said quietly. "This isn't just your job; it's my problem. I have the right to be with you and I have the right to know what's going on."

And Nik simply couldn't agree with her.

"You have that right when you have the training to back the desire," he informed her, barely managing to hide the anger rising inside him now. "Don't push this, Mikayla; you know you're not going to win. You're only going to end up getting yourself killed."

Once he got his hands on her, he was going to make

damned certain she understood who was the boss here. He'd be damned if he'd have her running all over town with a killer focused on her.

"At least I'll know I fought," she stated, the determination in her voice frankly frightening. "That's something some people can't do."

The connection closed. Nik waited, certain she hadn't hung up on him, just to learn that she had done just that.

Lowering the phone, he glanced at it with a glare. She had hung up on him. His jaw clenched as he punched in another number.

"Hi, baby," Tehya Talamosi came on the line. Jordan's assistant and all-around tormentor. "I heard Jordan cussing a few minutes ago. Are you getting a little some-some?"

One of these days. Nik decided Jordan was right, Tehya and duct tape would be good together.

"Tehya, if I give you a cell-phone number, could you GPS it?" he asked carefully.

"If it has GPS on it. What happened? Did you lose your little pretty?" she asked, obviously referring to Mikayla.

He gave Tehya the number slowly.

"Got it. Now are you going to answer me?"

"She may be misplaced for the moment," he gritted out the admission.

Tehya snickered. "Well, she just so happens to be at a quaint little coffee shop four buildings down from her shop."

He was going to kill her; it was that damned simple.

"Damn," Tehya breathed out.

"Damn?" The tone of her voice had his hand clenching on the steering wheel. "What's damn, Tehya?"

"Damn, she's with Bailey and Kira."

Nik blinked. For a second, pure abject male terror seared his insides. Jordan hadn't had time to send the other women; that meant they were being nosy. Nosy and most likely interfering. Those were not good combinations.

"She's what?"

"Currently having coffee with Bailey and Kira. I thought they were in D.C.?"

He disconnected and pressed his foot to the gas, risking a speeding ticket. Bailey and Kira with Mikayla? What the hell were they up to? Hadn't he kept his noses out of their relationships with his fellow agents? Hadn't he stood back, supported them where he could, and covered for them when they needed it?

What the hell were they doing?

The phone rang from the seat where he had tossed it.

"What?" he barked.

"You have your backup," Jordan growled.

"No." He was ready to grind his back teeth to dust. "Not those two, because they already have their own agenda here, and it's to interfere in my life. No."

He could almost feel Jordan's amusement. "Scared, Nik?"

"Fucking terrified," he snarled. "Do you think they're going to keep her out of trouble? Fuck no. I might as well just keep her with me while I'm questioning lowlifes and dodging bullets."

"That's always an option," Jordan agreed. "I could bring them back to base then."

He was going to strangle the phone. Then he was going to strangle Bailey and Kira. When he finished with them, he was going to fuck Mikayla until she was too damned tired to disagree with him.

Son of a bitch.

Bailey and Kira were both CIA brats, Bailey a former agent and Kira a former contract agent. Both were richer than Midas and neither one of them cared in the least about poking her damned nose in someone else's business.

"You did this," Nik accused Jordan furiously. "Admit it. You sicced those two on me before I even called, didn't you, Jordan?"

He wasn't above getting his laughs in wherever he could whenever he thought one of his agents was making what he considered the most dire of mistakes. Falling in love.

"You forget who you're talking to, Renegade." Jordan's tone held far too much self-satisfaction. "I'm the commander, remember?"

"Commander Malone, get fucked!" He hung up on his boss, praying the other man was stupid enough to have him pulled in now. Let Jordan send the entire fucking team after him. Once he got back to base, he was going to show his interfering commander exactly how matchmaking was truly done.

Did he think Nik didn't know his weakness? That the other men weren't well aware of exactly who Jordan couldn't keep his damned eyes off of?

Oh, they knew, and Nik was going to show the bastard the rules of playing matchmaker.

Jordan thought he was throwing roadblocks in Nik's path? That he was going to make things difficult enough that Nik would draw back from Mikayla?

It wasn't going to happen. But when he returned to base, Nik was going to see just how interfering Jordan could become.

Mikayla stared at the silent phone as it lay on the table before glancing back at her two new customers as they went over the books of designs Mikayla had put together.

Some were her own designs; others were on consignment. The gowns were by far the most expensive she had, as well as the most gorgeous.

"I love your style," Kira remarked as she glanced up with a smile, her gray eyes filled with vivacity as she tucked a strand of long black hair behind her ear. "I heard you were good, but this exceeds my expectations."

"And exactly how did you hear about me?" Mikayla asked as she picked up her water and sipped.

The two women seemed to know too much about her. They were smooth, graceful, but the way their eyes watched everything, the way they moved, the way they acted, reminded Mikayla of Nik.

"A party last week," Bailey Serborne Vincent answered. "Margaret Westfield was wearing a beautiful shimmery blue gown. I was completely jealous. She gave me your name."

Mikayla nodded. She'd done several gowns for Margaret Westfield.

"We have several charity events coming up this winter." Kira glanced at Bailey. The look the two women shared had Mikayla's eyes narrowing.

She wasn't stupid, and the other two women weren't even trying to hide the fact that they were amused by something.

"And you need gowns?" Mikayla guessed.

"Several," Bailey agreed, her green eyes appraising as she turned back to the design plates laid out on the table. "Three to be exact. And I do believe we're interested in having you make them. Do you think you could complete six gowns before October?"

"I could complete two by October and two by the first of the next two months. There's no way all six could be done by October, though. It will also require your availability for fittings on short notice."

The two women were quiet for long moments before Kira glanced at her friend, then nodded slowly. "Those arrangements are suitable." She pushed three plates forward from the book she was holding. "I'm interested in these, though I'd need an assurance I won't have to worry about anyone else wearing the same design anytime for the rest of the year."

She had nothing to worry about. The dresses she had chosen were three of the most expensive Mikayla had. They were her own designs and completely under her own control.

"That can be arranged." She wouldn't have to worry about rent on the shop for the next two years.

"I'd like to look at the designs a while longer," Bailey stated. "Could I come by the shop tomorrow and give you my choices? And of course I'd need the same assurance."

"I can only give that assurance if you choose the gowns I've designed," Mikayla stated.

Bailey nodded with a smiling, "Of course."

Talk about too good to be true.

She wasn't a great believer in coincidence, Mikayla admitted. These two women were damned good. They hadn't batted a lash while she was on the phone with Nik, but the call they had received right after her phone call had her suspicious instincts clamoring in warning.

"So, do the two of you know Nik Steele well?" she asked them.

They didn't act the least bit surprised. "We often travel among the same social sphere." Bailey smiled coolly. "Nik is an acquaintance of both our husbands, actually."

"And that's where you heard about my gowns?" Mikayla asked, fairly certain Margaret Westfield hadn't given her name. She was a friend of Maddix. That made a differene.

"No, actually, it's not." Kira smiled in amusement. "Nik would have never told us. Another mutual acquaintance happened to know where he was, and that he was helping a friend out here. Your name might have been mentioned. Gossip does travel fast, dear, and when Margaret Westfield mentioned you as well we decided to look you up."

"And you're here because of Nik why?" Mikayla asked curiously.

"Because Nik is a friend and we enjoy tormenting our friends." Bailey laughed. "Once he knows we were here, he's going to be—"

"Completely irate enough to call both your husbands," Nik growled behind them as he approached the table.

Tall, dressed in those wicked black leathers, with a scowl on his face and irritation glittering in his eyes.

He took a seat and stared at each of them in turn. Kira. Bailey. Mikayla.

Mikayla smiled back at him placidly.

"Hello, Nik. Ian and John send their regards." Bailey was all but laughing at him as Mikayla watched his eyes narrow, a muscle jumping in his jaw.

"I'm sure they did." His jaw tightened further before he turned back to Mikayla. "Are you ready to go now?"

Mikayla glanced at the other two women. "Is our business finished for the moment?"

"For the moment," Bailey agreed as she gathered up the plates. "I'll return these tomorrow, once I've made my choices, if that's all right with you?"

"Perfectly," Mikayla agreed as she rose to her feet,

followed by Nik. "I'll look forward to hearing from you."

"Thank you for meeting with us on such short notice," Kira expressed with a genuine warmth. "We'll be talking soon."

Mikayla just bet they would be, just as she was betting it wouldn't be all about dresses.

"You'll have to give me a ride," she told Nik as his hand settled at the small of her back and he led her through the café. "I walked over with Mrs. Richards and Mrs. Vincent."

"Not a problem." His tone was clipped and rough. The sound sent a shiver of anticipation up Mikayla's spine and she had no idea why.

"Good." She smiled back at him, making certain the curve of her lips was carefree and perky. "I'm sure it will be a fun ride."

His fingers seemed to tighten at her back and she swore his whole body tensed. Sex seemed to pour off him as they stepped onto the sidewalk and moved for the small parking area at the side of the café.

Steering her to the back of the parking lot, he led her to the monster black pickup backed into the parking space. Moving to the passenger side, she waited until he unlocked the door of the vehicle he'd started automatically as they left the café.

The door opened, he gripped her waist, lifted her onto the seat, then caught the back of her head and covered her lips with his own.

Instantly flames shot through her body. Her clit swelled, throbbed, her breasts felt electrified, and the breath seemed to stop in her lungs.

The kiss was a heady, heated stamp of ownership and possession. His tongue brushed over her lips, then forged past them to find her own. It stroked, licked, tasted, until Mikayla became so lost in the sensations she no longer cared where they were or why she was pissed with him to begin with.

This was what mattered. In that second, it was all that mattered. Holding him to her, loving him with every stroke of her tongue against his, every touch of his hair against her fingers as she delved into it.

The touch, the feel of him. Nothing else mattered. Nothing else could matter as she felt the flames, the hunger rising inside her.

Until his head pulled back and her eyes opened to stare into the flaming depths of the pale blue of his.

"You won't enjoy getting your way," he assured her, his voice thick and heavy with lust.

Mikayla leaned forward slowly, keeping her eyes locked with his, and touched his lips with her own softly as she said, "Bet me."

CHAPTER 14

Nik couldn't explain the emotions racing through him as he maneuvered the truck back to Mikayla's home. His hands were clenched tight around the steering wheel, tension mounting as he fought the tightness in his chest, the clenching of his abdomen. There was no way to fight the engorging of his cock.

He was iron hard, throbbing painfully as he fought the need to fuck her into submission.

His sexuality had always been one of his greatest curses, but he'd never in his life lost control of it. He controlled his hungers, his desires, not the other way around. Not until he met the sweet softness of an ethereal fairy.

He glanced over at her. She sat perfectly poised, her hands clasped in her lap atop the filmy, gauzy violet skirt of the summer dress she wore.

On her delicate feet she wore at least four-inch heels, which had given her legs a long, sleek look. He could push that skirt right up her thighs, he thought, and delve into the rich sweetness of her snug pussy.

She would be tight, even around his finger. Wet. Hot. She would take him. She was already primed for him.

What the hell was she doing to him?

The battle to restrain himself from touching her right now was almost lost. He could almost feel the hot, slick juices coating his fingers, easing his way inside her.

"You know this really isn't as bad as you're making it out to be," she finally spoke, her tone precise, stilted. "You act as though I've ripped your heart from your chest."

That was a fairly accurate summary. She was terrifying him with her courage and her refusal to allow him to protect her.

"This is something we need to discuss at the house," he gritted out between clenched teeth. "Just let it go for now, Mikayla."

Pulling over on the side of the interstate to fuck her silly wasn't an acceptable option. But if she kept pushing him, then it was going to be the only option. The need to touch her, to take her, to feel her safe and alive, wrapped around him, was making him desperate. Desperate to possess her, to feel her kiss, to feel the silk of her flesh beneath his hands.

What the hell was he allowing to happen to himself? Nik wondered as he took the Williamsport exit and quickly took the turn to Mikayla's house.

Within minutes he was pulling into the drive and shutting the vehicle off.

From the corner of his eye he watched as Mikayla picked up her purse and leather briefcase from the floor. He moved from the vehicle and strode to the passenger side to help her out. Once again, he noticed those damned high-heeled shoes that cupped her petite feet and lifted her a good four inches higher, placing her almost beneath his chin.

She had to be the tiniest woman he had ever had his hands on. Setting her carefully on the ground, he moved ahead of her as he drew the Glock from the holster at his back and held it carefully at his thigh.

Mikayla remained quiet, and it wasn't a contented quiet. He swore he could hear her fuming without her saying a word. Fuming and aroused. The arousal still glittered in her eyes; that kiss in the parking lot of the café had been enough to fire them both up.

Unlocking the door, Nik stepped into the house carefully and checked it thoroughly as Mikayla waited in the foyer. He needed the time to get a handle on his hunger as well as his emotions.

The harder he tried to stay away from her, the more the hunger for her built. The reckless courage she displayed, along with her impeccable manners and ladylike gentility, was a combination he couldn't seem to resist.

It was tearing him apart. She wanted more from him than he could give.

She wanted to be a part of her own protection, of her own life, and the thought of that terrified him. She terrified him in ways he couldn't explain. She had the power to destroy him.

And destruction wasn't a future he was looking forward to again.

He had hoped that the walk through the house would give him a chance to get his arousal, his need for her, under control. It wasn't helping, though. He swore his hands were almost shaking with the need to touch her; his cock was ready to burst from his pants.

Jaw clenched, he moved from the bedroom and back into the living room, where she waited.

She stood where he had left her by the closed door. Leaning against the wall, arms crossed beneath her breasts, she was clearly waiting with forced patience.

"Everything okay?" Her brows lifted as she tucked a heavy strand of hair behind her ear.

She had worn her hair loose today. It flowed down her back like heavy silk, tempting his hands with the remembered feel of it.

"It's clear," he told her as he moved toward her, knowing he was losing the battle to hold on to the restraint he needed. He was losing it all.

His hands were going to the snap and zipper of his leather pants as her eyes widened, darkening, her pink lips parting.

"Nik."

"Don't." He was in front of her, his fingers lying against her lips as he drew in a hard, deep breath. "For God's sake, Mikayla, leave me my sanity."

He didn't want to argue with her. He didn't want to feel her anger any longer. He wanted to feel her body against his, heated and warm. Her kiss beneath his lips. Her hands holding him to her.

"Why should I?" she whispered against his fingers. "You don't leave me any, Nik."

And he was going to make certain neither of them was going to have any sanity left.

As he lifted her against him, his lips descended on hers, the heated satin meeting his lips as her lips parted for him. Her hands held her to him by spearing into his hair as her arms wrapped around his neck.

She was like a flame in his arms. A flame he wanted to never see extinguished.

Lifting her from her feet, he placed her on the back of the chair that sat facing the room, its back to the foyer. It was an interesting arrangement and one that worked perfectly for his impatience.

Impatience. Hunger. God, what was she doing to him? She intoxicated him. She tore aside any civility he might have imagined he possessed and left him as primal as any male animal could be.

So primal that nothing mattered but having her, touching her, tasting her.

Pushing that skirt to her thighs as he tore his lips from hers and went to his knees in front of her.

Just a taste of her.

"I'm going to fall," she warned him, her voice trembling as he pushed her thighs apart and tore her panties from her.

Not that there was much to the panties. Damn her, that had to be the thinnest silk he'd ever touched.

"I got this," he promised.

He had this. With her legs over his shoulders, One hand behind her back and her hands in his hair. Yeah, he had this.

He slid his tongue through the sweetest, juiciest folds of flesh. The taste of her exploded against his tongue like ambrosia. Hell, it was better than vodka and went to his head faster.

He'd never gone to his knees for a woman in his life, but taking the time to actually get her to the bed, the couch, the counter, reclined, wasn't going to happen.

His need for her had risen too high.

She had managed to back him into a corner. She demanded participation. She demanded equality and there was nothing equal in their abilities to protect her.

There was this, though. Here he could lose himself in her. Here there was no danger to her, no fear of losing her.

There was just the feel and the taste of her.

He kissed the delicate knot of her clit. Drawing it between his lips and suckling it gently as her thighs tightened on his head and her cries filled his senses.

Pulling back, he licked, stroked, tasted each inch of the silken flesh as he felt her trembling in his hold. Flicking his tongue around her clit once again, he licked it, stroked it, drove her as high as possible before pulling back, easing her from the release he'd felt building in her body.

She was ready to come for him. He could feel it burning inside her, raging through her body. And he was so ready to taste the sweet excess of her pleasure flowing through her.

But not yet. Not yet. He wanted to feel her release while he was inside her, taking her. The sweet clench of her pussy around his dick was addictive. He swore he'd never felt pleasure so intensely as he did with Mikayla.

Rising to his feet, he gripped his cock as it pressed out from the opened front of his leather pants. Lifting her against him, he urged her legs around his hips, tucked the head of his cock against her, and pressed inside.

The pleasure was so intense he nearly lost his balance. Almost stumbling, he pressed her against the wall, his entire body on the edge of trembling as pure, sweet ecstasy began to consume the head of his cock.

Tender muscles parted slowly, gripping his flesh like a heated glove as it rippled over his cock with a million tiny pinpoints of pleasure.

"Sweet Mikayla," he groaned as he touched his forehead to hers, staring into the dark amethyst gaze and feeling as though she were sinking into his soul, as though he were sinking into hers. "Just hold me, baby. Just for a little while."

Her arms were tight around his neck, her legs wrapped around his hips as he forged deeper inside her, taking her by increments as he felt his chest tightening with the extremity of pure sensation racing through him.

"I'll hold you forever."

Forever. How did you tell a fairy that forever was an illusion? That they didn't have forever, they only had this moment. Forever was in memories only and God knew Nik didn't know if he could exist on just the memory of her.

He gripped the rounded globes of her rear, held her close, and rocked his hips against her, penetrating her deeper with every inward motion as he felt his head spinning with pleasure.

Damn, she was destroying him one touch at a time. Did she know what she did to him? Did she have any idea how she was locking herself inside his very spirit every time he touched her?

It didn't matter if she knew. That was what was happening. Each time his dick sank inside her, he could feel another part of his soul opening to her. Staring into her eyes, rocked by the physical as well as the emotional pleasure, Nik began to wonder if fate had finally caught up with him.

Live by the sword, die by the sword, he remembered hazily. He couldn't survive if that sword reached out to sever the life that glowed in Mikayla's beautiful eyes.

"Nik." She arched into him, her breathing rough, ragged, as little whimpers fell from her lips. "It's so good. Oh, God, it's so good."

She made him feel like fucking Superman when he knew he was no more than a man.

But the feeling was there, the knowledge that she saw him as more than what he was, saw him as no other woman ever had.

Trembling in his arms, she still held his gaze as her pussy gripped him tight and hot, so fucking sweet. The rippling caress of the clenching muscles was almost more than he could stand. His balls were tightening, the imminent release quaking through his muscles as he fought to hold back, just a little bit longer.

He needed to feel her just a few more minutes. Needed to be a part of her as much as possible. Just one more memory that he could hold on to.

As he rocked against her, his lips moved along her cheek, to her lips. He sipped at the swollen curves before his lips traveled along her jaw, to her neck, to the rounded curves of her breasts.

With one hand he cupped the side of her breast, lifted her nipple, and lowered his lips to it.

The strangled cry that left her lips had his cock pulsed, the release clawing at his balls as he licked over her nipple. God, he couldn't hold on much longer.

Sucking the tender tip into his mouth, he laved it with his tongue, tasted it with his senses, and gave himself over to the pure, sweet pleasure of her.

His hips moved faster, rocking harder into the tender flesh gripping him. Each desperate thrust inside the slick, hot interior drove him deeper into a morass of pure sensation.

She was holding him. Her arms and legs tightened around him as he drove into her, his cock thrusting into ever-tightening muscles as he felt her hurtling into her orgasm.

She cried out in ecstasy when it took her, his name a chant falling from her lips as he gripped her hips and raced headlong into the release waiting for him.

Silken fire consumed him. It tore up his spine, tightened around his balls, and drove the breath from his lungs as he felt his semen spurting deep and hard from the throbbing tip of his cock.

Unprotected.

A tortured growl tore from his chest at the realization that he'd forgotten to use a condom. That he was spilling himself inside the brilliant, vulnerable heat of her body.

But he couldn't pull back. He couldn't pull free of the grip encasing him. He drove deeper inside her instead, his seed spurting violently from his body, marking her, possessing her, as he groaned her name like a man demented from the pleasure.

And maybe he was. Maybe he'd lost his last grip on sanity, just as he'd lost his last thread of control, in her arms.

She lay against him, exhausted, little shudders of response still rippling over her body as Nik finally found the ability to think again.

And thinking wasn't something he wanted to do.

"I forgot," he whispered into her hair.

"Hmm?" He almost smiled at the curious little sound she made.

"I forgot the condom." He'd fucked up for both of them.

"It's okay," she sighed. "I'm protected."

He frowned at that, a strange spark of disappointment curling through him.

"You were a virgin," he stated. "Why are you protected?"

"Because I'm not stupid." Her lips brushed his shoulder in a lazy kiss. "I protect myself, Nik. I try not to leave it up to other people to take care of me. Now let me down; my legs are going numb." He heard the soft laughter in her voice as she pushed at his shoulders.

Lowering her gently to the floor, he watched as she wobbled a minute before sliding off the shoe she still wore and leaving it next to its mate on the floor.

"Wanna shower with me?"

She was decidedly disheveled. Her hair was mussed, her perfect pretty dress wrinkled and hanging off one shoulder where he'd pulled it down to get to her breast.

Her lips were swollen and reddened, her gaze slumberous and sexy as hell.

Fuck, she was reeling him in and she didn't even seem to be trying.

"Definitely; then we have to talk."

"About what? All the reasons why you don't want me with you through the day?" She smiled back at him softly. "Talk until you're blue in the face, Nik. If someone is going to keep shooting at me, then I'm going to be a part of figuring out why. It's my blood he's trying to spill here. At least give me the satisfaction of trying to figure out why."

She was going to be the fucking death of him. Even worse, he couldn't come up with an argument to counter that statement.

Not that he didn't try.

While they showered. While he watched Mikayla lotion her body, dry her hair, pull on lounging pants and a loose T-shirt. He fought with himself and every argument he could come up with, and still nothing could combat the statement she made.

"You have to follow my lead," he finally stated heavily as they sat across from each other in the living room, a pizza spread out on the coffee table in front of them. "I mean it, Mikayla. This isn't a game. It's not playtime and a killer isn't a joke. No matter what I tell you to do, you do it."

"I'm not stupid, Nik," she said somberly. "I know how to follow orders."

"I never imagined you were stupid," he breathed out roughly. "But no, Mikayla, if you don't like the orders, then you don't follow them. Don't pretend otherwise.

Whether you like the orders or not, you will follow them, do you understand that?"

He watched as her eyes narrowed suspiciously. "You won't give orders just to push me back and keep me out of the investigation?"

He only wished taking care of her would be that damned easy.

"I won't give you needless orders," he promised. "At the same time, if I think a situation is becoming or can become hazardous to you, then you will retreat to where you'll be safe. You'll agree to this or I'll have you locked in a room somewhere until it's over. It's that simple."

He was wondering if that wasn't the best thing to do now, rather than waiting. He was allowing her to endanger herself, and that wasn't sitting well with him.

"How dangerous has it been so far?" she asked him logically as she laid her pizza back in the box. "The danger has come from this investigation since you arrived, Nik. It's not going to stop, and what if they strike like they did the other night? While you're not around?"

"That's the only fucking reason I'm going along with this," he growled, anger surging inside him at the thought of the bastard who had shot through the store. "Because you don't know how to keep your nose out of this and let me handle it."

"Look, fighting over this isn't going to do either of us any good." Her shoulders hunched almost defensively. "Will you be around forever to protect me, Nik?"

He could only stare back at her. God knew he wanted to live his life protecting her, and he knew from experience that just wasn't possible. Shit happened. Love died. Innocence was lost and a man could lose his soul as a result.

"I didn't think so." There was no recrimination in

her tone, or in her look, only bleak acceptance. "If I sit back and let you protect me now, then I've lost valuable experience in protecting myself in the future. Don't take that away from me."

"And if you end up dead?" he asked her. "At least you'll have a life when this is over if you let me take care of it. Take shooting lessons after I leave. Take self-defense courses. . . ."

"They can't teach you in a class what I'll learn just watching you, being with you," she stated, determination glittering in her eyes. "And I won't have you in those classes, Nik. I'm not a child, and I'm not helpless. I won't be pushed into a corner with a pat on the head."

"You're too damned stubborn," he snapped.

"Fine, I'm too damned stubborn, but in this case you know I'm right; otherwise you would have already locked me in my room while you do whatever the hell it is that you do while you're away through the day. I want to be with you. I want to look these people in the eye, and if one of them is the one shooting at me then I want him to have to face me. I'm finished hiding."

She was finished hiding. "You mean you're finished being safe," he snapped back, an edge of anger slipping free in his voice.

"If that's how you want to see it, then fine. I'm tired of being safe," she countered. "But you can't look me in the eye and tell me I'm wrong, either."

No, he couldn't, and that just fucking pissed him off.

"What did you do today?" She lifted her drink and sipped at it as though the tension in the air weren't thick enough to strangle them both.

Rubbing at the back of his neck, he glared back at her.

"Come on, Nik." Fairy sweet and as innocent as a spring morning, she stared back at him reprovingly.

"Let's see how it works. If it doesn't work out, then we'll reassess the situation."

"In other words, you'll redefine your argument," he grunted.

A cheeky smile curled her lips. "That's an option. But I really don't want to die, so I'll always at least consider your side of the situation."

Well, at least he had that much. Shaking his head, he leaned back on the couch and stared at her as he attempted to find some damned way to counter her objections to staying safe.

It wasn't going to happen tonight.

"I questioned the new foreman, Jack Wallace," he told her. "He had some information I hadn't come across so far. I was going to check it out tomorrow. I haven't been able to confirm your friend Cronin's information, though."

Interest gleamed in her eyes. "And what information is that?"

He ran through it succinctly, finishing off with the information that he intended to question the disgruntled employee the next day.

"That should be safe enough for me to go with you." She smiled sweetly. "I know Jarvis Dalton. He's harmless."

"That's what neighbors said about the Son of Sam," Nik informed her as he tried to hold back his irritation.

The smile faded. Rising to her feet, she silently cleared the food away while he sat there and watched her, wondering what the hell he was supposed to do about her.

Any other woman he could walk away from. He would have put a bodyguard on her, done what he had to do, then left town just as silently as he had arrived.

But she wasn't any other woman.

She was his woman. Even if it was only for a little while. She was his.

"I'm going to bed." She stood at the kitchen doorway.

"I'll be in later." After she had gone to sleep. After he'd, he hoped, found a way to rebuild at least a few of the shields around his heart.

If she was going to deliberately place herself in danger, then he needed to prepare himself for the worst.

He wasn't prepared for the wounded look in those pretty eyes, though, before she turned and headed for the bedroom.

Moving to the guest bedroom, he collected his laptop and notes before returning to the couch to pull up as much information as possible on Jarvis Dalton.

He was going to have to find a killer faster than he'd ever imagined if he was going to keep his fairy safe and his soul from being destroyed.

Chapter 15

Something was different the next morning. Mikayla could sense it, feel it, as she stepped into the kitchen to find Nik preparing coffee and laying out a small platter of sweet breakfast rolls on the table.

"You didn't come to bed last night," she remarked as she watched him put the right amount of sugar in her cup, then creamer. Giving it a quick stir, he placed it on the small kitchen table before turning back for his own.

"I had work to do." His voice was as cool as a winter morning, his eyes as icy as the frozen North.

What had changed? she wondered. *How did he manage to go from desperate lover to cold, hard mercenary in the space of a few short hours?*

"What type of work?" She sat down at the table, watching carefully as he took his seat across from her and pulled a file from the other chair.

"Jarvis Dalton." The file was thick, heavy. "It seems he has problems holding down a job for long. He's worked for several construction firms between here and D.C., and if my information is correct he even worked for your father for a few months. He's a career misdemeanor criminal. Penny ante theft, shoplifting, burglary, terroristic threatening. The man has a rap sheet that proves his stupidity as well as his ineptitude."

"I didn't know he worked for Dad." There wasn't so much as a glimmer of warmth in Nik's eyes. "I rarely talk to him about business or his employees."

"How well do you know Jarvis?" Nik asked.

"He was a few classes higher than me in school." She sipped her coffee thoughtfully. "He's different. Really quiet. The last I heard, he was living in Nolan Village with his sister and niece since he served six months in jail for shoplifting. I heard he was fired from the construction job where Eddie was killed about three weeks before the murder, but I didn't hear why."

Nik nodded slowly. "I have the address to the apartment. We're going to see if we can't catch Jarvis before he leaves this morning." His gaze flicked over the lacy summer blouse she wore. "I'd change clothes if I were you. Jeans, T-shirt, and sneakers would work best."

She bit her lip nervously as she continued to watch him. There was something too cold, too hard, about him. As though the veneer of ice was only hiding a seething volcano. It made her nervous, made her wonder what that volcano actually consisted of.

Finishing the light breakfast, she moved from the table while Nik was going through the file he'd managed to somehow accumulate through the night. Retreating to her bedroom, she quickly changed clothes before braiding her hair, then lacing white sneakers on her feet.

She didn't often wear jeans and T-shirts. They weren't the best attire for the shop, and that was where she spent the majority of her time.

Returning to the kitchen, she found Nik waiting for her. The dishes were cleared away, the coffee cups rinsed, and he was waiting with an air of impatience as she walked into the room.

"Remember what I told you last night," he warned her. "If I say 'jump,' don't bother asking how high; just jump as high as possible. If you get in the way, this will be the last trip you make with me."

"I feel so welcome," she murmured as they left the house and Nik quickly set the alarm and locked the door behind them.

"Then I'm not using the proper tone of voice," he growled before catching her arm, swinging her around, and glaring down at her. "Get hurt and I promise you, you'll regret it for far more reasons than the obvious. Don't dare question an order I give, and if you even think of making a move I don't approve of beforehand I'll make a drive-by shooting look like a picnic in the park. Do you understand me?"

Her eyes narrowed. He was big, brawny, and giving her orders she didn't need.

"If you don't get out of my face you're going to find my knee in a very sensitive area of your body."

She had managed, as she spoke, to maneuver said knee until she was pressing against the heavy, thick bulge in his jeans.

His jaw tightened. So he was mad. Big deal. She was mad, too.

"This isn't playtime, Mikayla." He was almost snarling. He was cute, sexy as hell, but the fire burning beneath the ice in his eyes was almost mesmerizing.

"Then don't make it playtime, Nik." Her knee pressed more firmly into place. "Or we might be later leaving."

She didn't give him a chance to pull her away or to

retaliate with mockery, sarcasm, or male disgruntlement. Turning, she moved around the truck, leaned against it, and waited patiently for him to help her. The truck was a little too high.

"I don't feel like mountain climbing," she stated as he stared at her from the other side of the truck.

If his jaw became any tighter, it was going to crack.

He strode forcefully around the truck, opened the door, and lifted her into the passenger seat before closing the door and returning to the driver's side.

The drive to Jarvis Dalton and his sister's residence in Hagerstown was made quickly, if quietly, and filled with tension. Mikayla didn't even try to speak.

As the truck pulled into Nolan Village, Mikayla drew in a deep, slow breath. Parking, Nik left the truck, helped her out, then keeping carefully in front of her moved to the apartment where Jarvis and his sister lived.

Jarvis was the same beady-eyed little pervert Mikayla remembered. From the second she and Nik walked into the apartment, Jarvis's eyes didn't seem to want to leave the area of her breasts.

"So whatdya want?" Jarvis ran one hand over his greasy black hair as he ran the other hand over his bulky chest while staring at her breasts again.

Slimy dog.

Barefoot and clad only in sweatpants, Jarvis made his way along the stained carpet into a living room piled with pizza boxes, beer and soda cans, and a heavy layer of dust.

Nik pulled the black leather badge wallet from his back pocket and flashed the official identification. "FBI Agent Nik Steele. I have some questions for you."

"FBI." Jarvis blinked back at Nik before staring

blurrily back at Mikayla. "I didn't hear your boyfriend was FBI, Miki."

Nik gritted his teeth at Jarvis's nickname for Mikayla.

"My relationship with Mikayla isn't the issue," Nik informed the other man briskly. "You are."

"Me?" Jarvis scratched at his head, parting his oily hair. "Whatdya want from me?"

"I want to know where you were the night Eddie Foreman was killed," Nik stated as he stood in front of Mikayla just inside the door.

Mikayla watched as Jarvis turned, stalked across the room, then threw himself into a threadbare recliner, slouched back, and cupped himself between the thighs as he stared back at Mikayla.

"I was at a nightclub, man," he drawled with a yawn. "I was with friends, though I bet my friends were really there. Can Maddix Nelson say the same?"

"This isn't about Nelson; it's about you, Jarvis." Nik's voice became dark, dangerous, on the edge of deadly.

Like an animal sensing its death just around the corner, Jarvis sat up straighter, his small brown eyes staring back at Nik warily.

"How's it about me?" Jarvis swallowed, giving Nik his full attention now.

"Why were you at the job site the day Eddie was killed?" Nik stood tall, firm, his feet planted slightly apart, his arms relaxed at his sides, as he questioned Jarvis again.

The intimidation value was ratcheting. The way Nik stood, Jarvis could catch just the slightest glimpse of the Glock Nik carried at his side, beneath the light leather jacket he'd pulled on before he and Mikayla left the house.

"Look, I just needed my job back." Jarvis's gaze was trained on the area where the gun rested. "I wasn't there for no trouble and I didn't start none. I wanted my job back, we argued, and I left. No biggie."

"Why were you fired, Jarvis? What made Eddie let you go?" Nik's voice lowered, became darker.

"Because he was an ass," Jarvis breathed out roughly. "Some materials were missing and he had to blame someone. I didn't steal nothin'. I had no reason to. But he had to blame someone, so he fired me. If I'd stole 'em, then I wouldna come back like that."

"You were pissed at him then," Nik pressed.

"Hell, yeah, I was pissed." Jarvis's gaze flicked to Nik's face. "But I didn't kill him, man. I had no reason to kill him."

Fear was beginning to glitter in Jarvis's dark brown eyes and bead on his forehead as perspiration dampened it. He looked like a man facing a firing squad, and Mikayla couldn't blame him. If Nik had turned that look on her, then she would have probably gone running home to her parents.

"Did you see anything strange or unusual while you were there? Anything out of the ordinary?" Nik finally asked.

"Not that day." Jarvis shook his head. "That last week, though. I was there after work. Eddie was talkin' to some guy. Big guy. He looked familiar, but I couldn't get a good enough look. Dark curly hair, maybe a goatee, I'm not sure." He shook his head. "That's all I know, man. Ask Maddix Nelson if you need anything else. Everyone knows Mikayla don't lie for no one. If she says he shot Eddie, then you better fucking believe he shot Eddie." Jarvis nodded to Mikayla with a plea in his eyes, as though he were begging her to get Nik out of the apartment.

She almost rolled her eyes. Yeah, he was going to listen to her for sure. She didn't think so.

"Eddie, I find out you're lying to me and I'll be back," Nik promised, and there was no doubt in Mikayla's or Jarvis's mind that he meant every word of it.

Jarvis was still nodding as Nik turned, gripped Mikayla's arm, and they left the apartment.

"The bar won't be open until later," she told him as they walked back to the truck. "You intend to check out his alibi, right?"

She glanced up as Nik leveled a hard stare down at her.

"I'm not Jarvis," she informed him, irritation creeping into her voice. "That look doesn't scare me." Yet.

He grunted. As they crossed the yard he pointed the remote to the truck, and a second later it started with a smooth hum. It didn't take him long to walk around the truck, check it out, then open the door and lift her inside.

Mikayla buckled her seat belt and waited as he came around, got in the truck, and reversed out of the parking spot.

"Gina Foreman," he growled. "I called her this morning. She agreed to meet with us if we showed up before she went to work."

Mikayla's lips parted in surprise. "Gina? She wouldn't talk to me at all."

"I had some help," he informed her. "Her boss called her and gave her the go-ahead to talk to us."

"And you pulled this off how?" Mikayla asked sweetly, anger churning inside her now.

"My charming personality." His voice was dark and rough, the smile he shot her all teeth.

Yeah, she could see how that would work. No doubt his buddy Maddix Nelson had arranged that one.

Sometimes, Maddix made no sense whatsoever. For a killer, he was doing everything he could to cooperate with Nik, rather than trying to cover any information Nik might find.

Nik was snarly, growly, and uncommunicative as they drove to Gina Foreman's home. Mikayla was glad to see this part of the ride come to an end.

Gina met them at the door, her expression concerned, her eyes dark from weariness as she stood back and let them in.

"Please, sit down," she invited as they stepped into the worn, though spotless, living room. "I have to leave for work soon, so we'll need to hurry."

Mikayla perched on the edge of the couch as Nik sat back beside her and Gina took the chair across from them.

"I'm getting the house ready to sell," Gina sighed as she looked around. "It's lonely here alone."

"I'm sorry, Gina." Mikayla reached across the narrow coffee table to grip the other woman's hand as it lay in her lap.

"Thank you, Mikayla." Gina nodded as Mikayla pulled back. "And thank you and your family for the flowers as well. They were appreciated."

Nik refrained from staring at Mikayla in shock. This woman had refused to talk to Mikayla after the funeral, yet Mikayla acted as though she thought nothing of it? She had to be the most gracious person Nik had ever known. Even his own sisters would have been biting the other woman's head off at this moment.

"Mrs. Foreman, I just have a few questions," Nik promised as he leaned forward. "Was Eddie acting strangely before his death? Was anything unusual going on?"

Gina shook her head slowly, thoughtfully. "He was

often tense, yelled a lot. Though he was worse in the months before he was killed."

Nik bet he was. Eddie Foreman had been up to something; Nik could feel it. He just had to figure out what.

"Did he have enemies?" Nik probed.

Gina's lips curled mirthlessly. "Plenty. A lot of people didn't like him, Mr. Steele. He could be offensive."

"What about Jarvis Dalton?" Nik asked, wondering where the other man really tied into things. "Did he have problems with him?"

"Jarvis?" Surprise showed in the woman's face. "They were friends. Jarvis was one of the few friends Eddie had. As far as I know they had no problems."

To give Mikayla her due, her surprise didn't show on her face, though Nik felt her stiffen beside him.

"Did you know Eddie fired Jarvis a couple weeks before he was killed?"

"Fired Jarvis?" Gina stared at them in confusion. "Why would he do that?"

"According to Jarvis, Eddie accused him of stealing." Nik watched her face closely, her eyes. Gina Foreman acted like a woman who had no idea what he was talking about.

"I wouldn't put it past Jarvis to steal," she finally breathed out roughly. "But I didn't know about it."

"Was Eddie having money problems?" Nik probed further, trying to find an angle, any angle to push him in the right direction.

"Money was always tight; it still is." Gina shrugged. "But no more than usual."

"Did Eddie have an office?"

Gina nodded slowly. "He turned one of the bedrooms into an office."

"Could we check through it?" Nik asked her. "Maybe

there's something there that can help me figure out what happened."

"This way." Gina stood and led the way down a short hall to a bedroom. "Just please hurry; I have twenty minutes before I have to leave."

She turned and left the room and a second later Nik heard another door close, likely her bedroom. He turned to Mikayla.

"What do you think?"

She sighed deeply. "I think Jarvis was lying and Gina is telling the truth."

"What is Jarvis lying about?" Nik asked curiously as he moved to the cluttered desk.

"That I don't know," Mikayla answered softly. "I don't know him really well, but he kept shifting his eyes away from you, even though he was trying really hard not to." She winked back at Nik playfully. "He must watch too much *CSI.*"

"Ya think?" he grunted as he shot her an irritated look.

There was a hint of softening in the hardened attitude, though, as though the icy demeanor was deliberate. Sitting behind the wide desk Eddie had used, Nik began looking through the papers as Mikayla wandered through the room.

Eddie hadn't been big on neatness, she noticed. The office was piled with papers, magazines, a few books, and a lot of dust.

Moving back to the desk, she eased in behind the chair Nik was sitting in and laid her hand on his shoulder as he went through the papers, looking for what she wasn't certain. She doubted Nik even knew exactly what he was looking for.

His body tensed, though, as she braced herself with

her hand on his shoulder and leaned forward to watch what he was doing.

From beneath scraps of paper, business cards, time cards, and files of material lists Nik pulled a small index card free.

"Reed Holbrook" and three phone numbers. Home, cell, and office were listed.

"Reed Holbrook," she said softly. "That's the owner of Holbrook Construction out of D.C. If I'm not mistaken, Reed is a hometown boy, too. He and Maddix grew up in the same area of town."

"Do you know everyone in Hagerstown?" Nik frowned back at her.

Lifting her brows, she shot him a cheery smile. "Don't make the mistake of going to the store with me. It takes me hours to shop once I stop and say hello to everyone I know."

The look he gave her was one that baffled her for a few moments. As though he couldn't imagine having to deal with stopping to talk to anyone at a grocery store.

She was well known; she couldn't help it. She enjoyed people, and she enjoyed being social.

"It looks like we need to talk to Reed Holbrook then," Nik stated as he turned away from her and pocketed the card.

"Are we finished here then?" She stared around the room, wondering how they could possibly be certain they hadn't missed anything else.

"We're finished here." He nodded.

"We didn't go through everything," she pointed out.

"We'll have it all later." His voice was pitched low, carrying no farther than her, as she stared back at him in surprise, then excitement.

"We're sneaking back in tonight?" Mikayla could

feel the anticipation beginning to surge through her, even as he stared at her in something akin to horror.

The excitement glowing in her eyes, frankly, scared the shit out of him, Nik thought. The idea of breaking into the Foreman home and stealing papers had her all but rubbing her hands in glee.

He was creating a monster.

"No," he enunciated clearly. "We are not." Gripping her arm, he steered her to the doorway as a little pout shaped her lips.

"That's so not fair. You shouldn't do this stuff by yourself. You need a lookout." She was laughing at him. It was in her voice and in her eyes.

"Don't you have dresses to make?" he growled, wondering how the hell he was going to maintain the emotional distance he was trying to keep between them.

"Maybe this is more fun." Her brows arched as he opened the door and stepped into the short hall. "Besides, I called Bailey and Kira. They're going to meet me at the house this evening instead."

Gina Foreman was waiting for them in the living room, her gaze somber as they walked toward her.

"Did you find anything?" she asked.

"Nothing yet, Mrs. Foreman," Nik answered her.

She nodded slowly as her lips turned down with an edge of bitterness. "At least someone is trying to find out what happened. It gets hard working at the police station, wondering if the chief is lying, wondering what really happened." She shook her head as she shoved her hands into her jeans pockets. "It destroys your faith in people."

Nik watched as Mikayla crossed the room and wrapped her arms around the other woman as though a hug could fix anything. Everything.

"I'm sorry," he heard Mikayla whisper. "I'm so sorry, Gina."

The woman's arms went around her as Gina nodded, sniffed, and, strangely enough, seemed to find strength from that hug.

"You call me if you need me." Mikayla stepped back and gave the other woman's arms a brief rub. "I mean it. Come by the shop, whatever."

A timid, saddened smile pulled at Gina's lips. "Thank you, Mikayla." And she suddenly sounded as though somewhere, somehow, she had found hope.

Would he have felt differently after his daughter's death if he had felt such hope? Nik wondered as he and Mikayla left the house. Would he have made different choices, found other ways to strike back at the men who had killed his family?

If Mikayla had been a part of his life would she have shared her fairy charm with him and helped heal those shattered remnants of his soul?

It was possible, he admitted. She seemed to carry with her a capacity for love that astounded him. But even more, an ability to find softness within people that they didn't know existed.

Within Nik she had found emotions he'd never wanted to feel again. Emotions he feared could well and truly destroy him.

"I want to head to D.C., see if we can get in to see Holbrook," he stated as he took the I-70 interstate exit. "Foreman had to have been in close contact with him if he had his home number."

"Holbrook Construction doesn't have the reputation Nelson does, either," Mikayla mused as he glanced at her. "There's been several charges leveled against him for attempting to sabotage other jobs, bribing employees of other firms, and finding ways to force companies out of their contracts so he could pick them up. Nothing was proven, but the accusations are there."

"Then he could have been bribing Eddie Foreman," Nik guessed.

"Which gives Maddix Nelson a perfect motive for murder," she concluded sweetly.

Nik grimaced. He couldn't argue the point; if he didn't know Maddix, he would be at the top of Nik's suspect list. Hell, if he didn't know Maddix, then he would have been investigating everyone supposedly at that meeting.

When had he begun allowing personal associations to interfere with his job? Nik asked himself as he made a mental note to put Kira and Bailey on the chief of police and two council members. As Mikayla stated, Maddix had the perfect motive and his friends had some damned good reasons to lie for him. They were in bed with him where business was concerned, and that often made for damned fine alibis.

"If Maddix killed Eddie Foreman, then the best way to prove it is to follow the evidence trail," Nik told Mikayla. "It will lead us where we need to go. We'll talk to Holbrook, see what happens there; then I want to check Jarvis Dalton's alibi. He was lying; I'm just not sure what he was lying about."

"I don't think Jarvis is smart enough to pull off a murder, even one that simple." She shook her head before turning hurt eyes on Nik. "But Nik, I saw what happened. I saw Eddie die. I saw who killed him. Why can't you believe me?"

"It's not a matter of belief, Mikayla," he breathed out heavily. "It's a matter of evidence. But you're right: Maddix may have a hell of a motive. One thing is for damned sure. If he did it, I'll find out. And I'll make sure he pays for it."

"How could he not have done it?"

Nik shook his head. "Trust me, amazing things can be done with makeup and latex now. I know. Everyone knew you were coming to pick up Scotty. Anyone could have been waiting for an opportunity to kill Eddie and place the blame on Maddix." He held his hand up. "I'm not saying they did. I'm saying it's possible. I'll have Maddix checked out deeper, as well as his friends and neighbors. I won't overlook him. I'm following rumor and evidence at this point, which has to be done no matter who killed him."

"There were no attempts to kill me when no one believed me," she stated soberly. "The first attempt came after you began investigating me."

He nodded. He knew that, and it enraged him. The thought of one of those bullets actually striking her fragile body was enough to send terror racing through him. The world couldn't bear to lose Mikayla, he thought. Too many fairies had already been destroyed.

Hell, he couldn't keep thinking this way. She wasn't a fucking fairy; she was a tiny, independent, too-trusting woman, not some mythological creature of innocence.

That's what his head said; other parts of him, such as his heart, his soul, were saying something entirely different. Mikayla was the epitome of everything a woman shouldn't be in this day and age. Innocent, sweet, trusting, caring. Her very nature was going to end up getting her destroyed, and he was terrified there wasn't a damned thing he could do to stop it.

"Nik?" she interrupted his musings softly. "You didn't answer me. Why else would anyone try to kill me if it isn't Maddix?"

"Why would Maddix hire me if he didn't want the truth learned?" Nik countered. "I can't overlook that one, Mikayla. Maddix knows what I am, what I'm capable of, and he knows if he killed Eddie, then I'll find out. And he'll suffer."

It was a warning he'd already given the other man. It was a warning he would follow through with.

CHAPTER 16

Reed Holbrook refused to see them and Jarvis Dalton's alibi was a lie.

Mikayla watched Nik as the day progressed into evening and they returned to the house. Not long after Bailey and Kira arrived for measurements and the final decisions on the dresses they wanted. This only delayed Mikayla's chance to figure out his attitude.

He was stone cold. So cold, so icy, that the chill enveloped her and left her wishing she'd worn a jacket, despite the summer air.

From the moment he had made his statement concerning Maddix Nelson, Nik had only grown colder. She was walking in her home with Frosty the frickin' Snowman.

She stood in the foyer after his friends left, watching him silently as he watched her from the kitchen. She was tired. The drive to and from D.C. had been filled with enough tension to thicken the air and make breathing seem like work. Bailey and Kira's concerned curiosity while they were here hadn't helped matters in the least.

The colder Nik became, the more it hurt. He was

blocking her out, distancing himself from her. It felt like a breakup, except she'd given Nik far more than she had ever given another man. And it wasn't a breakup, because he was still here, tormenting her with his presence and the remembered feel of his hands against her flesh. The warmth of his body shielding her own.

What happened? The need to ask, to demand an explanation, was on the tip of her tongue, but the words wouldn't fall from her lips.

He was, at this moment, completely unapproachable.

"I'm going to shower."

She had to get away from him before she made a fool of herself. Before she demanded answers she had no right to demand. Before she cried, where she had no right to cry.

She had walked into this with her eyes wide open. He had warned her he couldn't love her, and she had promised herself she wouldn't love him.

As the hot water from the shower washed over her body, she reminded herself of that promise. She wasn't in love with him, she told herself. But if she wasn't in love, then why the hell did it hurt so bad? Why did her chest feel tight, her body heavy from the ache inside?

She leaned her head against the wall of the shower and fought back the tears. Two nights he'd spent apart from her, and she missed him to the point that sleep had been almost impossible the night before. She could feel another such night coming on.

She'd never imagined it could be so easy to get used to a man sleeping in the bed with her. She'd slept alone all her life. But sleeping with Nik had seemed as natural as breathing. And she missed him.

Sniffing back the tears that would have fallen, Mikayla finished her shower, dried her body and her hair before dressing in summer cotton lounging pants and a loose, sleeveless T-shirt.

Moving into the kitchen, she paused at the doorway, watching as Nik pulled out the casserole she'd put in the oven that morning and set the oven's timer back on.

It was still warm; the cheese, hamburger, and macaroni casserole scented the air and reminded Mikayla that they had eaten very little that day.

Within minutes they were sitting apart from each other, still silent, as they ate.

The tension was only growing between them. It wasn't an angry tension, but one thick enough to cut with a knife. Secrets shrouded it; silence intensified it.

It was a silence that wore on Mikayla's nerves and left her struggling to hold back the resentment she could feel growing inside her.

"What do we do next?" she finally asked as he sat back from his meal and appeared ready to leave the table.

His gaze flicked back to her, and what she saw in those few seconds rocked her to her soul.

The ice was there, but beneath it lurked a bleak sorrow, a dark agony that had her chest clenching in pain for him. As though the silent battle between them was touching shadows inside him that he had no desire to revisit.

The deaths of his wife and child? Mikayla wondered.

Had something renewed that nightmare inside him and left him remembering the pain he must have felt at their loss?

"Next we see about revisiting Jarvis and politely inquiring as to why his alibi didn't hold up. Then I'll need to see why Reed Holbrook preferred not to speak with us." There was a flash of predatory determination in Nik's gaze that sent a shiver up her spine. And she hadn't missed the adjustment from "we" to "I." He had no intention of taking her with him when he discussed this with Reed.

Mikayla could only shake her head. "I understand your reason for following the trail as you are, but you're not mentioning what part Maddix may have played in this."

"For the sake of argument we'll say Maddix did it." Nik leaned forward as he stared back at her implacably. "Right now, he's getting away with it. His alibi is solid. If you want to break that alibi, you follow the trail. It's that simple."

"Then there's a chance he killed Eddie because Eddie was working with Reed Holbrook?"

"And the fact that Reed is refusing point-blank to speak to us tells me there's a chance he has something to hide. It's beginning to appear as though that something could be the fact that he was paying Eddie Foreman to sabotage the job."

Mikayla stared back at Nik thoughtfully. "I think I remember something in the paper last year. There were several delays on the job because the foundation of the building had to be redone when the building inspector found a crack in the cement. I heard Maddix fired the entire cement crew when that happened."

Nik nodded. "We follow the trail and see where it goes."

"But you still don't think it's going to go back to Maddix," she guessed.

Nik shot her an irritated look before propping his arms on the table and staring back at her. "Mikayla, I believe you think you saw Maddix. I truly do. But Maddix Nelson is not a stupid man. He knew when he hired me I'd get to the bottom of this. He laid down a hell of a lot of money to ensure that I did. So no, I don't think he did it."

"Maybe he's smarter than you're giving him credit for," she suggested, trying to ignore the twinge of hurt the explanation sent rushing through her. "Maybe he knew what you'd do and he's planned for it."

Nik shrugged at that. "That's always possible. Not likely, but possible." The smile that crossed his lips had nothing to do with amusement and much to do with potential lethal intent.

It still left Mikayla confused. Personally, she thought questioning Maddix until he broke was a good idea. It worked on *CSI*, right? Though she knew it wouldn't work on Maddix, at least she would gain a measure of satisfaction.

"I need to take care of some things." Nik rose from his chair, pushed it in carefully, and stared back at her. "I'll be in the guest room working."

In other words, he intended to use work as an excuse not to sleep with her.

Mikayla watched as he left the room before rising and cleaning the dishes silently. She felt off balance now, uncertain what to do. She wanted to touch him, to hold him, to ease the bleak pain from the far corners of his gaze, but she had no idea how to do it. That left her alone, and she'd never realized how lonely alone could be until now.

Nik was on the verge of throwing something. It had been almost a decade since he'd put his fist through a wall, but the urge to do so now crawled through his system like a potent disease.

Distancing himself from Mikayla was killing him and hurting her. But that distance was all that was left to save his soul when this was over. Walking away from her would be impossible otherwise. Staying with her would only endanger her, and he couldn't face that, either.

He paced the small bedroom, his gaze rarely falling on the open laptop and the files he had pulled up earlier, before showering. Information on Reed Holbrook, Jarvis Dalton, Eddie Foreman, and Maddix Nelson were waiting for Nik's perusal.

He already suspected Eddie Foreman had been either stealing materials and substituting inferior grade or deliberately sabotaging the job for Reed Holbrook. Either way, as Maddix's current foreman had stated, it was a recipe guaranteed to fuel Maddix's temper but not enough to cause him to kill.

As he paced to the window and the heavy shades that blocked the view of the backyard, the cell phone at his hip vibrated.

Nik grabbed it like a lifeline, desperate to find something, anything, to keep him from crawling over Mikayla like a wild animal in need.

"Hey there, sexy," Kira drawled.

Nik heard her husband in the background, former Navy SEAL Ian Richards, laughingly protesting.

"What did they find?" Nik wasn't interested in their byplay; he was interested in Ian and John's secretive visit to the Foreman home. Frankly, tonight Nik couldn't handle it. It reminded him too damned much of what he didn't have with Mikayla.

Kira and Bailey's earlier visit had been strained. They had sensed the tension between him and Mikayla and he knew it. Questions were coming. They were questions he didn't want to ask.

"Interesting stuff," Kira stated. "Ian and John just got back from the Foreman home. Mixed in the mess of a filing system the man had was the blueprint of the job site he was killed on. There were some distinct X's marked on it. Ian said they were particular weak spots. Places where the foundation and skeleton would have to be strengthened by using specific materials. One of those locations was of the foundation that last year Nelson had to completely replace when the inspector found a crack forming in the cement. There were also vague notes that could have been referencing where lesser-grade materials were used in other areas. Ian and John's assessment is that he was deliberately sabotaging the building, and I agree with them."

Nik raked his fingers through his hair with a tight grimace. Evidence was mounting against Maddix, which meant Nik was going to be making another trip to talk to him. Unfortunately, this time Nik had a feeling he'd be taking Mikayla with him.

Hardheaded damned stubborn woman, he thought, she was going to be the death of him.

"Ian did a little research into Maddix," Kira continued. "He has a temper, and he and Eddie Foreman had gone head-to-head before, but Eddie was pissing a lot of people off before he died."

"He's pissing me off now," Nik growled.

"Maddix's alibi is solid from the reports you sent me and the follow-up Ian did today," Kira informed him. "Robert Cronin checked out as well, but the information he gave hasn't yet been confirmed by any of our contacts, though it is early for information there to be coming in. If Maddix was involved with the underground gambling world, then we'll know soon. Eddie Foreman was involved, though, even our contacts knew him, and they didn't like him any more than anyone else did. He owed everyone money."

"Mikayla's certain it was Maddix; that means we're looking for someone attempting to frame him for whatever reason. Let's go deeper into Eddie and Maddix's past, see what we can find out," Nik suggested.

"Tehya's already suggested that and is moving on it," Kira assured him.

"Tell her to put a rush on it," he sighed. "The next time the bastard shoots at Mikayla, it just might be fatal."

"She's an interesting young woman," Kira said softly. "I'm a damned good judge of character. Not once this evening did she even attempt to discuss you or whatever problems the two of you are having. She did a good job of hiding it as well, even as tired as she was. You have a treasure there, my friend."

"Don't start, Kira," Nik breathed out roughly.

"And it looked to me like you're becoming pretty involved." Her voice softened. "Are you going to break her heart, Nik?"

Was he? As far as he was concerned, there was no way around it, unless she wasn't in love with him. And he knew better. She wasn't clingy, whiny, or possessive, so far, but she was in love.

"If you have no more information, Kira, then I have to go," he told her without answering her question. "Let me know if Ian learns anything more."

"I'll be sure to, Nik." Her voice held that gentle, sympathetic tone that she reserved for animals and morons. He could only imagine which one she was thinking of.

Disconnecting, he laid his cell phone on the bedside table before rubbing at the back of his neck as he fought the irritation, the arousal that only grew inside him.

He could almost feel Mikayla's soft skin against his hands, his fingers flexing at the memory of the warmth of her, the snug heat of her pussy enveloping his dick.

He was as hard as iron. He had been as hard as iron

all day. His damned dick was going to end up getting him into the type of trouble that he didn't want to deal with. The type that would end up with him back in Mikayla's bed, and in a hell of a lot of trouble for both of them.

He paced the bedroom like a caged tiger, that hunger eating at him from the inside out as he fought the need to go to her, to ease the hurt and the confusion from her pretty eyes.

She was softening him; he could feel it, and he hated it. Softening meant looking at himself, seeing the shadows he knew existed inside his own soul. Remembering when he didn't want to remember.

"Nik?" A soft knock, Mikayla's low voice, and his senses seemed to go into overdrive.

The door opened slowly.

She stood there, long blond hair flowing around her, while amethyst eyes stared back at him with innocent hunger. She had changed from the lounging pants to a robe, and if he wasn't sorely mistaken, she was naked beneath it.

"Are you coming to bed?" Soft as a whisper, like fairy wings, her need reached out to stroke against his senses. "I miss you against me, Nik."

"Mikayla," he sighed her name. He should tell her no, he should walk away now.

So why wasn't he?

"Is it over so soon?" she asked him then, a hint of painful knowledge filling her gaze. "I didn't expect that."

"You don't want me tonight, Mikayla." He shook his head wearily.

"Why don't I?" she asked softly. "I've wanted you since the moment I saw you. Why would that change?"

The bleak despair she had sensed earlier shadowed his gaze once more.

"So fucking innocent." He felt like an animal, the need for her burning through his veins. "You have no idea the things I could ask for."

Nik was dying, fighting to hold back. She had no idea how hard holding back truly was.

A spark of anger should have lit her eyes rather than that spark of need that went beyond hunger or lust. That glimmer of something deep, something that pierced his soul and left him aching to lose himself in her silken embrace.

She stared back at him as she drew her lower lip between her teeth and gazed at him with that sweet, burning hunger. Then she did something he fully didn't expect. With incredible grace, her fingers loosened the belt to her robe as she shrugged, the silken violet material sliding over her shoulders, her arms, to pool on the floor at her feet.

Creamy pink-tipped breasts rose and feel quickly, the hardened nipples tempting his tongue as his fingers curled with the need to touch her.

He felt like an animal ready to pounce, the hunger raging through him with a desperation he wouldn't have believed possible. She was his. The innocence glittering in her eyes, the gentle warmth, the need, it was his. He was her first lover. He was her only lover. The need to mark her as his forever raged through with a force nearly impossible to control. To mark her body, her heart, her soul. To ensure she was always his.

He moved without thought. Thought was a thing of the past. Striding across the floor, Nik lifted his woman in his arms and strode down the hall to the bedroom and the bed where he had first claimed her. The bed where he had found the greatest pleasure imaginable.

His lips stole hers in a kiss that fired his blood the

second he picked her up. As she twined her arms around his neck, a low, delicate moan sent his senses crashing into pure need.

Lust, he forcibly reminded himself. It was lust. It wasn't need.

But it was need. A need that defied description. The hunger that tore through him made no sense, yet it felt as natural as breathing. It felt as needed as the air around him.

She was a flame burning in his arms, and he was helpless to do anything but burn with her.

Shouldering her door open, Nik carried her through it before kicking it closed behind them. He laid her on the bed, their lips parting as Nik fought to draw in enough air to sustain him. Enough to, he hoped, dilute the surging arousal. Nothing could dilute what he was feeling now. There was no force of earth or of nature that could possibly turn down the fire raging through him.

Stretching above her, Nik held his weight on his knees and elbows as he stretched her arms above her head and held them in place. The feel of her silken hands touching him frayed his control. At the moment, he needed his control.

His lips wandered down her neck, nipped and caressed with his lips as she arched beneath him with a decidedly feminine moan. Hard-tipped breasts brushed his chest, searing his flesh and making his mouth water with the need to taste, to stroke.

Moving lower, he licked over the rounded tops, ignored her strident little demands for more, and simply relished the taste and feel of her.

"Nik, you're killing me with the teasing," she whispered, her voice thick with arousal. "Please."

"Please what?" He could barely breathe. The hunger

raging through him tightened his chest and sent a fiery ache of longing surging through his senses.

"So pretty," he crooned, holding her wrists in one hand as he plumped a breast. His thumb raked over the hardened little tip; he felt her flinch from the pleasure and had to grit his teeth to keep from fucking her now.

"You feel so good," she whispered as her head ground against the pillow. "You make me lose my mind with the pleasure, Nik."

She was killing him. God, he needed to gag her if he was going to hold on to his control, because her innocent murmurs had his balls drawn tight, his cock throbbing with imminent release.

Brushing his lips over her nipple, Nik parted them to pull the succulent berry into his mouth and release the soft taste of female flesh. His female's flesh.

A shudder raced through her, vibrated against him, and had sweat popping out on his brow as her fingers bit into the wrist holding hers.

"Oh, yes," she moaned. "Oh, Nik." Her thighs tightened on his, her hips lifting to rub the mound of her pussy against his upper leg. "That's so good. Your mouth is so hot."

Damn her. How the hell was he supposed to keep his fucking wits with her pleasure-taking voice?

Raking his tongue over the nipple, he sucked at it ravenously, feeling her pleasure as she trembled and shuddered in his arms. Adrenaline was pumping through the veins, the proof of his effect on her tightening his muscles, thickening his dick, until he felt wracked by the hunger surging through his system.

His tongue lashed at the tender tip, drawing a cry from her lips as she arched tighter against him. Never had a woman given him her response so easily, so unconditionally.

"I want to touch you, too, Nik," she cried out as she tugged against his hold on her wrists. "I want to feel you. I want to taste you." Her thigh pressed against his cock. "Oh, God. Like you let me before. I want you in my mouth, too."

Fuck. Fuck.

He was going to come against her leg if she kept this shit up.

The memory of his cock in her mouth destroyed him. Releasing her breast, he jerked to his knees, pulled her up, and with one hand at the back of her head, the other gripping his dick, he pressed the flared crest against her cherry, kiss-reddened lips.

His neck arched back until he wondered if it would snap. Ecstasy tore through his veins as she sucked the throbbing head inside the liquid heat of her mouth. Her tongue lashed at it, as his had at her nipples. A second later, she rolled her tongue over it with lazy pleasure, the glitter of amethyst eyes peeking beneath her lashes as she rubbed against the underside of the crown.

Ah, hell. She was killing him.

She sucked him to the back of her mouth, licked and tasted him until he swore he was going to lose his mind to the pleasure. He couldn't believe the temptress who held him in her grip now.

Reaching down, he palmed a full, rounded breast in one hand as he held the back of her head with the other. His cock thrust in and out of her mouth, fucking her in slow, agonizing movements as he felt the come boiling in his balls.

Mikayla was shaking with the pleasure and the need rushing through her. She had never imagined she could be so brave, that she could take how he had touched her and turn it around to use it on him. To see that she was bringing him pleasure as he did to her.

She was on the verge of climax. She could feel her juices dampening her thighs, her clit throbbing in need. She wanted him as she had never wanted anything in her life.

Sucking the head of his cock as deep as possible, she shuddered again as he pulled back, leaving only the thick, heavy crest just inside her lips. She licked it, laved it, feeling his hand lower to his balls as his fingers tightened around them to hold back his release.

A release she wanted.

Using the tip of her tongue, she outlined the heavy width with her tongue as her nails raked along his inner thighs and she felt his body jerk a second before a heavy moan rumbled in his chest.

"Damn you," he growled. "Your mouth is so fucking hot, Mikayla. Sweet baby. Suck it harder, sweetheart."

She sucked deeper, harder, feeling the head of his cock throb as she tasted the essence of his release against her tongue. It was just a taste, so much less than what she needed.

As she licked, laved, and sucked at the hard flesh, Mikayla felt the calloused caress of his palm as it moved down her back, then over the rounded curve of her rear.

Sensuality washed through her once again, clenching her womb as she felt his fingers move into the narrow crease of her rear.

Those diabolical fingers pressed and played around the forbidden entrance there before dipping lower, sinking into the thick layer of juices that soaked her pussy before traveling back.

Mikayla felt as though she were burning alive. Feeling as though flames were licking at her flesh as he lubricated her rear entrance with the slick juices easing from her vagina.

"So sweet and tight," he growled as she fought to breathe through the caress. "I'll have you here one day, Mikayla. Right here." His finger sank slowly inside. "Until you're screaming from the pleasure, and begging for more."

Her nails bit into his thighs as she fought to hold on, to keep her balance. She wanted to steal his control, to steal that incredible restraint he used against her, but he was stealing hers instead.

Not that she had many defenses against his touch, but this one, this touch, destroyed her. It was forbidden, wickedly arousing, and completely dominant.

First one finger, then a second stretched her, burned her with a bite of pleasure/pain as a trembling moan slipped past her lips.

With each movement of her mouth on his cock, his fingers moved inside her ass, penetrating deep, scissoring and stretching her flesh as she felt the biting sensations racing to her clit.

"Mikayla, darling, playing like this is going to get you in trouble," he growled as her tongue rolled against the sensitive spot just beneath the head.

In retaliation Nik's fingers sank inside her again, thrust slow and easy, in careful rhythm with the cock thrusting beneath her lips.

She was dying. She was going to come and he wasn't touching her clit or her pussy. She was going to explode into fragments and there was nothing she could do to stop it.

"Damn it, Mikayla, I'm going to come," he snarled above her as his hand sank in her hair, his fingers gripping the strands as he began to thrust his cock in and out of her mouth with tighter, sharper strokes.

His cock seemed to harden between her lips, to thicken. His fingers were moving inside her, stroking nerve endings that still weren't accustomed to his touch.

Shaking, Mikayla could feel the need for release clamoring through her body even as she felt Nik stiffening. His thighs hardened, his cock throbbed, thickened, as he tried to pull her head back.

She wanted the taste of him. He wasn't stealing this from her, not now. Moaning in denial as she sucked deeper, harder, he rewarded her with a tortured groan and the hard, heated jets of his release spilling to her mouth.

The taste of him infused her senses, fired her needs, and flared through her body with sharp, electrified sensations of agonizing hunger.

She had never wanted, never needed, like she did now. The raging hunger tearing through her was nearly more than she could bear, definitely more than she could fight.

"Damn you, Mikayla." His voice was tortured as he pulled from her, his fingers slipping from her rear. "What the hell do you do to me?"

She had no idea what she did to him, but as he moved she knew he would destroy her.

"Stay there," he commanded, his voice harsh as he moved behind her, his lips pressing to her shoulder as he pressed her palms to the bed. "Right here, baby. Let me show you how I play."

How he played? She had no idea if she could survive it.

"You have the softest skin." His lips brushed down her spine. "So soft, and so sweet." He licked at the flesh just above one side of her rounded buttocks as she shivered in pleasure.

"And so wet." His fingers eased between her thighs.

"I can't wait to taste you again, Mikayla. I could live on the sweetness of your pussy."

She shuddered. She was going to come just from listening to him talk to her.

His lips roamed over the rounded curves of her rear as she fought to find the strength to hold herself up as he kissed and caressed from her rear to her thighs.

His tongue licked at the excess dampness that had spread to her thighs, a rumbling groan vibrating against her skin as she trembled at each lick.

"Sweet as fucking sugar," he murmured as she felt him move, turning.

A second later he was on his back, his head beneath her, his tongue swiping through the violently sensitive slit of her pussy.

Mikayla jerked, flinched, a cry tearing from her throat as his tongue surged inside her as it reached the sensitive entrance and licked at the snug, tender intimate tissue.

His fingers clenched at her hips, holding her in place as he fucked inside her with his tongue, laved around her clit, then returned to sink inside her once again.

She could never anticipate where each lick would go, which of her senses he would attempt to destroy with each caress. Fingers of thrilling, adrenaline-laced sensation began to race over her flesh. Perspiration gathered on her skin, rolled down her sides as his tongue forged through the intimate folds, fucked inside the clenching depths of her pussy, then moved to suck at the swollen bud of her clit as the strength drained slowly from her arms.

Tension mounted inside her, tightened her muscles, locked them in place. As his tongue pushed inside her again, licked, and stroked, the world began to explode around her in a series of vibrant, mind-destroying bursts that dragged strangled screams from her throat.

Gasping through each explosion, Mikayla needed just a second to catch her breath, to drag her senses from the ether, when she felt the hard, heavy, stretching thrust that began to stretch and burn the tender muscles of her pussy.

Back arching, her arms shaking as she fought to hold herself in place, Mikayla could only close her eyes and give herself to Nik.

His hands gripped her hips as the second fierce thrust buried him to the hilt, the head of his cock pressing deep and high inside her.

Delicate muscles still shuddered from her orgasm, caressing and milking the thick flesh as Mikayla felt uncontrollable tremors as they began to race through her.

Each breath became a struggle as whimpering cries began to tear from her. Nik gave her no time to accustom herself to the thick, hard flesh penetrating and possessing her.

Each deep, hard thrust tore a cry from her lips as she struggled to breathe. Her body sensitized. Her arms collapsed, spilling her upper body to the mattress as Nik came over her, his hips pumping against her, his lips falling to her.

"Sweet Mikayla," he growled as his teeth raked her neck and his hips slammed his cock inside her.

His fingers laced with hers as a scream tore from her throat.

"Lift your ass for me, baby," he groaned as her hips fell to the bed, her knees sliding from beneath her as her strength gave out. "Come on, Mikayla; it will be so much better."

Struggling, Mikayla lifted her hips, felt his teeth

nip at her neck, his cock pressing in, filling her, throbbing inside her.

Once he was buried, the thrusts became strokes, a deep, internal caress that pressed and probed and raked against nerve endings so sensitive Mikayla began to gasp for her breath and shake in reaction as she felt her orgasm building.

"I love fucking you," he groaned as his hips shifted and another strike of sensation raced to her clit. "The way your pussy milks my cock, flutters so sweetly against it, and then clenches like a little fist around it." His hips ground, rotated, and the world exploded.

Mikayla screamed as the orgasm tore through her, raced over her body, burned across her nerve endings, and sent fire raging through her clit, straight to her womb.

Behind her, Nik's teeth clenched at her shoulder as she felt his release begin spurting inside her, sending flares of minor quakes racing through her.

It was exquisite, soul destroying, and, Mikayla knew, ruining her for any man who could ever come after him.

Pleasure such as this could only come to a woman once in a lifetime. A combination of heart, body, and soul mingling in an ecstasy that sealed her heart forever.

As each tremor began to ease and a flush of sated contentment washed over Mikayla, an edge of shadowed future pain twisted deep inside her.

She had warned herself not to love him. She had promised herself she wouldn't love him.

But Mikayla knew, she loved him.

Heart, body, and soul. Star-crossed and without a future.

She was in love with Nik Steele.

CHAPTER 17

The night before faded to the next morning as they dressed and headed out.

Nik's tone was crisp, clear, as he outlined the day, beginning with Jarvis Dalton. The lover of the night before was nowhere in sight.

He was determined to keep that distance between them, and Mikayla wasn't going to fight it. She wouldn't go to him again; she wouldn't ask him back to her bed. She wouldn't refuse him if he came to her.

A woman had to have some pride, Mikayla told herself as they pulled into the parking spot in front of the apartment Jarvis Dalton shared with his sister.

"Stay behind me," Nik warned Mikayla as they exited the vehicle. "If you see a weapon, get your ass as close to the ground as possible while running to the truck. When you're safely inside, call nine-one-one."

She nodded. He'd given her the same directions that morning, as though she hadn't learned anything from him the day before.

Moving behind him to the front door, she stayed carefully back while he knocked.

Jarvis, the poor guy, opened the door as though there were no risk to Nik's return.

Mikayla had to bite her lip on a surprised cry as Nik's hand immediately wrapped around the other man's throat and quickly pushed him back into the apartment.

A strangled cry fell from Jarvis's lips as his eyes bulged, his body thrashing helplessly as Nik pinned him high enough against the wall that he struggled to keep his toes on the ground.

Mikayla closed the door quietly, her gaze moving around the room as she searched for weapons or any surprises that could be coming from any of the other rooms.

"Jarvis, Jarvis, Jarvis," Nik sighed. "Did I mention when I was here last that I hate liars? That I hate them so much that I just want to put a bullet through their brains?"

A terrified squeak left Jarvis's lips as he stared back at Nik in abject fear. Mikayla almost felt sorry for Jarvis.

"Why did you lie to me, Jarvis? You weren't at the bar you said you were at. Tell me how you made yourself look like Maddix when you killed Eddie."

Nik didn't truly believe Jarvis had killed Maddix, Mikayla knew. He simply wanted answers. He wanted to find the trail that led from Jarvis to Maddix.

Rabid fear leached into Jarvis's gaze. "Oh, God, man, no. You don't understand," he wheezed.

"I sure don't," Nik agreed. "So why not make me understand why you killed Eddie?"

"Fuck no, you don't understand. I didn't kill nobody."

"So make me understand," Nik suggested once more, his tone patient, deadly.

Jarvis shook almost violently. "Man, I was at a bar.

I swear I was. I was at Deer Park. I just want no one to know."

Silence reigned as Nik glanced back at Mikayla, obviously unaware of the bar. She didn't doubt he hadn't checked out that particular location.

"It's a gay bar," she informed him with a quirk of a smile. Surprise narrowed Nik's gaze as Jarvis tried to smile nervously back at her. "I've seen you there sometimes."

Nik's gaze swung back to her, that narrowed gaze slicing into hers.

"It's a nice bar." She shrugged. "They have good music and the guys there like to dance rather than anything further. At least with me." She arched her brows in amusement.

"You're lying to me, Jarvis." Nik turned back to him, his voice hardening.

"No, man, I swear," Jarvis cried out, the fear in his voice returning. "I'm not lying. No one on the job knew I was gay until Eddie found out. My boyfriend, he works for the government. His boss doesn't know he's gay. Eddie threatened to tell. I wasn't going to say nothin' about what I knew."

"Is that why Eddie fired you?" Nik questioned, his voice smooth, dark.

Jarvis tried to shake his head, but the fingers wrapped around his neck held him in place. "No. Eddie was having problems. . . ." He tried to swallow. "The money kind. He wanted me to use some inferior materials. Cut costs. He had some kind of racket going, but I don't know what."

Now this was interesting. Mikayla watched curiously, as fear began to loosen Jarvis's tongue.

"Stop lying to me, Jarvis," Nik ordered, his tone becoming more threatening. "You're pulling this story out of your ass. Otherwise you would have spilled it last time we spoke."

"I swear, it's not a lie. I wanted to find out who it was. I wanted time to work on it myself. I could make a buck or two." He tried to smile again. That curve wobbled in fear. "I wouldn't do it for him. For Eddie, that is. I told him I would at first; then I backed out. He was real pissed, maybe even scared. He said I was fucking him over. He fired me, then told me if I ever let anyone know what he wanted me to do, then he would tell them I was gay."

"You know I'm going to check this out, Jarvis," Nik warned him. "Just as I'm going to check your boyfriend out. What's his name?"

"Come on, man," Jarvis whined. "Don't do this to me. I want him to move me to D.C. with him. Cause him trouble and he never will."

"His name, Jarvis." Nik's fingers tightened once again around Jarvis's throat.

A tear slipped down Jarvis's cheek as misery filled his eyes. "Darnell." He gave the name Nik wanted. "Darnell Waters."

Mikayla's lips tightened at the name Jarvis gave. She hated to tell him that Darnell Waters would never move him to D.C. with him. Darnell Waters had a wife, a family, and a possible political career. He wouldn't risk the future being carefully mapped out for him by his senatorial father-in-law.

"Who else saw you there?" Nik growled. "Give me names or I'm going to make sure you hurt before I leave."

Jarvis's lips trembled, but he did as Nik ordered. Naming the bartender as well as several regulars whom Mikayla knew as well.

"Very good, Jarvis." Nik smiled, the hard, cold curve

chilling in the danger it represented as he released the other man and stepped back. "I will be checking this latest story out, you understand."

With his fingers massaging his throat, Jarvis nodded jerkily.

"Do you know if Eddie found anyone else to do the work he wanted you to do?" Nik asked as he moved to the door.

"I don't know." Jarvis's voice wavered. "But I know he was still scared that last day, when we argued. I knew Eddie, and I know there was fear in his eyes that day."

Nik didn't turn; he didn't ask more questions. Opening the door, he escorted Mikayla from the house and back to the truck.

"Do you believe him?" Mikayla asked as Nik backed out of the parking space and turned to leave.

"I think I do," Nik sighed. "And that just fucking pisses me off. Because he was damned good suspect material."

Mikayla's lips thinned. "He looks nothing like Maddix."

Nik nodded. "And he leads us right back to Maddix. I have no doubt in my mind Maddix wouldn't kill Eddie if he caught him attempting to sabotage that project."

Mikayla stared at Nik silently, nearly holding her breath.

"Now what?" she asked, wondering if he would even mention Maddix Nelson.

"Now?" Nik shot her a resigned look before turning the truck to the interstate. "We see if we can't catch Holbrook again; then we check out this newest tale of Mr. Dalton's."

But Reed Holbrook, this time, couldn't be contacted. According to his secretary, he was unavailable and she had no idea when he would be in the office.

It was more than obvious they were being avoided, and Mikayla could feel Nik's ire as he glared at Reed Holbrook's closed office doors.

Leaning his palms flat on the desk, Nik lowered his upper body until his face was only inches from the obviously wary secretary.

"Inform Mr. Holbrook he has twenty-four hours to contact me," Nik told her quietly. "After that, I know how to get nasty."

Rising, he lifted a pen from the desk, scribbled his name and cell-phone number on the pad on it, and turned away.

With his hand riding on Mikayla's lower back, he led her from the offices and back to the truck.

"Another wasted trip," Mikayla murmured as they headed back to Hagerstown.

"Supposedly." His voice was tight and hard.

"He obviously has no intention of talking to you," she pointed out. "He was seen meeting with Eddie; maybe he was the one Eddie was working for."

"Anything is possible," Nik growled as he slid a pair of dark sunglasses over his eyes and headed for the interstate.

"Why don't I just sit over here and keep my mouth shut while you continue to pout?" She crossed her arms over her breasts as she glared at his profile.

He had been like this most of the day. Short answers, his manner controlled and obviously patronizing. She was getting sick of it. She wasn't a child he needed to keep information from.

"Why would I be pouting, Mikayla?" His lips thinned, a muscle at the side of his jaw clenched and unclenched in obvious annoyance.

"I have no idea why you're pouting," she bit back in irritation. "But I have three brothers; I know the signs.

If you're still put out because I insisted on coming with you, then I personally think you're taking it to extremes."

"I'm certain you do," he agreed.

God, she hated it when her brothers did this to her, and it was even worse now that Nik was doing it.

"What is your problem then?" she huffed out. "It's not as though I'm asking you to take me into a war zone here. Nik, I have every right to be a part of this."

"You have no right to distract me, Mikayla." Anger simmered in his tone now. "You're my lover, not a mark, a suspect, or a client. For this moment in time you're my lover, and every minute you spend with me places you in more danger. Do you think I enjoy that?"

Nik could feel a dark awareness crawling through him ever since he had picked up the tail just out of D.C. They were being followed, and rather than stinging the bastard and jerking his balls off for information, Nik found himself trapped in the truck because Mikayla had insisted on accompanying him.

How the hell was he supposed to protect her like this? He couldn't work efficiently if he had to check his actions because of her presence.

"Do you think I enjoy hiding in a back room all day awaiting word? Pacing the floors while you decide what information you will and will not give me when you return?"

Pain and anger shadowed her voice, but he heard something more as well. Vulnerability, a sense of help-lessness. Her world had suddenly changed on her, as had her security. The battle to accept that was clear in her voice.

He glared back at her in frustration. "It's not like that," he argued. "I tell you what I know."

"What you know, not what happened, their expressions, their actions, or the tidbits of information they give out," she protested. "Nik, I need to be a part of this."

And he needed to protect her. The protective urge was eating him alive from the inside out.

Glancing at the mirrors again, he could still see the plain tan sedan that had shadowed them since they had left Hagerstown earlier in the day.

"You're doing that a lot," she said.

"Doing what?" He frowned back at her.

"Checking your mirrors. Are we being followed?"

Hell, she was more intuitive than he wanted to give her credit for.

"We picked up a tail earlier," he finally admitted. "One of Holbrook's flunkies, I'd guess."

He'd find out later, he promised himself. If he had to slip into Holbrook's bedroom and prick his balls with a blade, then he'd get the truth.

"Is he very close?" To give her credit, she didn't turn and look behind them.

"A few cars back." So far, whoever it was represented no threat, but Nik knew that could change at any time.

"Just give me the word and I'll duck," she promised. "But please stop acting like a five-year-old without his PSP. It really irritates me."

He almost laughed at the comment. The tone of voice was one that a woman would use only with small children or belligerent young men.

He was neither.

"What time does the bar open?" He changed the subject before his own irritation became more apparent.

"It will do you no good to arrive before ten," she told him. "The bar opens at six, but to make certain the regulars are there to question them it would be best to arrive later."

He had to agree with that, and he hated it.

"Dinner then," he sighed, checking the mirrors once again to locate their tail.

He was there, same position.

"Fine, dinner." Her voice lowered as she propped her elbow on the armrest and rubbed at her forehead.

The tension was like a live wire between them, sizzling with too much damned awareness. Arousal.

Taking her the night before hadn't stilled the hunger for her; it had done nothing to ease the ache that flared inside him. It did nothing to ease the hunger.

The hunger wasn't going to ease anytime soon, either. Nik admitted that hours later as they pulled into the parking lot of the nightclub Jarvis Dalton swore was his alibi.

The little bastard was too incompetent to have actually committed that murder. But a trail was a trail, and at this point Nik was becoming desperate to finish this. If he didn't get away from her, then he was going to lose his soul to her.

The fact that she had insisted on returning to the house to shower and change should have clued him into the fact that she was going to make him crazy tonight.

Seeing her dressed in that snug stretchy silk violet dress, her hair pulled to the crown of her head to cascade to her shoulders in luscious waves that still confused him. How had she managed those waves? Because he knew her hair was a beautiful straight ribbon of rough silk.

If he'd thought she looked like a fairy before, then she sure as hell looked like one now. One in four-inch-high sandals that made her feet look so much smaller and more delicate than ever before.

With his hand against her lower back he escorted her into the club, paid the entrance charge, and nearly grimaced at the clash of music as it assaulted his ears.

On the dance floor bodies gyrated and moved in synchronized seductive intent.

Moving along the edges of the dance floor, he followed Mikayla through the chaos to the long wooden bar. The journey there was a hell of a lot slower than he would have liked, though. It seemed Mikayla knew just as many people here as she knew anywhere else they went.

By the time they moved onto two of the empty bar stools, Nik was gritting his teeth in pure irritation. Between the invitations to dance, the offers of a drink, and the social chitchat, it took more than half an hour to get to their destination.

"Mikayla, sweetheart. Darling, did you make that perfect creation?" The bartender's nasal tone coupled with the approving look as his gaze went over the dress had no sexual connotations. "You didn't mention new designs, darling."

"Nothing new," Mikayla promised him before turning to Nik. "Nik, this is Kevin Mackey. He does some sewing for me sometimes."

"Precise, delicate stitches can make or break the creation," he told Nik seriously.

"Of course." Nik shot Mikayla a speaking look.

"Kevin, is Sam working tonight?" she asked, referring to the bartender Jarvis swore could alibi him.

"She should be in anytime." Kevin waved toward the bar area. "She called in late. Her girlfriend had a little meltdown. You know how it goes." Kevin rolled his eyes as he stroked the small patch of his short goatee before glancing down the bar. "Excuse me, dears. Customer."

Nik felt like rolling his eyes himself. He didn't think he could name a single mission quite like this one. He knew he'd never met another woman quite like Mikayla.

"Here you go." Kevin returned with an amused smile and a whisky, which he set in front of Nik.

Nik looked at the glass, then the bartender.

As Kevin lifted his brows, his petite face reflected amusement and he glanced down the bar.

An older man sat watching, lifted his own glass with a smile as he mouthed, *Enjoy.*

Nik turned to Mikayla.

She was watching the exchange with a smile and as Nik turned to her gave the other man a dainty four-fingered wave before she picked up the glass herself and shot the whisky back.

She didn't even grimace.

The facets of this woman were beginning to amaze him, and that wasn't a good thing.

"Mikayla, sweetheart, does your daddy know you're here?" The man from the end of the bar appeared at Nik's side.

"Ryan, if you tell Daddy I was here, then you're going to have to tell him you were here, and you know he's going to have that talk to you about picking up strange men again." She wagged a finger at him playfully as Nik stared back at her with narrowed eyes.

Ryan laughed. "Speaking of strange men, you going to introduce me?"

Mikayla's amethyst eyes gleamed with laughter. "Ryan Bhats, meet a very good friend of mine, Nik Steele," she introduced them. "Nik, Ryan Bhats, my third cousin and a general troublemaker."

"Mr. Bhats." Nik nodded.

"So you're the guy trying to find Eddie Foreman's killer," Ryan commented. "Bastard. Killing Foreman would have been okay if he hadn't drawn our Mikayla into it."

The fact that Eddie Foreman wasn't well liked wasn't the issue.

"Maybe you could help us, Ryan." Mikayla smiled. "Were you here the evening Eddie was killed?"

"I was. Got here when the doors opened with some friends." He nodded.

"Would you mind answering a few questions for us?" she asked.

Ryan turned to Nik, his gaze going over him slowly. Nik understood how a woman felt now when she complained of being looked at as though she were a piece of meat.

"Maybe," Ryan drawled. "Do you think tall, dark, and dangerous here would grace me with a dance?"

Nik turned, stared back at the other man, and it didn't take Ryan Bhats more than a second to figure out that wasn't going to happen.

Bhats grinned again. "What do you need, darlin'?"

"Jarvis Dalton," Nik answered for her. "He says he was here that night."

Ryan nodded slowly. "Yeah, he was. Showed up 'bout the same time I did, just at opening. About five thirty, I'd say."

"You're certain it was Jarvis?" Nik asked.

"Positive. He and his friend come here pretty regular. Darnell, I think his name is. Some guy from D.C. They were here until closing." He glanced at Mikayla. "You know how it is. We all just get together and bullshit sometimes. That was one of those nights."

"Thanks, Ryan." Mikayla smiled back at him.

"Look, sweetie, I know what you're going through. Maddix is a big fish, but I might have something that could help. It's just, ya know, I work for him, too." Ryan's hand settled on her shoulder and Nik had to grit his teeth to keep from knocking the touch away from her even as he waited for the information.

"Your name won't come into it," Nik informed him.

Ryan drew in a deep breath, dropped his hand, and looked around for a second. "Maddix says he was at a meeting. That was in the papers. Well, I saw Maddix as I was heading here. He was at the station just off the exit before you get to the job site. Seemed kind of strange, because he was using the ATM."

Nik stared at Bhats as his jaw set in potential fury. It kept coming back to Maddix. Each thread was slowly coming together to create a noose for the construction company owner's neck and Nik was beginning to wonder just what made Maddix think he could manipulate this.

Hell, Nik had been as certain of Maddix's innocence as he was of Mikayla's and learning he could be wrong enraged him. God help Maddix if Nik proved the other man had used not just him but also Mikayla to get away with murder. And as far as Nik was concerned, using Mikayla was a far greater crime.

"I think we're finished here." He rose from the bar, helped Mikayla down, and turned to Ryan Bhats. "Thank you, Mr. Bhats."

"Look, just keep my name outta this." Concern darkened the other man's eyes. "I like Mikayla. She's a good girl. But I have a job, I have a mortgage, and I enjoy my life, ya know?"

"Your name isn't a part of this," Nik promised before turning and urging Mikayla to the exit.

She was quiet, her expression somber as she glanced up at him.

He couldn't look back at her. He'd followed the line that she must have mistakenly identified Maddix. That somehow someone could have tricked her. It was beginning to look as though somehow Maddix Nelson had managed to trick him instead.

"Nik?" she questioned him as she stopped him outside the bar before they headed back to the parking lot.

God, he loved her eyes. Loved the scent of her, the feel of her. Hell, he even enjoyed the hell out of her being with him, questioning those involved, when he knew he shouldn't enjoy it. Yet having her with him was an experience he knew he would miss when it was over.

"When I prove it, he'll pay for it," Nik swore to her. "I promise you, Mikayla, I'll make sure he pays for every moment of fear, every second you were in danger."

"He'll pay for it anyway," she told Nik. "The proof will put him in prison."

He hoped.

"We have to break his alibi, but first I need more information," Nik told her. "Come on; let's get back to the house. I need to get on the computer."

He needed facts. He needed to find proof, not supposition, which was all he had at this moment.

"Then let's go." Walking ahead of him, she moved smoothly and gracefully, despite the height of the heels.

Shaking his head, he started to follow her. He should have stayed closer to her. He should have never let her get so much as an inch ahead of him.

He was jumping for her as he heard the motor rev, as lights suddenly blazed, blinding him as the car shot from a parking spot too close and with a sharp burst of speed headed for Mikayla.

His hand went for the gun at his side as his arm wrapped around Mikayla's waist and jerked her from her feet.

The car missed them by inches. Bearing the brunt of the fall on his back as Mikayla cried out, Nik was shooting at the car, rage coursing through him as a curse tore from his lips.

Rolling smoothly, he shielded Mikayla's body between him and a parked car before dragging her quickly between the parked vehicles.

She rolled with him. She didn't fight him. When he pushed her against the side of the car and came to one knee, weapon raised as the car screamed onto the main road.

The bastard had gotten away, but Nik was fairly damned certain he'd hit it at least once.

Assured there was no other threat, he turned back to Mikayla.

She was pressed against the side of the car, eyes wide, the perfect wavy updo falling to the side, covering one cheek and smeared with blood.

His hands were shaking as he brushed her hair back, relief searing him first as he glimpsed the long scratch that disappeared into her hair. On the heels of that relief came a rage so all consuming it nearly exploded inside him.

He was becoming sick and damned tired of these attempts against his woman. Someone was going to pay for it. When he found Eddie's killer, he'd find her assailant. He'd find the shooter, and by God, they were all going to pay.

CHAPTER 18

As far as Nik was concerned, it took too long to call the police department, report the attempted hit-and-run, and answer the questions the uninterested detective managed to ask.

It would have been Nik's preference to take her straight to the hospital, but that wasn't Mikayla's preference. She wanted to go home. And he wanted her home. He needed to hold on to her, just for a little while, to convince himself she was truly all right.

Kneeling in front of the prissy little chair she kept in her girly bathroom, he cleaned the scratch gently, checked it to ensure it wasn't deep enough to require that hospital visit.

The scratch was deep, but once he'd cleaned it, he was certain no stitches were needed.

"I'm sorry, baby," he said tenderly, as tender as his roughened, nearly ruined voice could be.

His stomach was tight with fear, with rage at the memory of the horror of watching that car speeding toward her, the knowledge that if he didn't move fast enough, then he could lose her.

He could have lost her, just as he had lost Nicolette.

Just as he had lost his life so long ago, the future he'd envisioned, he'd almost lost Mikayla as well.

Someone was desperate to see her dead. The strikes against her were becoming closer with each successive attempt, but still she stared back at him now with such trust. Trust and love. He could see the love in her eyes, and it tightened his chest, tore at the heart he'd never believed could be touched again, and sent hunger pounding through him.

And he still couldn't understand what made a woman so innocent, so tender, give her heart to a man who had warned her he could have no future with her.

"Why?" He couldn't hold the question back. He had to know. "Why aren't you asking me for anything, Mikayla? Commitment? Some kind of relationship? Are you waiting to hit me with it later?"

Hurt filled her gaze at the question. "You're my lover, Nik, not my possession. You said you had no promises to give me. You never lied to me. You were honest from the beginning. Would it be fair of me to ask for more now? Or later?"

She was breaking his heart. Nik wondered painfully if she had any idea what she was doing to him. She was tearing at the very foundations of the man he believed he was. The cold, hard, unfeeling man he wanted to be, had needed to be for the past ten years. He had no clue how he was going to manage to salvage his soul when it was time to walk away from her. God knew he couldn't stay. If he stayed, if he lost her later it would kill him.

And he knew Mikayla. She would want children. She would hunger for children. And Nik knew he could never, ever allow himself to take that risk again.

"Nik," she whispered, her voice aching with gentleness, with emotion. "I have you now, for this moment in time. However much you're willing to give me. I don't have the right to ask for more when you warned me up front that you had no more to give me."

Nik shook his head. She destroyed his defenses without even trying. She was locked inside him and he was damned if he knew how to get her out or how to protect himself against it.

"You deserve better, baby," he told her as he fought the emotions tearing through him. "The happily ever after, the white wedding you dream about. All of it, Mikayla. Why waste your innocence on a man who can give you nothing but his body?"

She gazed back at him with such somber love that she broke his heart.

"I haven't wasted my innocence, Nik." Tears filled her gaze, but she kept them carefully in check. "I gave it to you. And I know the memory of it will always be safe with you."

How the hell was he supposed to defend himself against her? There was a purity about her that he couldn't fight. An inner innocence that he never wanted to see her lose. A part he wondered if he wouldn't indeed carry inside himself now.

He'd never known anyone, anything, like Mikayla.

Lifting his hand, he cupped his fingers around her neck and pulled her to him. He needed the feel of her lips against his, her kiss warming his soul. He ached for her in ways he had no idea how to combat anymore. The hunger for the warmth of her tore at his control and filled him with such a demand for her touch that restraining himself was impossible.

She eased the nightmares inside him, as well as the ice he'd allowed to build in his soul since the death of his family. She filled him, she made him believe in fairy tales, and God alone knew how dangerous that made her to him.

His hands smoothed down her arms, feeling the softness of her silky flesh, the warmth of her against him. He needed her. One more memory to hold inside him, to store against the lonely nights to come.

Trailing his fingers up her arms once again, he stopped at the silky straps of her dress and eased them slowly down her arms.

He had to restrain his hands from shaking. Leaning back, he stared at the smooth, unblemished mounds of her swollen breasts as the material eased over them. Candy pink nipples were tight and hard, tempting him to taste them, to feel them against his tongue.

Lowering his head, Nik let his lips trail down the side of her neck, then the sweet curve of her breast. The taste of her filled his senses. It left him almost shaking as hunger and lust raced through his system.

How the hell was he supposed to ever survive walking away from her? The memory of her, the touch and taste of her, would forever haunt his memories.

Opening his eyes, he stared up at her as his lips found a sweet, hot nipple. He watched her face, watched it transform with pleasure as he let his tongue lick over the hard tip.

Amethyst eyes blazed with heated arousal. They were darkening, turning almost purple as she watched him. Her abandonment to the pleasure, to his touch and his hunger, never ceased to amaze him. Never ceased to humble him.

As his tongue caressed the delicate nipples, first one, then the other, his hands gripped the material of her dress and drew it to her hips.

She lifted for him, as though she felt the unspoken

need to remove the dress. Removing the dress, his hands pressed between her thighs, spreading them, letting his fingertips caress her flesh as he drew ever closer to the heated folds of her pussy beneath the black silk panties.

A little moan echoed around him as he gripped the band of her panties and pulled them free of her body as well.

Drawing back, he stared at the sweet perfection between her thighs. Soft wheat blond curls glistened with the juices from her pussy, darkening the curls.

"Look how pretty you are." His fingers brushed against the wet folds, his fingertips grazing over the honey that spilled from her. "Sweet and hot. Intoxicating."

Glancing up at her, he watched as her teeth caught her lower lip, her lashes lowering over her eyes as slumberous sensuality took hold of her.

His lips moved to the light rise and fall of her stomach. He licked at the sweet flesh as he moved lower, so desperate to taste her he was about to begin shaking with it.

Soft, curl-shrouded folds drew him, tempted him. The light glaze of her feminine honey was an addiction he refused to deny himself. The tight, swollen knot of her clit greeted his lips and tongue as he moved lower.

The sweetness of her exploded against his tongue as a groan tore from his lips. Heaven help him, he had no idea if he could hold on long enough to give her the pleasure he was aching to give her.

Parting the swollen folds of her pussy, he licked through the juice-soaked slit as she whimpered in pleasure. Her fingers threaded through his hair, holding him to her as he stroked his tongue along the intimate flesh, moving closer to the snug, juice-filled entrance he ached for.

Gripping her ankles in his hands, he lifted her delicate feet as she rested against the back of the chair. He placed her feet in the seat, opening her further, watching as the folds of her pussy parted, revealing the sweet, pink, glistening flesh.

He needed her. He was dying for her.

His tongue licked around her clit before he sucked it gently into his mouth, laved it, caressed it as her hips lifted to him, offering him more.

And he needed more. So much more.

Licking lower, drawing more and more of the honey to his tongue, he stroked, tasted, until he reach the snug entrance to her pussy.

And he lost his senses, lost his control. Thrusting his tongue inside her, he licked delicate flesh, stroked against the smooth walls of the sweetest pussy he'd ever known in his life.

His dick was so hard he was dying with need. His balls were drawn tight, pre-come dampening the tip as he fucked her with his tongue, groaning at the taste of her, the need that had her hips thrusting back at him until he felt her explode.

He felt it.

Her pussy clenched and tightened around his tongue. Heated spicy-sweet juices met his tongue as she cried his name, her hands tightening in his hair, trying to drag him closer.

He lost his breath at her response, at the complete abandonment she gave him. The way she filled him.

"Complete me, Mikayla," he begged as he tore at his pants, releasing the agonizingly hard flesh that strained against the zipper.

Hell, there were probably zipper tracks on the too-hard flesh.

Gripping the shaft, he straightened, pressed closer, until the head of his dick was pressing against the clenched opening. "One more time, little fairy, complete me."

Leaning back, he watched as he began to penetrate her. The heavy, wide flesh pressed inside, parting her as the folds of her pussy began to grip and hug the heavy erection.

He'd never known anything so beautiful as this. As this perfect innocence accepting him, lifting to him, crying out for him. Her hands gripped his arms as her neck arched, her hair falling around her shoulders as slumberous violet eyes stared back, locked with his gaze.

Her slick juices clung to his shaft, beading on her curls, slickening his dick. Fucking her was pure pleasure. It was pure rapture. It was sweet, hot ecstasy.

"There, baby," he crooned, his voice rough. "Let me have you, just like this. Just like this, Mikayla."

He pushed inside her, filled her, sinking in to the hilt as the tight muscles gripped him, flexed around his sensitive flesh until he swore he was dying from the pleasure.

He couldn't hold back. He was losing himself to her. He could feel it. Losing himself until nothing mattered but this. Nothing but holding her, fucking her until she was screaming his name, until he heard his own voice, choked and desperate, as she began coming around him.

Her pussy gripped him, stroked him. It held him tight as it rippled around him, her juices heating his flesh further as he erupted.

His semen spilled inside her, and a part of him ached, a part of him longed, for the forbidden, the impossible. For one broken second he could see her with his child, see that innocence, that purity, in the eyes of their child.

"Hold me, Mikayla," he whispered as he collapsed against her. "Sweet baby, just hold me."

And she held him. Held him in her arms. In her heart. In her soul.

"I'll always have this, Nik," she whispered, her voice weak, drowsy. "The memory of the greatest pleasure of my life."

Those words echoed through his head as he cleaned her gently and carried her to bed. Pulling her against him, he sheltered her against his body, felt her hand against his heart, her head on his shoulder, as she slipped into sleep.

She was safe here, he promised himself. Here in his arms was the only place he knew she was safe. A part of him was terrified to let her go, terrified to trust her to fate. Fate was a capricious, vindictive bitch and he knew it well. If he trusted this treasure to that whimsical being, then he would be left a broken shell of a man in ways he had never been before.

Smoothing her hair back from her face, he laid a kiss against the top of her head as his hand smoothed down her naked back.

It was a good thing he was keeping her with him. Her protection was his main priority. Finding the person responsible for this, for Eddie's death, for the attempts against her, was the only way to keep her safe when he had to leave.

He'd believed Maddix Nelson when he said he had nothing to do with Eddie Foreman's death. Nik had believed Maddix knew better than to screw him over like this, than to lie to him and expect to get away with it.

Maddix didn't know the organization Nik was a part of, but the other man was damned well aware of the fact that Nik wasn't going to be easy to manipulate.

The alibi Maddix had appeared solid. He was obviously not working alone.

As Nik stared up at the ceiling, his forehead creased into a frown. He had help here. Ian, Kira, and Bailey. They were in D.C. and they would return to Hagerstown if needed.

They were needed.

He had to get this taken care of. He had to return the security to Mikayla's life before he could walk away from her.

Walk away from her?

His jaw clenched at the thought. How the hell was he supposed to walk away from her? But how could he bear to stay with her? If something ever happened to her, an accident, a disease, if anything stole her from him once he came to breathe for her existence, then it would destroy him.

Laying another kiss against her brow, he eased slowly from the bed and padded silently to the guest room. Drawing on a pair of sweatpants, he picked up the cell phone from the dresser and hit the number for Kira Richards.

"Is she okay?" Kira answered quickly. "We heard the return on the attempted hit-and-run. Ian's been pacing the floor waiting for you to call."

Nik doubted Ian was pacing; most likely Kira was the one pacing. Ian was calmer, more certain that if Nik needed them he would call.

"Is Ian with you now?" Nik asked.

"He's here. Should I turn on the speakerphone?" Kira asked.

"Yes." Nik had to grit his teeth on the word. "Pulling in one of the members of the Elite Ops backup team wasn't easy for him.

"I'm here, Nik." Ian spoke a second later.

"All I saw was a black sedan, no plates," Nik stated. "I put at least two rounds in the vehicle. I need you to check for vehicle repairs. I could have heard glass shatter, so there's a chance I got the front or back window."

"I have it," Ian promised. "How are you doing with the investigation?"

Nik sat down heavily on the side of the bed. "It keeps leading back to Maddix," he admitted. "I'd thought he was smart enough not to try to use me. I could have been wrong."

"Everything I've found on Mikayla points to a very honest, forthright woman," Kira stated through the line. "She doesn't even finagle on her taxes. But if Maddix did this, then there's not even a hint of evidence that I've been able to find. Usually, the least you can get is a solid rumor."

Nik rubbed at the back of his neck. "It's not going to be easy to break his alibi," Nik admitted. "I'm following every lead I can find, but as I said, those leads are going back to Maddix. I'm heading back to Gina Foreman's tomorrow. In the meantime, Kira, see if you can find a financial trail for Eddie Foreman and Maddix Nelson that coincides somewhere other than Foreman's salary. After I meet with Gina, I've got to find a line in to Reed Holbrook. The man's avoiding me, and he ties in here somewhere."

There was a brief moment of silence.

"How does Reed Holbrook fit into this?" Ian asked.

"Do you know him?" Nik questioned softly.

"I know him," Ian answered.

"Mikayla and I found Reed's office, cell, and home numbers in Eddie Foreman's private office. There was also a witness who saw Reed and Eddie Foreman talking the day Eddie died. There are a lot of threads moving here, Ian; I need to track down as many as possible."

"I'll get you a meeting with Reed," Ian promised. "If he's involved with this, we'll figure it out."

"That's what I need, thanks."

"I'll get started on the financials," Kira promised. "It may take a few days, though."

"Get it as quickly as possible," Nik asked. "This needs to be finished, Kira. I've been here too long already."

He hadn't been here long enough. He didn't believe any amount of time with Mikayla would ever be enough. Leaving her would tear his soul from his chest, but better that, he told himself, than losing all he was to her and having her taken from him.

He disconnected the call moments later and moved back to Mikayla's bedroom. Laying the cell phone on the bedside table, he stared down at her, watching as the fragile light of the moon spilled through the small seam of the curtains to the bed and the woman.

If ever she looked like a fairy, then she did now. The moonlight loved her flesh, caressed it, bathed it in gold.

He was fucking waxing poetic, something else he'd never done in his life, that he had never done with any other woman.

Shedding the cotton pants, he moved back into the bed beside her, his lips quirking as she moved against him, a sleeping little groan falling from her lips as he pulled her against his chest once again.

Her head fell back to his shoulder, her hand to his chest, as he held her to him. He hadn't slept with a woman in over ten years. He'd fucked them. Enjoyed them. But not until Mikayla had he needed one in the bed beside him.

Not until one had penetrated that part of himself that he held in reserve.

Even his wife hadn't managed that. Not until Mikayla had Nik felt his heart slipping from his grasp with no idea how to protect it.

Only with Mikayla.

Chapter 19

"Are we going to be questioning Maddix Nelson anytime soon?" Mikayla asked as Nik sat at the kitchen table the next morning on the laptop.

"Not today."

The answer surprised her. Normally he didn't answer her when it came to certain questions. Maddix Nelson was one of those questions.

"What are we doing today then?" she asked as she poured more coffee, and waited for Nik's reply.

"Today we're going back to Gina Foreman's." Mikayla turned as he twisted around in his chair. "Jarvis said Eddie was trying to sell plans and sabotage the project. I didn't have that information when I sent some friends to go through the Foreman home office. I want to check it myself again."

She blinked back at him. "You had friends go through the office?"

"I do have friends." His brow arched with an edge of amusement.

"Well, of course you do." She cleared her throat, still staring back at him in surprise. "You didn't tell me you were having friends check out the office, though."

"My bad. I'll make sure I don't make that mistake again."

He turned back to the laptop and began scrolling through a file he'd pulled up.

"Your bad?" she asked slowly.

"My mistake." He shrugged.

"Who are your friends?" she asked, intensely curious.

He glanced over his shoulder. "I could tell you, but then they might have to kill one of us. I'm more valuable to them."

"But I'm nicer," she informed him archly. "Give me an hour and they would like me much better than they like you."

There was a brief chuckle. "I have no doubt of that."

Her eyes narrowed on him. "You're being too secretive again."

"I can't tell you who my friends are," he said as she pulled out the chair and sat down across from him. "What I can tell you is that if Eddie was up to something dirty, then the evidence is out there. We'll find it."

At least he was saying "we" and not "I."

"Good." Sipping her coffee, she sat back in the chair and watched him silently for several moments before saying, "When are we going to Gina's?"

He checked his watch. "A few more minutes. I want to time it just right."

"And what would you consider 'just right'?"

His lips quirked. "Just right is just before she leaves. I don't want her looking over my shoulder, and I'm hoping she'll trust you enough to let us stay in the house after she leaves."

Mikayla stared back at him worriedly. "I wouldn't bet on that happening."

He smiled back at her. "We'll see."
We'll see.

Three hours later, Mikayla stood with Nik on Gina Foreman's doorstep.

The door swung open to reveal a harried, drowsy Gina Foreman. Dark blond hair was mussed, chocolate brown eyes were sleepy, and it was apparent she had just come from bed.

So much for catching her before she went in to work.

"Mikayla?" Confusion filled Gina's voice. "Mr. Steele?"

"I'm sorry, Gina." Mikayla smiled. "We wanted to ask you a few more questions before you went to work."

Gina shook her head. "I called in this morning. I needed a personal day." She stood back. "But come in. I'll answer what I can."

Mikayla could feel the tension emanating from Nik as he moved in beside her.

"Would you like some coffee or something?" Gina tugged a ragged, threadbare brown robe tighter around her and pushed her hair back from her face as she rubbed her foot against her ankle.

"Nothing, Gina," Mikayla replied. "If you could just help us out a little."

"Sure." Moving to the small seating area, Gina sat down in a recliner and stared back at them inquisitively. "How can I help you?"

Nik and Mikayla sat on the couch across from her.

Now what did Nik have planned? Mikayla wondered. Gina wasn't exactly falling in line with the plan he had.

"Mrs. Foreman, did Eddie say anything about needing more money than normal? Did he do or say anything that could have indicated he would have an influx of cash coming?"

Gina frowned. "Like I told you before, Mr. Steele, Eddie always needed money. And if he had extra money coming, then he wouldn't have mentioned it to me." There was a glimmer of bitter cynicism in her dark gaze.

"Did Eddie play the lottery or gamble in any other way?" Nik questioned her.

Gina shrugged, her gaze becoming clearly upset now. "Look, Eddie stopped talking to me a long time ago, about money or anything else. I wasn't exactly his best friend."

It was spoken matter-of-factly, without anger, but with an underlying sense of disillusionment that was more powerful than anger could have been.

"Who was his best friend, Gina?" Nik leaned forward, his gaze intent as he watched her. "Who could we talk to who might know if Eddie was having any problems, Gina? Someone besides Jarvis?"

Gina sat back in her chair and stared back at them with a frown for long moments before sighing wearily.

"Steve Gainard."

Oh boy. Mikayla heard the name with a sense of discomfort.

"Steve was one of the only friends Eddie had who was decent. They'd been friends since high school, though Steve travels a lot, so that may have made it easier for Eddie to remain friends with him."

"You didn't mention him to us before," Nik pointed out.

Gina shook her head. "He wasn't in town. Steve just returned last night. He's an architect. He's been in London on a job for the past several months. He called me early this morning to let me know he was back and give me his condolences."

"Do you have his address, Mrs. Foreman?" Nik asked.

Gina frowned back at Mikayla. "Mikayla knows it; they used to date."

Mikayla bit her lip before turning to Nik with a bright smile. "Yeah, I know where he lives. She doesn't have to write the address down at all."

"Tell me," Nik muttered, his voice so low Mikayla was certain only she heard him. "Is there anyone you haven't dated?"

She smiled and shrugged. "You."

His eyes narrowed, but thankfully he simply turned back to Gina. "Mrs. Foreman, do you mind if we check out Eddie's office again?"

"Make yourself at home." She waved back to the office. "Someone else did last night. They broke in while I was at work and stole most of the paperwork. That's why I'm home today. I have to get the locks changed and a security system installed."

Mikayla glanced quickly at Nik as he rose to his feet and strode through the short hall to the office. Moving behind him, she reached the doorway just as he entered the office.

"Your friends?" she asked, careful to keep her voice low.

Nik shook his head. "Not my friends."

As Gina had stated, just about everything was gone. File drawers hung open, shelves had been emptied, and the mess that had been there days before was definitely limited now.

"Wow. Someone cleaned house," Mikayla murmured.

"No doubt." Icy disdain filled his voice now as Mikayla continued to stare around the room. "Maybe Steve will know something."

Bad idea. She should have never mentioned it.

Nik's gaze turned on her slowly, the ice in his pale blue eyes freezing the air around her.

"How serious was this relationship you had with Steve Gainard?"

How serious?

There was no question of being honest with Nik, but that honesty had the potential to make Nik's gaze even icier.

"Well, he may have been more serious about the relationship than I was," she admitted.

"Meaning?" Nik's voice lowered.

"Well, he might have asked me to marry him." She winced as she gave the information.

She didn't expect Nik's reaction. She expected icy anger, expected that distance that he'd placed between them to grow; what she didn't expect was to have him pull her into the room, lift her against him, and cover her lips in a kiss of pure possessive hunger.

Shock held her; dark, intent need washed through her like a tidal wave of hunger. There wasn't a chance in hell that she was going to fight this, no matter how brief it would be.

Her arms wrapped around his neck, her fingers tearing at the leather strap that held his hair back until the thick, soft strands fell over her hands.

As she lifted herself closer to him, her knees gripped his hips, the suddenly sensitive mound between her thighs rubbing against the heavy length of his cock. His fingers dug into her hair, gripping and holding him closer, her lips parting, her tongue meeting and stroking against his until he suddenly jerked back from her.

His gaze blazed down at her.

That wasn't pale ice; it was pure pale blue flames. White-hot. Possessive.

"As long as I'm here, you're mine," he growled. "Do you understand that, Mikayla?"

She shook her head slowly. "I'm not yours, Nik. At the moment, I choose to be with you. Just as I chose not to be with Steve."

Nik stared down at Mikayla in shock. This wasn't what he expected. This wasn't the reaction she should have given him. She was to agree she belonged to him. She was to accept that, not disagree with him.

Setting her slowly on her feet, Nik backed away; the urge to pick her up and carry her away back to her bed was nearly overpowering. He wanted to show her, wanted to prove to her, that she belonged to him well before they arrived on Steve Gainard's doorstep. Before he had to face the man who would most likely attempt to pick up the pieces of his relationship with Mikayla once he left.

"You'll be leaving," she whispered, standing in front of him, petite and determined, so strong, and yet so fragile. "Don't ask more from me than you're willing to give, Nik."

She turned and left him standing there. Dressed in butterscotch silk slacks, those sexy-as-hell high heels, and a matching butterscotch sleeveless knit top, she looked as sweet and fragile as the sunrise, but what he repeatedly forgot was the fact that she was just as strong and just as endearing as the sunrise as well.

And damned if he didn't feel as though he had just been put well and truly in his place.

Later, later, though, he promised himself, his time would come. Tonight, when he had her beneath him, when she was screaming his name in pleasure, then he would make certain she realized exactly who she belonged to.

* * *

Mikayla remained silent as they made the drive to Steve's home outside Hagerstown. The two-story glass and steel home he had built several years ago rested on the side of Sideling Hill, staring out on the valley below.

The winding blacktopped road was hell in the winter when ice and snow hit, but Steve, Mikayla knew, was rarely there in the winters.

He was home often in the summer, though, and the sight of the black Bentley parked in the drive as Nik and Mikayla pulled up to the house assured her Steve was there today.

She waited until Nik rounded the truck and opened the passenger door before turning and allowing him to help her from the vehicle.

Her hands gripped his powerful lower arms, and a quick peek into his face assured her that her last comment to him had struck home. Unfortunately, it had only served to increase the distance he placed between them.

She covered the hurt that caused, hid it deep inside, and fought against it. She didn't want promises from him, she reminded herself, but she was woman enough that it hurt to know that he expected her to give all she was to him while he was holding a part of himself back.

She considered it highly unfair that he would even consider it. He knew he was leaving her when this was over; she knew it. Did he have to demand everything when she knew he would lay it at her feet, return it to her, and walk away?

She had no regrets, she told herself. That didn't mean she didn't have her pride as well as her determination to ensure that she survived this little affair.

"Tell me about Gainard," Nik demanded as he

closed the truck door and touched her arm to keep her from moving ahead of him.

So why hadn't he asked that before they arrived?

Frowning, she stared up at him. "He's thirty-nine, a very successful architect with a firm in D.C. He's never been married and he has no children. We dated for about six months."

"Why didn't you go to bed with him if you dated that long?" Ice dripped from Nik's voice. "A man isn't going to waste six months on a woman he's not sleeping with."

"You don't think I'm worth getting to know first?" she asked, unable to hide the fact that it hurt. "I guess not. You found it pretty easy to get me there, didn't you?"

"That wasn't what I meant, Mikayla." His voice deepened, hardened. "I'm asking you why you waited when it was obvious he was interested in more than sex."

"It's not just about the sex, Nik," she snapped in irritation. "I wasn't ready; that didn't mean he wasn't."

"So why didn't you marry him?" The questions were going somewhere, she knew they were, she just wasn't certain where.

"What does this have to do with Eddie Foreman or Maddix Nelson?" Mikayla demanded as she glared back at Nik. "My personal relationship with anyone has nothing to do with why you're here."

Nik couldn't argue that, but he was damned if he could get it out of his mind. She had dated this man for six months, he had asked her to marry him, yet he hadn't slept with her. She hadn't slept with him, but Steve Gainard had thought he held enough of her heart to ask her to marry him.

It was eating at Nik, and he knew it shouldn't. He

had no right to demand anything from her, just as he had no right to worry about what she did when this was over, or who she did it with.

But it was burning inside him. Like a steady, pulsing flame it was searing his guts with a possessive fever he couldn't seem to control.

"You're right," he finally growled. "It has nothing to do with this."

Turning, he released her arm and settled his hand at her lower back instead, very much aware of the eyes watching them from behind a curtain at the front of the house.

Gina Foreman had most likely called Gainard and warned him Mikayla and Nik were arriving. And no doubt Gina had told the other man Nik was living with Mikayla. It seemed the whole damned city knew she was living with him. The woman had more eyes on her than anyone else he had ever known.

As they stepped onto the marble-capped porch, the front door opened decisively. Standing on the stoop was a somber blond male, his green gaze touching on Nik before he turned to Mikayla.

"Damn, you get prettier every time I see you," he said with a smile as he reached out, gripped her shoulders, and bent his head to kiss her cheek with lingering affection.

No, that wasn't fucking affection, Nik thought as anger tightened every muscle in his body. That was a warning to Nik. A warning that Steve had known Mikayla far longer, and better, and that he would be waiting to strike when Nik was no longer in the picture.

"Steve, it's good to see you." There was the slightest edge of discomfort in her voice. "I'd like you to meet Nik Steele," she introduced them. "He's investigating Eddie's murder."

Nik caught that. There was no "my boyfriend, Nik," "my man, Nik," not even a "my friend Nik." There was no possession whatsoever in her voice.

"Mr. Steele." Gainard's voice chilled, but his hand reached out in greeting. "Nice to meet you."

The handshake was brief, the two combatants very well aware of the stakes of the game.

"Come in." Gainard's hand settled on Mikayla's shoulder at the invitation. "There's coffee in the kitchen and Rosa has some of those pastries you like so well, Mikayla."

"I've missed Rosa." Mikayla's voice made Nik's back teeth clench. Familiarity and genuine warmth filled her voice and had him wishing he'd waited to come here. Waited until she wasn't with him.

"She's missed you as well," the other man informed her as he led them through a wide foyer to the back of the house. "We both have."

Strike one, Nik thought as he gave the other man an icy look. Nik was keeping tabs as of now; when the time was right, Gainard would figure out the mistake he was making fast.

Entering the kitchen, he waved them to a glass-topped table where the promised pastries and coffee waited.

"Gina said you have questions about Eddie," Gainard sighed as they sat down. "She called when he was killed. I was sorry I couldn't make it to the funeral."

"You knew Foreman well then?" Nik asked as he waved away Gainard's silent offer of coffee.

Mikayla, on the other hand, accepted the cup Gainard prepared as well as a small plate topped with a flaky fruit-topped croissant.

"I'd known him since high school." Gainard nodded. "We were thick as thieves until after college. Eddie went into construction and I joined an apprenticeship in London. When I returned several years later, he wasn't the same, but we were still friends."

"Did he have many enemies?" Nik wanted this over with and he wanted it over with fast.

Steve Gainard laughed at the question. "Plenty. Eddie was a helluva prick, Mr. Steele, if he had the chance. He collected enemies like a connoisseur. The damned man never could understand the value of more than a few friends."

"Yet you claim him as a friend?" Nik pointed out coldly.

"Let's say, I didn't give him a chance to be a prick," Steve answered as his gaze slid to Mikayla once again.

The darkening of the green eyes had Nik glancing to Mikayla where she was licking sweet, sticky fruit from the tip of her finger, her gaze on the pastry rather than the men.

"Mr. Gainard." Nik pulled his attention back. "Do you know any reason why Maddix Nelson or anyone else would want to kill Eddie?"

"Everyone." The other man laughed. "Just no one with the guts to do it. Even Maddix. He might hire someone to kill you, but he would never dirty his own hands to do it."

That was pretty much what Nik had believed until the past few days.

He caught Gainard glancing at Mikayla again, but thankfully her attention was now on them rather than the pastry.

"What about money problems?" Nik pressed.

"Plenty," he was told. "Eddie liked to gamble too much. He kept it quiet, always did, but he had a problem with it, and he wasn't very lucky."

"Did he ask you for money?"

Gainard breathed out heavily at the question. "Eddie and I had an understanding from college that he would never ask me for money. He wasted his cash, and I struggled to get through on part-time jobs and scholarships. He knew better than to hit me up. He broke that rule a few months ago when I was in town, though. When I wouldn't give it to him, he threatened to go to a loan shark we knew, Martin Kefler. I tried to talk him out of it, I hoped I had, but he never mentioned it again."

"Did he say why he needed the money?" Nik asked.

Steve's expression hardened as he shook his head. "I didn't want to know. You have to understand Eddie Foreman, Mr. Steele. Loan him a dollar and before you knew it he owed you more than he could ever pay. He lost a lot of friends like that in college. I wasn't going to be one of them."

"The loan shark, you say you know him?" Nik was getting damned tired of the other man glancing at Mikayla with that edge of hunger in his eyes. Gainard was acting like a fucking animal on the prowl.

"Martin Kefler." Gainard nodded. "He's a bookie, a pimp, and a loan shark. Jack of all illegal trades." He grimaced. "Another college acquaintance, though I'm certain Martin didn't graduate from those expensive business courses his crime family put him through. Eddie got himself in a lot of trouble with Kefler several years back as well. He managed to pay him off, but not before he acquired a few broken ribs and a nice little stay in the hospital."

"Isn't Kefler the same man Maddix Nelson nearly lost the property the building site is on to?" Mikayla asked then. "I remember something about his almost being outbid on the property?"

Gainard nodded. "The property owner had that

parcel up for auction rather than placing a price on it. He wanted a quick sell. Kefler wanted it, but I guess Maddix wanted it worse. Kefler wasn't happy when he lost it."

"What interest did he have in it?" Nik probed, wondering why a bookie would bother to bid on the property.

"It's a prime location," Steve informed him. "The owner wasn't real smart about selling it, but it was my understanding he had to sell fast. Kefler and Nelson both wanted it, but from what I understand Kefler didn't get notice of Nelson's last bid, for whatever reason. When he didn't come back with another offer, Nelson walked off with the property."

"What about Reed Holbrook?" Since the bastard was so full of information, Nik decided to probe further.

Gainard frowned thoughtfully as he rubbed at his jaw. "He owns a construction company in D.C. I don't know him as well; I haven't dealt with him as much. His business practices have been questioned several times, though. He's a shark. One of the worst if rumor can be believed. But that's about all I know about him."

Gainard's gaze slid back to Mikayla as she sipped her coffee. His eyes were locked on her lips, lips still just slightly kiss swollen from her exchange with Nik at the Foreman home.

The other man knew that redness for what it was. His gaze came back to Nik, a hint of anger in it.

Nik smiled. A slow, possessive curve of his lips as he stared back at the other man knowingly. He had what Gainard wanted, what the other man hadn't been able to possess, and if Nik was a betting man, he would bet Gainard had known about Mikayla's lover before he ever hit town.

A small part of Nik felt damned sorry for the other

man, though. Nik knew pure male fury would have been eating him alive if Mikayla were sitting here in front of him with a lover. There would be no way in hell Nik could be civilized enough to actually carry on a conversation with the other man.

"Thank you for your time, Mr. Gainard." Nik nodded as he rose to leave.

"Before we leave, I need to use the ladies' room," Mikayla announced as she rose as well and glanced at the other man. "Do you mind, Steve?"

"You know where it is, sweetheart." Gainard nodded, his tone softening, his look almost fucking lovesick. *Strike two, son of a bitch,* Nik thought as his fingers curled into fists.

"I'll meet you in the foyer," she told Nik as she moved through the kitchen to the far entrance and into another hall.

Silence filled the void as Nik followed Gainard to the foyer.

"She's a wonderful woman; I hope you know that," the other man said somberly after several minutes went by. "Don't break her heart."

The general consensus was that Nik was going to break her heart. He wondered if anyone knew what it would do to him to walk away.

"And if I do?" Nik bit out with an edge of anger.

"She doesn't deserve it." Steve shook his head. "But if you do, I'll be here, Steele, and I'll help her repair it. Is that what you want?"

Strike three, but Nik was damned if he could hit the bastard. He wanted to. The need to strike out and eliminate any competition raged inside him.

"What I want is none of your business," Nik informed him.

"What you do to her is," Gainard growled back. "I

heard about you before I ever stepped foot back in America, and I had you checked out, Steele. Does Mikayla know you're no more than a damned mercenary? A fucking expensive gun for hire? Why don't you hurry up, finish your job here, and get the hell out of her life. She doesn't need you messing it up."

Hell, he was going to end up pissing Mikayla off, Nik could feel it, because he was going to take this bastard's head off his shoulders.

The problem was, Gainard might not have all his information correct, but he was right in the fact that Mikayla didn't need the instability in her life that Nik would bring. He knew that. He wasn't trying to deny it. But having it thrown in his face was only pissing him off.

"Get your jealousy under control, Gainard," Nik finally responded with mocking amusement. "I promise, I can make you throw the first punch and I can make Mikayla feel damned sorry for me. Is that what you want?"

"When you're gone, and I know you'll be gone," he was told, the other man's tone low, furious, "I promise, I'll pick up the pieces. You might be her first love, but you won't be her last."

"Bet me." Nik only barely managed to disguise the shock at the instinctive words that burst from his lips a second before Mikayla walked back into the foyer.

He managed to get her out without growling like an animal or pounding on his chest like a Neanderthal. But just barely.

Possessiveness was suddenly a demon raging through him, pouring into his senses and opening a well of raging lust that he had no idea how to cap.

Suddenly he didn't know himself, had no clue how

to handle the needs nearly breaking his control or what to do with one fairy-sized little woman.

He had a feeling he was simply well and truly fucked.

Chapter 20

Martin Kefler had a rap sheet that would have made any crime boss father proud, Nik thought that night as he pored over the files Kira and Bailey were busy gathering and sending to him.

The youngest son of a major crime family, Martin had started out with his own stable of prostitutes at the tender age of seventeen. By twenty-one he was into drugs, money laundering, and loan-sharking.

The man was working on building himself a fortune if he could keep his family's greedy little fingers out of his particular pies. The information gathered showed Kefler owed his fellow crime bosses a hefty portion of his earnings, keeping him on the low scale of the power plays that were constantly waged within that particular family.

"Eddie wasn't very smart," Mikayla commented as she read over Nik's shoulder. "And Martin Kefler looks rather scary."

Nik glanced at the picture of Martin. The long face, heavy goatee, balding in the front of his thick wavy black hair, his large eyes, pale brows, and pale skin.

Nik had seen a lot shadier characters, but he could see where Mikayla had problems with this one.

"He's actually considered one of the nicer crime bosses," Nik stated mockingly. "He at least gives his clients a chance to pay up. Some of the others come after you if you're not paying early rather than on time."

Actually, that was more or less the truth, Nik thought. The reason Kefler was still on the lower tier was his kill ratio. He made the money, not the kills, while the rest of the family had no problems, and actually enjoyed, shedding blood.

Not that Martin was considered a good guy; he was simply not as bloodthirsty as the others.

"I know him."

Nik glanced up at her as she moved to the chair beside him, coffee cup in hand. She'd spent the better part of the evening in a back room working on a dress; now that she was back in the room with him, it seemed as if the life had returned.

Fucking soft shit, he thought. She was warping his mind.

"What the hell do you mean, you know him? You said you didn't know him."

"I didn't know his name." She shrugged. "I know his girlfriend's name, Eloise Lancaster. She orders some of my more daring designs. I like her."

Nik blinked back at Mikayla.

"Eloise is the lead singer with the Jezebels, they're playing in a little place in Frederick right now. She told me her boyfriend is there every weekend with her, if you want to know where to find him."

Mikayla said it so matter-of-factly, as though knowing the mistress of a dedicated crime boss was no big deal. Sweet, innocent, a recent virgin, and she acted as though her connection to a crime family was all in a day's work.

"You're not saying anything, Nik," she stated slowly.

He wasn't saying anything. God knew he shouldn't have been surprised. Hell, he'd sworn a long time ago that nothing could surprise him. But staring back at Mikayla, he admitted, he was surprised.

Hell, she would have made a perfect contact. She had clients from D.C. and two he knew of from LA. An exclusive, little-known shop that evidently pulled in clients he simply hadn't expected. Clients he hadn't even known she had.

"Where is this club this woman sings at?" he asked Mikayla.

She smiled. "Do I get to go with you?"

"No." He wasn't taking her anywhere close to Martin Kefler.

Her expression stilled. "Then find it on your own. I'm sure it won't take you long."

"I'm sure it won't," he agreed.

"See if he talks to you." She crossed one knee over the other and watched him knowingly. "According to Eloise, her boyfriend has a lot of people who want to talk to him but few he'll deal with."

"He'll deal with me," Nik promised her.

"Then I have a dress to finish. Good luck."

As she moved from the kitchen, he watched, feeling the warmth in the room leave with her.

For a moment, he was half-tempted to agree to take her. Hell, he wanted her there. But Mikayla had no business around men such as Martin Kefler.

The fact that she was associated with him through one of her customers wasn't the same, Nik told himself.

He'd managed to hurt her, though. His need to protect her was riding hard; the softness of her, the gentleness she brought to his life, was becoming more important, more imperative.

He didn't want her anywhere near Kefler.

As the thought dug into Nik's soul, his cell phone vibrated at his side.

"Steele," he answered quickly, keeping his voice quiet.

"I have some additional information," Ian informed him. "I was told to give this personally."

Nik's lips thinned as he glanced back to the hall Mikayla had disappeared through. "You'll have to come here."

She was behind on the dresses, Nik knew. Ian could make the trip here just as easily as Nik and Mikayla could make the trip to D.C.

"I'll bring Kira with me," Ian stated. "She can talk dresses with Ms. Martin while we discuss this. Give us about two hours for arrival. There's still a few things I have to clear up."

"I'll be waiting."

Nik disconnected the call before breathing out roughly and staring back at the file on Martin Kefler.

Mikayla was right. Getting a meet with Kefler wasn't easy. He was a wary son of a bitch, and a tough one to boot. She had the perfect in, because according to the information Nik was looking at, Kefler's mistress, Eloise Lancaster, was supposedly his only weakness.

Ms. Lancaster, lead singer for a female rock band named the Jezebels, had her own personal bodyguard, and more than one man had died for attempting to get too close to her. Men who thought striking out at the mistress was suitable revenge against the criminal they were dealing with.

Kefler had shown them differently and made an example of more than one of them.

Rising from the chair, Nik moved to the back room; standing at the open doorway, he watched as Mikayla pieced together material meticulously, a frown on her brow as she lifted her gaze to him.

He could see the anger still simmering there, as well as the hurt.

"Kira Richards and her husband, Ian, will be arriving in a few hours," he told Mikayla. "Ian and I have some business interests, and I think Kira wants to discuss dresses."

Mikayla's brow arched. She wasn't buying that explanation, and the proof of it was the skepticism in her narrowed gaze.

"That's fine," she finally answered before turning her attention back to the material.

"Mikayla, Kefler is too dangerous for me to allow you to accompany me," Nik tried to offset the anger he could feel brewing in her.

She paused again before lifting her head, those amethyst eyes shooting flames back at him now.

"Why don't you just tell me who's going to decide what's too dangerous for me or not too dangerous for me once you decide to ride right out of my life?" Graceful hands went to her hips in challenge. "You know what, Nik? I'm getting real sick of hearing what you think might be too dangerous for me when accompanying you means no more than going to a damned bar or a home office with you to meet with the boyfriend of one of my clients."

Her lips were set, her gaze piercing, as she glared back at Nik now.

"Kefler isn't someone I want you associated with."

Her brows shot up. "Since when is that your choice?"

"Since I became your lover, that's when."

Control went flying out the damned window as he

faced the defiance pouring from her. What the hell was it about this one tiny woman that made him fucking insane?

"Since you became my lover?" The question sounded torn from her.

Mikayla was ready to strangle on the anger pouring through her now if the fire in her eyes was any indication. "Since when does being my lover give you the right to order me around in any way? Trust me, Nik, you have no more rights now than you had the day you walked into town."

She didn't scream at him. Mikayla didn't scream. She didn't pout. She tried really hard not to cry when she was hurt or angry. But she did nothing to hide the pure disgust she felt at his autocratic decision that she simply wasn't going with him.

She could get him in to meet Martin Kefler, and it wasn't as though she weren't already associated with him in a slight way. There was no additional danger in her being with Nik.

"You don't want to understand this." His voice tightened, a sure sign that he was becoming furious himself, and she really didn't give a damn.

"It seems to me, I'm in more danger away from you, but you go right ahead and go meet Kefler by yourself. Maybe we'll get lucky and the next time someone tries to shoot at me they'll miss then, too."

His eyes were pure white-hot blue flames. Mikayla watched the transformation as though mesmerized the second it hit his eyes.

Her focus on that so visible fury distracted her, giving her less time to react when he stepped across the room and jerked her to him.

"Do you think I wouldn't leave you protected?"

"Babysat," she charged back at him, her head lifting,

her gaze staying locked on his. "You would have me babysat rather than having me with you. Thanks, Nik, for showing me how little the time we spend together means to you. I guess I truly am no more than just a ready fuck for you. Shame on me for believing differently."

Shock entered his gaze, as though he couldn't believe the word "fuck" had left her mouth. Well, she knew how to use four-letter words, too; she just preferred not to.

The reaction she received wasn't one she expected, though. Nik jerked her to him, pulling her body close and up until the hard proof of his erection pressed against her lower stomach. The anger churning within her suddenly morphed into arousal as she glimpsed the need suddenly flaming in his eyes.

"This is all you want, isn't it, Nik?" she whispered, wondering at the desperation she saw in his gaze now.

"There can't be anything else, damn you." Naked, furious need burned in his eyes.

It wasn't just lust. It wasn't hunger. It was a need, a burning, intense desperation that made little or no sense.

Her hands slapped against his chest before gripping the edges of his shirt. "Why? Tell me why! I don't want your promises, Nik, I don't want a commitment you can't give, but by God I want to know why."

It was exploding inside her, her chest, her head, striking through her soul with a pain she had no idea how to control. He didn't trust her; he wouldn't open up to her. The only thing he was willing to share was his body.

It should have been enough. She had promised him it would be enough.

"I can't." The words sounded torn from him, but the hunger that filled his gaze told her otherwise. "I can't give you that."

He wouldn't give it to her. He didn't want to give it to her.

All he had to give her was his body.

Her hands jerked apart, ripping open the buttons that held his shirt together to expose the hard, broad contours of his chest. The soft ping of buttons against the bare floor was little more than a knowledge of where the buttons were falling. Not that Mikayla really cared.

"Then give me what I can have," she cried painfully. "Stop taking all of you away from me, Nik."

All of him. She thought he was taking something from her. She had no idea how much he had already given her. How much he gave her each time he touched her, kissed her, possessed her.

Lowering his head, he ground his lips against hers, taking the parted curves and tasting her with his tongue. Stroking it against hers, he groaned into the kiss as he fought to pull back just a little bit, just enough to catch his breath, to hold on to his senses.

There was no holding on to his senses around Mikayla, though. Hell, he could barely remember his name as her hands locked in his hair. As she held him to her, her lips nipped at his first as she fought to take control of the kiss. It was a move that sent pure electric pleasure screaming across his nerve endings.

She was becoming a challenge he couldn't walk away from. Just when he thought he had a handle on her, just when he thought he could control her, she turned the tables on him.

She kept him on his toes, and that was the most dangerous thing she could do. It was the most effective way to steal her way into his heart.

It was that defiance in the face of all odds. Odds that said she was going to get her way. The challenge, the feminine determination to be a part of him, to hold him to her. To lock his soul to her own. And despite every defense he'd ever built against having a woman in his life, she was doing it.

Holding her kiss, he lifted her until her ass met the table. His fingers moved to the band of her silken slacks, released them hurriedly, then undid the zipper before stripping them and her panties from her.

The light shirt was easy to remove from her. She'd torn his shirt; he ripped hers from her back and gloried in the strangled cry of excitement that fell from her lips.

This hunger raged higher, hotter, than ever before. He couldn't hold himself back; he couldn't grasp the self-control he had managed to lose his grip on because of her.

She was a live fire in his arms, tempting him, drawing him into a web of such hunger and need that it ripped past his defenses, tearing through a part of his soul he'd believed was forever gone.

That part of him was raging how. It was burning out of control. It was tearing aside the veil of self-protection that was far thinner than he'd ever believed.

Naked now, her neck arching back as his lips traveled down along her jaw, her neck, to the pert, hard nipples reaching for his lips.

Or were his lips reaching for her nipples?

They were candied pink and so fucking sweet he wanted to drown in the taste of them. He wanted to intoxicate himself with her. He wanted to taste her until his senses were so sated with her that she would never torment him again. So sated that once he had to walk away, he would have her with him forever.

Drawing one of the tight pink tips into his mouth, he sucked it inside, flicking his tongue over it, laving it, loving it with every taste of her. He moaned with a hunger that went clear to his soul.

God help him, he would never be free of her. He would never be free because the more he tasted her, the more he needed her. The higher the hunger rose.

Trailing his lips from her nipples, along her stomach, Nik pressed her back along the table, spreading her thighs, lifting her legs, until the sweet, silken curl-shrouded folds of her pussy lifted to his lips.

Soft, delicate dark pink flesh was revealed as those folds parted. The tiny pearl of her clit revealed itself, the snug opening to the fist-tight portal of her pussy.

His dick was so damned hard it felt ready to burst. The need to thrust inside her was overpowered by only one thing.

The need to taste.

As he lowered his lips, his tongue swiped through the delicate slit, flickered around her clit, and relished the taste of feminine heat that exploded against it. Sweet, silken. Nik groaned at the exquisite taste of her.

Lifting his lashes, he watched as her eyes opened, held her sensually drowsy gaze as he let her watch him lick around her clit.

Fairy eyes. Amethyst and violet shifted in her eyes as she watched, her lips parting as her breasts rose and fell erratically.

Ah, God. Her hands were cupping her breasts, her fingers going for her nipples.

Nik curled his tongue around the delicate tissue of her clit before licking over it. Watching her, wondering how brave she would become, he kissed the little knot delicately before moving lower.

He wanted to taste the sweet dew easing from her pussy. Slick and hot, like the richest syrup.

His tongue flicked over the entrance.

Her fingers moved from her nipples, her hands smoothing down her stomach.

Fuck. She was going to destroy him. He could see it in her eyes. Naked challenge glittered in her eyes as her fingers eased lower, her hips lifting, her pussy growing wetter, hotter, beneath his tongue as her fingers reached her clit.

Delicate, graceful. A single fingertip rubbed against the side of the small knot as her expression began to go slack with sensual delight.

Slim hips rose and fell to his tongue as he pushed it inside the snug depths of her pussy. Silken muscles clenched on his tongue, fluttering like a butterfly's wings against his tongue.

His hands tore at the fastening of his jeans as her delicate feet pressed against his shoulders. Her hips arched fiercely, forcing his tongue deeper as he fucked into it with a muttered growl.

She made him feel like an animal. So hungry, so desperate, that nothing mattered but taking her, possessing her, marking her.

Fucking her until every part of himself lived within her. It was the only way to sate the craving crawling through him now.

As her fingers stroked her reddening clit, Nik pulled his tongue from the addictive recess of her feminine heat and lifted his head until he could catch those fingers in his mouth.

Sucking the sweetness from them, he nibbled at the tender tips, licked them, then lifted her fingers from her flesh.

Rising, Nik gripped her ankles, wrapping them around his hips as he came over her.

Excitement raged through Mikayla. It was burning

through her. The storm of sensation tearing through her had her heart racing, her pulse beating in her veins as Nik rose over her. His cock pressed against the folds of her pussy, parting her as he straightened, gripped her hips, and began to sink inside her.

She watched, her breath catching, tiny mewls of pleasure falling from her lips as she watched the head of his cock stretch her until the pleasure/pain of the entrance began to rage through her.

"Yeah, watch me fuck you, baby. See how that pretty pussy stretches for me."

The words. So explicit. So sensual. A wave of sensation tore through her at the sound of them, stoking the pleasure higher.

Her curl-shrouded folds parted for his cock, hugged the heavy shaft. She wanted him inside her. Fully. She wanted all of him. Oh, God, she wanted him inside her and he was going so damned slow.

Dizziness washed over her as the intensity of the sensations began to rock her. As she lifted her hands, her nails scraped down his abdomen, her knees bending back to take more of him, her eyes locking with his as he tightened before her.

She could barely breathe, the pleasure was so great now.

"What are you waiting for?" she cried out.

"You," he growled. "How fucking hot you make me, Mikayla. So fucking tight and sweet."

She was doing this to him. The pleasure gleamed in his eyes, hot and bright.

"Are you going to talk all night or fuck me now?" she moaned.

His gaze flared, his body tightening further. Drawing back, he pushed in hard, fast. Mikayla felt the scream that tore from her lips as pleasure began to slam inside her with the same force of the thrusts of his cock working inside her.

She watched him lose control. The cords of his neck tightened, standing out in stark relief as sweat began to bead on his forehead and shoulders. His hips began to move faster, stronger, his cock stretching her with a fiery burn as he impaled her to the hilt.

She felt his balls pressed against her for only a second. She felt his cock throbbing at her innermost walls for the smallest amount of time.

Pain and pleasure beat inside her, the burn both exhilarating and unbearable. Striking hard inside her, the flaming sensations began to explode and rupture through her pussy, her clit, her very womb. The orgasm was a detonation that sent a tidal wave of pure white-hot sensation tearing through her.

It destroyed her. It remade her. It flowed through her, wrapped around her, and as she felt Nik bucking hard and heavy inside her, his semen spurting, it swamped her senses and seared each delicate nerve ending in her body.

It was like dying and being reborn.

Collapsing back against her table, Mikayla fought to catch her breath, to find a semblance of sanity where she was certain no sanity could be found.

As the last of the tremors began to slowly recede inside her, Mikayla lifted her lashes, staring up as Nik slowly levered himself from her.

"Nik." She stopped him, her hand lifting weakly to her face. "If you do this without me, then whatever we have between us will be damaged."

"And no doubt, it would be best for both of us if it were simply destroyed."

She stared back at him, something crashing inside

her chest, restricting her heart as she felt him ease from her, the still-hard length of his cock deserting her, just as the warmth of his body did.

She couldn't speak.

She couldn't hold on to the pain that bloomed inside her with the force of a blow.

And she couldn't stop the tears from filling her eyes. They didn't fall. She would be damned if she was going to cry for him. She wasn't going to cry over him.

She felt sick inside. Her stomach was cramping with the pain, with the tears that wanted to fall.

Lifting herself slowly from the table, she ignored him, aware of him watching her, aware of the dark, brutal grief that reflected in his gaze. A grief that built inside her with a force she couldn't fight.

She was going to cry.

It almost tore free. It almost bled inside her.

"Mikayla." He caught her as she turned to rush from the room.

"Don't." Desperation shuddered through her. "Let me go."

"You don't understand," he whispered. "Listen to me, Mikayla. You don't know who I am. You don't know what I am. Don't love me, baby. Don't hurt us both like this."

She shook her head. How was she supposed to answer him? How was she supposed to survive the pain inside her when she knew that whatever it was that kept tugging them closer was something he wanted destroyed. He didn't want whatever she had to give. She had been right in what she had said before: he wanted nothing but the fuck.

"I can't let this happen." His voice was hardening.

"Then don't."

Jerking away from him, naked, fighting back tears,

she rushed from the sewing room for the safety of her bedroom.

In that moment she realized she had been hoping. Hoping so much. A part of her had been hiding that hope even from herself. A hope that Nik would at least allow a small measure of what she felt into his heart.

Just a little bit. She wasn't asking for much. Just enough that maybe he would think of her when he was gone. That maybe, oh God, maybe one day he would come back to her.

Rushing to the bathroom, she closed the door behind her, flattened her back to it, and let the first tear fall.

She wasn't going to cry for him. She was crying for herself.

CHAPTER 21

As Ian and Kira arrived at the house more than an hour later, Nik watched Mikayla warily. She was composed, no hint of the tears he knew she had shed in her eyes, and no hint of the anger.

It was as if what had happened in the sewing room, the pleasure, the pain, the nightmares resurfacing inside his mind, had never occurred.

But evidently his own composure wasn't nearly as strong as he thought.

"What's going on, Renegade?" Ian asked as they moved onto the back deck with a beer.

"You were the one who wanted to meet," Nik reminded him as he finished his second beer. "I could be in bed sleeping now. So, I'd say that's my question."

"Yeah, but I'm not the one who looks like a train wreck and Kira's not wearing makeup to hide the fact she's been crying," Ian pointed out.

Nik glanced back at him.

To look at him, no one would ever know that the former Navy SEAL was the son of a former South American drug cartel leader. Or that he had single-handedly brought his father down.

Ian Richards was one of the few men Nik trusted. He was also one of the few who knew Nik's secrets and the life he lived.

"She wants more than I can give," he stated as he gritted his teeth in frustration. "She thinks her life is a fucking game and going with me to meet Kefler is a damned walk in the park."

She thought she should be able to love him and that he should be able to love in return. How did a man go about convincing a fairy that fairy tales simply did not exist?

"She's nothing like Tatyiana, Nik."

Nik's fists clenched. He never spoke his deceased wife's name. He never thought it. The guilt of his own absence in their marriage had the power to make him want to cringe in shame and anger, and her name was only a reminder of the fact that his wife and daughter had died because of his neglect of his marriage.

"Mikayla doesn't seem like a woman who would allow you to forget you had a wife. She's proving now that she would insert herself where she feels she belongs," Ian continued.

"Do you think I don't know that?" Nik kept his back to the other man as he finished the beer quickly.

"Then what's the problem? She's a damned fine woman from what I hear. You could do a hell of a lot worse," Nik was advised.

"Who said I was looking?" Nik growled, anger surging inside him.

Ian chuckled. "That's when you find it, Nik. When it's the most inconvenient thing that could happen in your life."

"What was so important that you had to come here?" Nik turned back to Ian, careful to keep his expression unemotional, unaffected.

Ian's lips quirked into a rueful smile as he stared back at Nik through the darkness.

"Kefler is dangerous," Ian stated. "But for the meet you're requesting, it would be safe enough to take her. What you need to know is some information Kira and I uncovered. He's not just backing certain construction projects; a contact I found says he's out to help someone else break Nelson and take his business over. No one knows who the partner is, but it's someone Kefler thinks he can control."

Nik could feel his back teeth grinding in frustration. "Oh, but it's safe enough to take Mikayla to a meet and greet, right?"

Ian inclined his head. "No one's pretending he's a good guy, Nik, but he's a part of a network as well. One that's ensuring her safety."

Nik's eyes narrowed at the lowered tone and the information. That network could mean only one thing: Martin Kefler was a law enforcement informant.

"You know how it works," Ian continued. "He's given the white-glove treatment and certain leeway in exchange for services rendered. That doesn't mean he's not one of the meanest sharks in the pool, but it does mean he can be required to give certain favors."

"And the favor?" Nik growled.

"You need information and the assurance that no one in his little group will strike at your woman. You have that."

He should flat tell Ian now that Mikayla wasn't his. His lips were parting to do just that, but the words wouldn't come.

"I'll take that into consideration," Nik bit off.

Ian nodded slowly. "What are you fighting so hard, Nik? Do you think you don't deserve a life now?"

No, he didn't. He'd failed when it had mattered

most. When the only innocence he had known in his life had depended on him, he had failed.

"Let it go, Ian." The rage was beginning to spark inside Nik once again, a rage he remembered from that long-ago night when he had stained his hands with the blood of fellow soldiers and murdered the man who had been the cause of that destruction.

Nik had nearly died himself.

He had wanted to die, but he'd lived instead. To suffer? He'd often wondered. Was that why his soul had refused to simply drift away?

Ian breathed out heavily. "No one would begrudge you a little happiness after all these years, especially Nicolette."

Something crashed inside Nik's soul. He swore he felt something splinter in his heart, the pain went so deep.

"Let this go." He heard his own voice, heard the ice dripping from it, felt the fury threatening to engulf it.

"Yeah, sure, Nik, I'll let it go," Ian sighed. "But you're going to break that young woman's heart in there, and when you do, you'll suffer for it as well."

He was already suffering. God knew the pain was sinking sharpened talons so deep inside his flesh he wondered if he were bleeding from it.

"I want backup." He returned to the subject at hand. "When the meet comes down, I'll let you know. I want you there. Nothing matters but her." He stared back at the other man demandingly. "Do you understand that, Ian? No matter what happens, screw the others. She's all that matters."

Screw the Elite Ops, the organization Nik was a part of and the men who had pulled him out of hell and those who had paid a fortune to re-create him. The past ten years and the promises of faith he had made meant nothing when compared to the woman whose heart he was breaking.

"That goes without saying, Nik," Ian promised him. "A few of the guys from the backup team are close by on leave. We were getting together for a week before we went back on mission status. We're standing by for you. Just as Jordan is if you need him."

Yeah, Nik's commander would bitch and moan and cuss a blue streak, but he would do whatever he needed to do.

Nik nodded sharply.

"Anyway," Ian stated heavily. "What did you find out from Holbrook?"

"Confirmation Kefler is indeed backing him," Nik stated before relating details of the meeting to the other man.

"We're still working on the financials of everyone involved, but just from what I've seen so far, there was a hell of a lot of money being exchanged between Kefler and Holbrook. There are some other anomalies as well, but we're still working on those."

"There's something damned strange going on," Nik agreed. "And not just with the money. I can't fit the pieces together. If I look at it logically, Maddix has to be involved, but that alibi is going to be damned hard to break."

Ian nodded. "Stay on Holbrook and Kefler until we turn up something on the numbers," he advised. "You're going to need ammunition before you go to Nelson or the members of that alibi. Let's get our information together; then you can strike."

Then he would kill. If Maddix was the reason Mikayla was in danger, then nothing would save him from Nik.

His fists clenched at the thought. The thought that

Maddix might have used him against Mikayla, used him to make her look foolish, or like a liar, enraged him.

"What the hell do you think is going on with this, Nik?" Ian asked. "Ms. Martin's standing in the community is exemplary. None of the teenage high jinks her brothers and friends got into. No drinking, no drugs. She's quiet, dependable, and compassionate. And this has shed a shadow across that reputation she's obviously worked so hard to attain."

"Someone's using her," Nik stated. "The further this goes, the more apparent it becomes. To stop it, I have to find a killer."

"It doesn't make sense." Ian shook his head. "Her reputation could effectively destroy a normal alibi. If it was Maddix, why use a woman with her reputation?"

Nik shook his head before rubbing at the back of his neck. "That's one of the reasons I ruled out Maddix in the killing. He knows Mikayla. He knew her reputation. He knew she would be there. He knew she would recognize him. Why use her? Why bring me in? Until I can answer these questions, Ian, then this isn't finished."

"If Maddix is involved, then his alibis are involved as well," Ian mused.

"Which could be the reason why this investigation stays stalled. The chief of police, a major business owner as well as two city council members. But why use Mikayla?"

"Exactly. Why use Mikayla? Why use anyone if it's as simple as committing murder. He has an agenda. An agenda that includes Mikayla, and possibly includes me. He called me. He wanted me here specifically."

"You think he has anything on you?"

The Elite Ops had pasts. They had pasts that were

potentially fatal should anyone learn their secrets, or their weaknesses.

"See what you can find out." Nik turned, staring into the darkness as he considered exactly what a relatively small-town construction owner could know about him.

"I'm already working on it," Ian promised. "Until then, if I were you I'd not just keep my woman with me; I'd watch my back, too. There are too many improbabilities here, and that makes my neck itch."

An itching neck was never a good thing. That primal, defensive response to danger was guaranteed to put any soldier on edge. And what more was he than simply an advanced soldier?

"I'll take care of things here; you take care of the information end," Nik told him. "I'll take care of Mikayla."

"I know you'll take care of her," Ian sighed. "What worries me is your idea of the best way to do that."

"What the fuck does that mean?" Nik turned on him, his gaze slicing to where Ian stood across the back porch watching him.

"The best way to take care of a woman like Mikayla isn't storing her in a protective area while life passes her by. Leaving her won't save her, Nik."

"Neither will staying." The edge to his voice was sharp, furious. "What do you want, Ian? You think because marital bliss suits you that it suits the rest of the fucking world?"

Ian's lips quirked. "I think it eases the demons, Nik," he finally said. "And you have more than most. But if the demons make better bedfellows than that woman waiting inside, then that's your bad decision, not mine."

"Damned right," Nik snarled. "Remember that."

Ian's smile was rueful and tinged with a hint of compassion that just further pissed Nik off.

"This conversation is over," Nik informed him. "Find something else to talk about or get the hell out of here. I don't care which."

"I should have the information you need soon, Nik," Ian told him, his tone somber now. "And if you need to talk later, then I'll be there."

Nik gave his head a hard shake as a bitter laugh left his lips. "How long have we known each other, Ian?"

"A long time," Ian answered quietly.

"How many times have I needed a buddy powwow?"

"You've never asked for one, Nik," Ian stated. "But if a man ever needed one, then it was you. What happened to Nicolette wasn't your fault. But if blaming yourself helps you sleep better at night, then who am I to tell you different."

Before Nik could sneer in response Ian turned and stepped back into the house.

"Hey, cutie," Nik heard Kira, Ian's wife, greet him. "The dresses are going to be so beautiful. All the other high-society witches are going to be so jealous of me." Laughter filled her voice as she teased her husband, "And all the guys are going to be so jealous of you. I'm going to be hot." She made a sizzling sound as she stepped into her husband's embrace.

"You're always hot," he told her. "One of these days, those jealous bastards are going to come up missing eyes, though."

The teasing struck at Nik's soul, slicing through his heart with a jagged blade.

He could have that, with Mikayla. But for how long? How long before the job, his responsibilities, tore at their relationship? How long before she decided she needed a lover? . . . That thought fractured.

No, if Mikayla made the vows, she would uphold them. But love died when it wasn't nurtured. He wasn't free. The Elite Ops still had two more years of his life, and the missions were often near-suicide trips.

If he and Mikayla had a child, if an enemy found Mikayla, if she fell out of love with Nik, if she learned who and what he truly was, if she needed more than he could give . . .

If. So many ifs. So many that he knew there was nothing to do at the end of the road but walk in the other direction.

As he entered the kitchen, his gaze moved to her. She was just as pale as Ian said she was, and she looked tired. She needed to be sleeping rather than putting up with this. She needed to be making her dresses rather than fearing for her life.

She needed to be tucked close against Nik's body where he'd know she was safe.

Her gaze lifted to him as he stepped inside the room, her unusual eyes flaring with hunger and pain. Even after he'd hurt her, made her cry, still she wanted him.

Aching need and a fierce, almost furious desperation shadowed them now.

Damn her, she was tying herself to him. She was falling in love with him, if she hadn't already. Dealing with that knowledge was something he found harder to do than facing terrorists. Facing the hungry need he could sense inside her was like facing a bomb. Nuclear. With the potential to destroy more than just his sanity. It had the potential to destroy his very soul.

"Now that you're happy with your dress, we'll head back to the hotel." Ian grinned down at his wife as though she were the socializing little butterfly she pretended to be. The truth was, Kira Richards was probably just as dangerous as her husband. In some ways, more so, because a man wouldn't expect it coming from her.

"I'm ready." Kira's gaze turned to Nik. "Take care of her, Nik; I have a feeling she and I are going to become very good friends."

That statement was enough to send frissons of alarm scattering down his spine, but he gave her a tight nod anyway. He held back the awareness in Kira's statement that he'd always have a tie to Mikayla. Kira would keep up with her. She would keep Mikayla safe.

That didn't help him sleep at night, though.

Holding Mikayla in the darkness hours later, Nik smoothed his hand down her back, over the light, sleeveless gown she wore, as his eyes closed in agony.

There were few times in the past ten years that he had allowed himself to remember the fact that once he had loved his deceased wife. That he had trusted her, laughed with her. That he had lain in bed and dreamed of the future they would have together.

But it hadn't been the same, Nik admitted. There had always been a part of him that had wondered if his wife's affair with Anton had been fully dead.

Anton Vileski.

Nik's jaw clenched. She had been sleeping with Anton before Nik met her, but he hadn't learned of the affair until after their marriage. An affair that had supposedly been over before she met Nik.

He'd always wondered, though. He'd loved her more than he'd ever loved another woman at that time, but a part of him had always feared that his position inside the Russian federal government had been the reason she had married him. That she had married him for her lover.

Nik had never doubted Nicolette was his own,

though. From the moment of her birth, staring into her pale, pale blue eyes he'd known that tiny scrap of screaming humanity was his. And he had adored her. Cherished her.

And he had lost her.

Stroking his hand lower, his fingers met bare flesh where Mikayla's gown had ridden up above her hips. She was naked. There were no panties covering her, just sweet, warm, feminine flesh.

Memories of his deceased wife retreated beneath the warmth of Mikayla's bare flesh. The need to touch her became more important than the need to push back the unfamiliar emotions crowding inside him.

Those emotions he was finding only amped the pleasure, though. As his fingers moved over the curve of her rear to find the damp, slick folds of her pussy, they tightened his chest, his muscles, allowing nerve endings to pulse closer to the skin, to experience each nuance of touch.

As his fingers slid over the plump folds, he felt the heat rising inside him. His cock became immediately erect, pulsing, throbbing with an unsated hunger impossible to control as Mikayla shifted slowly awake beside him.

Without saying a word, she flowed against him, lifting, her hair falling around her to spread out around his face, her lips lowered to his.

It was a drowsy, sleepy kiss. One filled with slow, lazy hunger and heated need as one slender leg slid over his hips.

What she did next rocked him clear to his soul. Lifting above her, her hips moved, shifted until the hot folds of her pussy cupped the engorged head of his cock.

As she pressed down, the snug tissue parting, flexing around the sensitive crest, electricity began raging over his flesh. From the top of his head to his toes, sensation traveled like flames through him. It thundered through his veins. It raced through his chest.

Her pussy gripped his cock like a tight, sensual glove, milking it, loving it. Like the tightest little mouth sucking him deep and strong, she drew him into her.

Gripping her hips with his hands, Nik thrust powerfully against her, parting the tender tissue as she cried out above him and burying into her to the hilt.

It was fast, glorious. It was a rush of flames searing his flesh as he began powering inside her, driving her fast and hard into an orgasm that had her shaking, shuddering against him.

As he felt her pussy flexing and gripping him, Nik gave in to his own need. As his seed spurted inside her, Mikayla collapsed against him, breathing hard, trembling in his arms.

"I love you, Nik. I love you so much," she whispered. "So much."

The words exploded inside his head, fractured inside him, and tore one last, torturous jet of come from his cock. That final burst of pleasure shattered his senses as her words had shattered his soul.

She loved him.

CHAPTER 22

Had she actually whispered those words the night before? Had she told him that she loved him, or had that
simply been another dream?

The next day, as Nik and Mikayla entered the parking lot to Holbrook Construction, Mikayla fought to
remember what was real and what was simply a dream.

It wasn't as though it was the first time she had
dreamed of taking Nik, riding him to completion as she
whispered her love for him.

Nervous tension ratcheted inside her at the thought
that she could have revealed that secret to him. She
hadn't even wanted to admit it to herself until now.
Until there was the danger that she had dared to whisper those words to Nik.

Surely if she had said them he would have mentioned
it. Been angry, unnaturally cold, or something. He was
so determined that she not love him, that he not love her,
that surely he couldn't have ignored it.

He wasn't acting any differently, though. He was
acting as though it hadn't happened. As though nothing
were any different between them than it had been the
night before.

She was very well aware of the fact that Nik didn't want her love. So where did that leave her?

At least she was with him, she thought wearily. He hadn't argued over her accompanying him; he hadn't suggested she hide at the shop instead. That was his normal suggestion as they started each day.

"Holbrook isn't known for his control over his temper," Nik warned her as they moved toward the entrance. "Stay behind me, watch, and listen. If you think of anything, then get my attention and we'll discuss it where he can't hear it. Let's not give him the chance to one-up us."

"Do I ever mess up?" she asked.

"Never." His surprising admission nearly had her pausing in shock.

Gripping the door, he swung it open and stepped inside before drawing her to him. With his hand riding low on her back they moved to the receptionist's desk.

The blue jean–clad young woman sitting at the desk glanced up from a movie playing on the computer, her brown eyes widening as she stared at Nik warily.

The small nameplate on her desk read: "Tabitha Holbrook." Nepotism didn't always pay. Then the girl grimaced in distaste as she stared back at Nik.

That surprised Mikayla. She'd been in Maddix Nelson's office building several times, and never had she seen this.

"What do you want?" the receptionist's voice squeaked.

Mikayla nearly winced at the complete lack of protocol.

"Nik Steele. I'm here to see Reed Holbrook," Nik informed the receptionist, his dark, rough voice as casual as Mikayla had ever heard it.

It was obvious he was trying not to frighten the young girl.

The receptionist pressed a button on the call pad before speaking into the headset she wore. "Yeah, uh, there's a Nik Steele here to see Uncle Reed—" She blinked up at Nik as the person on the line obviously spoke. Mikayla could have sworn she paled.

"You want me to do what?" she hissed as she ducked her head. "Look, you want him told that, then you tell him. Not me. He's scary."

Mikayla glanced at Nik, noticed his frown, and hid a smile. Actually, she thought he looked pretty damned sexy.

"You tell him . . . ," Tabitha repeated.

Nik leaned forward, placed his hands flat on the desk, and Mikayla almost giggled when he scowled down at the receptionist, causing her to jump back in fear.

"Holbrook. Now. Tell him Senator Stanton advises him it's in his best interests to speak to us." Pure male dominance transformed Nik.

It reflected on his face and in his voice.

Pure arrogance. A force of nature. It was going to kill Mikayla to lose him, but what she was learning from him she would never forget. Determination, arrogance. And how to navigate more anger than she could have imagined she would have to face.

Nik used the senator's name, a calling card he'd debated leaving unused for this meeting. The senator had left a message on Nik's phone that morning that his name would get Nik in to see Holbrook if nothing else could.

Stanton was part of the founding Elite Ops organization. Though his participation wasn't known outside the secret group of agents, his power was still far-reaching.

Nik was still glaring into Tabitha Holbrook's frightened gaze when the doors behind her pushed open.

Reed Holbrook's personal assistant, Arlene Dayton, was harried. Shoulder-length black and gray hair was disheveled, dark gray eyes filled with irritation as her overly red lipsticked lips were thinned and held an angry line.

Mrs. Dayton was a far cry from Alison Chenkins, Maddix Nelson's personal assistant. There was clearly no professionalism here, no business protocol.

"Mr. Steele." Arlene Dayton's tone was just as harried as her appearance. "Mr. Holbrook has a very tight schedule, but he can give you five minutes if you'll come with me."

Nik straightened and turned back to Mikayla, his hand reaching out for her. She didn't hesitate to take it. The move clenched his chest even as he fought against the reaction and resulting emotions rising inside him.

The personal assistant led them through another room and then to Reed Holbrook's office.

Opening the doors, she stepped aside as they entered.

Holbrook stood behind his desk, his craggy face and wide goateed beard giving a harsh appearance. There were none of the neat, conscientious appearances here, that was for damned sure.

"I'd offer you a drink," Holbrook sneered. "But I didn't exactly invite the two of you here."

"Oh, that's okay, Reed," Nik answered. "A drink wasn't really what I was after to begin with."

Nik placed himself just in front of Mikayla as Reed snarled back at them while they took seats in front of the desk.

"I don't fucking have time to deal with this," Reed

bit out furiously as he threw himself back into his seat.

"But you made time to meet with Eddie Foreman on a Nelson construction project the day he died. Now you can take time to discuss it with me."

Reed rolled his eyes. "So what? Little fucker swore he'd make it worth my while. He didn't, so I left. So don't try pinning Nelson's actions on me. I didn't kill Eddie."

"How was he going to make it worth your while, Reed?" Nik asked with mocking curiosity. "What did Eddie have that he thought you would want?"

"He said he had some information, proof Nelson was using shoddy materials for a project. He wanted money for the proof, but he didn't have shit. I left."

Nik arched a brow. "He just wanted money? Was he having any problems with Nelson?"

"Little fucker was always after money, just like he was always looking for an angle he could cheat someone with."

"You sound like you dealt with him a lot," Nik stated conversely, watching the cunning and temper that flashed in Reed's gaze.

"Enough," Reed answered. "But not nearly as much as you want to pin on me. Now, if this is all, I have a meeting to leave for."

Reed rose to his feet, glaring back at Nik as he and Mikayla rose to their feet.

"Tell me, Reed, do your business partners, your brothers, know that several of your projects are backed by a known criminal figure?"

Reed's smile was slow, a cold shark's smile that reflected pure triumph. "It was their idea, Mr. Steele." He turned to Mikayla then.

"Ms. Martin, ask yourself a question," Reed ordered

as Nik stood back to allow Mikayla to move ahead of him.

"And that is?" she asked.

"Why would Maddix Nelson's mercenary, his hired hand, want to help the woman he was hired to incriminate as a liar? Do you think sleeping with him will convince him to deviate from the job he accepted?"

"Sleeping with me wouldn't cause him to deviate from anything," she said softly before turning away and heading for the door.

The silence that filled the room was heavy with recrimination and fury as Nik turned back to Reed Holbrook.

"Watch your back," Nik advised the other man softly. "Very diligently, very carefully, Holbrook, watch your back."

Being attuned to another's feelings was something Nik knew he had never asked for. It was something he wouldn't have wanted if it had been offered to him. But suddenly he found himself attuned. Attuned and aching because he knew Mikayla had been hurt.

Reed Holbrook had sliced into her heart with his question.

Nik's fingers clenched around the steering wheel. He was so fucking tired of watching other men decimate this little woman. Calm, gentle, composed. Mikayla, for all her strength and determination, hadn't lashed back at Holbrook. She'd lifted that stubborn little chin, narrowed her eyes, and delivered her parting shot without self-pity or tears.

"We can say all the rumors about Reed Holbrook are true," she commented. "He's not a very nice person, is he?"

The thread of rueful amusement in her voice had

Nik's gaze slicing to her before he pulled it back to the heavily traveled interstate they were on.

Her voice was amused, but he saw her eyes. They were hurt.

"I could use stronger language," he grunted.

"So what exactly did we learn, besides the fact that he's rude, overbearing, and ugly?"

Nik almost chuckled at the description. "We learned he's definitely involved with Kefler and Kefler was involved with Eddie. We're narrowing in on the common denominators that are linking several people."

"But are they linking to Maddix?" she sighed.

"Maddix has links to everyone but Kefler. If Eddie was working for Holbrook, or Kefler, to sabotage the job, then the delays would have been a major loss of cash for Maddix as well as those who have allied themselves to him. His alibis also have interests, one way or the other, in that job site or others that Maddix owns. Once we get the financials I've requested and look a little more deeply into Maddix's business activities, then I'll have more information."

"Did Maddix Nelson pay you to make me look like a liar?"

He had expected the question. He knew it was coming.

"Maddix paid me two hundred and eighty thousand dollars to find out why you were determined to convince everyone he committed murder," Nik answered her. "I wasn't hired to make you look like a liar, Mikayla. I was hired to find out why you were trying to make Maddix look like a killer."

"Because he is one," she said painfully.

"Then he miscalculated and spent a hell of a lot of money for nothing. Because I promise you, if he killed Eddie Foreman, then he'll pay. For nothing else, he'll pay for daring to drag you into it and endangering your life."

"What next then? Where do we go from here?"

Nik's jaw clenched. His next course of action was one he hated taking because he knew there was no way in hell he could keep Mikayla out of it.

"Kefler. Next, we talk to Kefler."

And he took care of making that appointment quickly, Mikayla thought as they pulled onto the exit to Hagerstown. Martin Kefler was waiting for them at his home office. According to Nik, Kefler claimed there wasn't a chance he was turning down a request from the woman his girlfriend spoke so highly of.

The fact that Nik wasn't happy to be taking Mikayla was apparent. His expression was hard, his gaze so icy it was brutal. He had drawn completely away from her now. She felt as though she were sitting in the truck alone, the man operating it now no more than a robot.

"Why?" she asked as they turned from the exit. "Why don't you want me with you, Nik?"

His jaw seemed to tighten further.

"You don't understand the danger," he answered, his rough voice darker, harder, than before as his hands clenched around the steering wheel.

"Explain it to me. I want to understand it, Nik. Then, when you're gone, I'll know."

He was silent for long seconds; then the muscle at his jaw flexed and tightened before he glanced at her with eyes filled with shadows.

"A long time ago," he said quietly, "I was married, Mikayla. I had a wife and a child."

His voice resonated with pain.

"You loved your wife." Mikayla's voice quavered with the knowledge that someone else had held his heart, and had broken it.

"I loved her." His voice was distant, marked with pain. "But my daughter, Nicolette, she was my life. From the moment of her birth, she captivated me." A rueful smile tugged at his lips for only a second.

"My wife didn't love me or our child as I loved them, though," he sighed. "Her association with a known criminal figure resulted in their deaths." He wouldn't look at Mikayla, but she could see the agony he fought to keep from his expression. "Losing them as I did nearly destroyed me, Mikayla. It tore pieces of my soul from my body when my child was killed." He pulled to a stop at a red light and stared back at her. "If I lost you in such a way, there would be nothing left of me to continue fighting. There would be nothing left to exact vengeance, or to continue breathing. You are a bright piece of innocence that the world should never lose. A part I know will always glow throughout the night. And you expect me to risk that so cavalierly?"

He jerked his gaze away from her and when the light turned green pulled out. But the tension in the air only thickened, only grew heavier, with the pain Nik kept locked deep inside him.

"One day, you're going to be out of my life," she said, feeling as though she were suffocating with the pain of the parting to come. "I won't cower in corners when you're gone, and I can't cower now. But I'm not stupid, either. I learn where I can, and I'll stand back where I must. But I won't hide, Nik. If I hide from life, then the lack of it will kill me."

It was so hard to make him understand, so hard to find the words to express how she felt. That she wanted, needed, to prove to him that she wasn't helpless, simply untrained. That she was a woman he could trust, whom he didn't have to protect from all of life's little bumps.

As though a part of her thought if she could prove that to him, then maybe, just maybe, he wouldn't leave when it was over.

"In this case, living could kill you," he stated bitterly as he gave her a hard, brief glance. "And you expect me to live with that on my conscience."

And it would do no good to tell him that he couldn't accept the blame.

Mikayla battled back the tears. "Take me home." She stared straight ahead. "Or to the shop. I'll wait for you there."

Nik almost closed his eyes in relief. She wasn't angry; she wasn't threatening. Maybe she was beginning to understand what he couldn't put into words. What it would do to him if he lost her because of her determination to accompany him.

Martin Kefler was a twin to Anton Vileski, the lover his deceased wife, Tatyiana, had taken so long ago. A two-bit criminal with an organization backing him. Kefler was doubly dangerous for the fact that he didn't have the power or the full backing of the crime family he came from. Just as Anton hadn't had.

Mikayla had no business being around them, no business being a part of this investigation.

Nik made the turn and drove back to her home after making a quick call to Ian. He wasn't leaving her alone, either. She was safer at home with Kira and Ian watching over her than she was with Nik at the Kefler home.

Pulling into the driveway, he saw Kira and Ian's car in the drive and silently sent a thank-you winging heavenward for the unquestioning loyalty Richards showed the Elite Ops. This wasn't a formal mission; the man could have turned his back on Nik.

Mikayla didn't speak as she and Nik moved from

the vehicle to the front porch where the other couple waited.

Nik noticed Mikayla avoiding the other two's eyes, the way she kept her gaze straight ahead as he opened the door. He and Ian went in first, the other man covering part of the house while Nik went through the other part.

He listened closely for any conversation between Mikayla and Kira and heard nothing. Mikayla had shut down after asking to return home, and Nik could think of nothing but her warning that something vital between them could be destroyed if he went to talk to Martin without her.

What she couldn't understand, what she didn't want to understand, was that there could be nothing lasting between her and Nik.

He'd signed his life away, and he hadn't done so lightly. The fact that in two years the contract with Elite Ops would be over didn't mean that the identity the Ops had created was over. That identity would never go away, and he would always have enemies because of it. Enemies more deadly than Martin Kefler could ever hope to be. Enemies Nik could never fully escape.

As Kira moved across the living room to meet her husband, Nik moved closer to Mikayla.

"Kira's going to stay with you," he told Mikayla as she lifted her somber gaze to meet his. "She's fully qualified to protect you."

Mikayla shook her head, and Nik knew to stop then. She didn't want to hear about protection. She didn't want to hear about him leaving without her.

"Be careful," she whispered as her hand lifted, silken fingers touching his cheek. "If something happened to you, because of me, then it would be no different."

No different than losing her would be to him.

The statement was unfinished but well understood.

He wanted to do so much more, but rather than doing what he wanted, what he needed, Nik gave a sharp nod and stepped out of the door onto the front porch.

He waited and in less than a minute Ian followed, the door closing behind him.

Nik stared into the darkening skyline, fighting back the overpowering urge to turn around, retrieve his woman, and take her along with him.

Possessive. It was that core of dominant possessiveness she'd awakened within him. He had no idea it existed there, and now he had no idea what the hell to do with it.

"Know what you're doing, bro?" Ian asked as he drew beside Nik.

"Bro?" Nik lifted his brow. Hearing the word coming from a forty-year-old man was damned strange.

Ian grinned. "Mr. Steele, do you know what you're doing to my friend?" he amended.

"No." He might as well be honest about it. "I have no fucking idea."

Moving down the steps, he made his way quickly back to the truck as Ian followed behind.

"I think I'd figure that out if I were you," Ian stated as he moved into the passenger seat. "That's a damned good woman you're walking away from."

"Shut the fuck up, Ian," Nik ordered shortly, reversing from the drive and hitting the gas hard as he accelerated down the street.

"Now there's appreciation," Ian drawled in amusement. "When you get your head out of your ass and realize what you're risking, let me know. You might get smart enough in time not to lose her, and then again, you might not."

Nik shot the other man a glare. "That's not possible. I won't risk her."

"You're not the first Elite Ops agent to fall in love and you won't be the last," Ian informed him. "I've watched four of you fall so far, and I'll be here to watch your commander go down fighting as well. Protecting your woman isn't your problem; it's protecting your heart."

Nik brought the truck to a hard stop in the middle of the street before turning back to the other man. "Get the fuck out or shut the fuck up."

Ian chuckled as he gave an easy shrug. "It's your funeral, my friend. Drive on. I'll say no more."

His funeral. Fuck, he'd never felt more alive in his life than he did when he was with Mikayla. Just her being in the truck with him was enough to make him feel exhilarated, on top of a sensory overload that made no fucking sense.

Accelerating once again, he fought to block Ian out, to get a handle on himself and the regret lacing through him. If Mikayla were there with him, the world would feel brighter, lighter. It would feel invigorated.

He would feel invigorated.

He'd been dead inside for so damned long that coming to live once again was damned painful. That was exactly what he felt as though he were doing, coming to fucking life.

As he and Ian pulled into the quarter-mile drive that led to Martin Kefler's three-story mansion, the stately brownstone looked too distinguished, too aristocratic, for the man Nik knew Martin Kefler to be.

As they pulled into the drive, double front doors opened and two black-suited bodyguards stepped out on the landing.

"We have a welcoming committee," Ian murmured.

Fuck, Nik was glad he left Mikayla home.

"Mr. Steele, Mr. Kefler is waiting inside. Could we have your weapons please?" One of the bodyguards held out his hand imperiously.

"I'm unarmed." Nik held his arms out while the other bodyguard produced a metal detector and began running it along the outline of his body.

He'd left his weapons in the truck. Kefler was dangerous but not nearly as dangerous as an Elite Ops agent and one of the most dangerous Navy SEALs America had ever produced.

Satisfied they weren't carrying, the bodyguards moved aside as Nik and Ian stepped into the luxuriously appointed marble-floored foyer.

They were escorted through the house into an office that could have belonged to any of the major CEOs in the world.

"Damn, and here we're told crime doesn't pay, Nik," Ian commented mockingly as the doors closed behind them, leaving them alone in the office with an illegitimate son of one of America's most dangerous crime bosses.

"Mr. Richards." Kefler rose to his feet, his penetrating hazel eyes staring back from an imperious face. "I must say, you do your father justice in your bearing as well as your insolence."

"Well, you know what they say, blood tells," Ian quipped sarcastically, though Nik was well aware of the fact that Ian's father, a former Colombian drug lord, was a sore spot with the other man.

"Do tell." Kefler's brows arched as he tugged at the expensive leather belt cinching the charcoal gray slacks at his waist.

Pushing the long sleeves of the silk white shirt up his arms, Kefler grinned before waving them to the chairs in front of his desk. "Have a seat, my friends. I must say, I feel rather privileged to be sitting in such august company. The son of perhaps one of the most lethal drug lords in Colombia, and a mercenary of such bloodthirsty tendencies that he could give even me a few uncomfortable moments."

Nik grunted at the mockery.

"I must say," Kefler continued, "I was pleased to learn you weren't bringing Ms. Martin. Her reputation is one any woman could envy. A trip here would perhaps sully it." Self-deprecation curved his lips before he glanced at them again. "What can I do for you?"

"As I'm sure you already know, I'm looking into the death of Eddie Foreman," Nik told him.

"I heard." Kefler nodded, his expression turning serious. "Just as I've heard Ms. Martin has been threatened several times. Eloise was distressed to hear that. So much so that I've been attempting to gain some information on the problem myself."

Nik arched a brow. "And did you learn anything?"

Kefler's lips quirked into a grin. "Not much, I'm afraid."

Nik stared back at him. "It seems I've learned a few things, though. Things such as the fact that Eddie owed you a lot of money and he wasn't paying."

Kefler blinked back at Nik. "A small amount," he admitted. "I must say, a few of my men were looking for him when we received word that he had been killed."

"Were you behind the murder?" Nik asked straightforwardly. With a man such as Kefler, subtlety wasn't always the answer.

Kefler shook his head with a grin. "If I'd caught him, I would have knocked him around a little, ya know? Made him hurt. He was useless to me dead."

"Perhaps it was an investment in teaching others to pay on time," Nik suggested.

"Naw, your girlfriend, now she would be an investment. A dead Eddie was just money outta my pocket. Killing him would be like slicing my own wrists. Besides, didn't Ms. Martin witness that murder? Seems to me she's of the opinion someone else killed him."

Nik ignored the reference. "What about Reed Holbrook? I understand you two are working together in certain business ventures."

Kefler's gaze narrowed on him. "What business is this of yours, Mr. Steele?"

"We're discussing Eddie and your connection to him, Kefler, not me," Nik reminded him.

Kefler gave a short laugh. "Good thing my honey likes yours; otherwise I'd have to kill you."

Nik ignored that as well. "Was Eddie trying to sell Holbrook information or sabotage the Nelson job on your orders?"

Kelfer's gaze reflected surprise. "I have no idea. But hey, everyone is trying to make a decent buck these days, right? The fucking economy sucks."

"Seems strange to me, Martin, the three of you make a very interesting little triangle."

"Yeah, ain't that some shit?" Martin laughed with sly humor.

He was getting nowhere here, Nik admitted. When it came right to it, the fact was all roads were leading back to Maddix, not away.

"Thanks for your time, Martin, and for wasting mine." He stood to his feet, watching from the corner of his eye as Ian followed suit. "We'll be leaving now."

"Steele." The other man rose slowly. "Look, all shit aside, my honey asked for my help here. She likes Ms. Martin more than she should, and I try to please her whenever I can. I can tell you this: you're chasing shadows. Word on the street is confusing with this one. The strangest tale I've heard so far is that whoever killed Eddie Foreman wasn't Maddix Nelson, but it was still Maddix Nelson. And that comes from a crackhead with more drugs in his veins than blood. Take it however you will."

He'd take it as it was. A lame-assed story from a crackhead who loved his drugs more than he loved living.

Nodding sharply, Nik turned and, followed by Ian, made his way from the house.

There were no more answers to be found this way, because those Nik had unearthed so far kept leading him back in one direction.

"What now?" Ian asked as they were driving from the mansion and heading back to Mikayla.

"Now, I find Maddix."

CHAPTER 23

Mikayla spent the time at the house in the sewing room with Kira sitting quietly on the sofa across from the worktable. She worked, trying to keep her mind off the fact that Nik wasn't there with her. That she wasn't with him.

What was he learning? she wondered. Had Martin Kefler even known anything that could have helped?

"Do you miss being at the shop every day?" Kira finally asked as she brushed thick black hair from her face and regarded Mikayla with serene gray eyes.

"I miss it," she admitted. And she did. "Once this is finished, I can go back."

"Will it ever be finished, Mikayla?" Kira asked then. "Do you think your life will ever return to what it was?"

"No."

Life couldn't be the same, it could never be as good, once this was over, because Nik would be gone.

"Letting go is hard," Kira said softly.

And it was. Mikayla had made the first step to letting him go this evening, and she had known inside exactly what she was doing. She was giving him the rest of the distance he needed to completely step away from her.

"You love him," Kira said then.

Glancing up at her, Mikayla saw the understanding in the other woman's gaze, as well as the compassion.

"Does it matter?" Mikayla finally sighed heavily as she tucked the edge of the material and pinned it into place. "If love isn't acknowledged, does it still exist?"

"Of course it does," Kira said gently. "As long as one person loves, Mikayla, then it always exists. The lack of acknowledgment doesn't cancel it out."

She shook her head. "It won't matter when he's gone," she said painfully. "Do you think he'll ever remember, Kira? That he'll look back and know what he left behind?"

She watched as the other woman sat forward slowly, her arms folding over the tops of her knees. "I don't know, Mikayala. What I do know is that Nik leads a very dangerous, very lonely life. I would think those memories would be something he would be unable to forget, especially during the darker times he faces."

"Is he a mercenary?" Mikayla wasn't entirely certain what he was, but she had a feeling he was much more than anyone wanted to admit.

"Of a sort," Kira agreed. "A very specialized one, though. Nik makes things happen. His expertise is in weapons, and in logistics. He would have made an excellent commander if that was the route he had wanted to take."

"Before his wife and child's deaths?" Mikayla needed to know as much about him as possible. As much as she could get from the few who knew him.

"Even then," Kira stated. "I've always thought Nik was a man searching for something he had never had.

Funny, though, when I saw him here the first time, he no longer gave that impression."

Mikayla's heart clenched. "He doesn't love me, though. If he loved me, Kira, he couldn't walk away."

Kira smiled at the statement. "Funny, I don't see him walking away, Mikayla."

Her lips parted to comment, to assure the other woman she could feel him already walking away, when the lights went out.

Mikayla immediately dropped to the floor. She'd been shot at enough that she wasn't about to remain standing.

"I have a light," she hissed to Kira as she scrambled to her appliance drawer and pulled free two small Maglites that she kept on hand for emergencies.

Kira was there beside her, her fingers slipping over one of the lights.

"Do you have a weapon?" The other woman's voice was quiet, carrying no farther than Mikayla's ears.

"Dad gave me a .22." She pulled the tiny six-shot gun from the drawer.

"Well, hell," Kira sighed. "At least it shoots bullets. Now come on. Stay close to me. We're going to slip out the back and make our way to my car."

"Call Nik."

"The phones are jammed; I hit the panic button to Ian's phone the second the lights went out and the call wouldn't go through. We're going to have to get out of here, then call once we get out of range of the jammer. Turn off the flashlight and stay close. The light will only give us away."

Mikayla's eyes were slowly adjusting to the dark, but with that came the shadows that seemed to shift and twine throughout the room.

Kira was calm, confident, as though it were no more than a game. Mikayla knew it was much more.

She could hear her heart beating in her eyes as her chest tightened, restricting her breathing. Panic was only a breath away as Kira, staying low, began to make her way to the opened doorway.

Swallowing past the tightness in her throat, Mikayla stayed close to Kira as they crawled quickly through the room and past the doorway.

"Ian will know something's up soon," she promised Mikayla. "We have a system. When my hourly ping doesn't hit his phone, then he'll know there's trouble."

"Ping?" Mikayla felt stupid asking the question.

"It's programmed into our cell phones, like a computer. Every hour when we're apart the phones ping each other automatically. If the signal doesn't go through on one end, then the phone alerts the other. It's a safeguard."

Mikayla nodded, though it made about as much sense as anything else did anymore.

Making their way through the short hall to the kitchen, Mikayla tried to make out whatever might or might not be in the shadows. Whoever had managed to cut the electricity could be waiting anywhere. No doubt with a weapon.

Now this was just getting ridiculous. It wasn't as though anyone believed she had seen Maddix kill Eddie Foreman. Why the hell was he determined to kill her now as well?

Moving up on the glass sliding doors, she slid in behind Kira at the edge of the door frame.

"Damn, you have no cover out there," Kira cursed as they stared out at the moonlit backyard and open deck. "Nik should have fixed this for you."

"He's been rather busy," Mikayla stated breathlessly.

She heard a small snort. "No doubt." And a second later the door began sliding open.

"We go out low," Kira ordered. "Slide out along the side and slip over the deck to the yard. If we can get to the side of the house, then we'll have more cover to the car."

"Okay." Yeah, that sounded like a plan. All they had to do was get over the deck. "I thought you said the front would be covered?"

"Any assailant worth his salt would have help, and they'd have all exits covered. Any prey worth their salt assumes all exits are covered and takes the line of best defense."

Mikayla would decide if that made sense later.

Breathing in deeply, she moved as Kira slipped out the door, following close behind and staying as low as possible.

The moon seemed as bright as daylight as Mikayla stared into the darkness desperately, trying to pinpoint the shadows. She could feel the panic, the fear, rising inside her. They weren't making it across the deck fast enough. She could feel it.

She was so focused on it that when the first crack of wood just to her left splintered, she didn't even know what it was.

"Run!" Kira didn't bother trying to be quiet.

Mikayla felt the other woman's hand grip her arm, jerking her across the deck as that *plop, plop* sound began pelting against the side of the house.

A window shattered above their heads as they reached the end of the deck. Kira pushed her over the side and as the other woman followed a hollow sound of pain came from her lips and she collapsed on the grass.

"Fuck me. Ian is going to be pissed," Kira groaned.

Mikayla knew what had happened. Gripping the other woman, Mikayla jerked her to her feet despite the curse that fell from Kira's lips.

She'd been shot. Mikayla could smell the blood, felt it as Kira fell against her, her wounded shoulder pressed against Mikayla's arm.

Mikayla fought to get Kira to the side of the house when the quiet sound of bullets striking around them began to enrage her. She fired into the darkness.

The pop of the little .22 wasn't loud enough to suit her, but a bullet was a bullet, right?

She doubted it, but she could hope it was.

She didn't realize she was crying as she struggled to drag Kira around the side of the house. Mikayla wouldn't have realized she was cursing if she hadn't heard the word "fuck" fall from her own lips.

Reaching the corner of the house, she threw Kira around the side of it. Wood splintered above Mikayla's head once again, raining small splinters of wood around her as she ducked and fought to drag Kira to her feet.

"Bastard got me in the leg," Kira cursed, her breathing heavy as Mikayla fought to catch her breath. "At least we have some cover here."

It was little enough. A small toolshed that they were tucked against. There was cover on two sides, leaving them too exposed.

"Kira, I'm sorry," Mikayla panted. There was no way out of it. She could feel the danger coming closer, death marking the very air as she fought to figure out what to do, which way to turn.

Things were happening too fast. She hadn't had a chance to do too many things. She hadn't told Nik she would always wait for him.

"Mikayla!" She heard him.

Jerking around, she saw him. Two tall, dark figures

were racing across the yard, weapons drawn, as sirens could be heard in the distance.

The steady, silenced strikes of bullets against the house had stopped. Whoever had waited in the darkness to pick her and Kira off like sitting ducks were gone now.

"Kira!" Ian was suddenly at the other woman's side, his voice calm, concerned.

"Two. Shoulder and leg." Kira was breathing roughly. "I might need help pretty fast, Ian."

"An ambulance is on its way, baby," Ian promised her as he tore his shirt off and began placing tourniquets around Kira's shoulder and thigh.

Mikayla felt Nik beside her. She hadn't moved. His hands were going over her, his gaze watching her in concern.

"They're gone?" she whispered as she stared back at him. "I didn't get to see who it was, Nik. I'm sorry."

His pale blue eyes were like white-hot flames in the darkness as the flash of lights began to fill the night and neighbors began filing from the houses.

"That's okay, I did." His face, his voice, was hard as stone. "I saw who it was, Mikayla. And I'll take care of it."

She shook her head slowly. "Don't leave me again Nik. *We'll* take care of it."

Nik prayed for the ice to return within his soul. He prayed like a broken man praying for death as he stared into Mikayla's shocked, horrified eyes.

The race to get to her and Kira once Ian's phone had emitted that hard, shrill pulse in the truck had nearly gotten both men killed. Nik had raced through town like a madman. All he could see was Mikayla's blood; all he could hear was her screams echoing in his head.

To find her alive was a prayer answered. To realize

just how many of his barriers against emotion had been destroyed was a nightmare.

Holding her close, he watched as the police and ambulance arrived. Kira was prepped for transport as the chief of police pulled up and watched, his expression stony, from the side of the street as another car pulled onto the curb.

Nik wasn't surprised to see his commander, Jordan Malone, step from the vehicle.

Robert Denover, the criminal investigator, stood to the side of the ambulance questioning Ian as Jordan moved to them. Nik had no intentions of being a part of this. He'd seen who had shot Kira, who had tried to shoot Mikayla, even as he and Ian had rushed from the truck, their own weapons drawn.

Nik couldn't believe it. A part of him had been certain, despite the evidence, that Maddix Nelson hadn't been involved in any of this. Only a stupid man would hire someone of Nik's reputation to investigate a murder he had committed.

But it had been Maddix. There had been someone with him, Nik had seen the other shadowed, unidentifiable figure, but he'd clearly seen Maddix.

"Don't mention that Ian and I saw anything," he warned Mikayla as the investigator glanced their way. "You only saw shadows and bullets, nothing else."

Mikayla nodded. "That is all I saw."

Her voice was still quivering as she trembled in Nik's arms. He should never have left her, he admitted. She would have been far better protected with him than she was without him. He should have known this would happen. He'd allowed both Ian's wife as well as his own woman to be placed in danger because of his own fears.

Because of his knowledge that he was growing too

close to her. That leaving her was going to be that much more difficult.

His arms tightened around her as Jordan moved to them.

"I need backup," Nik told Jordan. "Mikayla and I are heading to the Nelson home. I saw Maddix Nelson here tonight."

Jordan's gaze sliced to Mikayla. "Leave her with Ian."

"No." Mikayla's hands jerked up, gripping Nik's arm where it crossed over her breasts, holding her to him. "Not this time. I'm going, or I promise you everyone on this street will hear about it."

Nik grimaced. Jordan was right: the best thing to do would be to leave Mikayla with Ian. Jordan would ensure her protection, even from the police.

"Nik, you do this and I promise I'll slip away from him." Her voice was husky from the tears that Nik refused to allow himself to see. "I have the right to face him. You know I do."

"The right and the ability are two different things, Ms. Martin," Jordan informed her.

"Who the hell are you anyway?" Mikayla bit out, the fury in her voice catching Nik by surprise. "You don't tell me what to do and what not to do. The last I heard, I already have a father."

Nik noticed the almost-amused quirk to Jordan's lips as he glanced back at him.

"She's too damned stubborn," Jordan told Nik. "This isn't going to work."

Nik shook his head wearily. "We don't have a choice but to make it work. I can't afford the distraction right now. She goes with us."

And he prayed. Like a dying man praying for salvation, Nik began to pray.

*   *   *

Mikayla sat silently in the front seat of the truck as it pulled into the Nelson driveway several hours later. There should have been a sense of triumph, she thought as she stared at the lights blazing in the house. At the very least a sense of satisfaction.

Finally, Maddix Nelson would be brought to justice.

"Mikayla and I will go to the front door," Nik told Ian and Jordan as they sat in the back. "Slip around the back and come in behind us. Maddix doesn't know he was seen. He's not going to expect trouble if he just sees me and Mikayla."

The plan was simple. He and Mikayla would get into the house. Once he saw Maddix was alone, then Nik would let him know he was seen.

Nik had promised the other man retribution if he learned he was involved in this. The police would be called later. First, though, Nik would have his pound of flesh for Mikayla.

"Slip this into the back of your jeans." Flipping the safety on the small handgun he laid in Mikayla's hands, he stared back at her. "Keep your shirt pulled over it. Stay behind me, and if things go from sugar to shit, head for the nearest exit. Understand?"

She nodded, her amethyst eyes wide as excitement flushed her face.

Damn, he hoped he was right about this. Everything pointed to Maddix being alone in the house. He wouldn't expect Nik and Mikayla to be showing up if he had been seen. He should be off guard. That was all Nik needed to make certain Mikayla was safe.

"Let's go." He got out of the truck before coming around to help Mikayla out.

Jordan and Ian slipped out unnoticed, sliding into the darkness as Nik led Mikayla to the front door.

The doors opened as they approached them, a confused Maddix Nelson staring back at them in silence.

"Nik?" He looked at Mikayla. "I heard there were problems at Ms. Martin's home?"

"A shooter." Nik escorted Mikayla inside as Maddix stepped aside.

Mikayla stared around the foyer, her gaze searching, ears listening for anyone else who might be there.

"Come into the living room," Maddix said, a note of confusion still in his voice as he invited them into the room. "Is there something wrong?"

"A few things," Nik stated as they moved into the luxurious television room. "Are Glenda and Luke here?"

Maddix shook his head as he moved toward a well-appointed wet bar. "Glenda is out with friends and Luke hasn't been around for a day or so. He'll show up when he sobers up, I imagine." The hint of disgust in Maddix's voice wasn't feigned.

"Then you're alone?" Nik asked.

Maddix glanced up from the drinks. "Is that a problem?"

"Only if you weren't here when Mikayla was attacked," Nik stated coldly.

"Then we don't have a problem." Maddix shrugged. "Would you like a drink?"

"No, thanks. We're fine."

Maddix fixed his own as Mikayla watched him. Surely there would be some hint of nervousness, something other than confusion, as he fixed his drink, glancing at them with a frown.

"Nik, why are you and Ms. Martin here?" he finally asked as he moved to the butter-soft leather sofa in front of a cold fireplace and took a seat. "I'm going to assume it has something to do with the shooting."

Mikayla stayed close to Nik as he shifted and glanced to the open doorway.

"I saw you there, Maddix."

Maddix stared at them as though he couldn't process Nik's words. "Excuse me?"

"I saw you." Nik moved, sliding his hand to his side to release the weapon holstered there.

"I'd leave that gun there if I were you, Steele."

Mikayla swung around, her heart in her throat; the only thing overriding her fear was her anger as she saw Luke Nelson standing just inside the doorway, gun in hand and pointing to them.

"What the fuck is going on here?" Maddix moved slowly to his feet as Mikayla glanced at him, his gaze widening, shock and bemusement marking his face. The same bemusement she was beginning to feel herself.

Maddix acted innocent. Luke was definitely guilty of something, but he looked nothing like his father, physically; there was no way she or Nik could have mistaken him for Maddix if he had been the one at the house.

"Luke, put that damned gun away," Maddix ordered harshly. "What the hell is going on with you?"

Luke's smile could have rivaled Nik's for icy disdain.

"You're inherently stupid," Luke drawled. "I realized that before Mother ever divorced you. You'd think you'd be smarter with all the success you've had with the business Grandfather gave you when he retired."

Maddix's eyes narrowed. "What have you done, Luke?"

"Let's say I made my choice and picked the winning team." Stepping back, he glanced to the hall, and a second later Mikayla well understood how Maddix Nelson could be in two places at once.

The man who stepped into the door was his exact

likeness. He was even dressed in the same clothes Maddix was wearing.

"Good evening, Ms. Martin," he greeted her, his voice an exact match to Maddix's as well. "It seems my marksmanship isn't all it should be. Though if it were, where would my witnesses be?" He chuckled, a low, evil sound that sent a chill racing up her spine.

It was almost impossible to believe. Maddix Nelson had no brothers. How many times had she heard that Maddix Nelson was his father's sole heir when he had taken over the business? As though being an only child were a handicap.

If the look on Maddix's face was anything to go by, then the belief was mutual.

"Luke?" Maddix spoke to his son, but the disbelief and confusion in his voice were heavy.

Luke laughed. It was a mocking sound, heavy with cruelty.

"Maddix Nelson, meet your twin brother, Floyd Cantwell. Did you know your grandfather was the one who made the decision to split the two of you up at birth?" Luke's smile was hard, brutal. "To raise Floyd with the knowledge that he was the lesser son, the one he threw away? I understand how he feels."

Maddix pulled his gaze from the brother to the son. Mikayla could see the disbelief in Maddix's gaze, the agony, and the fear.

"I never threw you away," he whispered as though in shock.

"You threw me away for your first child, that fucking company you prize so highly," Luke snarled. "But I've decided you're not the best father and now I'm choosing the father I want. And I chose the new Maddix Nelson."

Maddix was pale, staring at his son as though he

had lost his mind, as though he had ripped his father's heart from his chest. She didn't think she had ever such pain on anyone's face in her life.

"This is going to be difficult to pull off, Luke," Nik stated then. "Your father isn't alone."

Luke grinned maniacally. "So? You and Maddix argued. He shot you and Mikayla; then you fired at him and killed him. Floyd will then show up as the Nelson heir, since my grandparents so kindly disowned me and my father intends to name that whore Glenda as his heir rather than me."

Maddix shook his head. "It was a threat. I just wanted you to see what you were throwing away," he whispered. "I have no other children, Luke."

"Glenda is trying to get pregnant," Luke raged. "That cow is trying to breed so you can throw me away like your father threw your brother away."

Maddix looked at his brother again and shook his head. "You should have come to me," he whispered. "I would have never disinherited you."

Mikayla watched as Floyd Cantwell smiled. "I will, when you're dead. I've lived my life in your shadow, Brother. I have no desire to live there any longer."

As Floyd Cantwell stepped farther into the room, it was easy to tell he thought he was in control. His hazel eyes were chillingly cold, as mean as Luke's and just as brutal.

Maddix looked as though he'd been struck clear to the soul. He stared at the brother he hadn't known he had like a man possessed, or one hungry for a connection.

"Did my parents know?" Maddix asked.

Floyd laughed. "No. According to the bitch that raised me, your parents believed I died at birth. There was a nice little funeral, the body of a child who had actually died at birth. It was really quite touching, I was told."

"By my grandfather?" Maddix's voice was hollow, so hollow that Mikayla found her heart breaking for him.

He was a man slowly being broken, by a son, a brother, whose loyalty should have exceeded their cruelty.

"By good ole Grandpop." He laughed before turning to Nik. "Strange, I had you investigated. I didn't imagine Maddix could actually come up with your fee. And I definitely expected someone more effective. You've been more concerned with that cheap piece of ass there than you are with the job," he stated as he motioned to Mikayla.

"We all have our weaknesses."

Mikayla knew the sound of Nik's voice, and she knew that now he was at his most dangerous. "Ineffective" wasn't a word she would have applied to Nik. And she could see by his face that calling her a cheap piece of ass hadn't been a good idea.

"I told him he should have hired someone who knew what they were doing," Luke snorted. "Thirty-five thousand dollars? A good private investigator costs more than that."

Thirty-five thousand? Mikayla looked at Maddix. Why had he lied?

"The economy sucks," Maddix stated. "Business isn't what it used to be."

"And I'm tired of suffering for it," Luke bit out angrily. "I live in poverty because you don't know how to run a business. But you can give that cow you married whatever she wants."

It was a normal refrain. Luke was always telling whoever would listen how his father refused to share his wealth or how his wealth lacked because of his intelligence.

Whichever, it seemed Maddix kept his son in the dark concerning any wealth he might actually have.

"I'm rather curious what makes you think you can get away with this," Nik stated. "Once Maddix is dead and Floyd shows up, people will suspect what happened with the Foreman murder."

"No one will suspect a thing." Floyd chuckled. "Maddix killed Eddie. Once it's done, I'll finish planting the needed evidence. Of course, if Maddix had cooperated rather than having that fucking meeting that night so suddenly, he would be in prison now and I'd be the owner of the company."

"Someone's delusional," Nik muttered.

Floyd's gaze sharpened with fury, lighting with rage as he glared back at Nik. "You're nothing more than a hired gun without a gun. I was watching you. You left your weapon with your friend. I saw you give it to him. Then you rushed right over here. How stupid was that?"

Stupid, Mikayla thought, because Ian had handed that weapon back to Nik in the truck.

"You tried to frame me for Eddie's murder?" Maddix's voice was soft, disillusioned. "Destroy me?"

"Of course." Floyd laughed. "And then I would have framed you for killing this little bitch if she hadn't been so damned lucky. The first time I shot at her at the job site a cloud moved and sent that damned sunlight right in my eye; the second time, she moved at the last second, the third time that damned car hit a pothole. Then Mr. Muscle here"—he waved at Nik—"managed to reach her before Luke could run her down with your car. She has more lives than a fucking cat."

"You could have told me you existed." Maddix

sounded as though he was choked. "I would have welcomed you."

Floyd sneered. "Fuck you. I was the castoff. Now the castoff is going to kill you."

The gun lifted. At that last second, Nik moved. Mikayla felt what was coming and could do nothing to stop it.

Nik pushed her to the floor, going down with her as gunfire began to echo around her. She heard curses, enraged and furious, as Nik moved.

Maddix went down, his eyes rounded with terror as he began trying to crawl across the floor to her. A bullet fired into the wood floor in front of him, chipping wood and causing him to fling himself to the side.

The lights went out, throwing the room into complete darkness as chaos and bullets swirled around her.

When silence finally reigned, Mikayla struggled to penetrate the shadows, to find Nik. Everything inside her was demanding that she call out to him, that she find him.

Rising to her knees, she stared around desperately, feeling her lips tremble, fear crawling through her system.

"You fucking whore!"

There was no way to avoid the arm that suddenly went around her neck, restricting her breaths as the sound of Luke's heavy breathing blasted in her ear.

Instantly blinding spots of light centered on them.

"I'll kill this bitch!" The words were screeched into her ear.

This was Luke. And she had never seen the pure evil that existed inside him.

"You're going to let her go or I'm going to kill you." Nik's voice came out of the darkness. "Don't make that happen, Luke."

"Fuck you, Steele!" His arm moved.

A shot rang out.

Mikayla felt Luke still, felt the sudden shock of his body that indicated something had happened before he crumpled behind her.

She was left standing in the middle of the room, her breathing harsh, heavy, for no more than a second. A lifetime. A brutal, freezing eternity before Nik's arms were suddenly around her. He pulled her against his chest, held her close to him, and she could swear she heard him breathe a prayer.

CHAPTER 24

Luke was dead, as was his uncle Floyd Cantwell. The two men hadn't known who they were dealing with when they faced Nik. An ineffective mercenary? She didn't think so. As she watched the black-masked men who filled the Nelson library hours later, she knew he was anything but a mercenary.

Maddix Nelson was slumped in a chair, his third glass of whisky in his hand, tears unashamedly dampening his cheeks. He'd lost everything in a very short amount of time. The brother he hadn't known he had, the son he hadn't known the true evil of. He was a man fighting just to believe the events of that evening.

The chief of police and the detective assigned to the case stood close to Maddix while Glenda stood at his side, silently weeping for him.

Say what one did about the woman, she genuinely seemed to care about Maddix.

His parents were on their way from Arizona. God only knew how they would handle the truth of what had happened to the child they had believed had died.

Nik stood with Jordan Malone and Ian Richards on the other side of the room, talking to four other men, all in black masks and black clothing. They were all tall, hard bodied, and hard-eyed as they surveyed the scene.

Clapping Nik on the back, each in turn, they walked through the patio doors as Mikayla watched, disappearing into the night as Ian and Jordan moved to where Maddix and the police sat.

Nik moved to her.

"We're leaving," he told her as he held his hand out to her. "I've given the investigator your statement. It's over, baby."

How could it truly be over when so much had been lost?

Taking his hand, she let him pull her to her feet, his arm wrapping around her as he led her to the door.

"I want to stop at the hospital and check on Kira." Mikayla wanted to cry until there were no tears left inside her.

"A friend has been at the hospital," he told her. "Ian checked on Kira; she's doing fine. She's resting and she'll have a few more scars to add to her collection, but she's going to be fine."

Mikayla nodded. So much for delaying the inevitable.

"We're going home, then?" she asked.

"We're going home," Nik agreed.

He handled her gently, lifting her into the truck and helping her buckle her seat belt because her hands were shaking so hard. She didn't want to go home. She didn't want to watch him leave her.

Pulling into the drive, Nik had to fight to hold back the fear still crawling through his system. Seeing Luke Nelson's arm around her neck, that gun pointing toward her, had nearly destroyed his soul. If anything had happened to her . . .

Leaving the truck, he moved around to the passenger side, opened the door, and helped her out. Clasping her waist with his hands, he nearly didn't set her on her feet. He almost carried her to the house, desperate to keep his hands on her.

He wasn't going to make it.

He could feel it. The fear and hunger were ripping through him, making it impossible for him to hold on to his self-control.

He didn't let her go.

Swinging her into his arms, feeling her hands grip his shoulders in surprise, Nik carried her to the house. Unlocking the door took a few seconds longer. Locking it back was almost forgotten as she buried her face in his neck and he felt her tears.

Tears she hadn't shed at the height of the danger. Tears she hadn't allowed him to see in the truck.

What would happen to him if he lost her?

Nik knew he would never be able to survive if Mikayla was taken from his arms.

He didn't set her down on her feet until he reached the bedroom. Then he still didn't put her on her feet. He laid her back on the bed and proceeded to slowly, easily, remove her clothing before tearing his own from his body.

He had to touch her. He had to feel her.

Ah, God.

"Never again." The words tore from Nik's throat as he came over her, his lips burrowing in her neck. "Never again, baby. Sweet God, it won't happen again."

There was no time for preliminaries, no time to get a handle on himself or to balance the combination of hunger, rage, and fear that whipped through his system.

His lips covered hers as he felt her arms wrap around

him, holding on to him tight, so tight. But nothing was as tight as the hold she had on his soul. Nothing as warm as the pure, sweet heat of her flesh against his, her lips moving beneath his, her tongue dancing with his.

"Sweet Mikayla," he groaned, his lips moving to her neck, his tongue stroking her flesh, tasting her as he moved desperately between her thighs, parting them, lifting them to his hips as he pressed against the slick, silken folds of her pussy.

Her flesh parted, giving and soft beneath the iron-hard head of his cock. Pressing inside her, he breathed out roughly as he felt her inner muscles begin to clench and tighten around him.

Nothing was so sweet, so beautiful, as his little fairy.

Lifting his head, staring down at her, he watched her face as he took her. Watched the soft heat that filled her gaze, the sensuality that overwhelmed her expression.

Sweet Lord, he could never live without this again. How the hell could he ever live without her touch, her laughter, without the pure unbridled hunger she filled him with?

"Hold me." The words were torn from him; he couldn't hold them back as she took him, the milking sweetness of her pussy wrapping around his cock. It flexed, rippled, held him like the sweetest, tightest glove.

"I'll always hold you." Her voice, her vow, washed over him, locked her inside his soul.

He had to leave her. When it was over, when he'd taken this last taste of sweetness that he would allow himself, then he had to leave. It was the only way to protect her. It was the only way to ensure . . .

How?

Pushing in to the hilt, he groaned her name. God

knew he meant to hold back. He needed to hold back. He needed to be strong enough to leave her, but how the hell was he supposed to do that?

Live without this?

His cock was buried in pure, liquid heat. It clenched around him; tight muscles stroked the sensitive head, tightened around the shaft as her juices dampened his balls.

He wanted to hold inside her forever, to feel nothing but her hot, tight pussy flexing around him. But each subtle stroke pierced his control, frayed it, until he had to move.

He'd go slow, he promised himself.

As he moved back, his teeth clenched at the slow drag of her silken grip against his cock.

He was losing it.

The pleasure was ripping through him. He couldn't handle it. He couldn't hold back.

"Fuck. Baby." The growl that tore from him came with a hard thrust of his hips, and then it was over.

Pushing inside her, stroking into her, he began throwing them both into the maelstrom of pure hot bliss.

It overtook him. He could feel it overtaking her. Her legs wrapped around his hips, her arms around his neck. With each thrust inside her, she arched upward with her hips, taking him deeper, taking him harder.

He was wild with the need for her. Crazy for her touch.

Nothing had ever hit him so hard or taken him with the power with which she was taking him, accepting him. He'd never known pleasure like he knew with her at the moment he felt her unraveling around him. Her pussy tightened, her juices flowed, and she shuddered in his arms as he felt her coming, felt her losing herself to the pleasure he gave her.

"I love you, Nik. Oh, God, Nik. I love you."

The pleasure she gave him.

His release tore through him. It ruptured inside him, spurting from his cock in hard, hot jets as he heard himself groan her name. Fought, held back the emotions ripping through him, and swore he had never known anything this powerful, this exquisite, in his life.

He'd never known love, but he knew it now.

Burying his head at her shoulder, he gave in to it, let it tear through him, let it have him.

And he knew without Mikayla there was no love, no laughter, there was no life.

Nik was gone when Mikayla awoke the next morning.

Rising from the bed, she felt her stomach tighten in panic and fear, felt the pain that tore through her.

Surely he wouldn't leave without telling her good-bye.

"He wouldn't," she whispered as she felt tears dampen her eyes.

He wouldn't just walk away.

Jerking her robe on, she rushed out of her room, to the guest room, threw open the door, and stared at a naked, clearly curious Nik as he turned to her.

He'd showered. There was a towel cinching his hard hips, emphasizing the tight, hard abs of his stomach.

And he was packing his bag.

Mikayla felt her lips tremble and hastily stilled them. She wasn't going to cry. She wasn't going to make him feel guilty because he couldn't love her.

That wasn't love, she told herself.

Her eyes turned once again to the leather bag and the clothes stacked beside it as he turned around, the fingers of one hand clenched.

"I was afraid you wouldn't say good-bye," she whispered.

His head tilted to the side, a little smile playing about his lips.

"Why would I do that, Mikayla?"

She shook her head, fighting back the tears. "I don't know."

She could feel the pain churning in her stomach now, the knowledge that she was losing every dream she had ever had. When he walked out, all the love she had dreamed of having, of feeling, would be gone.

"Mikayla." She watched as he moved to her, like a predator, like a fierce Viking warrior easing up to her.

She wanted to cry, and she swore to herself she wouldn't. When he lifted a hand and brushed her hair back, though, it was all she could do to hold the tears back.

"I'm not a mercenary," he stated.

Mikayla nodded. "I know."

His lips quirked.

"I'm away a lot. Being with a man like me wouldn't be easy."

He was making excuses?

"Please, Nik—"

"You said you loved me again last night, Mikayla," he said then.

And she had said she wouldn't ask for promises. But she hadn't asked for promises; she had only told him how she felt.

What did he expect her to say? That she was sorry? Well, she wasn't, and she wasn't about to lie about it.

"So I did." She was glaring back at him before she realized it. "It's too late to take it back now, so I guess you'll just have to live with it."

"I guess I will." His hand lifted again, cupped her cheek, his thumb brushing over her lips. "Say it again."

"What?" Confusion rocked her. "Say what?"

"That you love me."

Was this some new form of emotional torture?

"You know I love you—"

His thumb settled over her lips once more. "Say it the way you said it last night."

"I love you, Nik." She couldn't hold it back. It was the truth. If he needed to hear it before he walked out of her life . . .

"I love you, Mikayla."

She couldn't have heard him right. It wasn't possible.

"What?" She couldn't breathe. Had she heard him right? Was she losing her mind?

"Mikayla Martin, I love you," he whispered as he took her hand and slid slowly, with such male grace, into a perfect kneeling position.

She watched, entranced, uncertain, suddenly so filled with hope. . . .

"I called your father this morning." Nik took her hand. "And I asked his permission to marry the most perfect, the most beautiful fairy ever created." He slid a ring on her finger. "And now, I ask you, Mikayla. Will you marry me?"

Diamonds and emeralds graced a small gold band. It was obviously a much-loved heirloom, old and created with an eye for beauty as well as wealth.

"Nik." She stared back at him, uncertain, terrified she was only dreaming.

"Marry me, Mikayla," he said softly. "Don't make me go out into the cold again. I don't think I could live like that after knowing your warmth."

"Yes." She wasn't hesitating. If it was a dream, if she was hallucinating, then she wanted it all. "Oh, God, yes."

The dream was real. The ring on her finger, the man who rose to pull her into his embrace, the kiss that touched her lips.

"Your parents are on their way over," he groaned against her lips. "Those damned brothers of yours. Something about celebrating."

She wasn't hallucinating.

"I love you, Nik," she whispered against his lips. "Always."

"Always, little fairy," he whispered back. "I'll love you forever."

Epilogue

One year later

The bride wore antique white, and if the smooth silk looked just a little full at the stomach, then no one mentioned it.

The groom wore black, his long blond hair tied back, his expression fierce as he watched his bride walk slowly up the aisle.

He could feel his hands trying not to shake.

If ever she had looked like a fairy, then it was now. Ethereal, petite, and delicate. A dream he had never allowed himself to have until she was forced into his life.

Now, he would die for her. He would kill to keep her.

Her and the child she carried within her.

Their child.

Nik couldn't believe he had the courage, but his Mikayla was courage itself.

Determination.

Strength.

Love.

She was his soul, and he had no shame admitting it.

He stepped to her, her graceful fingers lying against his arm as he stared down at her.

His perfect, beautiful fairy.

Amethyst eyes stared up at him, sparkling with tears and with joy behind the antique lace of the veil.

It was her dream wedding. She was his dream bride.

"Dearly beloved, we are gathered here together . . ."

The priest's words droned on. The vows were in Nik's soul, tied to hers, wrapping them together with silken, unbreakable bonds.

His bride.

They called him Renegade, but his Mikayla would now call him husband. And to Nik, "husband" was a far better word.

"You may kiss the bride."

His fingers actually shook as he lifted the veil, curved his arm around her, pulled her to him, and in that kiss they sealed the vows they had made a year before.

To love forever.

Want more from the men of Elite Ops?

Look for the first novel in this series
from *New York Times* bestselling author
Lora Leigh

WILD CARD
ISBN: 978-0-312-94579-4

…and don't miss Leigh's sexy SEALs series

KILLER SECRETS
ISBN: 978-0-312-93994-6

HIDDEN AGENDAS
ISBN: 978-0-312-93993-9

DANGEROUS GAMES
ISBN: 978-0-312-93992-2

Available from St. Martin's Paperbacks

Want more from *New York Times* bestselling author
Lora Leigh?

Discover her red-hot Bound Hearts series

ONLY PLEASURE
ISBN: 978-0-312-36873-9

WICKED PLEASURE
ISBN: 978-0-312-36872-2

FORBIDDEN PLEASURE
ISBN: 978-0-312-36871-5

Available from St. Martin's Griffin

Sign up to read

"NIGHT HAWK"

A FREE never-before-released Elite Ops story
from *New York Times* bestselling author

Lora Leigh

Visit
www.stmartins.com/loraleigh
to learn more

1 *New York Times* bestselling author

LORA LEIGH

keeps the HOT reads coming…

Look for

LIVE WIRE

ISBN: 978-0-312-94584-8

Available in March 2011
from St. Martin's Paperbacks